PA

PPE

−6. APR. 1977

16 JUG 7

13. OCT. 1975   15 FEB 1978

−3. NOV. 975   03 NOV 1979

15 OCT

10 MAR 1978

−9. DEC. 1975   18 APR 1978   17 DEC 1979

27. JAN. 1976   26 JUN 1978   17 MAR 1980

−1. M 1976

18. JUN 1976   22 JUL 1978   17 OCT 1980

15 NOV 1980

14 1976   20 OCT 1978   06 MAY 1981

13. 1976

−3 FEB. 1977   2 MAR 1979

11 JUN 1981

LIKE MEN
BETRAYED

LIKE MEN BETRAYED

Frederic Raphael

JONATHAN CAPE
THIRTY BEDFORD SQUARE LONDON

FIRST PUBLISHED 1970
© 1970 BY VOLATIC LTD

JONATHAN CAPE LTD,
30 BEDFORD SQUARE, LONDON WCI

ISBN 0 224 61935 7

MADE AND PRINTED IN GREAT BRITAIN BY
BUTLER & TANNER LTD, FROME AND LONDON

Sometimes it crosses my mind that the things I write here are nothing other than images that prisoners or sailors tattoo on their skin.

(GEORGE SEFERIS: '*Logbook II*')

for Clive Donner

THEY HAD BEEN RETREATING ALL DAY ALONG MOUNTAIN paths in brilliant cold when they saw the shepherd up ahead, crouched like an Indian, in an orange goatskin coat. He sat under a hurdle sloped against the wind. The sky throbbed with silence. The planes which had been hunting them had withdrawn half an hour earlier. Soon they might be back. Artemis raised his hand; the men's footsteps slurred and stopped. Artemis climbed a torrent of dust and stones to where the old man was waiting.

'Good day, my friend. Hermes, the son of Eirene, sent me. He says that you can take us to the frontier.'

The old shepherd gaped at Artemis like the mouth of a drained leathern bottle. The men, to whom the halt was a tax exacted in pain from tired or wounded bodies (the boy Stelio was bled the colour of unbaked bread), advanced within earshot. They were split by separate apprehensions, less of death than of trickery. Artemis heard the tumble of slack as they mounted the slip to the old man's perch.

'Why doesn't he answer us, Captain?' asked Yorgis, the sergeant-major.

'Perhaps we should kick him a little, Captain.'

In the last weeks the men had called Artemis by his rank. It was the only obvious change he had noticed. Their endurance and their determination appeared unbroken. They would never agree to defeat since they had never clearly been defeated. They looked to Artemis not as their immediate salvation but because his intellect was their contact with what lay beyond them. He came from the capital; they were men of the country. They had never challenged his leadership; now, however, they insisted on it, which was something new. If they were not blaming him for the retreat, they refused to blame themselves.

Artemis understood this. Perhaps he had helped to make it true, by understanding it. How else could the men avoid the bitterness of their worsting by the Government, for whose conscripts they had so recently had an almost affectionate contempt, except by withdrawing again into that mysterious, even mindless solidarity from which Artemis and the other members of the Political Committee had tried to wean them? Artemis saw them shrink into the warrens of an impassive secrecy. They resumed their rude and unintelligible argot. They became positively anonymous; he began to mistake one for another. He accepted the necessity which drove them down into the catacombs of these impersonal hiding-places, but he could not join them there. He watched them go like a surface worker.

'Why does he pretend not to understand?' Stelio strained for enough harshness to convince him that he was still on the living side of the stream. 'Kick him, somebody.'

'He isn't pretending. He's dead.'

'Who killed him if he's dead?'

'Are you sure, Captain?'

Artemis touched his foot to the frame of the old man; the body toppled in the orange dust. Artemis turned and looked at his men. They stood round the body as they might have round the breakdown of a vehicle which was to take them to safety. 'We must rely on ourselves. Not to worry, we'll reach the frontier.' The men stared at the boulders lining the summit of their vision like unnamed tombs.

Paniotis, a stocky ex-sailor, with a thick rind of healing wound over his half-closed eye, a man on whom that distant bullet, incurred in the fighting round the capital five months earlier, inflicted a look of unappeased suspicion, aimed his kick at the empty old body. A stone rolled into the folds of the orange coat. Laughter splashed down the slope and rebounded in a low echo before peeling off into silence. 'You say we'll reach the frontier? How do we know what that will mean?' The old sailor, rotating on his misshapen hip, turned away with calculated ambiguity, as an actor with an incomplete speech joins in muttered conversation with the crowd to conceal the inconclusiveness of his line.

Artemis smiled. 'Explain yourself, Paniotis. You know of the decision. It was fully analysed when we first received the orders. You saw the sense of it then.' He clung to the vocabulary of the future, while Paniotis, frowning at the body before him, saw only the oracles, the sick entrails, of the past. The old sailor scowled like a captive manacled to a corpse. 'We shall cross the frontier and so be able to regroup, to re-equip, to heal our wounds before re-commencing the battle under circumstances more advantageous to us. We shall be safe from the Government and we shall be on friendly soil.'

Artemis repeated, with a dressing of humorous expression, the arguments of the Political Committee. Memories, unoiled by the certainty of action or the hope of victory, rotated rawly against each other in his mind and blazed behind his eyes. Guilt, of a kind, was his defence against despair, just as the men's (and there again was the terminology of *his* retreat) lay in their regressive solidarity.

'Friendly? Perhaps.' Paniotis turned the body with his foot, his face that of a fisherman who has wrestled all day to land a catch which has turned out to be worthless. His resentment, leaving the present unacknowledged and the future open, withdrew into the haunted past when those across the border were the traditional enemies, coming from an incomprehensible land of mosques and barbarous tongues. The men rustled in an autumn of suspicion. Paniotis, though never exactly popular with the mass of them, had a way of articulating their deepest, incorrigible feelings. They were approaching safety, it was said. The Political Committee and the Central Committee of those across the border had come to an undying and eternal understanding. They were comrades forged in the fire, promised the communiqué, and dedicated to the common cause. But what common cause, the old sailor demanded, was there under the bandage of words, between these two winds which had blown, since the earliest ballads, in contrary, conflicting gales, making the borderlands a by-word for rape and deceit? The future was made the natural descendant of the past by Paniotis's words. Artemis forced to resolution eyes which all but watered behind his thick glasses. He was in positive battle with the old sailor. Artemis's only weapon was his understanding. He knew Paniotis; Paniotis did not know him. He could accuse Paniotis of a breach of faith; Paniotis had not the mind to suspect Artemis. Artemis wrestled Paniotis to make him face his shame. And there, against the obvious odds, came the sign of it: Paniotis could not withstand his gaze, but blinked like a boy caught with his cock in his fist. His passion spurted despite his shame. The contradictions in him were embarrassingly funny to the others. They drew back from him. But how long would discipline master desire? It was a temporary victory convention had won over nature. 'Friendly! I hope you're right. For your sake, Captain, not for mine. Once we're across, we're across.'

'Well, that's undeniable, old friend, and no mistake.' Artemis combined the wit of the city with the bluffness of the country and again, for the moment, the coalition got its vote. The men laughed, but they loitered by the collapse of the oracle on which they had relied. It was in Artemis's mind to order them to advance, but the words stuck: he was warning himself (and how he dreaded that reduplication of internal commands!) that they might not follow and that then, too soon, he might come to the crisis which was building between them and which he must not allow to have form until they were within sight of the frontier or of death. Paniotis confronted him like a block of stone. Any physical challenge would be met and crushed. The dragon's teeth would shrivel into the ground which had given them flesh. The land would be as it was before the uprising. The victory of the Government would be complete. It was not vanity but correct analysis, as Brasidas would have called it unsmilingly, which made Artemis see, with terror and intensity, that he alone stood between these men and the end of their fight. The pride he found in this was quite impersonal. No one was less nostalgic for Bonapartism at that moment than Artemis, his knees thin against the shanks of his trousers, tears pricking behind his glasses, his jaw settled against the shred of cuticle which was the only sweetness in his mouth. The pages of the dictionary of his mind were blown over and over in the breeze of fear; the words, of which Bonapartism was only one, flicked his consciousness with the callousness of a ringmaster's whip. Yet he stood his ground with old Paniotis and the stone was moved.

One of the boys, square-shouldered as an archaic statue and with the same sly and enigmatic smile, Kosta, who slid his lustrous eyes left and right to catch anyone looking at him or mocking him, too short in the leg for his haughtiness to have the grace which might have made him irresistible, reached for the orange coat of the old shepherd and fingered it, savage and docile, as he might the pubic hair of a whore sitting unpaid on a bed in a brothel, knowing his right, sure of his manhood and yet awaiting rebuke. Yes, he allowed the curls of the wool to ring his fingers and his eyes were fixed on Artemis. Artemis was the woman. The pelt was something he had no right, had he, to refuse the boy? And Artemis, the cold as clear as a light in the roof of a bare room, a room unclothed for living, the room of a brothel, in which the cupboards contain nothing, where nothing personal is at home, faced the boy and his love of the boy, his desire for the boy whose manhood was so directly on display, and the cold was sharp as ice in his lungs. *Ce n'est pas moi que tu aimes:* the words came to him.

It was before the war. He was at the university. His betrothal had just been announced. His loneliness was plagued with desire. The days were full of announcements, laced with static, from loud-speakers bolted to the street lamps. The dictator, among whose supporters, 'provided he faces the question of wages', Artemis's parents were to be numbered and whose Minister of Marine was the father of Artemis's fiancée, had his portrait everywhere. He had been portrayed, whether through art or its bastard sister in-advertence, in a sepia tint, at once remote and imperial, re-miniscent of those photographs of royalty to be found, themselves bowing gently, in the back rooms of provincial cafés where brown, almost ecclesiastical chairs for functions that will never be held are stacked against the fly-specks. The dictator, in his ubiquitous posters, had the air of one already long gathered to his fathers. It was risky propaganda, but it gave to his assumption of office the rooted propriety of a dynasty, if only of that dynasty which his own arrival had interrupted. As he walked through the dust-whitened streets, Artemis had the illusion of living under the power of a ghost, whose victories were part of folklore and whose policies, both unquestionable and absurd, had imposed on the country, and especially on the capital, that semblance of appre-hensive virtue which can be observed in a sanatorium where the director's prescriptions contain more acid than sugar and where not to feel better is a symptom less of the need for better treatment than of a failure of proper effort. If the Marshal had done nothing to heal the country's divisions, he had at least bandaged them very tightly. He did not enrich himself, though his supporters were not above corruption, as Artemis would later discover and now only suspected, in the way that a sophisticated youth, brought up among the notables, learned to suspect his mistress of infidelity long before he had the good fortune to acquire her. Even his opponents referred to the Marshal as the Old Man. He had placed himself above Party by affecting to put the clock back to an Arcadian time when parties had not yet come into existence. Artemis then, in that white summer heat, lived among ghosts. He dreamed luminous dreams, free of the trammels of possibility. He wrote bitter and untiringly weary poems. His engagement, which had been advanced to before his graduation and military service, unnerved him by its remoteness. So a condemned man, he noted, remains unperturbed, unnaturally normal, at least between the time when sentence is passed and the day the executioner moves into the prison. He found Katerina herself neither unfamiliar nor unattractive, but she remained enclosed in the sealed envelope of her parents' wishes. He had agreed to marry her, rather as an invalid agrees to have his favourite dish cooked even though at the moment he has no appetite for it. He does not want to lose his reputation for finding it delicious, lest it is not offered again. Artemis had no quarrel with Katerina then; they had known each other so long and their union was so 'obvious' that nothing could stop it without a jolt. Artemis was studying French at the university and felt upon him all the weight of ambitious resentment which comes of reading the literature of a great power, of watching others gallop through the open spaces of rhetoric, swinging sabres of sharp and disrespectful wit at the thickets of superstition, while oneself is being pestered with the captious prescriptions of men who can neither be repudiated nor chastened but whose power, in a small and unregarded country, is as absolute as it is disgraceful. Between the young and any volatile future stood the small, dark-suited and tightly buttoned interns of power. The Marshal was at least not vindictive (he had released many whom the previous regime, for all its boast of popular backing, had locked up) and it was true, if lamented in clandestine student debate, that he was the one man likely to unite the military and those of military age against the enemies who were said to menace the country. The bluster of these enemies might sound laughable to the writers of editorials in the great foreign newspapers (which an amiable or parochial censorship still did not prevent from being bought at the narrow kiosks in the streets of the capital), but their glowering ambitions, comic-operatic as they might be to the major chancelleries, would be repelled only by a united country. The penalties of smallness were never so obvious as in that lonely summer. Rhetoric rumbled in the capital like the armoured vehicles it could not provide. The Marshal, to his astonished chagrin, had recently been refused by Paris certain armaments which had always been supplied in the past. The French Government, in its elegant and liberal reply, alluded to the risks of war in the area and said, as if in justification, that it had also refused a request from the Marshal's 'traditional enemy' across the border, when everyone knew that both countries needed the weapons to resist the Duce who was so loud in his threats towards the pair of them. Artemis was filled with bitterness before he had tasted sweetness. He was reading a volume of Maupassant, whose clarity he observed to conceal contradictions to match his own. The worldly manner put a candid face on the dark and unstylish caverns of Maupassant's pain, just as standard jokes and assumptions provided a common and amusing front for the uncoupled desires and private hungers of Artemis and his fellow-students.

One evening he went with some friends from the Faculty to a dramatic reading given at the French Institute by a famous husband and wife. Despite their devotion to the French language and to the fiery minds and profligate poets in whose terms they scanned the world, there was something dutiful in the students' presence and the atmosphere within the hall became taut with the unstable serenity of a congregation which is attending, for civil reasons, the religious service of an alien faith. Art, as Turgenev said, might be one of the things which unite men, but here it was being used to proclaim a unity which would have needed no observance had it not been breached. If the students were amused by the Marshal's chagrin, they were insulted by their country's rejection. They honoured France; they were peeved with the French. And then, on top of these contradictions, typical of those who boast their vigour and feel their impotence, came the characters of the two actors. Their delivery, a modified version of the traditional Comédie Française, seemed to exemplify the pretentious grandeur of a nation which at once advertised its greatness and was too petty to help its allies. What call was there, in this modest auditorium, for such baroque bombast? The students controlled themselves with a restraint more commonly mooted in Helen's anteroom where to postpone pleasure was said to render it more enjoyable, but finally they burst out with a prompt opportunism which too closely resembled premeditation. The national anthems of the two countries were played by the pianist who had accompanied a recital given by local French singers to allow their euphonious compatriots to spray their throats. The students suffered their own anthem in silence, but they joined in the French, at first decorously and then with aggressive emphasis on the phrase '*Aux armes, citoyens*'. Finally, they repeated that stirring formula over and over again, even when the pianist had left the platform, until '*Aux ARMES, citoyens*' came more and more thunderously from the tall empire windows of the Institute and people in the streets crowded, smiling uneasily, by the railings. The police had come next, of course, summoned by a Foreign Office official who could not wait to punish the students for expressing so exactly the sentiments of his own Government. In the midst of the chanting the audience was subjected to a final, dignified appeal by the famous couple, who returned to the stage in the name of the common humanity of art, an example of Turgenevian liberalism which, since hypocrisy revolts the young more than repression, released the obscenities which they had restrained all evening. The female member of the duet, whose sensibilities can hardly have been as innocent as the shepherdess costume which she had donned for the final excerpts from La Fontaine, implored them to be gentlemen with a tremulous coquettishness which drew peals of laughter. The poor woman lurched from roguishness to tears, caught her peasant costume on a splinter in the platform, tripped and ran. Her husband, who had exemplified all that was intended in the expression 'an ambassador of the arts', spread his arms, man to man, and then, according to some, lost patience and threw his persecutors a jerked gesture from the elbow unmistakably not of the repertoire. By now the police were in the hall. Fashionable women and dinner-jacketed men were hurried, like members of a chorus late on cue, out of the

17

side doors. The students, who had fired all their metaphorical bad eggs, were buttoning on a now rather sheepish and certainly un-militant garrulity when they found themselves faced with the black and unspent humour of those who had been sent to get them.

Through good fortune, in which there was a tincture of regret, Artemis did not find himself among those arrested that night. Dmitri Stratis led his cronies over the balustrade of one of the stage boxes (Artemis would remember the wounded look of a mackintoshed police officer, cheated of his portion) and down a corridor which took them into the library of the Institute. From the noise and alarm in the hall, the students found themselves in an arched cellar of books at the far end of which a grave gentle-man in a trim goatee was sniffing in several heavy volumes. The students had spent their derision; they asked politely if there was a way out. The librarian selected a key and allowed them to pass through the vestibule, where there was a bust of Rousseau, into a side street of a district famous for furs. The noise of the riot, in which both sides seemed to be striving for an effect neither was going quite to achieve, rose like the lights of a city and panelled the sky. Stratis deterred them from marching to the guns and directed them instead towards the harbour. He was their leader not because he possessed any originality of mind or ambition but because of his energy, his money and his refusal to take no for an answer. Artemis and those who succumbed to his greedy charm were not themselves socially unpresentable; he coerced them less by his privileged position than by his talent for coercion. It was not that he had bright ideas but that they had none. Artemis was a slim, dark and febrile young man, not athletic but good enough at the sports of his class, tennis, swimming and banter, never to lack companions. He was welcome in the houses of the educated and the ruling class, the so-called notables. He had a courtliness which commended him to the parents and a shy playfulness agree-able to the younger brothers and sisters of his contemporaries. He was hardly anyone's favourite, but everyone liked him. As for

Stratis, he was the son of his father. He followed his parents as the conclusion of a syllogism follows its premisses. Asteris Stratis was the proprietor of several newspapers renowned for surviving the crises which had closed his rivals right and left. He had been accused of agitating for the elimination of those who held opinions disagreeable to him. In fact his pleasure came not from the suppression of what he disliked but from the evidence it provided of his own nimbleness in remaining immune. He owned two main papers: the first was a daily of exhaustive pretentiousness, which seldom published pictures; the second a tabloid, published little else, revelling especially in calamities in more prosperous countries. The print of the *Times* was so small and so crotchety that its readers were convinced that nothing escaped its notice. Whatever was not in the paper could not possibly be of any consequence. The large sections devoted to religion, finance and the arts suggested an international outlook. Without the *Times*, the country would be overgrown with the weeds of parochialism. The paper gained a reputation abroad for the liberal spirit of its own Government in allowing it to attack the illiberalities of others. Its outspokenness was assumed to be enjoyed by the country at large. In this way Asteris Stratis was internationally respected for keeping the torch of liberty ablaze while at the same time making his fortune from a domestic scandal-sheet the existence of which was scarcely known by his grand admirers and which was notorious for its failure to publish any article or even letter critical of established authority. Between the upper and the nether millstone, the students said, nothing at all was crushed. Dmitri Stratis was as full of opinions as his father was wary of them. He liked to think of himself as a cavalier and Artemis seconded his Royalist postures, at that time outrageous to the authorities but not actually proscribed. The Marshal had recently, if grudgingly, announced that he would like to come to an accommodation with the Royal House; he had in mind the possibility of a Regency leading to the eventual accession of Crown Prince Paul. It was the return of King Boris, a foreign nobleman not especially dear to his adopted countrymen, that the Marshal was compelled to oppose, not so much because of any autocratic or improper actions on the king's part as because he was held responsible for the cession of certain 'border marches' to the traditional enemy. The treaty he negotiated had ended a ruinous war, but his officers claimed that it cheated them of a victory they had showed no signs of gaining. In him they had at last spotted an enemy over whom they might triumph. Boris, being a 'foreigner', was burdened by a patriotic conscience and was reluctant to humiliate his unsuccessful commanders; when he hesitated to cashier the incompetent, they wasted no time in pensioning him. The Marshal was said not to be a party to the plot, but he was certainly not its opponent. When the officers propelled him into office, he insisted his hands were 'clean'; he soon discovered that they were also tied. He proclaimed himself the fearless guardian of national freedom but he was more completely the prisoner of the officers than the king had been. If he resented their 'counsel', he could hardly question the judgment of those whose first act had been to install him in office. He had once advertised his contempt for public opinion, but it was in the comfortable, if deceptive light of sponsored adulation that he first proposed, under pressure from the officers, that a referendum be held over the future of the throne. The regime hoped to convince foreign Governments of its own stability by showing a happy majority in favour of a republic. The people guessed what the officers wanted and voted overwhelmingly for the monarchy they had never previously cherished. The Marshal congratulated them publicly on their decision and resolved privately never again to submit anything to it. He covered his miscalculation (at least he had never openly endorsed the republicanism of the extremists) by affecting to find a great moral difference between *the* king and *a* king. He thus managed to seem not less Royalist than the Royalists, merely more discriminating. He resembled a man who says he is prepared to embrace the Church but prefers to postpone salvation until he can get the confessor of his choice. The officers were against an early restoration. An unpopular king might be an embarrassment, a popular one would be a catastrophe. The crown prince, whose capabilities were unknown, became the symbol of hope both for the ordinary people and for the young bloods. Because the regime feared him, its opponents were his champions. The frustration of their ambition united them as surely as its fulfilment would divide them. Meanwhile the crown prince refused to disown his father (from whom, after all, his legitimacy derived) and his father showed no signs of renouncing the throne. The latter's dignified presence in one European court after another kept alive that hostility to the dictatorship which never attacked the dictator personally but sought to anathematize his regime. France's refusal to supply arms was a symptom of the republic's embarrassment at the eviction of a monarch. Boris himself announced that he would not rest until he had restored to his country the freedom so crudely filched from it and which he himself now elected to impersonate. The courts of Europe joined in his hopes. How agreeable to believe that princes were a condition of democracy! Furthermore, he was an expensive and demanding guest.

Artemis chose to find politics of no crucial interest. Political discussion was difficult in his parents' house. The atmosphere, though not oppressive, was clouded by a familiar and airless propriety, in which considered language and a thoughtfulness about larger issues was supposed to maintain in private that reputation for speculative subtlety and political perception which the country was inhibited from displaying in public. Sophocles Theodoros preferred to shudder at alternatives rather than to criticize the existing situation. He was scornful of measures that future ministers might take, but he thought one should 'wait and see' before attacking what was actually being done. Since any breach of 'patriotic unity' was measured on a scale which quickly graduated to treason, even those who had not approved of the Marshal's coup but whose prosperity was advanced by it had solidified behind him, less because of his practical virtues than because, with the fog which now blanked out the political scene, any new step in the silence sounded to them like a possible assassin. Artemis's father, whose building business had benefited from the public works programme, had previously been associated with a liberal movement whose most radical policy had been to recommend the solution of 'the language problem' which had polarized opinion ever since the Wars of Independence. They proposed wholesale adoption of the 'popular' dialect and the dropping of the 'high' language in which all Government and legal business was supposed to be transacted. This 'sublime reformism', as the extreme Left had called it, was intended to be more palliative than seditious. At the time, however, of the troubles which followed 'the king's peace', it managed to have the effect of radical action while being concerned, quite literally, only with talk. It affected to make a concession to the masses without damaging the notables. The inability to write the formal language (it was a jargon without spoken use) had previously barred the lower orders from careers in the legal or civil service. The sublime reformers declared that they wished to remove this barrier and to make 'the mother tongue' the official common language. Intelligent men might wonder how the unprivileged could think such an innovation sufficient to improve their opportunities or how the notables could fail to realize how many more obstacles than mere vocabulary barred any takeover by the illiterate. Nevertheless this issue, raised in order to de-fuse the social conflict, set off the explosions which brought the Marshal to the Sophia Palace. The Conservatives claimed that the country was being 'withdrawn from civilization' since it would no longer have a language 'capable of literature' and joined forces with the Monarchists (whose bloodthirsty partisanship Boris loyally disowned) against the 'egalitarianism of banality'. The masses on the other hand found so good a slogan in 'Let the People Speak' that the Left was forced to inscribe it on its banners and march on the palace where they demanded the abdication of the king. When His Majesty refused to be provoked, he lost the support of those who would have died to sustain his folly but were dismayed by his wisdom. The reconciliation programme of the Liberals proved more divisive than the intransigence of those they hoped to reconcile. They themselves were attacked from both sides. Their claim that they had no part in the quarrel, only in its resolution, infuriated the Left by its 'sell-out' and the Right by its 'cowardice'. The referee was exhorted to join the game if he wanted to prove his impartiality.

Sophocles Theodoros had favoured the Liberals in the hope of seeming 'responsible' without having any responsibilities. He had doubted the wisdom of demanding that the language question be solved as a matter of urgency. An issue raised to pacify excited opponents should always be made to seem more, not less, complicated than it really is. To suggest an easy answer to a question which might have consumed the energies of the conflicting parties for months was an act of inappropriate sincerity. It was now too late. The riots spread to the major cities. Since he had continued to refuse to lend his voice to either side, the king was universally charged with improper partisanship. The army, in the name of the Nation, stepped in to restore order. The king announced that he would never yield to force and shortly afterwards left the country. In his absence, what more appropriate scapegoat could there now be than a party without popular backing? The Liberals were the first to be proscribed and their organization disbanded. Sophocles Theodoros signed the dignified message of 'disappointment' at their treatment, but he was relieved to have been punished so lightly and to have been seen to be punished. He found it convenient to think that if justice had to be seen to be done then what was seen to be done was necessarily just. His own humiliation became evidence of the magnanimity of the regime. Sophocles Theodoros had felt obliged to take an interest in politics rather as certain successful men, who have never cared for sport, acquire racehorses in the belief that they are expected to show their colours and from an innocuous ambition to saddle a winner. They do not expect to get kicked and are bashfully aggrieved when they find that they do not necessarily win. Sophocles Theodoros was happy to have been warned off; the whole enterprise had consumed more money (it cost Liberals more to bribe journalists than anyone) and more time than he could afford. While he could not fail to protest at the disbanding of the Liberals, he would have been dismayed by their reinstatement. If he saved his conscience by letting it be known that he would not kowtow to the Marshal, he was quick to say that he knew that he could rely on the Old Man, as the impersonation of the military sense of chivalry, to respect his opponents' honest (by which he promised an entirely inactive) dissent. It was less Sophocles's opinions which gave life its crushing air of procrastination in the Theodoros household than the copious reasons he would offer for not yet finding it opportune to present them. For what were they waiting? 'Things may get better', he would say, 'and they may get worse' – the kind of cryptically prudent tautology which made indecision sound like shrewd diagnosis and the postponement of treatment like the promise of stern medicine. Artemis perceived the vanity of his father's statements, but the weight of the family, an institution historically more stable than the State and which therefore received a more unquestioning allegiance, pressed so unconscionably and yet so consistently that it had already become, before Artemis was old enough to be aware of it, almost as natural a toll upon him as gravity. However absurd might seem the library of a man who rarely opened a book, and the affectations of connoisseurship in someone who could point in his collection of antiquities to some of the most costly fakes manufactured in the city, the moral and economic authority of the family remained almost as unchallengeable as kinship itself. The text of the book of life, the tradition claimed, was largely established; all that the brightest young man could be allowed to propose were the smallest possible emendations to it. He could gain a reputation for wit (the standard form of audacity in rigid societies) by the originality of his readings, but only if they left the sense unchanged. The respect which the students showed to the library of the French Institute was not accidental; that kind of serried venerability played upon them all. Inheritance, which was the heart of the tradition to which even the most boisterous were prepared to make loyal reference, lay ahead of them as certainly as whores, business and marriage. Their sportive championship of the young crown prince, of whose real character and qualities they had no reliable knowledge, devolved more from their sense of wanting a leading man, some Rupert to whose service they might rally and for whom, if need be, they might risk their lives without the tiresome necessity of a more commonplace and responsible allegiance, than from any notion of what he might actually do for the country at large. They never left the capital except to go swimming at fashionable resorts or to shoot on the estates of the richest of their companions. Offered a choice between dying for a ridiculous or for a worthy cause they would choose the former. Flippancy, after all, is a sign of individuality; worthiness comes in battalions. If the young men of Dmitri Stratis's stamp lacked the patience for morals, they had all the energy needed for gestures. Their casual and inconsistent outrageousness – now baiting the police, now a band of strikers – seemed like a challenge to the prevailing order, but it was a symptom more of their desire to shuffle the cards for themselves than of any wish to alter the rules of the game. When they wished to evict the old, as their most daring songs asserted, it was not for the sake of justice but in the hope of novelty. It is hard for young men to believe that there is not some wisdom in the arrangements which put money in their pockets. If they were not yet recruited, for the most part, to the business from which this wealth came, they knew its methods and were intrigued by its opportunities. When they sneered at injustice it was because of the hypocrisy of those who defended it, not the sufferings of those on whom it was practised. They were happy to be generous, since generosity is next to lordliness, and their swagger had the animal charm, looked at amiably, of beasts who have yet to use their teeth and whose vigour is, for the present, limited to ragging each other. Boredom was their constant fear and 'boring' their most opprobrious epithet. By dwelling on the aesthetic virtues or failings of what surrounded them they managed to believe themselves both outspokenly disenchanted and justifiably indifferent. The Marshal's regime seemed, by the time Artemis was a member of Dmitri's set, to have become at once innocuous and intolerable. Their disapproval took the form of yawning as loudly as they dared whenever they saw the Old Man's portrait. What rich young men find beyond endurance always has something to do with style. For the rest, their cushions are plump enough to make life supportable and their pillow-fights seldom provoke the intervention of the authorities. Dmitri, on the night of the recital, was able to dissociate himself from any obligation to take his share of the blows by laughing uproariously (laughter was an action with him, not a response) at the ease with which they had evaded the police and by treating the whole episode, as a result of which fifty-two students were barred from the university and eight sent to a penal colony for three months (after beating up a doorman), as if it were a comedy successfully mounted by an impresario of whom the smart *boulevardier* would certainly be hearing more. In this evasive frivolity Artemis did not join, not from any conscious disapproval of the evening's course (it *had* been exciting) but through a habitual inability to find pleasure in group emotions. For his solemnity Dmitri dubbed him 'the owl'.

As they walked away from the noise of the recital, Dmitri thumped him on the back and laughed, his heavy head lowered to Artemis's face, his eyes as encouraging as a prompter's. Did he sense in the younger man a criticism of his dexterity in turning the evening from a political confrontation to a prank, the humour of which derived from how silkily the jokers could disappear up the city's sleeve and leave others to fill the pack? Was it for accusations of cowardice that big Dmitri was fishing when he said, 'What's wrong with you, you young owl?' Artemis had not until then thought one way or the other about Dmitri's morals, but this sneering importunity cracked his complacency. He felt at once the cold wind of an immense solitude. Freedom came down on him like one of those summer chills from which the cloaking attentions of his nurse had always been used to protect him.

'I know what I need,' said Dmitri, 'and that's a fuck. That's what I need, a nice little lady-friend.' The conjunction of vulgarity and genteelism was typical; Dmitri preferred outrage to pleasure. When he had a woman he liked to think that he was fucking her in the presence of those whom it would disgust. The courtesy which he showed his mother (and he would do nothing, naturally, which might endanger his prospects) was tinged with an irony which she could not follow. She would ask him, 'Are you all right, Dimmy, you're not ill? You haven't caught something?' when his secretive charm derived from his amusement that if she had seen him twenty minutes earlier, he would have been stuffing a big tart. 'I'm all right, mother, don't worry about me,' he would say to her, kissing her gaunt cheek with the identical kiss he had bestowed on the woman whose cunt he had rented for a couple of silver coins discovered in the lining of his suit. 'The owl is in love,' Dmitri said, 'and he's saving his load for the big night. Or has the big night taken place already? Has Katie already tasted the joys of the spear perhaps, who knows?' Dmitri had a curious way of lurching at one, owing to a once dislocated hip, and he would wave his hands, the fingers splayed like those of an actor who specializes in exquisites. 'Come, Artemis, we're your friends, the companions of your youthful lust. Tell us, do!' Artemis took the little finger of the hand which was conducting this private cadenza (with the same insolence as a conductor beating time for a soloist who is out of form) and twisted it. Dmitri thought for a moment that he had adequate time to humour such petty violence before deciding on some massive counter-measure. In that ill-considered second he found himself delivered into the owl's power. As if it were some exercise which he had been practising privately for a long time, with a frown of dedication, as if he were striving for an exact quotation, Artemis bent and twisted that hairy little finger until Dmitri, with a gasp and a terrible smile, bumped down on one knee, a bad loser who has dropped the ball in a game of forfeits. He remained there, confident that he would be up on the next round, astonished at the concentration

27

of all feeling in that one little finger. When he attempted to summon the massive forces of the rest of his body he found them fled. His little finger represented his entire strength and it was powerless. The others, Yanni, Niki, Konstantine, whoever, stood ahead of them, looking back up the narrow street. An old man, in traditional costume, was eating a yoghurt at a café table perched on the narrow pavement. He watched the slow wrestling in the roadway with the unaffected mundaneness of a fact challenged by a metaphor. Dmitri found the whole thing ridiculous. Only laughter was left to him, like the radio station in the hands of a country which has already been overrun. In those last moments of breath he did not know whether to broadcast vengeful defiance or civilized capitulation. Artemis, the gaslight glinting on the roundels of his spectacles, kept up the pressure. Dmitri squealed and was on his back in the road, kicking, curling, ramping like an overturned caterpillar, helpless in the hands of his arched adversary. 'All right, all *right*'; he tried to laugh. The broadcasting station itself was now filled with the din of the invaders. Dmitri Stratis was turned on his face. His hand was locked behind him. His face was against the wall of the road with its crust of dried droppings. And then he was over again. Artemis was turning him towards the gutter where the damp droppings had been shovelled. 'Artemy,' cried the giant, flailing his legs, at once suppliant and desperate. His policy resembled that of defeated belligerents who send their mildest and most respected statesmen to plead for an honourable peace while attempting to mount a last and if necessary treacherous resistance at home. 'Stop this. It's enough.' Artemis twisted his victim sharply and now Dmitri could see the shit. His bulging eyes belonged to a panicky horse in a romantic painting. His chin grated on a flint in the wall of his cell. 'Stop, please. I beg you.' The resistance was over. 'Artemy, I apologize. I apologize.' His mouth slid round his head, it looked, as he was wheeled into the gutter. Artemis had his tongue out for the tricky moment, the chef twisting an egged escalope in the breadcrumbs. Dmitri was choking, gasping, his hips convulsing in a fat parody of the fuck he had said he needed. Artemis held him to his deserts for a second and then walked away, unhurried as a bullfighter. Dmitri coughed in a long regular sequence of moans, each one of equal duration and intensity, like a dog choked on its lead, the sobbing of someone who could not manage tears. He seemed like some mortified Caliban, acquainted at last with his distance from humanity. He gazed with accusation at Artemis, his creator and his tormentor. And Artemis returned the curious and sheepish frown of an animal who has just given birth to this new and weak-kneed Dmitri as he stumbled to his feet and learned to walk. Dmitri took strength as quickly as a new-born buffalo. He was instantly ready to keep up with the herd. His hide thickened as remarkably as his body recovered its strength. The others waited for him. No country remains for long without a ruler nor any ruler long without courtiers. 'You rolled me in the shit,' he said. 'You rolled me in the shit, Artemy.'

Artemis said, 'You insulted my fiancée.'

'I did,' said Dmitri, 'and I was wrong.' His face wore something of the wonderful surprise of a clumsy man who finds he has executed a graceful dance-step. His feet even seemed smaller. 'I apologize.' He led out his hand to Artemis. 'Artemy, I apologize.'

'That's all right,' said Artemis. 'Don't worry about it.'

'Now I must find somewhere to wash.' Artemis had thought that Dmitri might find it impossible to recover his dignity, but he had more resources or less shame than his friend imagined. He was accustomed to come out of a bedroom in a brothel and continue in a loud voice his conversation with the woman he had just had. He would adjust his genitals as the woman might the contents of her bag. This habitual shamelessness served him well after his bout with Artemis, which took on, in retrospect, something of the sensuality, that intense mindlessness, which would lead Dmitri to bestow upon the body of a bought woman the caresses a man might normally reserve for the tenderest love-making. 'I like the taste of cunt, Artemy,' he would shout afterwards, 'what about you?' Now he drew on the conventions of the brothel-party to regularize the occasion, to prove how unextraordinary had been his tumble with Artemis and how unaltered it left everything. 'I must find somewhere to wash,' he repeated with accusing good humour, as if he expected Artemis to produce an enamel bowl, a rind of soap and a threadbare hand-towel. Flakes of shit were still visible on his face. Artemis did go so far as to produce a handkerchief and Dmitri cleaned himself provisionally in the mirroring window of a confectioner's. Bins of home-made boiled sweets and glass mangers of nuts filled his profile. Artemis walked quietly beside the revived rowdiness of his friends. Though he lacked any vestige of anger, he felt himself remote from the others to whom Dmitri, wasting no time now, was quick to commend himself by his sportsmanship and his determination to make a joke of his humiliation, thus brushing aside before it could rise any barrier caused by embarrassment at an unmentionable abasement. 'You know what I'm going to do for you, Artemy, to show how sorry I am? I'm going to take you down to Helen's and stand you Veronique, what do you say? Can I offer anything better?'

'Thank you, Dimmy, but I shall go home, I think. I have work to do.'

'Oh Artemy, I've apologized. Please don't be angry.'

'I assure you I am not in the least angry. I'm tired and I want to go home.'

The others looked at each other, inclined to take Dmitri's side, though not wanting, here in the banking district, to have too loud an argument about their destination. The excitement of the evening had separated them and the prospect of a common fuck promised to repair their unity. Nothing was said, after Artemis's exemplary treatment of Dmitri, concerning the chastity of fiancées, but tactful reticence is more divisive than any banter. They left Artemis alone and his loneliness was the consequence. Like the man in the Regency drawing-room, if he departed now he would be leaving his reputation behind him. 'It'll do you good, Artemy. You'll sleep better and you'll work better in the morning.' Artemis was won, like a girl, and shrugged: very well. 'Bravo!

30

Bravo!' He agreed to join in this last excursion to Helen's with all the indulgent purposefulness of one who had resolved to give up masturbation after his eighteenth birthday. Meanwhile the proscribed pleasure enjoys a final boom.

They came to a fountain in a small square surrounded with the myriad offices of small businessmen, each of whom crammed his staff into the smallest possible space. Every window in the tall buildings was shared by several cramped tables, each pressed to partitions which divided the face of the glass and quartered the interior like the slats of a wine merchant's carton. All was now empty, of course, since it was near midnight, but the stacked and dog-eared catalogues, the upright and funereally shrouded typewriters, the stiff black daffodils of the telephones, seemed to offer to the young men, who sat on the fountain's edge while Dmitri made a business of washing himself, the image of a claustrophobic future at the service of sepulchral offices which would long survive and never mark their passing. 'Perhaps there'll be a war,' Konni Plakeotis said. It was as if he had spoken their real grievance against the Marshal, not that he was the foolish old soldier who might lead them into 'adventures' but that he was indeed the strong man whose stern profile might not only stave off foreign enemies but also impose domestic necessity. The hazards of war did not attract these young and comfortable blades, but neither did an immutable peace.

Dmitri made bubbling noises and sloshed like a seal. He came up with the blinded, touching look of a man bereft of his spectacles and pawed for them on the edge of the marble. Normally Konni might have nudged them into the water, but now he hooked them over the old walrus's ears. Dmitri turned, pink and clean, to face the polished white breasts of a watered nymph in the centre of the fountain. He waded forward, wetting his expensive knees, and kissed each embossed nipple with a loud smack. Then he toiled back through the underlit water, levered himself over the parapet and planted clean footmarks on the cobbles. He sat down with the confidence of a lover in front of a woman he has more than satisfied, and attended to his toes, brushed the pebbles from his soles before resuming his socks and attaching them to the elastic suspenders which he had put in his top pocket.

Helen's brothel was in the harbour, but it was not a brothel for seamen. The prices were too high. The place was, in fact, no more exclusive than its tariff (anyone who could afford it was allowed in), but Helen believed that she fulfilled her duty to her girls by limiting their acquaintance to those who were personally recommended, which meant in practice those who could meet the price. She despised street-walking; her girls paraded in the uncurtained saloon under an elaborate chandelier. The men lounged on wide divans and made their selection. Each young man who went there liked to think that he had stumbled on something rather different. Since it was a good walk from the centre of the capital one was unlikely to be embarrassed by finding that he patronized the same establishment as his father. In order to reach Helen's it was necessary to pass through the rougher quarters of the harbour where short-time women tottered under the eyes of their pimps and slim sailors who wore an air of prophylactic disillusion as they followed those broad haunches to narrow rendezvous. Dmitri was addicted to the district. He knew the bars; he knew the cellars; he knew some of the pimps by name and liked nothing better than to ask over the heads of the women, who stood stilted on painful heels, wincing at each tiny step, how business was and whether anyone had had this girl or that during the last hour. Dmitri could make a visit to Helen's a demonstration of good taste by showing his companions how profoundly lower than Helen's the real depths were.

While passing through this district, where the light itself seemed to have a more lurid tone, as if it came from a circuit quite different from that of the city, Artemis was filled with a familiar emotion of violence and shame. It was not a shame which had its origins in sexual fear or desire (its strands were more distinct to him than they had ever been before) but in the sense of economic power. Dmitri's crowd walked without apprehension in the

32

roughest neighbourhood of the city and liked to suppose that it was their charm, their quickwittedness, even their physical strength which secured them from attack. Artemis now realized that it was as milch cows that they were welcome. The pimps and bully-boys could easily have set upon them and robbed them, but it was easier and less dangerous, since there were no consequences, to take from them in instalments what might have been grabbed at once. Even in the lowest dive these sons of the notables were recognized for the mould from which they came. Dmitri's swagger was not a provocation; it was a guarantee. The likeliest risk came from the sailors, from the 'honest' element, since it was possible that they would be unaware of the resources behind these strolling and arrogant young men. As for the violence, Artemis felt it all around him, not because he feared attack but because it was the logic of the district. Violence was the reliable currency here as gold was in the palm-shaded residences and policed apartment houses around Independence Square. What frightened and excited Artemis was the shallowness of motive. Dmitri might imagine vast resources of evil in this smelly and infamous area. It amused him and Niki and the others to have drinks in bars where famous pimps and suspected murderers congregated. They liked to imagine their own sisters being dragged into sordid service, forced to suck-off lascars,* for then it seemed to them that they were walking with danger and daring across appalling abysses on rotten planks. The thrilling horrors of the possible made tolerable the *longueurs* of the actual. They were comforted to think, as men are who look back and see a long queue stretching behind them for some film they were not previously sure they wanted to see, that their situation was envied. An acquaintance with low life spiced the artificialities of society. For the rest of their lives they would believe that the time they put in at the brothels gave them a knowledge of life impossible to the women they married. The cunts of prostitutes swallowed their youthful lust without the necessity of protestations of love, while the extremes of indulgent devotion lavished on them by their mothers convinced them of the infinite and dutiful gullibility of women and of their right to it. The whore was proof of the stupidity of emotional expenditure as a means of getting what money and power could more simply secure, the mother of a woman's readiness to give devotion in return for hypocrisy. Marriage was a practical partnership not always cynically contracted, but without any emotional guarantees: one stayed with one's wife, but one was not limited to her. The business of a family and the family business were coupled in one transaction. The girl was made palatable, but her nubility did not long survive the nuptials. She had children and she grew fat. As soon as possible she transferred to the children the love which drew so little response from the husband who associated cunt with cash. The father withdrew to his accounts and replaced sensuality with greed. Dmitri and his friends foresaw their embittered future and, like the old priests who hoped to avert earthquakes with bull-roarers, tried to put it off by loud and outrageous demonstrations. They were fascinated by the present-dwelling potentates of the underworld. They were as flattered to be offered a glass of *anis* by a performer in one of the exhibitions mounted for tourists as a parvenu asked to taste the wine for a vintner's banquet. They would sit with a drug pedlar or a long-nailed boy who greased his arse for Turks or for the plump sons of domineering fathers and ask questions of him with the reverence their ancestors offered the oracle. The priestess drew her answers from the depths of the earth, the pimp from the depths of depravity. The wisdom of those who had no illusions rang indisputably true to those who would question only at the risk of their fortunes the morality which the present company did not hesitate to deride. Dmitri and his pals envied the freedom of the harbour riff-raff. Artemis, though he could not deny the pulse in his loins, was less bewitched. If he was aware of the flimsiness of his father's intellect and the flabbiness of his values, he could not conceal from himself the rich variety of manoeuvre, even of nuance, in the world of wealth. Irony and subtlety, wit and patience made sense in Vassili Street where it could bide its time. Low life was alluring not because it was more honest but because it was less complicated. It spoke in a language without figures of speech. The young men who made such loud use of its bold slang had joined a nocturnal army. They went to whores as others did to wars. Nakedness was the uniform which made them equals; fucking their common baptism.

They came down past a row of smoking doorways where skewered entrails were spitting over open drawers of charcoal. Large men with aromatic hands and singed hair fished for olives in jars of brine. The regime had embarked on a transformation of the sea-front against which steamers clustered under banners advertising islands. Mounds of earth, jewelled with red lamps, were piled between the tram tracks. Wells, with boarded sides, descended the darkness. Abandoned at night except for a watchman, the place had the air of an operation in which a number of brutal incisions have been made by surgeons who, having lost confidence in the treatment, take advantage of the collapse of the patient to steal away for another look at the book. It was rumoured that the works would never be completed. Sophocles Theodoros had refused to tender for them; the harbour authority could not promise a sufficient profit. It was galling to belong to a country which was incapable of repairing its own sewers, which had no means of containing its own foulness and whose rich men, as distant from its arsehole as the top of their heads, could deny it their resources. The stench seemed to tickle Niki and Dmitri, whose guffaws applauded the scandal. The crown prince, thought Artemis, might make all the difference. A clean example would shake the selfishness of the notables.

The noise of the students' footsteps drumming on the unevenly supported boards seemed to give rise to a strange, whispered echo. Artemis saw that all along the dark shadows under the shuttered shops (a few of which, first class with white cables, diminutive lifebelts and shiny storm clothes, looked for the captains of smart yachts who came to spend clean notes and receive agreed bills) men and women and children were bundled like dirty laundry. The young men had wakened some of them; the disturbance rippled through the others. 'Emigrants,' said Konstantine. Artemis looked at his friend with tears in his eyes. Konni's parents had lived for a long time in a foreign country from which they had been repatriated as a result of 'the king's peace'. His family had many branches and he had had no difficulty in settling into the social life of the capital, but there was about him an abstractedness, a pallor, which made aunts wonder whether he might not be delicate. He was capable of immense dash (he had once scored a brilliant goal in their last year in school, a goal so insolently contrived and so exactly shot home that he was spoken of as a possible international) and of singular lethargy, a kind of drugged sloth which earned the nickname 'the Indian'. Once he had actually failed to turn up for a trial match which might have taken him on a world tour. Was he away, on those occasions, on some spiritual visit to the lands which the famous treaty had removed from his father? Or was his casualness an early sign of that not unusual malaise which afflicts the brilliant in a country where their energies are doctored by polite rituals until early promise peters out in gracious gestures, fleshy jowls and uncompleted theses? 'It's a crime,' said Artemis, including in his passion the agreement which had evicted Konni's parents from their land. Konni shrugged. Artemis gripped the other's arm. Konni turned his glaucous eyes on his friend and peeled his pale, olive lips from his teeth. He stood still, watching Artemis, who reeled, as if shot, against the rough shutters of a shoe-shop. Artemis felt that he had never seen Konni before in his life. How could he have endured to see such beauty and not to have recognized it? His body throbbed and shook like an engine inadequately bolted to the bed on which it stands. It was the most remarkable and shattering moment of his life. Konni had scarcely been his friend, it was mere habit to speak of him so, and now he stood, in a dark-blue suit and rather pointed, scuffed shoes (he liked to kick stones), in the crumbling mess of those inept excavations, his hair steeply pitched on his narrow head, his large pale grey eyes watching with an amused gentleness that seemed to understand and license all of Artemis's feelings, while Dmitri and the others hopped on ahead, past the susurrating mass who waited for the steamer which was to take them to a distant land whose wealth they took for granted and whose prosperity required only their presence for them to share it.

'What do you want to do?'

'Do you want to go to Helen's?'

Konni shrugged, smiled, as usual.

'I don't.'

'What do you want to do?'

'Let's go somewhere.'

'As you like.'

'Do you mean that?'

'Yes, of course. I mean it.'

'Konni ... '

'What?'

'Something has happened to me.'

'I know.'

'Do you? Do you truly?'

'Yes.'

'I don't think I can move for a moment.'

'I'll wait.'

'Will you help me?'

'Yes.' Konni came and sheltered Artemis from the mild evening which seemed to blow on him like a gale, until his teeth rattled in his skull.

'I love you,' Artemis said.

'Yes. I see. I know.'

'I feel I've never seen you before. I'm frightened, Konni. I have to tell you. I know I shouldn't – '

'Tell me that you love me?'

'How afraid I am. How helpless without you.'

'In case I hurt you?'

'I love you.'

'Don't worry, Artemy, please.'

'Do you have any feeling for me? Never have I wanted anyone as I want you.'

'Yes. I've been watching you tonight.'

'Then perhaps it's not only me. Perhaps I'm not alone in what I feel – '

'Perhaps not.'

'You're not mocking me?'

That slim face, those huge eyes, that steep foliage of glossy hair, all shook slightly, gently before Artemis's blanched gaze. 'Come.' It seemed to Artemis that he had never heard a word so tenderly spoken. He started to cry. A cruise ship, immense with lights, the birthday cake of some god, blazing with myriads of candles, had drifted into the gulf before them and now swung on its cable in the oily water, filling the depths with its molten image.

They walked quickly, their shoulders scarcely touching. Artemis was able once again practically to control his limbs but he stumbled and hurried awkwardly, like someone with a brimming bowl, who now hastens to get it safely to its destination and now slows so as not to slop it. He dreaded a change in Konni or in himself. They came to a steep street, parallel to that in which the entrails sizzled, and Konni led the way. Artemis felt his love growing for the other. Konni's very existence seemed something of immense wonder. The street was dark. Could there be no hotel? Artemis summoned all his imagination, as if by sheer desire he could create what he wanted out of grime and brick and wood. They came to a narrow doorway with a lettered bulb above it loaded with dead flies: HOTEL. A urine-smelling passageway where boxes of tomato paste were stacked took them up tiled steps towards a pale light. Two women, stockings rolled down to their knees, their thighs ajar, their mouths stabbed on to chalky faces, were sitting on wooden chairs. A gate-legged table between them was topped by a tin tray advertising beer. Seeing the two boys, they closed their knees, drew down their dresses and adopted expressions of ungenerous entreaty. Konni and Artemis felt (and each knew the other felt) a surge not of disgust but of love for these

38

two harpies. They had so much to spare that they had time to embrace these thick, oily and repulsive old cunts, at least in their minds, and find them touching. One of the women called 'Spiro', harshly, before the two of them rose to their feet and began to smile. Artemis now lost that all-embracing emotion and his ironic sense warned him that he would be unable to resist these two women's cheap assumptions and that he would spend his desire with one or the other. Shame told him that he deserved the punishment. Dreams always ended in degradation. But Konni, whom he loved, for whom he longed now to die (or better, to please), had taken both of the women by their shoulders and drawn them to him. He was whispering to them, and, miraculously, they had not abused him, they were not shrilling insults or swinging their slack-fleshed arms. They listened as if to an angel and by the time Spiro the cripple, creaking on his metal leg like an ill-saddled donkey, had come to the desk and found a key, everything was arranged. The two women watched Konni and Artemis go down the patchily plastered passage towards a numbered room, over tiles which ran out into mere concrete, and whispered to the cripple, one of them holding his gartered shirt-sleeve until everything had been said. The room was cracked diagonally across the wall next to the bed. There was a tin bidet on a rusty stand and a basin with a single tap in which a jug of brown water was standing. The shutters were closed. It was stifling. The bed had a narrow sheet on it, too narrow to conceal the ulcerated mattress. Konni nodded and gave the man plenty of money. The door shut. The two were alone. Artemis said, 'I love you. It's never happened to me before. I know I've seen you many times. I've liked you, but now I love you.'

'I understand. I know.'

'What I mean to say is, I have never imagined this. I have never imagined anything of this kind before. I know they say it's quite common, but I want you to know that it is entirely new to me. Entirely.'

Konni came and stood in front of Artemis. He looked into his face and seemed to find an immense landscape there. He leaned slightly forward and brushed his face against the other's shoulder. Artemis was wearing a dark suit of an expensive and cool material. They stood there, bodies leaning as lightly as two playing-cards at the beginning of a card-house, when the faintest breeze is enough to ruin everything. Then Konni caressed his friend's face (as if it had been he whose desire had brought them here), a caress which did not arouse but reassured, which promised. He sat down on the bed. Artemis knelt on the floor and hugged Konni's knees. He felt Konni's face pressing on the top of his head and he looked up and they kissed. Konni stood and took off his coat and his shirt. Artemis waited for him, yes, as he used to wait for the whores at Helen's to be naked before he would consent to remove even his coat. Konni guessed even this perhaps and even this did not amaze or revolt him. He stood naked in front of Artemis, with only a gold signet-ring on his body. Artemis gulped and tears again trickled down his face. 'Come.' Artemis sat awkwardly on the bed beside his naked friend, longing now to kiss that pale belly and the branching ribs. Artemis stood to remove his trousers and when he turned Konni was lying on the bed full length, his hips turned from the other. Artemis looked up at the glaring light in the ceiling. He kissed Konni's shoulder and the hollow of his back and then turned him towards him, on to his back, and took his lips across his friend's pulsing belly and stroked his hair against the other's sex. He felt Konni's hand on his shoulder pressing him down and drawing him back towards his lips, so that as his own mouth touched Konni's swelling cock he could taste his lover's tongue on his flesh. Scissors of tenderness and murderous desire cut through his brain, tore his mouth open till he could see himself sleeve his lover's body within the moist, gulping passion of his own. The smell of Konni's loins deluged his nostrils. He tasted with his eyes, he smelt with his tongue, he saw with his fingers. The whole vocabulary of his life tilted and slewed like film in the decrepit projector of one of those summer cinemas for which the capital was famous, where you could sit and sip water ices and clap the projectionist. 'Je t'aime,' he choked, 'je t'aime, je t'aime.' His nails took the pulse of his lover's desire. His head was bursting with the fear that it would all end. He jerked like a hooked fish as Konni's lips sipped his belly and his fingers found their destination. He twisted in terror and saw his lover's naked mouth, yawning with longing, his eyes drugged, like the Indian's with a dream beyond time, and he flung himself into the other's arms and kissed that soft, warm mouth and drowned his tongue in it, thrusting himself away only to say, 'Je veux mourir. Je veux mourir, Konni, mon amour.' Konni, whose head now looked as if it had changed shape, as if it was as broad as before it had been narrow, the cheeks flushed, the mouth hung with saliva, the tongue lolling and thick, smiled the smile of a beautiful mythical being and, with the firm extension of his arm drove Artemis's head downwards and drew his sex towards him. 'Je veux finir, mon amour,' said Konni. 'Je veux finir.' The words, which seemed to endorse Artemis's, which seemed in their choice of the same language to which Artemis himself had been, not so remarkably, inclined, were like a fresh and final caress which charged with immensity the phallus Artemis drew into himself and exempted from time the infinite second that followed.

Artemis waited for some revulsion. He had laid out in the blinding light of his amputated consciousness all the possible reactions to this incredible pleasure. But the clinical, the dirty, the derisive descriptions of his behaviour, of their caresses, which had scattered like sparrows to distant branches, did not, as he had feared, flutter back to darken his immediate memory. He did not remember; he remained in the present. There was a different light in the room as he turned to watch his lover, from whose mouth the thick proof of their passion ran on to the grey sheet like blanched blood, so that Artemis felt, as if such passions had been common with him, a sort of anger with the universe, actually quite new to him, that the stuff should have no further use in their love, could lead to nothing. Guiltily, simply because he feared to offend Konni, he allowed it to run from his lips too and felt it glutinous and chilly on the hot air. His guilt had no practical application, for soon he felt his friend's fingers touch his hair and smile, the fingers, and his desire was instantly rising again. He flung his arms round Konni and kissed him again and again and his eyes searched the heavy-lidded opacity of his lover's to see what they should do now. Should words come now? Should they discuss what they would do next? How he longed to please Konni, with anything, anything, as long as there was something he wanted! But it was more than a desire to please, this love, it was a new nakedness, a new opportunity, so that remorse and anxiety stayed distant from it. The lovers enjoyed the cracked privacy of that room, giggled, for the first time, at the thought that perhaps the two oily women were watching them through one of the chinks in the plaster. They even considered, whether for real amusement or to tease each other, inviting the women to join them, to watch, to enjoy them, though not actually to come to bed with them. The bed was too narrow and too rickety. No, they wanted to be watched not because they could not find pleasure without it but simply because they were so happy in each other that they could imagine offering scraps of their love to others who would never taste its perfection. As to their embraces, they continued between dozes, until the first smudges of light began to dull the bulb (they had opened the shutters on to the dust-pollened well, thick with old pipes, behind the hotel) and were even ready, in theory, to feed the mosquitoes, at least before they heard the first monitory whine, the first deadly silence. 'Il faut que nous nous en allions,' said Artemis. He looked down for the last time at his lover's body, slim on the bed, his sex coiled like a comma in his bearded groin. He bent to kiss the crusted belly, the flat nipples, the bruised lips. 'Tu viens?' Konni turned and groaned, smiling, and reached and flicked his lover's wrinkled prick. 'Qu'est-ce qu'on va faire?' Artemis wondered as they drew on their clothes. Desire again commanded him. He loved Konni. He was sure of it.

'Tu vas te marier.'

Artemis turned and kissed Konni crushingly on the mouth and

throat and held his arms to his sides. He wanted now to own the boy whose tenderness he had so venerated. Konni rose, seemed actually to grow taller, slimmer against this assault. And immediately Artemis was on his knees on the beastly floor, demanding with his dressed fingers (so different did they seem with the cuffs back over them) the desire he hoped to arouse in the other. Konni put conventional fingers through Artemis's hair and pushed his head away from his suit. 'Not now.'

Artemis stood up, brushing his trousers. 'I must see you again.'

'Yes. Of course. Why not?' Why was it that Artemis was almost brutal, as if with a whore, where all night he had been gorged with tenderness? Was it something that came from him or was it that, as he now suspected, something had been changed by Konni, even willed by him? Were they both puppets of whatever ageless appetite had twisted them together like a butcher's sausages? Artemis turned out the light and they stood in the sunless light, the colour of the grey sheet which decked the bed. 'You paid for the room,' Artemis said. 'I must give you something.'

'I paid two hundred.'

Artemis took out a wad of notes, pinned together by the same clerk he went to every week, and handed Konni one. Konni took it. 'Thanks.'

Artemis said, 'Je t'aime.'

And Konni replied, 'Ce n'est pas moi que tu aimes.'

And what had Artemis said then? What did it matter? He had said, 'Alors, qu'est-ce que tu crois que j'aime?' His language was now French, foreign, harshly enunciated, the language not of love but of diplomacy.

Konni had said, 'Oh! Voyez-vous. Disons ... par exemple, le pouvoir.'

Out there on the mountain Kosta wore only tattered khaki trousers, car-tyre sandals with leather laces and a blue shirt taken from a village line, open at the neck for the Byzantine cross that shone on his breast. Over his shoulders were two huntsman's bandoliers studded with bullets. The black mouth of a captured machine-gun hung downwards, like an inedible fish, the tail under his armpit. On his buckled belt hung four grenades. Artemis feared that he sentimentalized the boy, though his love for him had never had and never demanded physical expression. He suspected (was this the reason for his continuing fascination with him?) that Kosta would kill him if he revealed his passion. He would kill him, it might be, not because he found the desire disgusting but because to kill one who loved him would be the greatest pleasure he could find in him. They had been many days on the march. Perhaps the wildness of Artemis's imagination was the measure of his hunger and his exhaustion. He digested and lived on words instead of food. He was never in doubt of his ability to control himself, but he had reached the point of inner turmoil where even his dreams were composed of documents. The walls of his mind were papered with texts. It grew more and more difficult to distinguish which were of his own and which of official authorship.

Paniotis, the old sailor settled with the tiller over his hip, stood behind Kosta as the young man retained his position over the body of the dead shepherd. Paniotis was responsible for the course things were taking without seeming to move, doing no more than lean his weight, imperceptibly, into the current. Kosta held Paniotis in special regard, a father to whom he looked not for protection (he was so impudent in his courage that Artemis had had to reprimand him for egotism) but for approval. He took up the actions of the older man and capped them with a kind of vigilant, even tender, rivalry which earned from Paniotis only the tribute of an exaggerated gruffness. Kosta matched himself to the other, as a striding lover will match his footsteps to the shorter ones of his beloved. Their teasing competition resembled the ritual exchanges of the old pastoral improvisers. When they were in camp, salacious stories were muttered under camouflage netting, incident following incident, triumph triumph, derision derision, the two of them lashing at each other and yet twins in the common

44

scansion which united their performance. Artemis was impatient with the drama on which they were now almost capriciously embarked. All around them the auditorium of the hills and the high peaks of the gods seemed to offer a timeless theatre for their performance, but in the distance, like doors closing, the thud of artillery, perhaps of bombs, ran a curtain of sound between them and the illusion of eternity. Artemis frowned at the sky for the planes and then had once more to face Kosta's tiresome aggression. The fall of the explosive reminded Artemis of trucks tipping stones into the brown cavity of one of his father's building sites on child-hood afternoons, when he would sit in his push-chair in front of Eleutheria, a water ice in his fist and a lace sunshade clamped to the handle of the chair. Kosta took hold of the goatskin coat and spilled the old man from it. As if trapped in the folds, a last moan seemed to escape the falling body. Kosta, the conjurer on a visit to a distant village, drew the coat free, shook it to give it bulk (and make his trick more impressive) and slung it, with a quick glance at his audience, over Paniotis's shoulders. Then he laughed. 'No, no!' Paniotis shrugged himself out of the coat and tried to press it on Kosta, but the younger man clamped the skins again over Paniotis's shoulder and held them there, a paper-hanger waiting for the paste to dry. Paniotis smiled, almost simpered, frowning in the light, as if his photograph were being taken.

Stelio, who liked to believe that he stood to Kosta as the hand-some soldier did to Paniotis, bent, knees to the side, with the awkward decision which betrayed his fear of breaking the panel of blood over his wound, and took the dagger from the corpse's waist. It had a silver haft and a curved scabbard embossed with thick, vivid embroidery. Stelio presented it to Kosta's belt. In pulling it free he had loosened the thick folds of the shepherd's crimson cummerbund, revealing a silver hook and eye and a twist of new thread as startling as a touch of modern paint at the smoke-wracked base of a village icon. Artemis understood in a new way the surgery of civil war; desecration, too, was a kind of therapy. He had wondered at times how he would keep his men to the politically motivated ruthlessness on which the command had decided. At first he was surprised that they never hesitated to commit what the Government press called 'outrages and crimes' and what the Political Committee called 'acts designed to polarize the struggle'. Perhaps the committee itself was strengthened in its policy by the longing to shuck the burdens of piety which lay as thickly on the country as the layers of artefacts through which summer parties of local amateurs and diligent foreigners once liked to burrow. Artemis had never supposed that there could be pure motives, only correct actions. The darkness of interpretations could not obscure the clear necessity of what actually needed to be done. He liked to think that he had finished with the inhibitions of style, the sterility of personal standards. Kosta's uncontrollable bravery neither impressed nor intimidated him. It did not make him doubt whether he was fit for command. He was fit for it because he had been appointed to it. To return to the idea of generalship through personal combat was to try to live again in one of those ticketed layers of the past which assiduous archaeologists left exposed, like frogs' innards after a dissection, to fascinate or disgust the living. Kosta's education was incomplete. Perhaps the period across the border would change all that. Perhaps then there would be time for the long operation of severing the handsome youth from his vanity.

Adonis, a pale-faced, small-headed man with the rumpled expression of a new-born calf, who had spent his youth in the furnaces of a coppersmith, doubled to the bellows, his lungs roasting in the hot breath of the fire, his elbows green with ore, and who seemed astonished and even alarmed by his height when he stood straight in the air, so that he crouched even under the roof of the sky – Adonis reached for the end of the sash and pulled the corpse over and over on the brown ground, flouring it in dust, until the crimson cummerbund fluttered in his hand. Kosta gave him the comic look a professional throws an amateur who has tried his trick. The body rolled to Artemis's feet; its cheek lay against his sandal. 'Let's go,' he said, modulating his voice as carefully as a singer coming in on the mildest of cues, and turned to the slope. He ascended undramatically, pausing now and again like a naturalist who senses the butterfly he seeks, suspecting the capstones of the ridges all about him, refusing only, though without any gesture of dogmatic purpose, to look back at the men. They must follow without being ordered; he could not waste the ammunition of his authority on so trivial an incident. They were capable, these unbeaten but defeated men, of either a great deal or of very little more. The alternatives were posted on the walls of Artemis's mind like the claims of new parties at an election. He reached the peak of the ridge. The men maybe imagined that they were testing him, that they would now see how he could cope with their callous challenge, but their nervous glances at each other, their scarcely concealed amusement at seeing their commander under the knife, and their choice of this ground on which to provoke him, were, if they were, as misjudged as the tactics which sought to conquer Antaeus by bearing him down to the ground. Artemis, alone on the ridge, girded by a thousand pointless stones, any one of which might be his tomb, was strengthened by the weight of the men against him. If, by some old logic, he willed them to follow him, he also knew that they would. He knew they would because it was no matter to him if they did or not. If he failed, he would merely be a failure. Failure would not shame him. He had no ambition. Power and ambition are not always linked. He was not making a revolution on his own. These men had their own responsibility. It was none of his job to force them. He hoped they would come. His vanity was not involved, even though, in the knowledge that all did not depend on him, he had timed his move, his manner and even his thoughts (little believing that they were necessarily unwinged) to draw the men after him. He would not be *satisfied* by their following him. He was angry and he was strong. He was alone on the peak and bent his mind, like a god, to bring these men together up the hillside. How far were they from the frontier? He stood, trousers furled in the wind, and consulted the poor map of the country, coming

47

apart at the hinges, which he had taken from the wall of a garage they had burned in a lowland village. He tried to recognize in the ancient commercial map some feature of the rumpled landscape which stood around him, to trace in the ill-printed lines the profiles of the mountains. He walked along the ridge, still alone, as if it were a longitude of time, and then allowed himself to go, as smoothly as tipped sheep's milk from a peasant's pursed pannier, over the lip and into the farther valley. He frowned at the future, at the possible shadow of the border over ahead of him, like a man who frowns a surgeon into administering the curative pain for which he has come. He was alone in a quickly steepening V of umber rocks whose upper rims were still polished gold but whose shining faces were now beyond him. The sun was sliding into the peaks to his left, melting a golden track in the pale sky, a hot wire through ice. The luxury of loneliness, the positive gift which the men had thrown at him, made him gasp. How could a country be at once so small and so immense, so unable to accommodate its people and so lunatically empty?

Artemis turned inland, so that his shadow went ahead of him, and his jaw hardened. 'It must be resisted,' he said aloud. 'It must be resisted.' He concentrated, as if he were preparing a public speech, on a correct analysis of the situation. He must not allow himself to slip into a sentimentality which gave to these senseless stones some rights, some destiny, some purpose. He must not slip into a passive patriotism of regret any more than he must allow his men to regress, as awareness of their purgatory came over them, to the point that the whole grammar of their revolutionary education was lost on them and they decomposed into those neutral symbols of folklore: peasants, labourers and sailors. He must not think that there was any virtue in saving them from blood and disillusion in order that they should remain righteous illustrations in an affable chapter of parish history. 'Avanti!' The cold of evening measured Artemis's chest with a quick, tactless rap. The Sten gun on his shoulder slipped into the crook of his arm and the suggestion it put in his mind stiffened his anger to positive intention.

He felt in his pouch for a clip. But before he had time to act, the shadows of the men began to form a fence behind his own. 'Have you decided, Captain?' asked Paniotis, as if it had been agreed between them that Artemis should go forward on his own to consider the ground. Artemis accepted the fiction and pointed down the path into the thickness of the valley. He shifted his Sten on to his shoulder again and led the way.

He walked back through the wakening docks under a sky thick and grey as an army blanket, though he could sense the sun which would make a kiln of the morning until it broke open the dome of clouds and fired the city. Konni had said, 'I must run. I have a lecture.' Artemis nodded and took the other's pale bony hand and shook it. They went separate ways. Heavy carts, with nodding horses, groaned and rattled along the foreshore; steamers were lowing like stalled animals in the tideless water. Occasionally a lorry, with its engine open to the eye like the genitals of an unbuttoned idiot, came noisily along. Its driver looked down, with all the arrogance of the entrepreneur whose colours he was wearing, on the handcarts and bulging sacks of those who stumbled in, after having risen at three in the morning by the light of a rag lamp, from the outlying farms. Artemis thought of Konni only because it occurred to him how little he was thinking about him. His passion was spent as cleanly as a gambler's wad. He had neither desire nor regret. Was it really power he wanted? If a man did not hide his weaknesses, he would be cut down at once, which is why we brood on insults and dismiss flattery. Everyone is other than he pretends and looks for his true nature in the malicious insights of others, while a lingering and indulgent love, for instance a mother's, disgusts one with its presumptuous blindness. Power? Granted, the wealth of his family, which would come to him, contained a charge of power such as few enjoyed and yet it had never pleased him to imagine his inheritance. What other power was available? Physical power, despite his smart conquest of Dmitri and his quick skill in finding how to please another man (surely no

49

cleverer a trick than learning to shave in a mirror), was beyond him: the days of champions were finished. Achilles might stay in his tent for all the machinery of modern war needed him. (Artemis had read some of the literature which came from the great dictatorships and which found in the dumb proletariat of steel, the muscle of powerful engines, a more reliable and more disciplined force for making history than the uncertain flesh and blood of the people whose will they claimed to carry out.) The liberation which he did feel from the tyranny of desire, the simple fact of a night of love, was surely too provisional to be relied upon; it released in him a sense of his own potential, it uncoiled his thoughts from the spiralling columbine of sexual fantasy, but that was very different from turning them to ambition or greed. What had Konni meant? The difficulty in finding a solution to that question revived his desire for his lover. Perhaps it was exactly this to which Konni had alluded, to the terms on which their relationship would be encouraged to develop. Was he saying that Artemis could not sustain the love which his lips had promised and that he could prolong it only by combining it with the urge to come out on top? Artemis shuddered in the cloying warmth of the unborn day and stopped by a café where workers were leaving their lunchboxes or bread wrapped in a clean rag, placing them on a wall lined with deal shelves which had once, perhaps, been intended for the hats of prosperous patrons. Artemis's tailored clothes, although rumpled, attracted the glances of the men, but they were in too much of a hurry to waste energy even in deriding a gentleman. On the counter was a glass blister of suspiciously old-looking quoits of bread sprinkled with sesame seed. The one he had indicated broke under his cautious nibble into quite delicious sweetness and freshness. The faces along the counter, whose aversion from him he had taken to be deliberate and deserved, now became luminously dear to him, as if the banal hoop of bread had contained some drug which had driven colour and nerve into the gallery of portraits above the unpolished bar. He left the café with a nod which might have signified that he now knew where to find it and that they could expect him to be a regular from now on. He walked behind a group of men towards the furniture factory where they worked. He tracked them more like a spy or a shameless tourist than like an admirer. Perhaps he had become what he tried for several weeks to remain, a simple student.

He avoided Konni out of shame, not at his passion but at its disappearance. He began to work so hard that his mother feared that he would destroy himself. She supposed that he was fighting his desire for Katerina and she maddened him by a sublime tenderness which seemed to connive at a vice he did not actually find necessary. As for Konni, he had perhaps gone away with his parents to one of their family estates on one of the larger islands, for he was not to be seen in the library or with Dmitri Stratis in any of their usual meeting-places. When Artemis did go out, he found the company of his old friends less displeasing than disappointing. All tension had departed from his life. He was courteous with a deeper and less ironic courtesy; his scholarship was neither as racy nor as showy as before. Now that he was convinced that the university could never provide him with whatever he was seeking, they spoke of him as a future professor. He even began, to the delight of his family, to take an interest in his father's business.

The Marshal's regime had become more and more tranquil during the course of the summer. Every day of calm was counted to its credit and yet an uneasiness matched and complemented the calm. The regime had no cumulative strength; it did not capitalize itself. It was as if a mysterious drought made men say of the day not that it was fine but that it had brought no rain. Without any incident of importance, without a single explosion to bruise the clear skin of its record, an edginess began to ruffle the even complexion of the city. The police, who must have known the wisdom of appearing sure of themselves, began to blow their whistles too urgently. Even in Independence Square they shouted and pushed fashionable people for nothing more serious than causing the deceleration of an official car. The crowd was piqued rather than cowed by this unnecessary force. Who were these small men whose progress was so pressing? The rich began to speak of a government of 'unknowns' and the middle classes, who had faced with resignation a regime in which both the wealthy and the military were combined and who had not dared, whether in crowded offices or in the once-garrulous political cafés, to say anything which might endanger either their liberty or their jobs, now sensed that they could as well, and with more sincerity, curry favour by sarcasm as previously they were bound to seek it through obsequiousness.

Dinner in the Theodoros household became an anxious occasion, as if there was someone sick in the family whose death might come at any moment and whose survival, while officially desirable, put a greater strain on the company than would the news they were supposed to dread. No one could make any plans, Sophocles Theodoros would grumble, the *Times* folded by his plate, its ink smudged as if by the passage of too many uneasy eyes, with things in their present state. If another industrialist was present and asked for amplification of Sophocles's views, the head of the family brushed up his moustache with his napkin and adopted an expression as near that of the Marshal as possible before declaring that he agreed with the regularization of the machinery of the State (from which it could be taken that he had nothing against the secret police or dictatorship as such), but that he wondered how long things could continue, whether in this country or any other, without some clue being offered to the public at large of the overall strategy of those who had assumed supreme power. This impersonation of the Marshal, which included mumbled asides, lowering of spectacles and all the repertoire of benignity on which the dictator's eulogists were instructed to dwell, appeared to be the most slavish endorsement of the Old Man's political naivety, but Artemis, sitting in his clean suit, his white collar, his silver tie with its gold slide, well down the table near his sister Eudoxia and his younger brother Demosthenes, understood that his father had donned the most sly of all disguises when criticizing the great: the mask of identity. 'What, after all,' the builder would go on, 'are the lesser men, the mere mortals who conduct, let's be frank, the

52

dull but daily and essential business of a state, what are they to tell their workpeople when an ugly situation threatens? Are they to believe in the strong talk of the Government, for instance when it comes to dealing with the question of wages (to mention only the most obvious issue), or are they to do what they see a great many of their colleagues and, needless to say, competitors doing, that is to say more or less openly evading the spirit and sometimes, I must be very honest without naming names, the letter of the law? Now this is a state of affairs which cannot continue for very long. It undermines faith in the Government and in the financial stability of the currency. As soon as we have that, we have what we can see today in a number of places' – by which, thought Artemis, he must mean here, since he is incapable of seeing farther than the end of his nose, that again being why he attaches so much importance to the condition of his moustache – 'the use of public policy to supplement the wealth of those who pretend to support it but do so only because they themselves have found ways of circumventing it. How long can Governments which have no policy other than that of bolting down the safety-valve continue to persuade even those who wish them well that they are in command not only of the streets but also, far more important in the long run, of the hearts and minds of their citizens?' If someone did not interrupt him, either with some supplementary evidence of the astuteness of his diagnosis or with more food, Sophocles Theodoros was capable of heaping rhetorical question on rhetorical question until, like the regime whose abilities he revealed himself more and more elaborately to be doubting, he was left marooned in an isolation of his own making, where self-inflation and dread of the silence which would follow his increasingly portentous monologue demanded the same nervous void-filling to which the Marshal and his uninteresting associates, once praised for their anonymous capacity for hard work and now sneered at for their lack of social grace, had been driven in the administration of public affairs. 'Already in certain places, we see that the strength of the authorities, far from increasing their self-confidence, actually seems to undermine it. As they remove their enemies, they become afraid of their shadows. And when the shadows are removed, it's the turn of friends to feel the breath of suspicion. Can a regime which feeds more and more on itself expect to survive? Soon they will be amputating their own hands and then wondering why they are clumsier now than they were before!' On some bold image of this kind, Sophocles Theodoros would stop, bite his napkin, look at his watch and accuse his wife of having kept them too long at table.

Several hours later, after the women had withdrawn, Sophocles and his friends would settle themselves in the brown leather-seated comfort of his study, where a large roll-topped desk occupied the corner under the icons, the same desk at which his grandfather had sat when Theodoros and Sons occupied a single room in a cramped corner of the harbour (not far from where Helen's now was), and there, over black cigars, new cups of coffee and a bottle of French brandy, the real grievances were unwrapped, like special sweets saved for a smaller company. 'Asteris is making a packet,' Sophocles would start, 'now will you tell me please, my dear Niki, how does one make a packet today, honestly, I mean? Are such things possible?' Artemis did not always excuse himself to attend to his studies, as he had in his first years at the university, when he was glad to have an excuse for escaping the tyrannous tedium of his father's conversation, but lately had taken to staying with the men, thus gaining a reputation with his elders for adapting himself to future responsibilities. Though his father joined in this general approval, his smile was frosted with an element of private irritation, as if he feared that Artemis was eager to be done with him. 'How can you bear to spend any *more* time with them?' Demosthenes, his younger brother, would ask him. 'I don't know,' Artemis answered, not so much evasively as him-self a victim of the same perplexity. It had something in common with a twelve-year-old's contemptuous following of a girl he would swear he disliked, this mindless pursuit of what lacked any explicable interest for him. Later he might tell himself that he had been spying or proving the vanity of his father's way of life, but for the present he asked the most solemn questions and followed every twist of the self-justifying or plaintive answers as if they contained the essence of mature wisdom. He believed that he felt a growing affection for his father. He began to understand his ideas and his fears so well that he could not but think that he shared them. He was persuaded that it was a real scandal that interest rates were rising so high that investment, even on the part of the Government, investment in essential works (those which Theodoros and Sons were capable of undertaking) had actually been diverted into foreign bonds. This was a fact Sophocles had on the highest authority. It meant that the country was being bled in order to stimulate the growth of a foreign economy. Could such things be tolerated? When the Minister of Marine himself, with whom miracles of circumlocution were necessary before such matters could be broached, began to speak of the Marshal's health giving rise to serious concern, frankness became less treacherous than 'constructive'. Not that anyone ventured a direct criticism of the Old Man, but he came to be so uniquely beyond reproach that he was elevated into as much of an irrelevance, 'in this imperfect world', as a God capable only of contemplating His own infinite goodness.

When he had taken his examinations and was waiting for the results, Katerina's family asked Artemis and his parents to come to their island for a week-end. The date for the marriage had not yet been fixed. The rendezvous thus had the aspect both of a modern social occasion and of a negotiation between two chieftains. Katerina's father was still Minister of Marine (he considered it his duty not to deprive the Marshal of his services) and a naval whaler took them out to the *Pegasus*, his own private yacht, built for him, it so happened, by a contractor with whom his ministry had placed an order. The Minister, conscious of the new morality, had insisted on making payment for it in full (a gesture on which the *Times* had congratulated him), but the head of the yard, conscious of other traditions, had found it possible to make the full price a very low one.

The journey began with a tense wait for the Minister. The captain of the yacht consulted his wrist as if he were in command of a liner which had to catch the tide. The *Pegasus* was anchored so close to the shore that the whaler seemed as superfluous as a doorman's umbrella on a fine day: there was nothing that Artemis could see to prevent the yacht coming alongside the quay, but he observed the show in high spirits, happy to giggle with Katerina as they leaned against the drooping rope-rail on the top deck and watched for the official car. Katerina read the Paris fashion magazines; she was wearing a blue-belted white suit, sailor-style, with square shoulders, big blue buttons and a long skirt which she amused herself by twisting so that it flowed round her brown legs now this way and now that. Artemis loved her with intense relief that she was so attractive to him. Her hair was pulled back under a white and blue band and her eyes were so full of humour and optimism, of an innocence which her attempts at chic made all the more enchanting, that Artemis longed to kiss her lips even when they were pettish with orders to the tall, lugubrious steward who had promised her lemonade. The sheer privilege of their position delighted him. They were on top of the world, lording it on the poop, with no one to question them. The mothers were inspecting cabins and marshalling the younger children (Katerina's younger sister Eleni and Artemis's brother and sister were, of course, on board), while everyone else fidgeted for the Minister.

'Do you love me, Artemy?'

'I love you very very much.'

She twisted her hips, back and forth, grinning, her hands with their long silvered nails propped on the hairy powdered cord in front of her. She turned and bulged her eyes at him with challenging intensity, offering to stare him out. He stared back, through his scholarly spectacles; his lips, narrow, almost colourless, but budded at the centre with the promise of a sensual nature, suggested that aroused attention which the eyes, trapped behind the lenses, could not. As for Katerina, she blazed with glee and promises. Suddenly she pushed her chin forward, eyes still glowing and unblinking. 'You blinked,' she said, as she might have said 'out' on the tennis court, between assertion and query. 'I did *not* blink.' He repressed the urge to throw his head back and, as in the yes-no game, lose precisely through the vigour with which he protested that he had not.

'I dreamed about you last night, Artemy.'

'Did you? What did you dream?'

'I dreamed that you wanted us to be married right away. I dreamed that we were married and that we were moving into our house, only it was not our house, it was a little house near the harbour – '

'You don't say.'

'The house of my old nurse, Marousa's house, did you ever know Marousa? She had a little house down the harbour. Near where the whores are. I went there only once. When Papa found out that Marousa had taken me there he got rid of her. I cried and cried. It was a lovely little house, with pots of geraniums on the roof. The roof was as high as you could go – surprise, I know! – but above it there were floors and floors of factories and tenements. It was like a little marigold in a field full of thistles. Isn't that touching?'

'Touching.'

'You're so sarcastic! I never had anyone like Marousa. Did you blink just then, by any chance, you didn't, did you?'

'I believe in your dream. Let's get married now. This minute. Can the captains of yachts marry people? No, I did *not* blink.'

'Papa is the captain of the *Pegasus*. The captain who runs it steps down when Papa comes aboard.'

'Well, then, we'll ask your Papa to marry us. Is that against the rules?'

'We can't, Artemy my love.'

'I know. I know.'

The staring game withered; a prolonged hooting startled the morning. The Minister's car had found the wrong gate, at the far end of the enclosure. A sailor, in white spats which gave him the air of the front half of a blancoed camel, was running to tell the chauffeur to back and come round to where a petty officer and several smart ratings had stationed themselves. The hooting continued. In the back of the official car, the Minister sat with a sheaf of papers in front of his face, in a pose at once relaxed and faintly absurd. Like one of those postcards which alter their expression according to the angle, he had the appearance both of calm authority and of shortsighted timidity. The rating began to remonstrate with the chauffeur, but then the papers were lowered and the Minister gestured incontrovertibly. The rating shrugged and tried to heave apart the heavy wire gates closing the way, in spite of the padlock and chain which married them. The Minister recrossed his white-flannelled legs and resumed his papers. The sailor reported back to the petty officer who looked round for someone to bully. Finally a harbour policeman was found to be responsible. The guard of honour was marched over to the gates which, now happily divorced, were rolled back on rusty castors to admit the Honourable George Dimitriades. The Minister lowered his papers with the surprised air of someone who has impatiently inspected every station on the line and yet can pretend when he reaches his destination that the journey has gone in a moment, so absorbed has he been in more important things. The door of the car was opened, before it had even stopped, by a hot petty officer. The Minister did not emerge, despite the urgent activity in the whaler, the priming of the bosun's pipe and all the customary frenzies of delay. The Minister wished to ponder certain decisions.

Another, smaller, official car, with one bumper crumpled yet highly polished, stopped inside the unusual entrance. Five men – four of them small and bulging, the fifth, who might have been the brother of the steward who was coming at last with the lemonade, tall and mournful, all carrying briefcases – encircled the Minister's car. Several others, of mixed height, none of them tall and all in thick suits, one carrying a canvas case and another an umbrella (although the sun was now at its zenith and making oily patterns on the black-blue roof of the limousine), joined them until they formed a spaced crowd of fifteen or so people around the Minister, who now began to crawl the long tunnel out of his seat. This crowd had something of the dolorous expectation of displeasure to be found in a provincial orchestra which has forgotten its music. They stood with bowed heads, each isolated by fear of dismissal, common resistance broken in the furtive hope that whatever thunderbolts might be unleashed would fall on the head of a colleague and not on his own. How delightful and how impossible to believe that they might produce wicked flutes and tambourines, bagpipes and a jaunty violin, that the umbrella might unfold into some weird and haunting roarer and that they might in devilish unison affront the gruesome air!

Eager to share the secret of this conceit, Artemis glanced at his fiancée and saw in her eyes, deferentially turned up in tribute to her important father, while her beaded upper lip drooped into the sparkling top of the lemonade, a matronly warning against any lack of respect. She was positively inspecting the guard and he could imagine that she was capable of reporting to the commander any man who, even at the very fringes of the scene, showed an iota of slackness. His desire for her was not checked by his awareness of her capacity for priggish malice. On the contrary, her body, which had always seemed to him so light and girlish, took on the heavier lines of aroused sensuality. As she leaned over the glaucous lemonade, her eyes rolling, he imagined the fall of her breasts as she crouched over him, their weight against his ribs and the hoarse proximity of her whisper as her lips came down to him. The immediate future collapsed and gave him an impatience which was perhaps largely sensual but which allowed him, seeing how merely arbitrary the present formalities appeared in its light, to speculate on the absurdities of this rich comedy. He became critical in an airy way, without losing that new respectability of which his father had so querulously approved and without any inclination to entertain an alternative style. Leaning flirtatiously against the soft linen of his sailor fiancée, he grew as frivolous and as carefree as the lightest juvenile in a translated success. He was transformed into the most proper of modest suitors, so that when Katerina's mother appeared, enormous in a violet dress of Wagnerian dimensions, her body so swathed in its myriad layers of oscillating lightness that it was as if a bad painter, with no hope of plausible anatomy beneath it, had covered her in an agreeable shade and relied on the small slippered feet and ringed fingers to make credible the existence of a body to which no underlying outline could plausibly be supplied (a woman whom one might impolitely imagine lifting up, as she herself did a doll in her own boudoir, to reveal a black telephone in her boneless recesses), that most breathless of cavilling ladies could put her white-gloved hand on his arm and ask how her 'very dear Artemis' was feeling and whether he had any complaints against her daughter. 'If Katerina is not nice to you, if she tires you, you're to tell me. Your dear mother, whom I am learning to like so much, has been telling me about your examinations and how brilliantly you've done and how much it's taken out of you. So you must not allow Katerina to exhaust you. She is such a lively girl. Remember, you always have a friend in me.'

On the dock the Minister, vigilant to the last syllable for his country's proper administration, was handing sheets of paper to one man after another. When he had finished informing his minions of their duties he shook hands with each one, his reluctance to make any guarantees of indulgence obvious in the elaborate preparation of his hand which preceded each curt dismissal and in the expression of inexorable disapproval with which he greeted their bows. Was he now going to come aboard? He turned away, even as the bosun was fretting his lips, and consulted the tall man over his shoulder. He nodded and nodded and surveyed the unarmed orchestra of his assistants, equipped now with music but not with instruments, as if he had just been informed of their deliberate infamy. He waved a terrible hand as much as to say that the whole thing would have to be referred to a military court, accepted his fishing-rods and his umbrella (promptly taken from him by a sailor), buttoned the gold buttons on his double-breasted blue blazer and stepped over to where the whaler was shaking like a ballerina who has held a pose long after she was promised that the curtain would come down.

'Are you all right, my dear Artemy, if you don't mind me calling you that, have they given you some lemonade? You are to treat this yacht as if it were your own, I know the Minister will tell you the same thing. You must not make yourself ill waiting for something you could perfectly well insist on having.' Artemis consulted the powdered face and yellowing eyes of his future mother-in-law, eyes which were set in the ruched recesses of her face like jewels in the inexpert artefacts of a dark age. What could she mean? Katerina had subsided into the dutiful daughter and was standing, correcting Eleni with endless whispered instructions, by the head of the gangplank up which the Minister, with many a last word, was climbing. Eleni was thirteen, slim, her face narrow, her black eyes bursting from a face that appeared not yet to have put on enough flesh to curtain them. She wore a dress made by someone in the house from the same material as her mother's. It was tight across her chest and had a wide sash tied in a traditional knot, the ends falling against her girlish but distinctly hairy legs. Her hair was shorter than Katerina's and tied with a violet ribbon. She wore white gloves and carried a violet parasol. How could such an image of rectitude require the ceaseless admonition which Katerina was forcing on her? Artemis was caught in a huge yawn as the Minister, done with reproaches and cautions, allowed the railing to be latched behind him and, as if it were the first of his pleasures rather than the last of his duties, kissed his wife's cheek.

They sailed through the rusty traffic of the harbour and out in the gulf. Luncheon was served on the afterdeck. The coastline opened like the pages of a school history which is marked only with the triumphs of the nation's arms and elides the misdeeds of its heroes into a comforting parade of their distant achievements. The Minister and Sophocles Theodoros ticked off the victories, the birthplace of a notable, the shrines of the country's golden age, as each little harbour or hill town, becoming in white, swam past them. What was real about the country, they decided, was its age-less inventiveness, its warrior spirit, its incomparable beauty. All present discontents were so much cloud, so much insubstantial dross which, whatever was done, would surely pass away, leaving as pure as their present view the unalterable nobility of their native land. 'How small and unimportant, my dear Sophocles, are the unseemly squabbles of public men, I don't exclude myself, when seen against what has always been and will always be here! I believe that in the end, whisper it if we must, seeing how we've let ourselves go, it is men like that – ' and he indicated a fisherman, standing in the bottom of a square-ended dinghy, remote from the land and yet as at home as a peasant in his field – ' men without our culture, without I have to say it nervous and grandiose ambitions, our city ways, that's all I mean, men like that who make this country what it is and who have more wisdom in their bodies than we have in our clever and calculating minds. My dear, considering they had a week's notice, it seems to me the galley is not at its quickest today. The Marshal is going to make an important speech next week, by the way, Sophocles, I had a word with him this morn-ing.' 'I'm very relieved to hear it,' said Sophocles Theodoros; 'he can't allow things to go on as they are and I'm sure he knows it.' 'He knows it better than anyone,' said the Minister, with the air of one who had told him. 'The Old Man, in spite of everything, had an amazing grasp of things, amazing.' 'He's an amazing man,' said the Minister's wife, as if she had been listening to blatant sedition and meant to put an end to it. So they coasted on, as con-fident of their deserved place upon the waters and as well stocked with comfortable notions as the lockers the storesman had so care-fully filled while at the same time making for himself whatever small dividend was possible through the connivance of the chandler.

They dined in the saloon after a welcome afternoon of fly-free heat, a blazing change from the buzzing furnace of the city. The night seemed scarcely cooler; Artemis fell asleep with the taste of exhaustion in his mouth, only to wake, it seemed seconds later, startled by the silence. The engines had stopped. They were drifting into harbour. He looked at his watch: it was four in the morning. The captain had been instructed to disturb no one. The hooter had not been blown, since the island was private to the Minister, although regulations demanded it on any landfall. Artemis's tiredness had dropped from him. None of the other passengers stirred. He left the elegantly panelled and accoutred cupboard which constituted his cabin and went on deck. The anchor had been lowered and had scored a phosphorescent scratch in the dappled skin of the harbour. On the bridge a light showed only over the chart which a white-coated officer, his cap pushed back, was consulting with his elbows and upper arms leaning on the table. A sailor in bare feet had watched the second anchor home and was snaking slack on to its coil. He finished and went forward. A smoky moon revealed a long beach and an empty plain narrowing to the knees of the mountains which presided over the island.

Beside the arcaded front of a café the harbourmaster was staring out at the *Pegasus*. She was not going to dock, but he feared that something might be sprung on him. He went, frowning, past white cubic shops and houses and opened his office with a key from a loaded ring. He struck a match for the lamp but it burned his fingers before he ceased watching the yacht whose owner ignored the rules of the sea but would demand his conformity to those of subservience. He was a neat man, Stavros Evangeli; he had been mate on a deep-sea trawler until T.B. forced him to change his uniform for the brown suit and leather briefcase of the official. He had seen his responsibilities scaled down to timid duty; he could not rebel, but his resentment had the slow malice of a resourceful man reduced to the exercise of brooding accuracy. The island was eating him like rust on an anchored hulk. The population was barely two hundred. Apart from the Minister's estate and those who served it, there were a few farmers, who made a scratchy living, a few fishermen, for ever finding reasons not to sail, and the few merchants who traded with the boats and the village. Evangeli came of a class whose competence had no place in this isolated society. He had the education to handle steamers and the wit to read foreign books (he had once worked a British tanker), but he was viewed with suspicion by the islanders and was limited for conversation to the manager of the ice factory, a large building slopped with rust behind his office. He had married the manager's daughter. The ice factory had been financed by the Minister. He looked on it as his most signal benefaction to the island; it enabled the fishermen from the region – those from the near-by islands came in for ice – to crate their fish for the capital, where the best prices could be obtained. The fishermen were not grateful; they were not so stupid not to use it, but they grumbled at the exacting opportunity it gave them. The journey to the capital required accountancy and wit which they were reluctant to supply. Evangeli, who supervised the safety and efficiency of the harbour, and his father-in-law, who ran a public amenity honestly and well, had no unquestioned place in the community they served.

Artemis turned and was mesmerized for a few minutes by the blink of the small lighthouse on the other point; then, thinking of the Stendhal he had not brought with him, he went towards the saloon where a glass-fronted library of uniform bindings promised amusement. A cabin door opened as he passed and he heard, 'Artemy'. 'What are you doing awake?' 'Doing? Nothing. I woke, that's all. I think I must have heard you creaking.' 'I don't creak.' 'Well, I must've heard something. Come into my cabin a minute?' 'Eleni, what're you saying?' The girl was wearing a nightgown down to the ground; her face was rumpled on one side from the hard pillow, her lips puffy and flaking. Her wrists were elongated from the sleeves of her nightgown, which was gartered in two bows on her forearms. 'You'll get us both into trouble.' 'No, I won't. We can't both get into trouble, can we?' 'You've been dreaming.' 'Yes, I have. About you. We've never talked properly before, have we?' 'Nor improperly.' 'No. I love doing things

64

you're not supposed to do, don't you?' 'It can be very agreeable.' 'Do come in. Just for a little. There's something I want to ask you.' He allowed himself to be drawn to the door of the cabin, which he saw to be larger than his. She pulled him inside and he peered into the darkness. Something in the air, a heavy, powdered smell, told him that Eleni did not sleep alone. A sighing figure was stretched, doped with sleep and food but full of somnolent reproaches, on the lower bunk: the Minister's wife. Artemis backed into the corridor. 'I can't. What if your mother wakes? I can't possibly, Eleni.' 'Would you have come if I'd been alone then?' 'Aren't you a flirt? Yes, of course I would.' She made him a child again. 'What is it you want to ask me?' 'I'll tell you what: why don't you wait and marry me?' 'I was wondering the same thing myself.' 'Were you really?' 'Of course. But you know the answer: such things aren't possible. Older sisters must marry first.' 'We could always find someone for Katerina.' 'Someone has already been found for Katerina.' He indicated himself. 'What we shall have to do is find someone for you. Not that I expect there to be any difficulty.' 'But I love *you*! I don't want you to find anyone.' A sigh rumbled inside the cabin and then a garbled sound of Eleni being called, or rather challenged, all in a tone muted by sleep, but enough for their meeting to end. Eleni blew Artemis a kiss he was quick to return and disappeared.

Artemis looked at the other doors along the corridor. Katerina was at the end. He turned and began, his heart pounding, to approach her cabin. The yacht creaked like a house full of watchmen. Artemis was breathless with fear. There was a certain world in which everything one did was wrong. He reacted with tremulous insolence, now striding to justify one story, now tiptoeing in order to avoid having to offer any. Katerina's cabin door was bracketed open for the breeze. He put his nose to it. The warmth of the veiled interior breathed at him like another face pressed against his own. 'Katerina?' His love was asleep, his soft request unheard. There was nothing soft in his desires. He could picture her thinly covered (possibly naked?) body restless in the narrow bunk and he turned sullenly, hand in pocket, back towards his own door. There was no danger in the boat now, only a predictable creaking such as one finds in a ghost story whose lack of surprise one has already forecast. His desire did not recede. He went back to Katerina's door and listened, as if he now suspected that she was teasing him. There was no sound but the yawning of the yacht at its anchor. He returned to his cabin and shut the door and lay on his bunk. He drew off his trousers and gazed at his erection, recognizing how unimportant had been his passion for Konni, unimportant in the sense that it told him nothing about his nature (he had not dreamed about a man since that night, though he had thought about Konni) and certainly in the sense that he was not its prisoner. He caressed himself and responded to his own promptings so readily that he was positively conscious of a growing affection for himself. He raised himself on the bunk and tried to reach himself with his lips, rather as a child will see if he can still get his toes in his mouth, but he was just unable to complete the circle. His penis began to throb and he concluded his pleasure with a patronizing caress (suddenly brought to climax by the image of Katerina naked with her knees held to her chin) and fell asleep.

Artemis had looked forward to the island. The strain of his examinations, the conflict of indifference and obsession over Konni, the unresolved tensions of political rumour, Dmitri's loud insistence, these would all be far away and he would have Katerina to concentrate his attention and desire. The duel of lust and coldness had driven him to a style of bitter formality from which only the prospect of an early marriage seemed to offer respite. His longing for Katerina did not abate, but he grew impatient with the protracted rituals (something was always being carried with great difficulty from one part of the island to another, from one terrace to another, one room to another) he found to be attendant on living with the Minister. Because his moods were too subtle to be noticed in this preserve of the complacent, he failed to stir the older generation with his air of studious impatience. Katerina alone felt its draught. She was uncertain how to react. Sometimes she felt as much imprisoned as Artemis, while later she could resent a lack of forthrightness in him (as when her mother asked him, 'Is my little Artemy enjoying himself?') which led him to reply with banal acquiescence to questions on which she knew hm passionate. When they were with the family he cursed their inability to be alone together, but when she contrived to search him out on the rocks and suggested a walk he snapped that the gong would soon be going for some endless meal. They could cut the meal, couldn't they? Artemis shook his head: there would only be a row.

'Are you worried about your exams?' she asked, crouching down beside him. 'The results?' He was in a pair of belted black woollen swimming-trunks and a black vest. She was wearing a white dress and silk-covered pumps. She did not like to allow anything to rub against the rocks. He sensed this and invited her, not without the malice which so often accompanied his desire, to sit down beside him if she wanted. She shook her head: 'I said I was going to walk up to the village. No one said anything, by the way – '

'Freedom!'

'Why are you being like this now we're here? You wrote me that note, that sweet note and now you act as though you wished you weren't here at all. Why?'

He glowered at the scuffed waters of the harbour and then glanced, sun on his glasses, at the white house, with its castellated grandeur, lording it among watered trees and flowering shrubs on the low hill which rose behind them. The hill had been augmented by rock and earth to give its gardens a more outstanding appearance. In the bay, under the caustic gleam of the church with its dovecote belfry, a rusty sailing-barge, streaked like a cow with its own discharge, deckhouse of unpainted planks, sails of soiled sheets, was loading crates with a crotchety donkey engine. 'I wish we were alone,' Artemis said.

'We are alone, silly.'

'You haven't any idea of the kind of aloneness I mean. I don't want to beg crumbs of time from someone else's schedule. This isn't what I mean by alone.'

'You aren't very nice to me, are you? I shall begin to think you don't want me.'

He leaned away, teasing and insolent, knees ajar, shoulders tilted back, chin in the air, and looked at her through one eye. His desire for her was outstanding, but she elected not to notice. 'We're prisoners,' he said, closing his body abruptly like a box and leaning forward over his feet. 'We're prisoners and you've been one all your life, which is why you're not even aware of it.'

Katerina was beaten with alternate rods of indignation and excitement. If she let go of Artemis she would lapse into the torpor from which he was so callously wrenching her, but if she hung on to him she might lose something of the beauty, the comfortable symmetry, in which she had dawdled so long. It was all a game, she told herself. Artemis was, of course, only playing at these cruel tricks and would soon come to terms once the marriage contract was agreed.

'Aren't you a prisoner then as well?'

'I am a prisoner aware of his prison. You're not. I've torn off my blindfold. You still wear yours.'

'You don't want to marry me, do you?'

'Do you want to marry me?'

'If I didn't I should tell Papa and that would be an end of it.'

He burst out laughing. 'What greater proof could there possibly be?'

'Oh you've been reading too many French novels. We all know how clever you are. You haven't answered my question, though. Do you want to marry me or don't you?'

'I want you. But as for wanting to *marry* you … That's a business question, isn't it?'

'And you're not interested in business!'

He gripped her arms and unbalanced her on to the calloused rocks. 'I'm not at all sure yet what I'm interested in.'

She snorted deliberately. 'Well, that's not a very decisive declaration! I was expecting something a lot more final than that!'

68

He stood up, thin and discomfited, while she sat there, plumply poised, her skirt over her shins, as winsome as a trade calendar, with the same smile of cardboard invitation and appliqué coquettishness.

'Have I hurt his feelings? Have I?'

He crouched down beside her. 'I should like – '

'Tell me. Tell me.' Her eyes flashed too, but like a lighthouse, too publicly, with a snappy, challenging demand which signalled to him the style of their available future. It amused her to seem both dutiful and wanton, decorous and shameless, prim and outrageous. Her virgin body, inadequately dipped in the stream of forgetfulness, remembered the caresses it was supposed never to have known. 'What would you like to do?'

'You want to hear the words?'

'I know the words,' she said. 'I've known the words as long as you have.'

'I doubt it. I doubt if you do, not that it matters.'

The gong rumbled on the terrace, where the lugubrious steward was now the butler. The Dimitriades brought the indoor staff, just as they did their vegetables, from the capital with them.

'You'd better go in. It's lunchtime.'

'Aren't you coming?'

'I don't have to.'

'But you have to send me, don't you? Which is exactly the same thing. You know nobody will say anything if you don't go, but you know there'll probably be some kind of trouble if I don't. You want me to be conventional and you think you needn't be yourself. But wanting me to be *is* being conventional. You're as bad as I am. Worse!' She stuck her tongue out at him, a glossy wet tongue, as if he were an unpopular doctor, and went over the rocks nimbly towards the stone steps, each with its staple white border, which took her up to the garden gate. Artemis considered many actions and then hurried on tiptoe over the hot rocks so as not to be late for lunch.

He sat opposite Katerina, but refused to look at her. They ate under a stretched blue sail which left only a low bar of light between it and the white wall on the far side of the tiled terrace. 'I hope you young people are feeling like some activity,' the Minister said, 'because there are plans afoot for an expedition tomorrow.'

'Artemy!'

'Mother?'

'Mr Dimitriades asked you a question.'

'Me, mother? I'm sorry. What question was that?'

The tall steward had brought a majolica bowl heaped with fists of meat cooked in vine leaves and covered with a thick, slightly curdled lemon sauce. The afternoon seemed to creak, as though they were still aboard the yacht. The sailcloth snapped in the wind, like the fall of a cane on flesh.

'You may not know this – though you, Artemis, almost certainly will – but this island, today boasting hardly more than two hundred souls, was once a considerable centre, with no less than twenty thousand inhabitants.'

'Twenty thousand!' said Artemis's mother to his brother Demosthenes.

'I'm speaking now of three thousand or so years ago, of course, during our Golden Age. At that time the trade routes of the ancient world crossed and recrossed in this area and continued to do so, I may say, well into the dark age which followed. Eventually, of course, famine, war and more powerful rivals completed the ruin which the end of the classical era had begun.'

The Minister's wife sighed: it might have been yesterday.

'Of course it is really you, my dear Sophocles, who should be telling this story, since your knowledge of our former glories far outstrips my own.'

'Not at all,' said Sophocles Theodoros. 'By no means. You tell it as well as it could be told.' He refused a second offering of vine leaves with emphatic disapproval.

'It is really your presence, Sophocles my dear friend, which has made me resolve to make a start on a project which has long beguiled my fancy.' Artemis was unable to face a second portion; he scraped his chair with a shriek over the tiles and unlaced his legs. The Minister paused and then went on, 'Most people quite naturally assume that the old city was situated here, where this house (which was actually constructed, in its original form, by the Venetians for their Governor) and its neighbours stand, but that is, in my view, totally erroneous. The ancient city was not here at all!'

'Of course not,' said Sophocles Theodoros.

The Minister stared at his guest. 'Where did you hear that?'

'Obviously not,' said Artemis's father, brushing his moustache and lifting his jaw to confront any impertinent view to the contrary; 'how could it have been?'

'I am aware,' said the Minister, now looking with the greatest curiosity, as if at some potsherd which confuted the received ideas of centuries of archaeological orthodoxy, at a platter of roasted lamb surrounded with fingers of crusty potato; 'I am aware' – and he looked with paternalistic warning and regret at the curved steward, on whose lips there lingered, with the most languid docility, the faintly ironic smile of one who had not forgotten some ancient uprising of the helots (nor its savage repression) – 'I am, as I say, aware that most people, even those who should know better but who give their opinions without a really thorough topographical knowledge of the island, believe that the ancient city was here, in the harbour. Well, how could it have been?'

Sophocles Theodoros, to whom this question was so forcibly put, looked penitent.

'How could it have been, my dear Sophocles Theodoros, when twenty thousand souls could never have been crammed, however uncomfortably, into the confines of this bay? And yet you will find this assumption in the most up-to-date textbooks of foreign scholars, men who ought to know a great deal better, if I may say so. Because it's here now, it must have been here then. Rubbish! You may not be aware of how it is that I have come to own large tracts, I might say virtually all, of this unfortunate island. It is not true, as you may have been told, that it has always been in my family. I own the substantial areas I do because in very large part they have been forced upon me. I don't know how true it is of other men of – what shall we say? – position, but I have never wanted to own more than a very small piece of property, enough for my family and a measure of privacy. Those who accuse us, and they exist, of buying up land cheaply, of forcing men to leave the countryside or the islands, I'm talking now of the kind of person who used to write for the gutter press in the old days and who now finds nothing better to do than snipe from the sidelines (I don't know if you're aware that a number of highly scurrilous news-sheets are now being printed abroad and smuggled into the country, we had a case only a week ago), well, that sort of person has no idea of the basic mentality of the peasant. He's not half as attached to the land as the scratchy pen of the journalists would have you think. Give him a decent living and he'll hang on like grim death to what's his, that I'll grant you, but show him a better life elsewhere and he wants nothing better than a chance to up sticks and go. Most of the property that I own here has been, and let me explain before you laugh, young Artemis, because I know you university students, most of what I own here has been forced on me against my will. Now laugh if you like, but I'll explain and then I think you'll see the point, as my old lecturers used to say, they probably still do, because the point is this, I was the only person they could turn to as a possible buyer. Without me, they'd still be tied to unproductive lands, useless worked-out terraces of dusty soil you couldn't grow enough on to feed the horse that ploughed it, they'd admit it themselves if they were here. There's nobody more talked about or less understood than the peasant. I'm not talking about only our own peasants, I'm talking about the peasant in the whole of our culture, as far west as the pillars of Hercules, as you classicists would say, Sophocles Theodoros, my dear old friend. Nothing ties him to the land except his own help-lessness, his own hopelessness. The traditions which you young Royalists admire – oh I know your views! – the traditions of endurance and respect for the old ways, the peasants would give them up like that, I can promise you, if they were given a chance to better themselves. Better off in the countryside? Don't you believe it, my young friend, you go and see for yourself before you start generalizing. Things aren't always as they're said to be. The peasants on this island, they may have seemed contented before I built this place and settled here (my grandfather came from here, I'm not denying that of course, why should I?) but the fact was it was the contentment of despair, I don't think that's pitching it too high.'

'They were in the depths,' said his wife, in a tone of righteous contradiction. 'They didn't know what to do. I see no sense in denying it.'

'I realized that I couldn't simply restore this house (it had fallen into pitiful neglect, they were stabling animals in the saloon) and staff it and expect everything to continue as before. The beauty of islands is that they have unity. The beauty and the challenge, as you may one day discover.' Artemis, in a vision of scorching brilliance, realized that he and Katerina were the intended heirs to this millstone of an estate and, perhaps, to the whole masonry of rhetoric which faced it. 'One cannot take one corner of an island and turn it into a paradise and ignore the other three which remain a desert. To come into one's inheritance is not, as I thought when I was your age, to receive a fortune, if one is lucky enough to do that, but to come to a sense of one's inescapable responsibilities, to realize the unity of human society and to make one's peace with it. The misfortunes of our country, which I am still confident can be put right, come, I am afraid, not least from those who, for whatever understandable motives, close their eyes to the public weal and concentrate on their individual enrichment or even, because however much we venerate it, not even the family is world enough, on that of their blood. Believe me, and you know this as well as any man, Sophocles Theodoros, I am no richer for being Minister of Marine. It has not been – how could it, with the Marshal at the helm? – a source of personal aggrandisement, but I have accepted my duties the more willingly because of my experience here, on this island, this has been the best university I could have attended. There was no cow cheese made here until I introduced a herd of Guernseys eight years ago. This cheese was unheard of. They made their own cheese, goat cheese, you still find it in the peasants' homes of course, but they made no cheese from cow's milk (I want you to taste this, my dear Mrs Theodoros, you won't regret it) and now they export it even to several of the larger islands. Isn't that good? Made here on the island.'

'It was most certainly *not* brought from the capital,' said the Minister's wife.

'What do you think of the wine, young man, young bridegroom-to-be, what do you say to the wine? It hasn't made you sleepy, has it?'

'The wine? No, not at all,' said Artemis, in the startlingly loud tone of a wireless hurriedly turned up (for a bulletin one has missed) and as quickly reduced. For the first time since the beginning of the meal he looked across at Katerina. With a baleful expression, he reached slyly for her foot with his, like someone groping in the skirts of an ornate festival cracker for a touch of the hidden but common brown paper that can alone snap the tedium of the occasion. She affected to turn reproachfully from him, hungry for another helping of her father's words, of which there was no shortage. Artemis's foot touched that of Eleni, who smiled instantly, and then found Katerina's, which moved a fraction away before allowing Artemis to brace his instep against hers. She turned her foot to give the impression of restricted flight, but actually offered a broader, more stretched expanse of ankle and foot to his cowed caress.

'Where was I?' the Minister demanded, as if some protracted interruption, uncalled-for and unprincipled, had lost him the line of his discourse.

'You were about to tell us, I think, sir, about the plans you had for an expedition.'

There followed a silence such as might have greeted some

ignoble sacrilege. It appeared that everything which had been fed into all the mouths present during the entire meal had been stored in some oral annexe from which it was now returned to be exhaustively masticated.

'I love expeditions, don't you, Artemy?' giggled Eleni.

'That's more than enough from you at table, Eleni, I've told you about interrupting your father. Whatever next?'

'The peasants', said the Minister, 'used very frequently – '

Katerina's laughter began, like a fire in a tin waste-paper basket, with every sign of being easily controlled, hardly more enduring than a sneeze, perhaps even disguisable as one, but it rose into devastating bloom, causing those about her to rear back, and became uproarious. The Minister looked critical of the fruit. Sophocles Theodoros had never been so engrossed by the filigree work on an antique salt cellar, while his wife had something inextricable in her eye. Leaning way back, the Minister's wife noticed one of the gardener's children – 'Michali,' she called him sharply – eating the grapes from a vine which covered a terrace normally out of sight. This parade of centrifugal interests might have continued long enough for Katerina to come to terms with propriety, had not Eleni joined in again just as the thing seemed to be dying down. The whole family turned their energies on crushing her, as though a pair of silk curtains had caught fire as well: the thing was no longer a joke. 'Katerina, please,' said her mother, looking furious at Eleni, 'I know this is a light-hearted family affair, but I think we must have an explanation. What *were* you laughing at? Not your father?'

Artemis relished his uninvolved, even judicial position. Through his small round lenses he frowned at the blushing embers of Katerina's outburst.

'Artemis was tickling me under the table,' Katerina said. Innocence was chased from Artemis's face by the simpering expression of a hitherto beardless boy flatteringly exposed in a rustic comedy as the father of the mayor's grandchild.

'And what about you, Eleni? What have you got to laugh at?'

Here the Minister's wife was sure something criminal would be uncovered.

'He was tickling me too,' said Eleni.

After a notable silence, the Minister said, 'Children, children, eh, Sophocles Theodoros, my old friend?'

'Indeed, indeed,' replied the father of the candidate bridegroom, the laughter of mature indulgence hurriedly muffling the hysteria of the young. Artemis alone had laughed neither with the children nor with the adults.

'How pleasant it is', said George Dimitriades, wiping away invisible tears of honest good humour, 'to be among family, simply among family!' He rose from the table, to which fingers of sunlight were reaching from under the sailcloth like a pick-pocket into the folds of a fat man's coat tails, and crossed to the coffered door which led to the 'saloon'. This room, from which another terrace opened overlooking the harbour, was largely of glass and had the chintz sofas and armchairs, the air of caged dust the Minister had admired in the conservatories of grand seaside hotels in England, where business had sometimes taken him. His sports clothes were from an English tailor in the capital. He had for that other seagoing nation a respect verging on the senti-mental. The Labrador which had greeted him with extravagantly circuitous affection on the quayside was called Nelson, its mate Emma.

An atmosphere of adjourned tedium lay upon the afternoon. Tiredness was drawn on like the vestments of a ritual. Artemis walked down the cool corridor to his room, where he took a copy of *Les Fleurs du Mal* from his suitcase, not entirely escaping the absurd pinch of conscience which made an accepted text at the university a risqué book at home. The contraction of life which would follow the licensed freedom, such as it was, of student life pressed in upon him like the walls of Edgar Allan Poe's dungeon. He was unable to breathe in the tightening embrace of his room and bundled himself, bent almost double under the lowering ceil-ing, out into the passage. He wished all of a sudden that he was not of his own country. Any nationality seemed better than that which clamped him to the life he looked bound to lead. Any adventure was better than the imposed safety of a mould pressed over and whitening his flesh. He went out like a criminal in search of his crime.

He escaped the house as he had so often, in school days, escaped from his parents, shaking with determination and terror, hoping to be caught before it came to the testing-point (as on the first occasion he made a rendezvous with Dmitri to go to Helen's) and longing equally for the opportunities of an unpatronized life. He reached the linen room and saw that its shutters were ajar, giving on to a section of the garden stepped with soft shelves of geraniums whose acrid smell – newly squeezed cadmium red applied over the direct reek of cat spray – filled the tiled white room and settled like pollen on the grey doors of closed cupboards. The room was coated with an invisible impregnation of redness, reminiscent of the children's books whose grey sheets could be painted with water and which then bloomed with magic colour. Whether through the force of this memory or for some more physiological motive (or for some other reason), Artemis was aware of his full bladder. He closed the door of the linen room behind him. The smell of the geraniums, blushing and suggestive, surged about him. He opened the linen cupboard to his left and saw the clean sheets, the folded towels, the pillow-cases, all in careful alignment and stacked to the top of each shelf. The shelves themselves were of deal board, still measured with the ticks of the local craftsman. He could see as clearly as a sequence from a film the emptiness of the room, unplastered, unboarded, grey with the cement blocks of its basic construction and then its prompt coating with the smoothness of the present plaster, the nailing of the boards, the instructions given to the barefoot carpenter who was to supply the cupboards and his marking of the deal on which these imported sheets and shaggy towels were to rest, the arrival of the unpainted doors on a boat from the capital, the whole assembly and the eventual bitter arguments about payment.

Before he could stop himself, as if this too were part of this film of the past unravelling itself in front of his eyes, Artemis was pissing on the fat folds of the linen. He splashed on to the smooth paint of the doors, rebounded among the towels and soaked into the nap, leaving only a few drops to reach and pool on the tiled floor. He stood, feet apart, cock out, and spent all there was. He gazed at the drenched linen and the extra drops which were now seeping through on to the ground and thought, with accurate shyness 'Now I'm a delinquent.' And like a delinquent, honouring his role, he closed the cupboard, so that only the small gleam of wet showed below it, and climbed out of the window, pulling it together behind him. He sprang down the crimson steps to the wall of the Minister's grounds, vaulted the wall, his hand on a soft moist pad of creeper (recently watered), and found himself in a dried river, banked with rough stones, floored with dust and boulders. He thought himself alone and almost tripped over a small animal hunched under the lee of the wall. At first it seemed the ungainly hybrid of a nightmare. He had dreamed on several occasions of a simple but quite large seaside village made of beige huts, they might have been adobe, on whose roofs there lodged some freakish creatures, in most respects human, but with four legs, the back two so elongated as to resemble those of a man, and a scantily furred tail, small rather pointed head (half-horse, half-monkey) and upstanding ears. It was difficult to decide whether they were prisoners of the dull villagers whose own quarters lacked amenities or whether, scampering about the place, though officially confined to the rooftops, they exacted so much from the villagers, both in the way of foodstuffs, stolen or thrown as sops, and in the effort necessary to confine them to their insecure enclosures, that progress was impossible for those on whom they were visited. Were these ungainly but agile beasts vermin or victims? On whom did the decision depend? No doubt on the dreamer alone; but he was usually so sickened by the vision that he could not approach close enough with his locked lens to question or to observe the habits of these macabrely perched inhabitants. He felt for the villagers, who tried to go about their dusty business as if unaware of the scampering company above their heads, a contempt which accused them both of filthiness, in allowing this alternative form of life to shadow their own, and of inhumanity, since they were doing nothing to redeem those whose conditions were so repellent. He wondered how they could eat or sleep with the slither and scuffle of those alien feet on their roofs, how they could stomach their food when the houses were ringed with garbage and droppings, how they could continue to speak in their usual commonplaces when another world squeaked and gibbered over every branch of the village. Here then, on the floor of the walled path, crouched and dirty, its rump cocked in the air, staring up at him with whiteless brown eyes was one of these creatures. It was the gardener's boy taking a shit. The eyes, peering up from an unexpected level, wore that expression of mindless effort because of the brown tail falling below the pointed buttocks. The boy's ankles were shackled by his tattered shorts; his feet splayed in the dust, found room to play with flakes of rock between his toes. He wore a loose cotton vest, full of holes and out of shape. 'It's Michali, isn't it?' The boy had finished and was drawing his pants over his hips. 'How old are you?' 'Twelve,' the boy replied. 'Twelve?' How could this midget, crouched so small that he seemed some kind of smooth, skinned rabbit, how could he be twelve? 'Goodbye,' said the boy and was gone, as if with companions, so joyous, so gleeful, so like one of a herd was his skipping run. Artemis was left by the crop of shit at which bluebottles were already making their first tentative runs. He pressed petulantly up the hill towards the village, slapping at the shining green flies which sizzled round his head. He was already a landlord. The problem of discipline disturbed him, though there had been no crisis, rather as a financier, observing no more than an error in a stock-exchange tape, something corrected upwards almost at once, discovers a trend in what others accept as an accident and begins to reconsider from basics the long-term prospects of the market.

The larger part of the island's population lived in the village which saddled the ridge between two peaks. Gazing down into the plain to the right of the harbour and over the ridge into the hinterland, it was hard to believe that there were not many more than the two hundred inhabitants the Minister had mentioned. White houses were dotted here and there as far as the eye could distinguish. The fact was, most of the islanders had several places, not through any pleasant excess but because they had always to be on the move from vineyards and vegetable plots to olive and almond trees and then back to the village in the cold weather. The island was a lung which breathed in and out with the seasons. Many of what seemed houses were churches. The island boasted the usual magic number of three hundred and sixty-five, which meant only that every saint had his shrine, the kept promise of some barren mother, frightened fisherman or pious child. Two hundred people! And yet Artemis, gazing out over the flat beach towards the other islands which lay hull-down, a somnolent fleet anchored in the fleecy sea, found no peace in the place. The Minister's house, by some inversion of perspective, appeared larger from here than from close by. With its concave ungrassed roofs (most of the peasants' houses were topped with rammed earth from which grass and withered wild flowers stood out like hairs from an old woman's chin), neat terraces, whitened steps, watered arbours and red flowers, it planted a bold and self-confident standard on the barren rock. Although Artemis was now above it, a similar inversion of scale pointed out more clearly than before how, enthroned on its hillock, it dominated the plain and the harbour. He remembered that it was from this angle, from some sort of unincluded eminence, that he had first seen in his nightmare the crouched prisoners whose agile brutishness so disturbed him.

The sun was below the mountains now, leaving a scorched crater in the deepening sky where Aphrodite had lit a first unsteady candle. Artemis looked up at the star and nodded, as if at the incorrigible promptness of an old friend. In less than an hour they would be safe from all but blind ill-fortune. The shadows were pouring down like cooling lava. They had almost reached the floor of the valley when they heard the sound of the returning aircraft. Yorgis, without even looking at Artemis, indicated a small stone hut with a collapsed tussock roof and pushed the men under its sagging lintel. Artemis squeezed Yorgis inside and stayed in the opening, a rag stuck in the mouth of a jar. Above them, through the parted strands of the roof, the men could see a too-bright section of sky. The day seemed to be returning. The planes grew louder. The first passed so wide of them that only Artemis could see how it melted into a skeleton against the fire of the invisible sun. The next two came closer, but the valley was so abrupt that they were quickly over. It would take more panicky men than these to disclose themselves to so aimless a patrol. 'Do they think we're boys?' said Yorgis, snatching a cigarette paper from Yanni, a thick and uncomplaining dockyard worker, who merely muttered, 'I wasn't going to smoke it.' Yorgis showed him the back of his hand and then pinched his thigh, just above the knee, and shook his leg. 'Cunt.' The fourth plane made the soldiers laugh again their old affectionate, derisive, victorious laugh. How could one hate such an enemy? It came in very low, crabbing like a blind man reaching for a wall, one of its engines feathered, its tarnished paint clearly visible in all its overlapping sections like a clown's make-up, the concentric hoops of its original allegiance ineptly painted out with the colours of the monarchy. Suddenly they could see a man in the opening in the side of the plane. He was working. 'Another cunt.' He was having a difficult time, but finally he succeeded. A large cube fell out of the opening, followed by another. They hit the far side of the valley and burst like heavy pillows into white flock. The men roared with laughter. The planes had gone. 'Stay here for the moment,' said Artemis. 'Yorgi!' 'Captain?' 'I'm going to see what this is all about.' 'They're dropping us bog paper,' said Kosta. 'Oh well, Kostaki, there have to be some shits in every unit.' They laughed, but the division between humour and anger was being worn away by an acid fuse. Artemis left them. 'Bring us some to mop up Yanni with, Captain.' Artemis stumbled across the valley, with its flukes of light, and reached where the crates had exploded. It was as though a crowd had dispersed, leaving its programmes in the gutter of this remote hillside.

Soldiers, Fellow-Citizens! The hour of national reconciliation is here. The war in which you have fought is over. The people have decided. The country wants peace. The country has fought for peace. The country will have peace.

Those of you who are still fighting, do you know that your leaders are already in safety? They are not sharing your dangers. They are already in comfort. They have learned the lesson of their adventures. Why do you risk your lives for men who risk nothing for you?

Where are you marching, you who have borne so much for those who are betraying you? Can you believe that there is a welcome waiting for you across the border? They will castrate you once they have you in their power, just as they castrated the armies of Paul the Brave when he trusted himself to them. Is it as eunuchs that you want to pass the rest of your lives in the concentration-camps of our traditional enemies?

Fellow-citizens, honest men, working men, there is an alternative. The only alternative. It is to remain in your fatherland. Are you brothers to the barbarians that you seek their hearths and not your own? Do you trust those whose language is gibberish to you and not your own blood? Let us be frank with each other. Our country has been devastated by this unnecessary fratricidal war. Bravery and brutality have gone hand in hand. The bravery is that of our people. The brutality has been imported by those who have already scampered across the border. Why trust them?

Where are you marching? Why are you marching? Is it in the hope of a better life for our people? That life is at hand.

Thanks to the generosity of friends who ask nothing but the right to help us. Freedom is what you have turned your backs on. Fellow-citizens, return to your homes. It is where you belong.

We do not wish to mislead you. The Government is now in control of all major centres and the whole of the heartland. Those sections of the country – largely uninhabited and uninhabitable – which still remain in rebel hands are being systematically cleared. We know where you are. That you are reading this is evidence of the truth of that claim. Therefore we have no need to plead with you or to come to terms. We can impose our terms. Our terms are those of a reconciliation. With certain exceptions.

Artemis sat on the hard ridge where the pamphlets had fallen and cleaned his spectacles before continuing.

The laws distinguish between those who commit crimes knowingly and those who have been misled. Many of you fought bravely in the war against the invader. The King and his Government are aware of your courage. We have not forgotten. But neither can we forget that certain of your leaders, men of proved criminal record, have still to render their account to civilization.

Soldiers, workers, peasants! Bring these men to us. We appeal to you who long only to see your families, who want a new fatherland to rise from the tragedy of these last wasted years, have no mercy on those who have deceived you! We give you our solemn word that these men and these men alone, the real criminals, are wanted by us. The rest of you, whom circumstances or misguided idealism has brought to rebellion, are sure of a free pardon. Tell your comrades. Your hands, your brains, your courage are needed in the struggle ahead. For a free nation, for a just nation, return to your homes and your duty!

★

Artemis lay back amid the white sheets, his particular copy still in his hand. The sky was thickening, the air gummy with returning scents and the threat of frost. Artemis was tired. The mattress of pamphlets under his shoulders and head was irresistibly seductive. He had to sleep. He had to think. He woke, hardly a second later. Yorgis was standing over him.

'Sleep here till two o'clock,' Artemis announced, 'and then we start out across the mountains. The moon will be up, but I don't think they'll do any night-flying.'

'And what's all this, then?'

'They've dumped some old song-sheets. Probably to lighten the plane.'

'Stelio is bad. His wound has opened again. I think we should leave him.'

'No,' said Artemis. 'No. Out of the question.'

'What are these things, Captain?'

'Pamphlets. They must have been flying to Boreopolis and had to lighten ship.'

'You should get some sleep, Captain. I'll take the first turn.'

'Leave those where they are, Yorgi. The men are tired. I don't want them straining their eyes reading fiction at this time of night.' Artemis gave a little laugh and stood up. The sergeant-major blinked at his speech. It might have been the first quirk of madness. The two men resembled, for a moment, models bought at different times by a boy who has misjudged the scale of the first: they did not belong in the same box. 'We should reach the border tomorrow some time. I don't see how we can fail to do so. One day's march and we're there.'

The sergeant-major seemed to grow larger and, simultaneously, less distinct in the now quickly waning light. He became part of the landscape glimmering around Artemis. The hut had melted into the bottom of the valley. The men's voices rustled like herded sheep. 'By God, Yorgi, I wish we were among them,' he said. 'By God, I do.'

They had once been so close. They had stood on the brink of the

84

capital. It needed only a decisive movement and they would have been pouring into the centre of things. Whereas now, now the plagiarized exhortations of a pasteboard Government had to be concealed, he supposed, from his weary and embittered soldiers whose irony was their only armour. The choice had gone from their lives. Action was a drain, not a challenge. Only Artemis's mind, searching like a sore tongue for the scraps between its teeth, tried over and over to engage itself on the thin gristle of argument which was all it could find to feed on. The gods had left the peaks. He had cheered their eviction. Words alone, the baked bricks of man's intellectual engineering, could make sense in this wilderness. The men had tired of them. He was tiring of them himself. And yet his dreams were walled with them, like those renovated shops which decorators paste with newsprint because they are cheating on lining paper. By God, he was wrong to make wishes. Now was the time to stand by the decisions which had been made. Now traitors were revealed or destroyed. This was the time, Artemy, you always looked forward to. And yet that great hod of manufactured bricks weighed too heavily on him. He longed to pitch it into dust. Why should he support it? It was time to live like an animal. Why were arguments always correct? What would happen if he led these men into the hills, uninhabitants of an uninhabitable land, and they lived there like mountain lions, as they had in the days of the Germans, in the great days? Traitor, Artemis, is that what men should call you? Watch out, watch out. This thing was thoroughly discussed.

Brasidas had argued like this: 'If we could have taken the capital and won the war, of course we would have done so. No one denies this. But it doesn't follow that what has happened is not the best thing. I'm not speaking now in terms of what we should say to the outside world. I'm not asking you to smile in any knowing way. The period of retreat which we have decided on, those of us who made the original appraisal, taking into account all the military and political factors, is an undeniable necessity. We have no need to exhaust ourselves any further with agonizing on that subject. The matter is closed. We withdraw. Good! Now let us proceed to an understanding of the historical perspective of this retreat. You must not imagine that I am unaware of the tone I adopt. I am not as much of a stylist as some of you, but I am not incapable of choosing a racier form of speech, something *un peu plus journaliste*. I adopt this language because I want to divorce this issue from incidental circumstances. The country must understand – that is to say the language of our people must come to terms with – the forces at work in its particular destiny. The inability of one Government after another ever since Independence either to solve or to ignore the language question – whether the popular or the 'High' language is the true language, I take it this is what we mean by the language question – this failure is, comrades, more than accidental, on that I'm sure we are agreed. Now if it is more than accidental it cannot be assimilated entirely into the modes of the social struggles of other countries. It denotes not only the unresolved contradictions to be expected in our particular situation, it also draws attention to the correctness of the doctrine of self-determination within the framework of Socialism. When we ask ourselves what we shall be doing during the long months, perhaps years, of retreat, real and symbolic, on which we are about to embark, is there not some justice in the apparently ludicrous answer that we shall be purifying our language, resolving in the creation of a new grammar the empty conflict of past generations who hoped with arguments or polemics alone to find room in one country for two conflicting logics? Let us consider the agreeable-seeming possibility that we could have taken the city and proclaimed a Socialist republic. This could have happened, I think, this hypothetical triumph of arms, only as the result of an agreement of some kind with the other side. It would have been a victory, not a revolution. A victory and not a revolution. This victory would have led to a coalition. Only in that way could we have been sure of a period of non-interference. Of course we would eventually have found ways of eliminating the bourgeois elements in the coalition. We need not feel ashamed to admit our intentions. Nevertheless the result would have been to allow the survival of certain concepts, to perpetuate the dualities implicit in our language, and so to trap ourselves once more in formalistic problems. We might – I hope we would – have overcome our enemies before they had time to effect a dialectical opposition to us which might have led to a false synthesis, but there could well have been a quite imperceptible distortion of the line, rather as a plane can seem to fly straight and yet, thanks to the uneven traction of the two propellers, finds itself over the sea when the navigator believes it to be heading for dry land.

'Now I come to the crux of the matter, comrades. It is tempting to think that as we retreat we should recruit as many friends as possible, lose no chance to endear ourselves to those in whose memories we must live until the time comes for our return. Comrades, this coalitionism of the spirit is a deep error. Without pleasure in saying so, I say this: we shall brand the country, not caress it. A caress is soon forgotten; a burn lasts forever. Our existence is not an episode in our country's history. We will not and we must not accept an honoured place in the history books of our enemies. Our retreat must not be a withdrawal into the annals of folklore. Here I may allude to the suggestion that the fight against the Germans was a fight for freedom, that both sides 'have their honour'. The fact that both some of those who now support the monarchy and we ourselves were involved together in this fight reveals only its historically parenthetic nature. The attempts of the capitalists to erect into a final confrontation the squabbles which originated between various of their cliques reveals their weariness and their cynicism. They want to believe that the battle is over. They have exhausted their moral strength. It is for us to demonstrate to them that, on the contrary, the battle has hardly begun.'

Brasidas was not a prepossessing man. He was solidly fleshed, rather pale, broad-hipped and short-fingered. His eyes were small and pale brown, his eyebrows ginger, his nose tilted back and rather delicate above curt but pouting lips. His ears stuck out and came almost to a point at the top. Because of his unlikely shape (narrow shoulders, big behind) his khaki never fitted him, but his frankly admitted absence from most of the battles against the invader did not blind Artemis to the almost oblivious coolness he showed under fire. Some of the old partisans were inclined to use his relatively late arrival slyly against him, rather as avowedly broadminded people will secretly refer to a man as queer and, even when they are quick to add that they have no objection to his morals, leave no doubt that they mean it to be a taint of a kind. Brasidas was a doctor. He had been studying abroad when the Germans conquered the country and had fought under other colours until near the end of the patriotic war when he was smuggled back to join the Political Committee and also because a doctor was needed. The forces controlling the capital in the name of the Allies refused him entry. He had had to land by fishing-boat. He was an ideologue, as no one who listened to him could doubt, but he was not a parrot. Certain of his 'formulations' (the precise architecture of his categorical thinking appealed to Artemis rather as boy's clothes of the most severe cut are all the more attractive on a girl whose feminity has already been revealed to us) verged very deliberately on heresy. It took courage as well as clearsightedness to suggest to a group of men whose whole consciousness was formed by the struggle against the Germans that their efforts were merely parenthetical. It not only challenged their achievements, it opened the way for a line opposed in principle (and what more dangerous opposition was there?) to that handed down by those on whose good offices the revolutionary army depended. When Brasidas emphasized the transitory nature of the patriotic war he was giving his life into the hands of his audience. No greater declaration of solemn dedication could have been given by any late-comer than this open play with a conceivable deviation. No blood-brotherhood could have been more moving to Artemis than this proof of unselfish commitment. Despite himself, it made Artemis think of Jesus. He too had given to His disciples the evidence on which He could be convicted.

Judas, in using it, justified the insight of his master and revealed the wit of the most unspectacular and the most sublime of His sacrifices, His genuine offer of equality as a man.

What made Brasidas's delivery of himself into his comrades' hands so moving was the ease with which, as Artemis saw, he could have remained remote and secure. The other members of the Political Committee had reason to fear his arrival. He was plainly a nominee of powerful external forces. He had the authority not only of his appointment but also of his doctorate. His almost professorial detachment from the commonplaces of fear made him a byword for reliability. Yet he disdained thanks and sneered at the idea of the saintliness of medicine. His indifference to praise made others ashamed of their own desire for it; his habitual bravery seemed cold to those whose pleasure it was to rehearse old battles; his breadth of outlook made his comrades aware of their own narrowness. He was given the unindulgent respect the ordinary pays to the clever. His stature was as grudgingly admitted as his fall would be gleefully regretted. He was like a scholarship boy in a house of louts. The shafts of light which he brought to their lives filled them sometimes with an exciting radiance, but in the long run they would remember only that he gave them a headache. Artemis, in his peripheral position as a Candidate Member of the Political Committee, noticed the yawns and mindless nods of Brasidas's colleagues and his heart went out to the yellowish doctor, with his severe passion for worrying a question to its conclusion. He was capable of unnerving detachment. He showed consideration for women, but no sympathy for those who either pined for their own or imagined they had conquerors' rights over those of others. 'Let me recommend the habit of masturbation,' he once said on the Political Committee, apparently unaware of the proud appetites of Alexander Pavlides, the old chieftain as he liked to think of himself, the mountain goat, terror of the plains. 'Better five minutes daydreaming than an hour's absence from duty.' Pavlides growled like a lion advised of the charm of vegetables. 'Reason', Brasidas would say, 'is not surrounded with courtiers.' During those weeks when they had hung like a rainless cloudbank on the fringes of the capital, weeks of frustration and sporadic impetuousness when the wind seemed set to drive into the city and then changed once more, Brasidas had held the committee together, not with charm, which might have been easier, but with unmitigated intelligence. Wild plans broke on the rock of his determination that gestures were the enemies of progress. 'Down with the folkloric!' was his slogan in a land encrusted with it. It was whispered of him that he had never set foot in the country before his arrival in the fishing-boat. Artemis Theodoros wrestled with a tendency to worship. 'If you say so,' he had remarked on one occasion when Brasidas had once again tried to persuade him of the futility of an attack which would bring the capitalists down on them in overwhelming strength. 'No,' said Brasidas with a positively foreign vigour, 'no, my dear Theodoros, not *if* I say so. *Because* I say so.' It was the nearest to a joke that Artemis remembered him ever coming. As he spoke, he indicated the gulf where the sliced superstructure of an aircraft carrier was floating to its anchor.

'Are you angry with me?'

'Angry? With you? Now why should that be?'

'Because of what I said at lunch, about you tickling me.'

'Oh that. No, of course not.'

'I've been looking for you everywhere. I fell asleep and when I woke you were nowhere to be found. I was really very frightened. I shouldn't be telling you this, I suppose. Mama would say it was unwise.'

'When will you start to tell me things?'

'You sound angry, Artemy. If you are, please tell me. Where have you been?'

'For a walk. I didn't want to rest. I walked to the village and then down into the plain.'

'What were you thinking about?'

'I don't know. Truly I can't say. My head seems full of phrases, ideas, all jumbled like a broken kaleidoscope. I can't tell you anything. It's strange, but no one could even torture out of me what I've been thinking.'

'Why should anyone torture you, Artemy? What dramatic ideas you have! Do you really think anyone cares that much what goes on in your head?'

'I care very much what goes on in yours.'

'Ah, that's because you want to believe evil of me.'

'Evil? Of you? I don't think I do.'

'You want to believe that I don't love you. That I only want to marry you because Papa and Mama want it. You want to believe that I'm a puppet. You're only interested in what's in my head because you like to think it's sawdust. You wouldn't like it if I was really independent.'

'And what would independent mean? In love with someone else?'

'Artemy, are we to marry? They're discussing dates and contracts. They seem to take it much more seriously than you do. I want to love you, but I'm afraid of you. I feel as if you only want me so that you can hurt me.'

'When have I hurt you?'

'Please understand. I never said you had hurt me. On the contrary, you're very charming to me. It's funny how charming you can be. I can never explain it to people. You're like a little owl sometimes.'

'Where did you get that from?'

'Artemy, don't. I didn't get it from anyone. Why are you so suspicious? It's not necessary to get it from anyone when someone looks as much like an owl as you do. I love you, I really do, I really believe I do. Only what is this marriage we're going to have, Artemy? That's what I want you to tell me.'

'You're right. We shouldn't marry. No one should marry me. I'm not ready for it. We should tell them that it's absurd. Neither of us wants it. It's an absurdity.'

She had seen him walking away from the house along the beach which gave the harbour a hem of sand. She had waved and run down to the gate and across to him. Now they were on their way to the far point of the bay. A vivid lemon light fell on the scorched fields behind the beach where a ruined farm was staked with almond trees. Behind the farm a path climbed into a stone hill pitted with cavities. It was towards this path that Artemis was now cutting, his jaw taut with the anger he had denied. The girl stopped at his ferocity. 'Artemy ... ' He did not slacken. She turned back to the house. The tall steward was taking tea to the mothers, who were sitting on a terrace above a fall of green and purple foliage. Artemis strode on through the stubble. Katerina called him again and then ran after him. The stiff grass snatched at her skirt and scourged her legs. She stumbled and fell into a quicker run, arms swinging. 'Artemy ... '

He stopped in the shadow of the deserted farm. The roof tree had broken. Caked earth and bamboo canes had spilled into the mouth of the main building. Steps led up to a stone terrace beneath which there was dark access to a cellar, an unusual luxury in the island.

'You hate me,' she said. 'Why? Why? Tell me. Why is it an absurdity? That we should marry. Tell me why.'

'Because I'm not a man.'

'Yes, you are.' She insisted on his manhood. She was holding on to him. She saw the abyss on all sides. He had to support her. 'What do you want me to do?' She demanded that there be something. 'You only have to tell me.'

'I knew you wouldn't understand.'

'The brothel doesn't prove anything. Nothing that happens there means anything. I know you're a man.'

'I haven't experienced any difficulty fucking prostitutes. I don't expect to have any problem with you.'

Ah, she was torn. She would like to have flown at him and from him. He had raped her mind. Her head was full of blood. She was blinded, angry and desperate like a boxer, dreading the premature end of a fight he knows he must lose, dreading mercy more than a beating, yet enraged by the butt which has split him. She gasped and flailed her fisted arms at him. She wanted him and she wanted to punish him. Tears served for blood. Her eyes were blinded with them. Her mouth was open, red and stretched with outrage. 'I hate you. I hate you. I hate you.'

'Good,' he said, 'good. At least you can begin to be a woman even if you don't know what it is to make me a man.'

'What do you *want* of me?'

He stood in the dark corner of the fallen room, switching a split bamboo cane against his leg like a boy in a petulant episode of a game his companions have failed to complete as planned. 'Why do you have to come after me? Did they send you?'

'We're supposed to spend our lives together. And you treat me like a – like a servant, like a nobody, like worse than nobody. You make me nothing. Why?'

'You should thank me. You should thank me that I made you let go of your nurse's hand and walk. So you fall and you gash your knees. Good! Gash them. Be hurt. You should thank me.'

'Artemis, what's happened? Just tell me what's happened. Why have you turned against me like this? Don't you like it here? Has Father said something? I know Mama can be maddening. Is there someone else?'

Again he laughed, one gasp of derision. 'Someone else? No. There's no one else and if there were it might as well be you. But what about some*thing* else? Has that ever occurred to you? I don't exist. I don't exist. I'm nothing. I can't marry because I don't exist. Your whole idea of existence is centred here' – and he clapped his hand over his groin – 'in spite of your scented airs I see it here' – and he gripped her lower lip and crushed it forward between his thumb and forefinger – 'I see it in all your calculations, a belief that a man only wants the one thing you accuse him of wanting. It suits you to think so. Before you've even felt a cock you want to believe it's all we want. I tell you, woman, I can get all of that' – he stiffened his arm and brought it up with a jerk from the elbow – 'all of that I want with this' – he threw a fistful of change at her feet – 'and it'd be better than I could get from you in a lifetime of your generosity, your noble knees up. I'm not interested in your gifts. I don't want them, so think again. And now what are you thinking? When you stop admiring your breasts and your belly in the mirror of my desire, what do you think of then? Your big eyes become like the eyes of a cow in the slaughterhouse when the knives come out. You look up at the hooks and you see the butcher at the door, his back against the closed door and the sunshine shut out and now what are you thinking of but flight, running, running home, running anywhere where there are no knives to cut the flesh, the pretty self-loved flesh you wear around you like the muslin sack sewn round a peasant's baggage? It would be better for you, Katerina, if you lost your virginity as the boys lose theirs, down at Helen's. It would be better for you to be fucked by a stranger, along with all your twittering friends, all of you, on your fourteenth birthdays, better have your cunts pierced than your ears and have done with that damned nonsense. I'd sooner marry you if you'd been married before. If you were less of this beauty and more of a person. Your precious hymen means nothing to me. Put your finger through it any time you like. I don't want it. It's no crown to me.' He had her by the ear like a stalled pig. 'Now, shall we marry, my beloved Katerina? Shall we unite our families? I have no family. I want no family. You'll not get fat to please me, that I promise you. I want to meet no son of mine at the crossroads. Let's have some new plays in the national repertoire, shall we?'

'I don't know how you can talk like this to me,' she said. Her tone was mild, however, almost as if he had paid her some unexpected compliment. She drew again and again on a strand of hair and caressed her eyebrow as if it had suddenly stuck out like an unwanted trafficator. 'You've said awful things, terrible things, things I never expected anyone to say to me in my whole life.'

'Apologies. I had too much wine at lunch.' He pitched the bamboo back among the rubble.

'Don't despise me, Artemy. I know I'm not worth much, but don't despise me.'

'I don't, it's all right.'

'By going back. By being polite and offhand and courteous again. I will try to be what you want.'

'That just shows how little you understand of what I've been trying to say. I tell you there's nothing *I* want, because I don't exist. Make yourself what you think you should be, not what you think I want.'

'I'm not as clever as you,' she accused him. 'You'll have to help me. You can't just abandon me without any maps, without anything. If you're going to be a man, be one, I agree, but don't expect me to be one too.'

'It's not a question of sex.' Artemis walked past her and on up the path which led over the hill to the farther shore of the island. There was little sign of human life except for the stone walls which defined boundaries, often of property belonging to those who had left for America or who were already dead and without heirs. One man did nothing on the island except repair these mortarless but durable walls.

They reached the shoulders of the slope and saw the fall away to the cliffs ahead of them. The sound of the sea boomed below their view.

'You were so happy on *Pegasus*. I thought you seemed so happy. And now you're so bitter. What's happened? Has something happened?'

'How trivial you make me! What's happened is that I can see the trap we're in and you can't. You humour me. "Yes, I see the trap, I do, Artemy, I do",' he mimicked her. 'You don't, you can't. You're part of it.'

'Do you want to push me over the cliff, is that what you want? Do you want me to kill myself to prove I love you?'

'What is this love of yours? Explain it to me, this tender emotion or whatever it is.'

'You talk as if you've never felt it. Whereas only yesterday you told me how much you loved me.'

'I did, did I? When was that?'

'Artemy, don't. Now you make me embarrassed even to call you by your name. That's cruel of you. What am I to call you?'

'This name ... what is it, this Artemy, when you've said it what have you named? A man, a person, a parcel of flesh, what? I'm nothing, Katerina, because I've done nothing. I'm nothing because I'm afraid. Fear is the negation of manhood and I'm full of fear. "Fear of what, Artemy?" I'll tell you. Fear of knowing only too well exactly what is going to happen to me, fear of the predictability of my life. The fear of being afraid only of accidents. Of whose lives can predictions be made? Of slaves, Katerina. And I'm to be a slave – of that!' He indicated the house which was behind the hill. 'And you likewise. Now why should that cause us to smile, to smile like fools?'

They came to the edge of the cliff. It was nothing like as high as it threatened. A trail led down, through the abrupt crust of earth and desiccated scrub, on to a broad beach bisected by a spit of rock running out into the sea. It had sand on both sides of it but – and here was Katerina's modest surprise – the sea broke in slashing breakers on the one side and lapped mildly on the other. 'I always think of this beach as being like you, Artemy. Your face has two sides too. An angry and a gentle one.'

'I'm sorry. I've been cruel. All anger turns to accusation when one is a prisoner. And all love to self-pity.'

'Do you still go with prostitutes? Tell me.'

'Do you think I'm going to trace my answers in the sand because I'm too timid to give them? No, I don't. I don't.' He saw her smile, and added, 'I don't know why.'

'Do you still want to?'

'I only said that to hurt you.'

'No, I realize that I don't matter to you that much that way.'

'Oh now ... my dear!'

'I mean, I know you can always ... find other women.'

'But I don't want to,' he said. 'I don't want to marry you like a cynic. I shan't do that, Katerina. I may want to hurt you, but I don't want to pain you. I want us to be married. If you do.'

'If I do!'

'If I asked you to come away with me now, would you? And never see anyone you know again except me? Well?'

They were walking along the spit between the two beaches. Artemis threw the question back at her and was suddenly skipping quite gaily, a child who has 'thought of a good one' in a word game. She made no reply until they came almost to the point where the spit ran out and the sea closed over its spine. Then she confronted him. 'You want me to deny myself,' she said. 'Why should I? What are you offering me that I should never see anyone else? And anyway what would you do? Would you see no one either? What should we live on?'

'No one you *know*, I said. Not no one ever. It goes on, you know, this, on under the sea. If one's legs were long enough one could probably walk to the next island. Poor Katerina!'

'No,' she said, 'not after all the things you've said this afternoon, not "poor Katerina" as well. And don't change the subject.'

He said, 'I should really like to kill myself.'

'Well, don't let me detain you.' She turned back towards the land. He sat on the end of the rocks where they dwindled into damp weed and threw pebbles into the thick sea, first one side, then the other. She did not hesitate, but climbed straight up the apron of grass which ran to the edge of the shore and reached the skyline. He sat there crossly and then, catching sight of her against the blue, her body stretched with effort, jaw thrust up, hair blown, skirt wrapped round her brown legs, he cursed his own garrulous stupidity and clenched his fists in the air. Was she waiting for him? He could imagine her dawdling on the ridge now, pretending to have discovered some interesting natural object, a fragment of pottery or some pretty insect she would certainly have had a servant squash if it had appeared on the terrace. She would be bending to it in the position of a sprinter at the outset of a race, showing him the taut, rounded lines of her haunches. Artemis stretched and then swung round as if, tired of gloom, he had made some definite resolution about the way things should go, a gesture demonstrably full of relief at the girl's departure and confidence in his own lonely destiny. There was no sign of Katerina on the ridge.

He considered his move. The shore was deserted, devoid now of form or symbolism, two stretches of sand curving under unimpressive cliffs, veering away out of sight to his right before sweeping out to form one of the headlands which sheltered the harbour, continuing to his left towards a collapsed promontory which failed to make it to a flat disc of rock perhaps five hundred metres round, over which the sea just managed to rise. He slouched along the sand towards the point and then cut sharply back and ran, with hobbled urgency, afraid that perhaps he was being watched, towards where Katerina had disappeared. From the top there was again no sign of her. She could not have regained the house already, but the hot, overbearing sun gave no shade of a clue. He set out along the path towards the house, passing the ruined farm on his left, his head scribbled with gnats, and kicked his way on towards the dull beach below him. Suddenly he was violently stung on the back of the neck. He clapped his hand there and swatted a fleck of dust. He steadied himself, smiled at the sun and walked slowly on. A shower of tiny stones and dried earth spattered round him. Now he showed surprise. He pivoted on his heel, heard a clap of laughter like a peasant woman's, and ran, zigzagging towards the fallen farmhouse. More and more clods spudded out at him, but he stormed up the path and into the main room. She had retreated to the back, under the sag of broken bamboo, her dress powdered with dust, her face streaked with strands of hair, mouth ajar, fists full of unspent ammunition. He ducked, wincing, as she hurled what she had at him, spitting 'Beast, brute', and then she snatched up a bamboo and came towards him swinging it, till he had to be a circus horse to avoid it. 'Katerina, Katerina,' he remonstrated with her. ' "Katerina, Katerina!" ' It was her turn to mimic him. She slashed him on the calf and then across the shoulders, aiming at his face. 'Have you gone out of your mind?' He grabbed at her and pulled the cane out of her hand, yanking it so that it scored her palm before he freed it. He bent the bamboo into splinters and hurled it rattling into a dusty corner. She pouted and spat at him. He put his arm round her waist and drew her against him, hard. She strained away, but only far enough to keep a clear view of him, like a parent who holds a returning child at arm's length, saying, 'Let me get a look at you,' and then closed her eyes and with a moan fastened her lips on his and let him kiss first her mouth and eyes and then her throat. She raised her arms and put them round his neck and sighed. He twisted away from her and she opened her drooping lids like a little girl unfairly awakened. 'What's the matter?' 'We'd better go back.' She began to cry. 'Katerina, don't.' 'You've humiliated me. That's what you wanted to do all along, isn't it?' 'No. It's because I don't want to humiliate you that I say we should go.' 'You think of making love as a form of humiliation.' 'Making love? This? Today is too confused. What do you think you mean by "make love" anyway?' 'What you do with the girls at the brothel. What everyone means. Everything.' 'No, Katerina.' 'I want to be like them,' she said. 'You'd buy me there. Why won't you have me here?' 'You're romancing, you're dreaming.' 'You don't want me.' 'You poor child!' He really pitied her then, her swollen, disagreeable face, her sullen eyes. 'My precious Katerina.' She laughed as his eyes filled with tears, again that harsh jeering laugh of the peasant at a rival's pain. 'You're really as conventional as they come, aren't you? You're as easy to shock as anyone I know! Not your precious Katerina! Not in a cowshed! Not on a dirty floor!' And she laughed again. She had the spent face of an old priestess, exhausted by greedy pilgrims. He dreaded her nakedness. 'You'd sooner die!' Her body would be corrugated with lines, her breasts skinny and dangling, nipples on cords of flesh, her belly creased, her thighs wizened. 'I love you,' he said. 'Katerina, I love you. I said it yesterday and I say it again today. I love you.' She looked at him and shuddered. 'I shall never escape you,' she said. 'I know it. It's no good.' He was ashamed of the triumph he felt. He was as sly and self-loving as a businessman who has used an old friendship to make a smart deal. It was a coming of age, this particular pride. His cock gave a little twitch of congratulation. She was arranging herself to go back to the house. He went to her and undid the buttons of her white blouse almost as if he were helping her to dress again, so that before she realized he was helping her arms out. He raised her arm and tasted the tuft of hair under it and then moved his lips and tongue over the strand of muscle that lifted her breast. Then he raised his face to hers and kissed her lips again. The blurp-blurp of a hooter jolted their privacy. A yacht was entering the harbour.

Katerina went forward to the sunny edge of the room, and shaded her eyes. Artemis was struck by the recollected beauty which shone on her face. There was no trace of the dust which had dulled her. 'I wonder who it is,' Katerina said. 'Papa didn't mention anyone coming.' She turned, almost as if to a servant, and raised her eyebrows at Artemis. He came forward and brought her to face him. They began at the same time to kiss each other blindly, each twisting the other's lips between their teeth, to be the first to taste sweet blood. He drew her into the shadows and helped her step out of her skirt, while in an absurd way she shook and protested, the virgin.

'Artemy ... ?' It might have been dark and she afraid that it was someone else.

'I love you.' He drew her slip over her head and she unlatched her brassière and her breasts swung free an instant before he was kissing them. 'I love you.'

There was another blurp on the hooter, a strangely personal and cheeky note it had for so mechanical a sound. She stood there as if she was quite used to the strange ways of lovers, though she had never before allowed him to caress her breasts. It required an effort in him to tell himself that, after all, they were nothing new to her. 'Well?' She twisted to find her skirt and he said, 'Come to me tonight.' 'Cheek!' she said. 'Oh come on,' he muttered, annoyed at this belated archness and at the stickiness on his belly. 'Do you really think I'm going to come to your room? I'm a well-brought-up young girl. You can come to mine.'

So, not without an uneven lurch on his part, they walked back towards the house. The new yacht was quite close in; they frowned at a shouting figure at the prow. 'Artemy!' 'Oh God,' said Artemis, 'it's Dmitri. There's no mistaking that fog-horn. What the hell does he want?' Katerina was bending to some purple shells along the tideline. She looked up with that heavy drugged expression he always thought of as 'mindless', a sullen, devoted look which excited and mortified him. He knew so precisely what she was thinking that they burst out laughing simultaneously, while Dmitri went on waving. 'Hey, Artemy! It's me. Big Chief Sitting Bear to Little Owl, can you hear me?'

'You didn't ask him here, did you?'

'Me?' she said. 'Dmitri Stratis? Catch me!'

The new guests produced a busy enough response in the household to cover Artemis's listlessness. He lay on the bed counting the bamboo rods the Minister's mason had employed nostalgically to underpin the concrete roof. A pale lizard stood pulsing on its round feet in the angle of the wall. He smiled at it and felt some kinship with its surreptitious domesticity. (It amused him to concoct polysyllabic little poems, fragments towards an anthology.) The creature seemed unafraid when he clapped his hands. He went across to inspect it, dawdling to give it time to escape, but it flattened itself, throbbing against the rough wall, eyes full of him. He reached it and said, 'Come!', presuming on their acquaintance, when it twitched and, to his horror, dropped its tail, jerking, at his feet, before scuttling up the wall and into a crack where the plaster met the wattles. At the same time he heard a loud shriek, angry voices and the unmistakable wop of a blow; more shouts, more screams and more blows followed. He ran out into the passage. A door was open on the far side. He ran into the room to which it gave access and threw out the shutters. The wailing and the crack of the strap had not stopped. He heard a commotion at the far end of the corridor, one voice inviting another to confirm what the first had reported, its tone both plaintive and accusing. He leaned out of the window, but again saw nothing. The wailing was uninterrupted now. The beating was over. He heard a movement behind him, but could not turn to apologize. He was enormously sexually aroused. 'My dear little Artemy, are you looking for someone?' It was Katerina's mother.

'No, not exactly, I – '

'I was just making sure that the guest rooms had been properly prepared. You've heard what happened, I suppose? That gardener's boy again. I can't tell you how wicked he's been. Indescribable. That was what the noise was all about. I don't know what we're going to do about him. I truly believe there's wickedness pure and unadulterated in him. He'll end up on the gallows.'

Dmitri had come with his parents (his father carried fresh copies of the *Times* for the Minister) and an Englishman, Michael Shaw, who had just taken a first in Greats at Oxford and had coxed the university boat though he had failed to get his blue, and whose father was attached to the British Embassy in the capital. Dmitri's mother was a slim and elegant woman with that untouchable courtliness of manner which seems to require other women to complement it. She was accompanied by a French-speaking woman, dark and guttural with a deeply lined face under tragic eyes drunk with horror. She had recently lost her husband in an incident on their estate in Algeria. Dmitri told Artemis after dinner, when they went for a walk along the beach, now cold to the feet, that her husband had been cut in pieces in front of her and his genitals forced into her mouth. The French had bombed the village from which the raiders had been thought to come. Artemis said, 'Thank you for waiting till after dinner.' Dmitri said, 'Well, and how goes it with you, my little owl?' 'How do you come to be here, Stratis?' 'Ask my parents. I'm merely the helmsman. They set the course. However, I daresay the three wise men have some plan or other that one of them will probably let out prematurely, so causing all three of them to run away from it like a botched burglary. Meanwhile, *I* have news for you. Our plans are advancing. Next week I go to Paris. Then we shall see.' 'What are you talking about?' 'The king, it is said, has been warned by his doctors that his heart is in an unreliable condition, I go to persuade the crown prince to make his father abdicate in his favour. With that under our belts, we can go forward to the next stage. Your presence in Paris might make all the difference.' '*Mine*? What could I possibly do?' 'My dear Artemy, a man with your tongue in his head! We must prepare the Quai d'Orsay. A new constitution on our side, a renewal of arms shipments on theirs. How long do you think we have, in heaven's name?' 'Dmitri, your jokes –' Dmitri crushed Artemis's shoulder between his fingers. 'There's no joke in this. There's comedy, I warrant you, when the old men discover that it is our plot and not theirs which is to come to something. Do you know what I think? I think that that prize buffoon George Dimitriades plans to have himself put forward as the Marshal's successor under the slogan "A Time For Action". That's the rumour. Fuck a pig, Artemy, have you ever heard of anything like that? Talking of that ever delightful subject, how is our beautiful Katerina?' 'Katerina is very well, as you can see for yourself.' 'Oh don't sound so possessive, Artemy, it's so boring. Anyway, I have my eye on the Algerian lady. Imagine that mouth! It excites me disgracefully, I'm afraid. Those lips!' 'Stratis Dmitri, you're a revolting specimen of humanity.' 'But at least I am one, Theodoros Artemis. I don't hide my humanity. Tell me, honestly, what have you been doing with it since you stopped coming to Helen's?' He rubbed a column of air in inquisitive mime. 'Nothing.' 'Ah, in that case you must be carrying quite a load!' Dmitri cupped his hand for a moment and weighed Artemis's groin. 'Look, lay off, lout.' 'You really are in love with the fair Katerina, then? Konni told me how you suddenly grew scrupulous that night. Very touching.' The light was so poor that it was impossible to catch the intonation of Dmitri's grin. Aphrodite glimmered in the satin sky. 'I don't remember saying anything to Konni.' 'He remembers. When's the date, by the way?' 'It hasn't been finally agreed. In the autumn, I think. I'm not sure whether we shouldn't wait till after I've done my *service militaire*, but the families don't think so.' Artemis was dejected by the servile tone which Dmitri's presence imposed on him. 'Are you with us or not, Artemy?' 'In what respect?' 'I take the view that we must grasp our opportunity. If we can be the spearhead of the forces restoring the monarchy, but a vigorous youthful monarchy, a monarchy –' 'Dmitri, no leading articles, not on the beach, please.' 'Artemis, you're in love. Believe me, that is something I understand. Something I respect. Something, to tell you the truth, I rather envy. But are you going to allow love to dominate your whole life? I tell you, you owe it to your wife, to the sons she will give you, to remake this country, to take a hand in things. We are the only free men capable of acting in the present crisis. The Marshal can't last much longer. It's us or the seniles, it's as simple as that. Why are we free? Because we've got the money. I'm not striking any moral attitudes. But we can go to Paris and George Mareotis, for example, can't. The army's paralysed, as usual, with a Marshal in the palace. None of those pregnant heroes dares make a move without an order in writing. I know you'd sooner shut yourself up in an ivory tower with your Happy Few and be damned to us, but we need your brain, my little Artemy, and that cunning little face of yours, we can use that too. You think the affairs of our poor little country beneath you. I've heard you talking: you wish you were a Frenchman. And what are the French doing? Sitting in their cafés wishing they were Russians! You can be our Mavrocordato if you'd let yourself. Even our Byron. Some of those poems of yours aren't half bad in my view.' 'What in hell do you know about my poems?' 'Konni happened to let me see the ones you sent him.' 'Did he just?' 'Don't be angry because your friends admire you. That's a form of cowardice and you're not a coward, I know that as well as anyone.' 'What action can we possibly take? Look here, we ought to be getting back, people're going to wonder where we are.' 'Let them wonder! Artemy, your cynicism about our country is like a sickness. It must be treated. You think you're above politics, but I tell you, you're relying on paper, you're relying on the seniles, whether you think it or not, on my father and your father and Katerina's father, all old birds who can scarcely get it up any more unless it's costing them a packet. Did you know, Helen was telling me, it's not the young girls that excite them, the old fools, it's the expensive ones? It depresses them to be left with change. So she makes damned sure they aren't, as you can imagine. She misses you. And so does that little Pilar, the Spanish one. Christ, I had her the other evening. I don't know how you can leave her alone. She did a thing with me, I don't know if she's ever done it with you – from the way she was talking she probably has – ' 'I'm going back.' 'Artemy, listen to me. I want to ask you man to man. Will you go to Paris for us?' 'Us?' 'The New Patriotic Committee. You know who I mean.' 'I have no idea at all whom you mean. If you ask me, it all sounds like a shooting party that hasn't got any guns and hasn't booked any stands and isn't going to get farther than the bar on the corner – or Helen's, more likely. And anyway, I thought you were going. Now you talk as if you want me to go alone. No, thank you very much.' 'We can't go in a party, in a deputation, that would be ridiculous. Even the Marshal's secret police would be on to that one.' 'I can't believe for one moment that they aren't on to you already. In fact, there are probably more of them than there are of you in on this.' 'You don't understand politics, especially the politics of our own poor little country. You may be right. The police may be in on it. But there is one thing that lasts longer than any regime in this country. One party above all parties and that is money. Money is the only institution that outlasts institutions. And we have it, or will have it. It would be worse for us if the police didn't know who we were and how strong we were, because, believe me, we shall be their paymasters and just as well they know it. They'll come down on us in one set of circumstances and one only: if they think we haven't got a majority holding. On the other hand, tact still matters: we must avoid embarrassing them. We mustn't challenge them before we are in a position to pension them, because that hurts a policeman's dignity. He likes to think that he has the last word and when we're in power we shall want him to have the same confidence and we shall want the people to have it too. Believe me, I've discussed this matter with Commissioner Ralli, in the most general terms, and we understand each other perfectly. Artemy, I'm older than you. I shall be twenty-seven next year. At my age Alexander had conquered half Asia. You're younger than I am, but you've finished with childish things, although this engagement business makes you feel like a boy – no, I mean that quite sincerely, I'm not mocking you, I know how it feels. Only I intend to be prime minister of this country by the time I'm forty. At the latest. In a situation of the kind we have at present it's futile to hope for power through popular support. The notables have a unique position here and we must face it. It is from our ranks that the leaders of change have to emerge. What are your political principles? The principles of Stendhal, am I right?'

'I don't know,' said Artemis, crushed by his inability to articulate his revulsion at Dmitri's rhetoric. They had stopped on a low bridge which crossed a drain under the wall of the Minister's house. The sound of a native guitar imposed a regular stitch on the hem of the evening. Was it Katerina laughing up there on the terrace? Did he hear her inquiring for him? Or was it Eleni, pitching the pebble of her voice into the well of the darkness and listening for the echo? How impossibly cut off from him they seemed, with the big Dmitri settled like a peasant's bundle on the wall beside him! 'Stendhal's politics? What were they? A detached, ironical tolerance, a dignified dance with disillusion, an awareness of the probable ordinariness of princes and the possible princeliness of the ordinary. Is that a set of principles? I wouldn't say so exactly.'

'Minister of Education!' said Dmitri. 'I'm going to appoint you Minister of Education as soon as I get the chance. A revolution through the classroom. The final solution of the Language Question! You're capable of it, Artemy. Perhaps the only man who is. You can keep your professorship. I know very well there's talk of you as the youngest professor in our history. I wouldn't want to deprive you of the honour. "The princeliness of the ordinary!"

By God, it's the very slogan we need. The very thing to explain to the mass of the people what we stand for. If it weren't for your blasted respect for the truth, I'd make you Minister of Information as well. The first thing, and first things first, Artemy, is to make it clear to the crown prince that we are the prime force behind those who see him as the salvation of the country. He must be brought to realize that without us his chances are nil. And strangely enough, I think that's perfectly true.'

'But who are we?' asked Artemis in a tone of wheedling refutation which again made him frown.

'We are the heirs of the future. Why are you marrying this girl and not Pilar who uses her backside better than most girls use their heads? Is it for the joys of her virginity or the thrill of her epigrams? Come now, Artemis, this is a dynastic matter and you know it very well. You're with us whether you like it or not.'

'You're wrong,' Artemis said gloomily.

'Let's go into the harbour and get some wine. I can see you want to talk.'

'Let's go back. I've no wish to talk at all. And very little chance either.'

'That's unfair. Autocracy isn't my programme and never has been. You're afraid of her already. Oh well, I admit it, I don't know anything about love. The kind of love I like is the kind you can get with a fat wallet any time you feel like it, pronto. It leaves the decks clear, that's the advantage of it, though I know literature's against me. Well, most literary men have got more excuses than deeds to their credit, if you ask me. They live on the margin most of them, don't they, illuminate the capital letters and leave the fine print of actual life to others? But you're not literary really, Artemis, and I'll tell you why: you don't want to be admired. No one can be literary and not crave admiration. Whereas you run from it. You know you're capable of something better than a footnote or two and a few elegant quatrains. Only you don't know what, am I not right? You'd like to think it's cunt you want, but I'm telling you even the most beautiful quim in the

world won't satisfy you for ever. I'm talking about you personally. Postpone it as you will with fine scruples and speeches, in the
end you come and that's it. No, Artemy, you're meant for bigger
and more permanent things. Can you deny it?'

'I can't do what you ask, Dmitri. Because I don't have any idea
whom to approach. I should never get past the doorman. I haven't
the nerve to pass myself off as the representative of a movement
that doesn't exist, offering terms to a king who has no country.
I don't believe I could keep a straight face.'

'Now you're coming to the point. Now you're beginning to face
things. Good! We can talk like men. First of all, your objections
– as you secretly hoped they would be, if my guess is right – are
completely specious. No revolutionary movement ever represented the people for whom it claimed to speak. All revolutionary
movements are fictions. They originate in idealism – or cynicism –
and they grow on illusions. That is to say, on the hopes of one side
and the fears of the other. They become real because they offer
portraits of the future. Any prediction, as the oracles proved, will
keep you in business as long as it's delivered confidently enough.
You needn't worry about which door of the Quai d'Orsay to
knock on because you won't have to knock on any. A member
of the French secret service will contact you as soon as you get
to your hotel. The Deuxième are very worried about their Government's failure to arm us as they promised. They want to
believe in us, just as the people whom we represent do – or will
as soon as they are aware of our existence, in their case because it
will help them to prove the ineptitude or worse of their own
enemies at home. Allow them to build us up, my dear Artemy,
allow them to make us important. Are you not aware that every
sovereign in Europe wears more foreign than domestic honours
on his breast? And the moral of that is, a man is as brave as other
people's cowardice insists that he must be. Let us merely declare
our purpose and there'll be no shortage of allies to carry us
through. It applies here as well, as you'll see the moment our names
are linked with the successful return of the crown prince, as they

most certainly will be, due to my intention to assume the editor-ship of the *Times* early in the new year. My father has insisted on my taking over since he believes, of course, that he will be Foreign Minister by then. Which indeed he may well be, for as long as a week or even two. Long enough to have his photograph taken against the Sophia Palace and a large supply of emblematic writ-ing-paper delivered to his office. Well now, what do you say, Artemy? Will you go?'

'I'll think about it.'

'Good! In that case I shall depend on you. When you apply for your passport, you can tell the authorities that you are going to do research at the Bibliothèque Nationale under M. Beyle. They'll believe you.'

'What –' Artemis began and then stood up and craned his neck towards the terrace where laughter had replaced music. Then the guitar began again, to cheers, and the girls took up the tune of an old patriotic song to which they had learned silly words at the Lycée. 'What do you seriously and truly propose to do when –' he broke off again, pursing his lips at the absurdity.

'When what? Speak up.'

'When you become prime minister? What do you stand for, Dmitri, honestly?'

'The will to govern. That is all a people asks of its Government. I have it.' And at that moment, with the unshapely bulk of Dmitri blocking the stars, Artemis had to admit that he believed him. 'The hypocrisy,' Dmitri added as they went through the little gate on to the Minister's hill, 'the hypocrisy can come later.'

Eleni and Katerina rolled their eyes to take in Artemis and Dmitri but continued, smiling, with their song, increasing the volume in accusation of the recent absentees. Michael Shaw was sitting with a glass of brandy in front of him, the only audience, while one of the yacht's crew, Kosta by name, a handsome young man of nineteen, played the guitar. Dmitri took the basket-clad brandy bottle and poured himself an ostentatious tot. He brought another to Artemis and toasted him with deliberate complicity. 'Here's to it, my Artemy.' Artemis included the health of the company and drank. In the chintzed saloon, the three fathers were smoking cigars by the unlit fire. At the other end of the room, near the doors which gave on to the far terrace, the ladies were sitting round a table set with glasses of lemon tea, a plate of sticky cakes (and empty ruffed containers) and a *bonbonnière* of sugared almonds.

Michael Shaw was a narrow-shouldered young man with a pointed face and a beaked mouth; he had the unreliable charm of a crocodile that had yet to taste flesh. The cautious fluency with which he spoke his hosts' language, pausing now and again for corrections that were superfluous, made clear at once the degree of his affection for their country and the comparatively minor place it held in the general scheme of his knowledge. When the music stopped, the young guitarist stood up to go, but Shaw addressed him with inquiring, fluent praise, and he agreed to play a little more. 'The banality of our own popular music makes me hungry for yours,' Shaw explained to the rest of them. 'I'm looking forward very much to this expedition tomorrow. Shall we be starting very early?'

'It's two or three hours across the mountains,' Katerina said, 'at the least, so I should think we shall have to or there won't be any point.'

'I intend to stay there for several days, though, don't you? I thought that was understood. We can't really hope to strike gold right away.'

'I'm willing,' Dmitri said, 'what about you, Artemy?'

'I suppose so,' Artemis said.

'I don't suppose they'll let us stay,' Eleni said.

'I don't suppose they'll let *you* stay. If Artemy stays I shall stay, that's quite certain.'

'That will be charming,' said Michael Shaw. 'I was very interested in what your father was saying at dinner. Do you think he's right about the site of the original settlement? He sounded very convincing to a stranger. His ideas would certainly tie in with the prevailing winds. That coast would make a much more sensible anchorage than here. And I was talking to someone in the village before dinner, I don't know if you've heard this story, but they say that a large number of artefacts and some marble sculpture have been turned up in that vicinity, although most of it is smuggled away and sold in the capital to avoid confiscation. Have you heard this story?'

There was a tap on the window of the saloon. It was Eleni's bedtime. Katerina stretched and said with a moan, 'I think I'll go and have a bath.'

'Katerina is going to wash off tomorrow's dust before it even has time to settle,' said Dmitri. 'It's probably a very good idea. I think I'll join you, my dear. In a manner of speaking, of course. In a manner of speaking, Artemy.'

Katerina said, 'Don't you worry! Anyway, there wouldn't be any room in the tub for anyone with you.'

'Now we are reaching the realm of the empirical, my dear, and that is something we would probably be better to leave alone. Impossibility – correct me, Artemy – can always be refuted by the single instance. There are ways in which even the largest forms can be accommodated in the smallest, surprising as it may seem.'

Katerina said, 'I haven't any idea what you're talking about.' She shook hands with Michael, said good night to Kosta, kissed Artemis on either cheek (as did Eleni) and went to the door at the ladies' end of the saloon. Dmitri shook hands all round and followed her, but when she left the women Dmitri stayed, leaning over the Algerian woman so that his nankeen jacket's lapels brushed against her shoulder. Michael Shaw said, 'Your fiancée is very beautiful.'

'Yes. She is.'

'You'll live in the capital, of course, when you're married.'

'I imagine so.'

'You haven't yet decided what you're going to do?'

'Good night.' Kosta had packed up his guitar and was ready to leave.

'You're sleeping on the yacht?'

'Yes, sir. Shall I wait for you?'

'No, no, you go on. I can always give someone a shout or get someone to take me. I'm not sure what the arrangements are. You go on. I understand you're thinking of teaching. Or is it true that you're going to travel first?' Shaw now, for the first time, ceased to smile, though he slid his lips uncomfortably back from his teeth as if they had lost their muscle. 'Dmitri tells me that you're a certainty for the prize of the year.'

'Dmitri has a tendency to exaggeration.'

'Have you ever thought of travelling to England? Or even more specifically to Oxford?'

'I'm about to be married. And then I have the army waiting for me.'

'You haven't thought of a diplomatic career? You must come and dine with my father when you're back in the capital. Why don't you come to Oxford for a year or two? Our French School is perfectly reputable, I'm told, and you could perhaps teach your language as a sideline. These things aren't difficult to arrange. I shall probably be accepting a Fellowship myself at All Souls. You could be sure of friends.'

'Why are you offering me all these things?'

'We're alone. I'll tell you very frankly. I believe that things are going to get a great deal worse before they get any better. Here, I mean, at this end of the world. This might be a very good time to take a prudent sabbatical.' Shaw drew over one of the deck-chairs with its back to the saloon. The mothers of Artemis and Katerina were rising, like reluctant balloons, while Dmitri pulled a chair next to the tragic widow, who accepted a black cigarette from him. Dmitri's own mother, her skirt high across her knee, was sitting flung away from the table, her legs crossed, feet far apart like the points of an open scissors, the far shoe loose and flapping, fingers stroking the ankle. She gave the impression of being at once aggrieved and aggressive, her chin high, her jaw stretched in the reflecting surface of the window. Her bangled wrist hung limp almost to the floor. The Algerian woman watched her with haunted, imploring eyes, as if the other woman had taken from her something for which only mute appeal was possible, something both very well known to her and unmentionable. Dmitri was addressing her in French: 'I'm overwhelmed, Madame Janvier, with the sense of your tragedy. You must forgive me, but I can't drive it out of my mind. It would be too facile to speak of compassion, perhaps too greedy to speak of love, but speak I must of an emotion which commands me every time I am near you. It is for that reason that I have avoided you until now.' Dmitri's mother looked back at him, her chin still raised haughtily, rather as a woman international will look over the hand of a young bridge player, agreeably surprised (and slightly disappointed) if he has failed to make an error. She turned away again and moved her hand from her ankle to her throat, which she stroked with something of the same almost callous appraisal. 'You may perhaps have supposed that I was indifferent to your presence. Not at all. I am profoundly moved by it. Your eyes haunt my dreams. I beg of you to think of me as your friend.' He moved closer to her, interrupting her view of his mother who shook her bangles and checked the gold charms on one of them, glancing round the shadows like someone who has been robbed before. 'Like it or not, Madame, you have been visited with a remarkable and bewitching beauty. Perhaps it is the last cruel twist of fate, but it is something which I would betray myself by not telling you.' He took the woman's hand and held it up, a curator to whom something really rather special had been offered unexpectedly. Her eyes were larger than ever, swimming in the brackish lymph from which they seemed bound at any moment to burst. Dmitri's mother rose and said, 'Good! I go to bed,' so harshly in her own language that she could have been rupturing a long silence. The other woman gazed at her more imploringly than ever, but Thalia Stratis kissed her back into her seat, exchanged embraces with her son and left the two of them alone.

Meanwhile on the terrace Shaw had poured more brandy for

himself and Artemis, whose ears were filled with the murmur of Dmitri's monologue.

'I find the atmosphere of your country both tragic and enchanting,' Shaw was saying. Artemis smiled, 'Antiquities amuse you.' 'Not merely that. If you're referring to enchantment. I like its remoteness, its astonishing largeness. It is at the same time packed and deserted. A living paradox. Loaded with history and yet light in its carrying of it. I suppose, above all, I find its sexual atmosphere an enormous contrast. A minute ago I was talking about you coming to England. Now you'll think I'm trying to seduce you into coming to somewhere stuffy and lacking in vitality. Of course I was thinking in political terms. I hope you know what I mean. England has interests in this part of the world. It wouldn't do to have the wrong people in the saddle. Or the right people jolted out of the saddle. It's a curious thing, patriotism, don't you think, Theodoros, I mean the contradictory impulses one has about one's own country? At times I think there's nothing I would like better than to see England brought down in fire and ruin and then, for the most Quixotic reasons, I find myself defending the very institutions I despise. I talk of bringing you to England in one breath and then I find myself dreaming of staying here all my life the next. What do you make of that, eh?'

'I assume you to be homosexual,' Artemis said.

'I beg your pardon?' Shaw had pushed back his chair roughly and was standing, his teeth sliding in and out of his furious lips. 'What did you say?'

'Have I offended you?'

'As we are both guests in this house,' Shaw said, 'I shall assume that I did not hear what you said. As for my own remarks, of course I stand by them. I cannot promise you that I can remain on the same footing with you as before, but I would nevertheless do my best to help you if you choose to come to Oxford.'

'I shouldn't leave my own country,' Artemis said.

The last full meeting of the Political Committee took place when the Revolutionary Army commanded both the harbour and the main airport, from the hills above the capital. It was assumed that the men would be allowed to rest, while supplies caught up with them from the high plateaux north of the central district and from the territory of the 'traditional enemy' whose Government had opened it to them. The conviction that a clinching attack would be mounted during the next few weeks was so general that some slackness had weakened certain sections of the army. Brasidas, fresh from a meeting in the north with representatives of friendly powers, introduced his remarks by alluding to this distressing tendency. He had an indoor look about him which contrasted with the weathered, even melodramatic, walnut features of Alexander Pavlides and with the rosy complexion of the general, whose white moustaches and full head of hair made him a walking premonition of coming winter.

In the mountains the general stood naked every morning outside his tent and braced himself for a bucket of icy water. His skin had the appearance of a stripped rabbit's (that uncreased silken rose madder), but he had the spring of untrapped energy about him. He came from a district which had suffered from the economic consequences of the old Marshal's naive tyranny. His family had been its largest land-owners and composed its traditional aristocracy, though their claims hardly went much further back than the War of Independence, when the bravery and the ruthlessness of their followers had not only rooted out the foreign masters but had eliminated any who might dispute with them the honours or the spoils of victory. The Marshal, who never lost a soldier's faith in the trustworthiness of soldiers, had grown conscious, with an old man's querulous perspicacity (he notices only what he guesses may irritate him), of the discontent which was at home in the countryside and assumed that dishonest (by which he meant non-military) men must be behind it. What better person could there be to appoint as commissioner than one of his own stamp, both a native of the district and someone whose interests the reported abuses were bound to damage? The Marshal's Office gave Major

Papastavrou a brief which went further than it might have, had they known of his intention to fulfil it. The *Times*, as was hoped in the president's secretariat, printed it in full, with an editorial insisting that it was evidence of the seriousness both of the condition of the rural areas and of the Marshal's determination to deal with it. The editorial praised so comprehensively the mere idea of the major's commission that the Marshal's men dismissed as superfluous any need actually to do anything. To meet rumours of trouble, rumours of remedy would normally suffice.

Andreas Papastavrou, the youngest of three sons, arrived in his family's hereditary fief with little more ideology than the resolution of a new commanding officer who has been appointed to cope with disturbances (resulting perhaps from the death of cadets on an exercise of excessive severity) in a distant camp. He would put things right because he could re-establish confidence, not because he had a more radical or humane temper than those whose misbehaviour he was delegated to correct. Andreas was aware of this tradition for investigating officers and might normally have been obedient to it, but he found a situation beyond the normal. Those whom he might have rebuked for an unwise exercise of power he discovered to be powerless. The squeals heard in the capital had been a chorus of both the governed and the governors. The province was in despair. Andreas Papastavrou was bewildered. His letters to the capital were received with the fulsome incomprehension of those who took it that his bewilderment was a rehearsed prelude to the usual meticulous indifference. Since he belonged to the class whose interests the Marshal took to be identical with those of the country, the Old Man congratulated the young officer on his diligence and imagined it both safe and 'progressive' to encourage him to pursue his investigations. A sharper man might have assigned him to the parachute corps, a pioneering branch where headstrong officers could prove their willingness to die for their country without the need to provide an external enemy for them. The Government, however, was too exhausted by the problems of the present to have imagination for the dangers of the future. The Marshal's men had taken power to expose the corruption, obscurantism and venality of their predecessors. They had been determined to simplify the machinery of administration. They had taken the praise of the notables as genuine encouragement; only when their 'National Resurgence' had gone beyond the possibility of retreat did they guess that what they had heard was the flattery of court orators and not the plaudits of relieved patriots. When the machinery of bureaucracy proved more complicated than they had thought, they chose to regard complications, whatever their origins, as a form of treachery. They took power as simple soldiers; events proved them simpler civilians. Those who served them were forced to pretend to make progress and so were burdened with the difficulties not only of administration but also of duplicity. The Government was further and further divorced from its hired officials, and its committees, which were now sitting round every hole in the path of the country's advance, were too intimidated to deny progress and too circumscribed to achieve it. The Marshal was allowed to believe that his subordinates had 'conquered' problems they had barely broached and became impatient for the next stage to be completed before the planks had been laid for the first. As soldiers, the Marshal's officers had always believed that theirs was the most testing art; they began to believe that anyone who failed in his task was betraying them and anyone who succeeded was making fools of them. Their social programme became a postponement of bankruptcy, paper promises to cover basic deficiencies. Nothing could save their public reputations but a call to arms; hoping for war, they prepared for peace. Andreas was left, as a result, to compile an ever more devastating denunciation of his own class, his industry unchecked either by the caution a bureaucrat might have displayed towards the Marshal or by the tact a career officer would perhaps have shown to a civilian administration. Inhibited neither by self-interest nor by opportunism, he proceeded without premeditation to demolish the myth of paternalism on which his own family's wealth was founded. He never understood, until it was too late to withdraw, that he was condemning the branch on which the Papastavrous had long rested. By then he was so disgusted by its rottenness that he was driven to sharpen the teeth of his saw. His anger had been directed first at the peasants who had adopted a know-nothing fatalism which enraged him to the point where he was driven to phrase his own questions more and more tendentiously. Only when he had aroused his own mind to a full and irreversible consciousness of the peasants' condition did he realize that his irritated impersonation of their grievances had led him to become the traitor to his class interests which his family and their like would later accuse him of being. Andreas Papastavrou was acquainted, by this appointed means, and much to his alarm, while early in his forties, with a loneliness which his upbringing and training gave him no machinery to understand. He took a small village house some distance from his father's principal holdings and insisted on doing all the cleaning and washing himself. Fearing that he was going to be poisoned, he expelled all the domestic staff. He ate little and prepared what he did eat so ineptly that he contracted severe dysentery. He refused to have a doctor called (there was none within a hundred kilometres) and turned away the sensible diet kind ladies brought to his door. He grew so weak that he had to discontinue his inquiries. His fear that he was being watched grew foundations, like a marsh tree which first spreads its shade and then sends down the roots to support it, for the villagers grew morbidly curious about this aristocrat who was shitting himself to death in their midst. His apparently voluntary martyrdom (what rich man suffers when he need not?) deprived him of the frightened sympathy his rank might have demanded or his condition deserved. He was a freak. By the time that he was in real need of help there was no one left who felt either bound enough or frightened enough to give it. He knew not only pain but that desolation – remote even from the consolations of the inevitable – which arises from deliberately marooning oneself on a calvary and a cross of one's own construction. He watched his own symptoms with the dispassionate attention of a scientist who has infected himself with a disgusting complaint of which its earlier victims have failed to give a satisfactory account. He became through agony what he could not be through birth: a helpless worm on the face of the earth, ignored, filthy and priggishly outcast by all within sight and sniff of him. His clothes were fouled with shit and blood. His legs were caked like a pig's. The house which he had tried to clean was his sty, the papers on which he worked as if in a trance were soiled by the sordid evidence of his misery. It might seem a sentimentality to say that he was happy, yet he welcomed his disease (and so came to conquer it) because he saw that it was forcing a complete, if terrible, nudity on him. His flesh fell away like his illusions, his confidence dwindled into the mute mutterings of a baby. He experienced infancy at an age when most men are beyond it. By the good fortune of an excruciating humiliation, he recovered a loop in time and was able to confess himself a child. In the end, blood-slimed and ulcerous, he dragged himself through the village, down past the café where the old men sat with their pipes and their tasselled caps, to the rubbish tip where, amid dogs as skinny as himself, he collapsed. He saw in this ungracious and unmerciful degradation nothing either expiatory or ennobling. And with the same clarity he saw that it could not end like this; his survival seemed to him to be linked with an assumption not of guilt, which would have been uncharacteristic, but of readiness. His lonely sufferings gave him no sense of mission. He did not recover to a knowledge of what he must do. He was still without weapons, just as he was now without armour. His illness, as soon as he began to recover from it, became a good reason for relieving him of his duties. He was sent back to his family estates on half pay, with orders to report when he felt strong enough. Andreas spent the time doing further work on the history which his illness would excuse the authorities for ignoring. He was without respect either from the military or from the local people. In a society which valued potency as the incarnation of a man's will he was derided as impotent. He became so. His older brother Vassili bribed a local widow to make advances to him.

Andreas, out of a meekness which had become his only vestment, imagined that she needed the reassurance of finding someone more wretched than herself and allowed her to come to his bed, only to find that he was unable to procure an erection. His paranoia took on a new and beautiful form: he believed himself transparent. To create for himself the conditions which might make this belief plausible, he became intensely secretive, addicted to disguise. He would, in the accepted sense, disappear for days.

Vassili was an active and energetic man. He was a bully only in the habitual style of his caste: he expressed himself through his possessions and through the possessions of others. He would have defended Andreas literally to the death against anyone who insulted him as a Papastavrou; he would have been outraged at the smallest hint that he could connive at his brother's death, but he resented the laws of inheritance guaranteeing Andreas a share which his puny performance did nothing to justify. Since playing on a man's nerves could be no crime in a code where men were supposed to have no nerves, he continually cursed his brother for the weakness which a sophisticate might have accused him of wishing upon him. He saw in Andreas's slyness something like the laughter-provoking convulsions of a donkey that has plunged from a safe if narrow path in flight from a surge of bees, only to break his back on the unnecessary rocks below. In fact Andreas already felt within him the promise of new strength. He was a muscle awaiting its function. If he looked as weak as an unstrung puppet, he was a puppet who had had the strength to sever his own strings. When war came he rejoined the army. Within a few days the doubts that hung over him were forgotten in the immensity of the crisis. He was thrown into the fire without much concern whether or not he emerged; he came out steel. The story was not simple, but the effect, from outside, was unmistakable. Major Papastavrou was gazetted colonel within two months and major-general a month later. A brigade of almost untrained conscripts stormed the walls of occupied Boreopolis with the bayonet under his personal command. He was the first into the city. He had assumed the appearance of a career officer in the Sandhurst style, but his men were touched to discover how unlike the swaggering and casualty-accepting staff man he actually was. It was as if his brass-hat's moustache and livid complexion were the last of his disguises. He kept them on.

Brasidas had said, 'The men have the idea that this is going to be their last battle. They must be educated away from this dangerous view. There will never be a last battle.'

Artemis imagined that he was about to hear yet another exhortation from foreign sources on the necessity of continuing 'vigilance'. Perhaps, like all military men, both Brasidas and the general dreaded the end of the fighting and hoped, by postulating new and more dangerous invisible enemies, to find a use for the simpler logics of war in the more complicated 'struggles' of peace. Brasidas said, 'The information which I have received is from the highest sources. The capitalists are resolved on intervention. Their fleet is already approaching the Cape and will be in the gulf within two days. In these circumstances, you must take my word for it – since it is something which our friends have considered to the fullest possible extent – our army is incapable of imposing a solution by force of arms. If help were to be given us, it would have to come across the mountains and it would probably be destroyed from the air before it could ever reach us.'

'Why don't we attack at once, tonight?'

'Who speaks here but the brave young Theodoros?'

'And I agree with him,' said Alexander Pavlides, the hawk denied a field full of young rabbits.

Brasidas said, 'It will take at least a week to pacify the city, even according to the general's most optimistic estimates. Isn't that so, Comrade General?'

The general fondled his moustaches and then nodded.

'We can tell the men what is at stake,' said Pavlides, 'and they'll fight like tigers. I believe we could take the city tonight. I'm with young Theodoros.'

'You have a faction,' said Brasidas to Artemis.

'And I support him,' said Carlo Brancusi, who had deserted to the partisans and had fought with them against the Germans.

'A foreign legion almost,' sneered Brasidas. 'A foreign legion,' he went on more tenderly but less convincingly, 'with which I should be happy to fight on any adventure. But, my friends, this is not an adventure. Do I have to tell you of the care and seriousness with which our friends have considered the situation? The military side alone, in actual fact, is decisive: we cannot succeed even on that preliminary plane – '

'You've yet to prove that,' said Pavlides. 'I don't accept it.'

'Let us hear the general's views. The man who took Boreopolis two weeks before the defenders expected to see his advance guard deserves some attention. General?'

'I've had conversations on the telephone with our friends, as well as Comrade Brasidas's personal report. While I accept your feelings and, as always, am willing to hear them stated, they remain merely feelings. In so far as they are for action, for victory and against pessimism and defeat, we all share them. It's merely a question of when we are ready to abandon feelings and rely again, as ever, on reason. Take your time by all means, but when you're ready face the facts. Do you suppose that I would lose a second in talk if we could complete our victory simply by committing our men to battle? The question of how scandalous it is of the capitalist powers to intervene is a rhetorical irrelevance. We know that they will intervene. The idea of a *fait accompli*, even if it were possible, is a sentimentality. It is not military realities which dominate the situation but political ones – '

'I thought the military side alone was going to prove decisive – ' Pavlides hissed at Brasidas.

'Hold on, my bold hawk,' said the general. 'Hover a little longer before you pounce. If I may correct Comrade Brasidas, there can be no real division between the two areas of debate, but what he means is true: our men will be in a military trap, if we commit them, because we ourselves will have fallen into a political one. The powers who wish things to return to the previous state of affairs do not have time on their side. We do. They have stirred themselves for one last attempt to hold the tide and they have the strength at this moment to do it. If we meet them at their strongest with all of our men massed in one attack, we shall present them with the opportunity of which they have dreamed. Our strength, as our tactics have shown, derives from a strategy of dispersal. Allow ourselves to be enclosed in the city and their material strength will crush us. Let us take to the country and to the mountains and we go to ground like Antaeus, to rise again stronger than ever. If we attack, we do so for the sake of vanity, Artemis my young friend, Alexander and Carlo, can you not see this? We give him the battle of which he dreams, on his ground and to his measure. Perhaps we could defeat him. Perhaps a great and famous victory might be brought off. With you, my dear Alexander, all things are possible. Oh no, I mean that. But greatness and fame are not the standards by which the future will judge us. It is disappointing. But disappointment, my dear young friend, is not a revolutionary emotion.'

'It's a man's emotion,' said Pavlides.

Brasidas hesitated. 'Comrades, I hope you will bear with me if I attempt once more to place things clearly in perspective. If a vote is taken, then it must be for retreat. The message from our friends leaves no alternative.'

Artemis, up there in the mountains, after all the events of the long retreat, recognized in himself the unsnuffed flame of what should have been beaten out of him. He walked up and down in the darkness of that unclosed coffin of a valley, drawing together the threads of old arguments, his head whirling with useless, gigantic images, dervishes of midday brilliance that sought to drag him round in a useless, exhausting dance of reminiscence, mouths stretched in yawns of silent and jeering laughter that teased him to join them. Once the Political Committee had come to its abrupt conclusion, it was as if no argument had ever taken place. The decision had now to be conveyed to the army. Artemis dreaded the first onslaught of his men's doubts, when they would use his own phrases against him. How would he manage to be fluent in self-contradiction? He had no difficulty at all. It was an exercise in pure unselfishness which stripped his own idea of himself. He imagined that he would have to dissemble, but there was more than reason in his arguments, there was passion. And yet only a few days later he was again questioning Brasidas, again offering to that pale and attentive man the objections whose emptiness he had already exposed among his own company. Was he a hypocrite? Brasidas smiled, the doctor who has been told the unique symptom which is, in fact, as common as oedema. How can a man criticize others for their foolishness in holding to an idea he later finds alive in his own mind? 'How can he not do so?' Brasidas asked. 'Isn't the situation in which we now find ourselves one in which such situations are bound to occur? Isn't the traitor within ourselves at his most obstinate in our generation? It is as traitors that most of us were raised. We try constantly to return to the comfort of old ideas, just as all our lives we long to sink back into the comfort of the breast, into the mindlessness of sensuality. Old Pavlides is not proving his manhood but his childishness with these girls with whom he imagines himself so virile. It is to toys that we run back when we believe again in the old gods with whom we know we ought to break. You see, Artemy, this retreat is really an advance. That is what I have been trying to tell you. It would be less frightening if it were really a retreat. But it is extremely frightening because we are marching away from the womb. When you tell your men of the futility of their objections, you impersonate the future. You are right not because you have access to some uncheckable source of knowledge but because you are thinking in clear and direct terms, in terms which can be checked by the analysis not only of your own intelligence but by that of others. Correct thinking is thinking which is capable of being corrected. Artemis, to tell you the truth I distrust the rhetoric of our movement least when it is most abstract, most susceptible of parody in the bourgeois press. Then I think we are working towards a vocabulary of honesty; it is the rhetoric which resembles theirs which disgusts me. The rhetoric of victories and bravery. To me this phase of revolutionary warfare is almost an irrelevance. It's too easy. My mind is constantly on the future. One must become familiar with it, you know, precisely – so that one may greet it in due course as a friend. I see victory as quite certain, which is why this so-called retreat fails to perturb me. But how are we to proceed after victory, if victory becomes the destination of our rhetoric?

'When you argue with all the purity of conviction for a view you later find distasteful and unconvincing you are like a runner who feels sick after his great effort. Has he then not run fast because he is now exhausted? When he throws his arms round his defeated adversary and hugs him, does he regret his effort? We fall back constantly to embrace again what we have just outpaced. It is a recognizable individual failing. And so our struggle must be like a relay. As you fall on your beaten opponent, the baton passes and you no longer matter. The race has gone on and you are still running at your fullest power, your cause at least, what you have given yourself for. It is for this reason that we shall run away from the capitalists – you know what I mean – because they have no unity, they have no swift logic that is caught by one generation after another. They begin again each time and they race each other as well as us. They seek the private glories and satisfactions which must not concern us. Ah, how convenient if it were as easy as that! Things are less perfect. Because each of us too carries inside him the traitor that wants to glorify himself, to whom his own feelings and his own longings are, being locked in himself, more profound and more important than the race. He longs for a winning-post and the comfort of a tired opponent to embrace. He longs for the end and there can be no end. And his opponent, that selfish capitalist, unspiked with the heroic shoes of the coming revolution, he too is a man like us and he too carries a traitor, the traitorous desire to belong to us, to be at one with others and so finally with himself. He believes that he craves the prizes and the glory, but he longs also to be with us. At times, as the Christians saw, there is something riper for glory in the sinner than in the saved. The vital thing, Artemis, is to remain in public, at the judgment of reason. Neither pride nor desire is a trustworthy argument.' Brasidas stopped and seemed to be waiting for Artemis to say something. Artemis was hypnotized by those pale eyes and that unhealthy, liverish complexion. Brasidas's lips drooped slightly open, forward, like a fish's. He had about his ungainly and uncharming person a disturbing and compelling radiance. He took Artemis's hand in his. 'Coldness is our warmth, Artemy, and warmth our coldness.'

Stelio died in the night. His wound broke open. When Artemis woke, it was time to move: past two. The men came out of the hut, catching white breath in mittened hands. They stood round the dead boy, nodding. Artemis could not shake off his anger. He had wrapped himself in it to sleep and it clung to him like a thin, damp blanket. The ironical smile of Brasidas seemed to hang above the cold blade of the mountain and Artemis wrestled as with an unwanted lover to whom something has been promised, the nostalgia for death against which Brasidas had warned him: the sentimentality of a soldier's grave.

'Why didn't you come?'

They had been plodding for over an hour in the growing heat before Katerina could force the head of her donkey alongside the mincing step of Artemis's mule.

'Artemy?'

'I couldn't,' he said.

'What happened?'

'Were you waiting?'

'Yes, I was waiting for you.'

'I can't explain now. Don't ask me now.'

'You didn't want me? Or did you just fall asleep and forget all about it? Which is really the same.'

'We'll talk about it later.' The gully was thronged with the bobbing animals. The three 'triumvirs', as Dmitri called them, had coasted in the yacht round to the beach the peasant had given Katerina's father and which he took to be the site of the ancient city. The young people preferred the illusion of an expedition. It was a chance to see the interior. Michael Shaw craned his head this way and that, though he seemed to Artemis to be more greedy for knowledge of his companions than for a traveller's impression of the landscape through which the muleteer was leading them. Dmitri was astride a small donkey, his feet dangling almost to the fat shingles which filled the walled pathway. Now and again he would point to the white barrel of a chapel on a ledge above a beekeeper's hives or to the perch of a monastery still wearing a shredded boa of cloud. Michael would agree as if some thesis had received fresh confirmation.

'You don't love me.'

'Wait, Katerina, I beg you.'

'I waited.'

'There were too many people in the house. I want to be alone with you. I want you not to be listening for footsteps.'

'In spite of everything, you do think of me, Artemy!'

'I think of you more than you think of yourself. I see you more clearly than you see yourself. I see more in the future than simple choices.'

'Are you threatening me or promising me? Sometimes I wish I knew.'

'You were disappointed for the wrong reason. Like a child who picks green olives, you knew all along the fruit wasn't going to be ripe. Perhaps that's what you hoped for – an excuse for feeling sick.'

'Now you're the one who's changing the subject.'

'I want you to cry out when I love you,' said Artemis. 'I want you to realize that you're alone. Quite alone. And with me. Without anyone. That's why I couldn't come.'

'What's that, Artemy?'

'Nothing to do with you, Dmitri Stratis,' shouted Katerina. 'Isn't he sickening?'

'So, do you understand now? With that in the house, how could I come to you?'

'I never think about anybody else when I'm with you.'

'That's hardly true,' said Artemis. 'From our conversation yesterday.'

'I only think about them when they're not around. When they are, I don't notice them. I realize how insignificant they are. You're afraid of them really, aren't you? You want to cut them out because they threaten you.'

'Perhaps they remind me of myself. And that's why.'

'I'm thirsty,' Eleni said. 'Isn't anyone else thirsty? I'm dry.'

'Poor Eleni is dry,' Artemis was glad to say. 'We'd better stop and water her.'

'We shan't get there till this afternoon at this rate,' Michael said. 'I'm really dying to see what there is.'

'Vanity,' Artemis said. 'A site for vanity. If we discover anything it'll go to the credit of the minister, and if we don't we shall be accused of digging in the wrong place! But then perhaps that's what you want.'

They had reached a green section of the valley irrigated by a network of clayey channels. Paniotis the muleteer, whose beige face had the expression of a man waiting for a surprise which would never come, expelled air noisily between fattened lips and the animals slowed and blinked. They bent from the path and found shade under the metallic leaves of an arbutus. The river bed was wider here; tufty bushes grew on islets given off by currents of silt. Four farmhouses stood in line behind traditional walls. One had a thick fig tree, a stone bench round it, in the centre of the yard. Paniotis kicked down a balloon of thorns which the owner had piled in the entrance and the animals were tutted through. 'I like playing the conqueror,' said Dmitri as he lurched through, drawing up his feet like an excited woman to avoid being bruised on the gateposts.

'Be careful you don't ride for a fall,' Katerina called to him. 'He's so conceited. He makes me sick.'

A picnic had been packed by the servants before they left the house. Paniotis opened the bags and laid them on the seat. Michael Shaw began to question Paniotis in his cautious, fluent argot.

Eleni said, 'I knew it. They haven't sent enough water. Artemy, do you think there's a well? There must be a well.'

Artemis shrugged and was ready to be obliging. He and Eleni might have been the same age. She was the only person he could look at happily this morning. Impotence scourged him to sullen and inexpressible disgust, while Dmitri grabbed the day for himself as he did anything that did not actively and violently resist him. Artemis took Eleni by the hand, with a furious glance to match the bland look which Dmitri threw him, and went with her behind the house. There was loud laughter from the others (Dmitri fortissimo) as they disappeared.

'He's very amusing, isn't he?' said Eleni.

'Dmitri Stratis?'

'He makes everyone laugh. I always like it when he comes. I don't know why.'

'Did you know he was coming here?'

'Oh look at all these grapes! Oh, it does seem a shame, no one living here. I should love to come down here and live all by my-self, wouldn't you?'

'You'd soon get tired of it.'

'No, I shouldn't. I hate the capital. I'm always being made to do and be things I don't want.'

They found a well brimming with silvery stones and glazed with dust. A bent bucket with a pursed rim had been slung in the opening of a disused oven.

'It's a shame,' Eleni said, 'these lovely houses and no one living in them! They just let them go. Don't you think it's a shame?'

'You sound very accusing.' Artemis rattled the bucket to shake rust and balled spiders out of it. 'But do you really think they should keep this place up just so that you shouldn't be disappointed when you come to visit it? Why should people give their lives to make a nice landscape for you and me?'

'Oh Artemy!' Eleni stared at him with marvelling eyes. 'I do believe you're angry with me.'

'No. But the others, they slight this place by ignoring what's happened to it, and you – and I, Eleni – we slight it by wanting everything to be just right when we choose to visit it so that we shan't feel ashamed about it. No, it's not a little thing. Why do you think that the authorities make everyone clean the villages before the king or the Marshal comes through? It's to preserve the good conscience of the notables.'

'Artemy, I think you're turning into a Communist!'

'Eleni, I give you one piece of advice: it's better to be serious than not. You did know the Stratis were coming, didn't you? Who told you?'

'I just happened to hear that perhaps they'd be coming.'

'When did you? In the capital, before we even set out?'

'Does it really matter?'

'And did Katerina know?'

'I may have told her. She may have known. I don't know. You are going to marry Katerina, aren't you?'

'This water's filthy, Eleni, I don't think you should drink it. It'll give you tummy-ache.'

'You're not angry with me any more, are you?'

'No, of course not.'

'I was afraid you weren't. Do you hate the notables then?'

'I feel powerless,' Artemis said. 'I feel absolutely pointless and yet – all this is very nice, sitting here with you, talking, riding, going on this expedition, I like it very much. I'd be dishonest if I didn't admit it. And yet I feel so ashamed, Eleni, so ashamed at being unable to act. We shall never get anything decent out of this well unless we clean it.'

'I don't mind. Let's just put our feet in it and let them drink!'

'Eleni, I believe you're a wicked little flirt. Your mother wouldn't like it if she knew you were alone with men.'

'Ah, but you're practically in the family, aren't you? Have they fixed the date yet?' She paddled her long, narrow, brown feet in the speckled lid of water on the top of the fallen well.

'You know very well they haven't. The old men have been too busy with their politics, which was the real reason for this trip in the first place.'

'Oh, now I understand! You want the whole thing to have been for your sake, yours and Katerina's. You're annoyed because you're not the centre of attraction.'

'Eleni, you're mischievous as well as wicked. I shall have to warn your mother and father – '

'You wouldn't.' She jerked her feet out of the water and planted their stamp on the dry panels of dressed stone next to where he was sitting. 'I'll kill you if you do. Artemy, do you really think there's no hope for you?'

'Did I say that?' He attempted the casual and reasonable manner of someone who merely plays with discontent and who would not like anyone else to take any risks in a game which he may abandon at any moment. 'No, I don't think things are quite as hopeless as that. I said I felt powerless. Perhaps power will come one day.'

'What is power?'

'Ah yes ... I don't know. The obvious answer is obvious. The other one is the absence of helplessness. That's what's meant by the people taking power. In a society in which the people had power they would not feel helpless. That doesn't mean they'd all be driving around in limousines.'

'My father's a terrible fool sometimes, isn't he?'

'Eleni, you're a dangerous girl. You're very dangerous indeed. I'm not sure that I trust you.' And he was not sure that he did. Her eyes were dazzling with the joy of their isolation, with the readiness with which temptations and teases sprang to her mind. She squirmed on the warm stones and plaited wet chains of footmarks on the dry dust, re-dipping her feet like a village baker his brush and setting out the equations with renewed zest. 'I think you're capable of making a great deal of trouble.' He smiled at her and was aware, with a slyness which made him dread the approach of any of the others, that he too was enjoying this ambiguous interlude. Eleni seemed actively to be promoting her own growth, stretching her toes, drawing up her shoulders, rotating her head all as if in accordance with some programme, some compulsion to obey a regime, rather as older women will stroke their necks or wriggle their hips when they find themselves sitting on a hard surface, and so seem to flatter their companions by their excitement when they are merely concerned to iron a wrinkle or unseat a bulge. Artemis was close enough to her in age to accept this separate energy of the girl's and yet to be challenged and excited by it. He saw the freedom of her growth as something which quickened the crass scene that had so depressed him that morning, the garrulous conglomeration of the family and its guests, deprived of their separate vivid qualities like the colours of a muddy painter jostling on an ill-furnished canvas. Separation, to which Eleni had so immediately alluded when she saw the cottage, recommended itself as the only hope. He felt splashed with the colours of the rest of them and wondered how long it would take for their tints to die away on him and for his own particular shade to emerge. Was that all sentiment and egotism? Were there perhaps no colours particular to an individual? Man had no plumage. 'You mustn't take me too seriously,' he said.

'Oh, but I want to. Who else can I? Not Daddy, not Mummy. Dmitri Stratis?'

'You like him, don't you?'

'He's funny.'

'Well, there you are. Trust those who make you laugh, they won't hurt you. Possibly. I tell you the trouble with me, Eleni, and that is, when I'm alone I don't seem to be angry any more. I become rather sad and thoughtful but I'm not angry. I don't welcome my solitude. So how can I trust the emotion that makes me want to tear myself away? Maybe it's the tearing I like and not the being away. That's what makes me wonder how straight I am. Do you see what's so frightening? The fear that one makes oneself a prisoner because one wants to shake the bars, but not to be free.'

He laughed. 'Do you realize we speak a language that few people can speak? A few million. We're locked in a way of thinking and talking that means we can't move very far away without being exiled. No wonder we talk so much, and no wonder we try to live so many lives – it's the only way we have of populating the place! And yet this island ... You know it's a scandal, the emigration, it's a scandal, you know that, don't you? The people who're going to America, they'll turn the whole of our country into an island like this, a place they'll revisit once or twice in a lifetime, with their pockets full of dollars, and they'll say, just like we have, "Isn't it a shame they let it go?" There's a great drama going on in the capital, perhaps that's what the triumvirs are talking about, because some of the Government have been investing our money in foreign bonds and taking the interest instead of making the money "work" here, do you know what I mean? Well, they actually manage to be grateful at the same time – publicly grateful – to the Americans for taking all these people and converting them into their own currency, because that's what it amounts to, without any interest!' He frowned at her, but she had left him and was plaiting wet chains across the uneven threshing-floor beyond the well.

'I did it,' she said, 'just!'

'Did what?'

'Got to the other side before you stopped talking. You do talk well. I love to hear you.'

'Eleni, you're a baby.'

'I'm sorry. Are you angry?'

'Don't sound so hopeful. Oh, probably you were right not to listen. There's something self-indulgent in talking too frankly, even too intelligently, to children, at trying to force speeches on them like food into babies.'

'One of the women at the house brings her baby with her to work and I see her feeding it sometimes and she spoons that glue into it, it's like a man plastering a hole in a wall. One after the other. It makes me sick.'

'Have you drunk the well dry?' It was Michael Shaw, unpeeling a smile like a dutiful son preparing a banana for his sick mother. 'Or what?'

'The water's delicious,' Artemis said. 'It has the flavour of Eleni's feet, only a *soupçon*, but ... '

'Sounds heavenly! Is it not drinking?'

'It's all right,' Eleni said.

'Your sister's been wondering what's happened to you.'

'To which of us?' Eleni wondered.

'Both, I dare say. No, I think she's discovered something your mother's packed she didn't know about and you like.'

'Hmm!' Eleni was not convinced but was so delighted to think that Katerina might be jealous that she threw an elaborately significant look at Artemis and skipped round to the far side of the house where Dmitri's voice greeted her as if she were the next event at a sports meeting.

'I was hoping to see you,' Shaw said, kneeling to investigate the well and sniffing the bucket at the same time. 'Has she really had her feet in this?'

'You've been drinking the wine, haven't you? They all put their feet in that. Or does the colour of the wine disinfect the feet? She has very beautiful feet, Eleni.'

'I'm afraid I don't go bull on feet,' Shaw said. 'Look here, I think I owe you an apology. The way I behaved last night. I've been thinking about it. I hope you weren't offended.'

'*I* wasn't offended.'

'Do you think one will come to any harm?' Shaw had a handful of water and was holding it to his face.

'It depends how badly you want it. I don't think I can advise you.' How ancient and how wily this Englishman made him feel! He disliked him as one can dislike a colour not for its own sake but because it cheapens the tone next to it. 'You want me to give you the wrong advice, don't you?'

'Not at all, you're quite right.' He threw down a blot on to Eleni's drying prints. 'You're quite right, it's not worth it. You know, England's a hell of a place to live. It breaks you into pieces,

134

like a stained-glass window, and solders you together again with lead. There are no great clear sheets in England. No unity.'

'Mosaic is our standard form of ecclesiastical decoration,' Artemis said. 'And you can't see through that at all.'

'One mustn't press analogies too hard. I was a fool last night and I hope you'll forgive me. You see we have to be bloody careful in England. You're always defending yourself against people who want to destroy you. Here it's quite different. I know the great God Pan is dead, but – ' His leer seemed incidental, a squint of the mouth. The sun was almost directly overhead. Pillars of heat bore up the roof of the sky. 'But you aren't perpetually in fear of your own selves here, like we are. I wish I was one of you.'

'Of whom exactly?'

'A native. I wish I could share your life. I know that sounds a contradiction, since I was telling you how you should come to England, but then I was thinking politically, you understand what I mean. From the personal point of view, this is the life for me. The gods may be dead, but they're at least buried here, they lend you their salts! They're in here and it makes a difference. I always wished Julian had brought it off, the Apostate. How much more generous the old religion was than the new! We live in a pluralistic society with a monotheistic metaphysic. How *can* it work? Christianity has stopped being ruthless and as soon as it does that it's pointless as well. It gives one nothing but a mouldy conscience. We must have either complete homogeneity or complete liberty, don't you agree, Artemis? And here, as far as I can gather, there's still something of the latter. Oh, the Marshal, I know! But that's for those who want to play that game, the basic thing is there's still something untamed here, something shameless, Artemis, and that's what we never manage to be, not in England. Not and proud at the same time. When we drink we don't get drunk, we get hangovers.'

'Your shame comes from the possession of more power than you can use. What you think is our shamelessness comes from our sense of having less than we need. It's the same with the virility you

135

think you admire in your working classes. You envy them their chains, not their strength. You envy them their mindlessness, not their wits. Your pity and your envy are the same things. What you can never do is to admit them as equals. It's easier to worship a man than to know him.'

'Well, well,' Shaw laughed, 'a follower of English literature! But don't you agree there's something primary about the sexual thing, that we shall never get ourselves right as a society until we stop damaging ourselves and each other as human beings? Isn't there a kind of blood-poisoning, a sort of national haemophilia which rots us from birth? Something that is passed on by women and shows its symptoms only in men. Isn't there a new basic awareness needed, a new unthought process before we ever come to institutions? Why build new hospitals and new mortuaries – and the one is usually damned close to the other, by the way – and never try to cure the disease?'

'These are things you never say at home. At home you talk about politics. And here, where politics are the dangerous things, you are outspoken about sex, on which a stranger's views, provided the examples aren't too gaudy, are always amusing.'

'You despise me now, don't you? I took rather a superior attitude to you, I dare say you thought, when we first met and now you think I'm turning out a hypocrite. Listen, I'll be honest with you. I'd like to be, if you'll let me. Thank you.' With a gesture of careless generosity, Artemis had offered him the untracked landscape up to the stiff knees of the hills. It was his to colonize. 'I've spent nearly the whole of my life so far passing exams, learning things to allow me to pass the next test. I was always telling myself that there would be time for me to discover myself when I'd discovered everything else. I'd be what was left, if you know what I mean. I don't know if I'm right, but from what people say about you you've had a similar sort of experience and yet – if you don't mind me saying so – you seem so much more certain of yourself as a person, so much less – and that's why I used the expression – ashamed. You speak out. I wish I could. You're quite right, it's easy to be outspoken in someone else's country, to see their lives in clear and distinct tones and admire them with the same sort of – I don't know – self-effacement with which one hates one's own people. All the time what one longs for is to be unknown oneself.'

'To be murdered,' Artemis said, seeing now the dejection of this precise and condescending figure who dabbled his hands in the shallow well, his feet in blue socks and sandals, his ankles glazed with mosquito bites.

'I don't think it goes quite as far as that.'

'One looks to the working class or to foreigners because they're enemies, not because one admires them. One longs to be raped and that means murdered, except that one will still be there to witness one's own … destruction.'

'I was foolish to be angry.' Shaw turned, dabbing water on to his hot forehead and cheeks, and grinned up at Artemis who was magisterial on the long bench above the threshing-floor. 'I mean, you were right. I'm not interested in women. I can't imagine ever wanting to live with one. It would be like – ' He threw a clod of earth into the well where it spread at once into a brown stain. 'It would be like drowning. I should have nothing left of myself.'

'Do you have a lover?' Artemis asked, more daring than Shaw imagined. The latter was ready to admire him now with all the gratitude given to those who allow us to speak freely of what disgusts us. Here was a man, Michael liked to think, who might revive or bring to life in him (since he had never found it a source of more than dread) a pride in his singular state.

'How easy you make it sound, Artemis! No one could ever say that to me in England without making it sound like a police inquiry. A lover. How beautiful you make that sound! No, I never think of love. I've never spoken to a man with whom I've had … relations – except to fix his price. They're rather famous for it, our guardsmen, you know.'

'You're waiting for something,' Artemis said. 'You give the impression that you can tell us what's going to happen, but I believe you want to be told yourself. You're asking questions all the time with your statements. You have the kind of confidence which betrays itself too late. People will give you power because you seem certain and they'll turn on you as soon as you reveal your humanity.'

'That's exactly our situation in England, exactly. We use force to declare our weakness, but no one recognizes it as you do. No one stops us and we're forced to live in our masks for ever. We grow fat because we want to be admired for being slim. Well, this is a funny show! I was supposed to persuade you to join us and here I am begging to join you.'

'That s not possible, I'm afraid.'

'I know. I know. Sad! Do *you* have a lover, Artemis?'

'I'm engaged to Katerina.'

'Homosexuality as an admitted part of life, it hardly seems possible, that's why I couldn't resist ... asking. It's not the thing we miss, it's the possibility of enjoying it, of accepting oneself. It doesn't matter how accepted it is within a certain group. It's enough to ruin one's life, a limitation not an experience. It's not so here. And so it doesn't mark you. It isn't part of your record. Well, there we are. It seems very petty to sit here and complain, with all the things that're happening. I can't see war not coming, can you? And somehow the things seem to go together. Fighting comes as such a relief. The state of peace is like a state of siege. Guns on the horizon! Do you find me ugly? Unattractive?'

Artemis watched him.

'You do. I'm sorry. I've embarrassed you.'

'On the contrary. You've embarrassed yourself. Just as you offended yourself last night on the terrace. You drive yourself to the ditch and then you daren't cross it. A lover mustn't ask if he's lovely. You're trying to fall in love with yourself, my friend, and can't quite bring yourself to it. Oh no, you're right. It's the beginning of self-realization. My having a lover, why should that interest you? You're asking me where you can find one. First you must find yourself.'

'It's true,' Shaw said. 'Not very helpful, but true. Well, we should go or – '

'I hate the past,' Artemis said. 'What vanity, don't you see that, to believe ourselves superior simply because we dig it out? I despise all these secrets and these grubbing vanities. Sometimes I think we should concrete over the whole thing. Do you really think we're going to find gods? We're going to find slaves and flesh their bones with our fantasies. It's sickening. Worse – morbid.'

'Well, I must say!' It was Katerina herself. 'So this is your idea of our all going somewhere together! You're being about as rude as you can be.'

'It's my fault,' Shaw began. 'We were just coming and then we started to talk.'

'If you don't want to come, why don't you go back to the house?'

'We're coming,' Artemis said.

'If you must sulk.'

'Katerina, I'm not sulking. I'm ready to go.'

'You're being hateful just because Dmitri Stratis is here. I think that's very childish and unnecessary of you. I didn't ask him to come. Although, as it is, I'm really very glad he has!'

'I hope it costs you your neck,' Artemis hissed at her as he went past. She was stunned for a minute and then she ran after him wildly, knowing that she could not catch him before he rejoined the others. Shaw stared at the empty fields and the threshing-floor with its chaff of two seasons before. It was true, he shuddered, that he longed for his own extinction, but he came of a culture too rich to acquiesce in its own confounding and so he had to confound the world. His ambition came from his inability to stand himself. He shivered in the heat and turned on his lumpy blue feet, hating the feel of his blistered toes, his teeth exposed like the pits of split fruit, to rejoin the expedition.

The yacht was already standing in the bay when they bobbed over the last ridge and saw the beach below them. 'The young finish last as usual!' cried the Minister when they reached the parents, who had spread themselves under a sunshade at the west end of the bay.

'But more frequently,' whispered Dmitri to Artemis.

'Now then, where are our scholars? Where are our intellectuals? Mr Shaw, we look to you and to Artemis, of course, to tell us where to start.'

'Not at all,' said Shaw. 'We may have some theoretical ideas, but you have the instincts. Where have they found traces in the past?'

Artemis walked away. The Minister, in his yachting gear, would have done better to pull out a pistol and shoot the Englishman than to allow himself to be spoken to like a child, but he smiled and took Shaw by the arm as if a compliment had been paid him. And at that, Artemis had to walk away, like a lieutenant too compromised to prevent his general from being duped by a well-paid spy.

'Why are you being so horrible? Everyone's talking about you! You're behaving worse than I've ever known you. Why? Because of last night, is that it?'

'Last night?'

'Are you ashamed, because you didn't come, is that what's the matter?'

'No, I'm not in the least ashamed. I explained to you. I advise you not to try to take advantage of my not coming.'

'You advise me? What right have you got to give me advice? You're humiliating me in front of everyone. Everyone.'

'I've been for a walk. What is it I've failed to do?'

'Been for a walk! You've deliberately turned your back on everyone. You're making me look a fool and that's one thing I won't forgive. Oh, you're so pompous sometimes, so self-satisfied. What's the matter with you?'

'Cease to speak to me in that manner, Katerina.'

'I mean nothing to you, that's the truth of it, nothing, that's why you treat me like this. Are you afraid of me or what?'

'If you meant nothing to me, I should have nothing to say to you except the things it pleased you to hear. The truth is, Katerina, you want to be nothing. You accuse me of being towards you the very opposite of what I am. I tried to think of you as a woman capable of marriage to a man, but you're not. You're an animal capable only of finding a master.'

'You're the most brutal, horrible person I've ever met. As for animals, you're the animal. You're the pig. Your language. Talking to me like you did. It's practically criminal. It's practically an assault. If you think I'm going to waste myself on you – You think you're a lot more ... more unusual than you really are. You're not the only man in the world.'

'You're free,' Artemis said. 'You're free to do as you please. Marry Dmitri. I shan't prevent you.'

'*Dmitri*, what do you think I am? Prevent me! What do you think I am? Someone who can switch about like a train when it comes to a junction, just throw the lever and off I go on a new track. I wouldn't marry Dmitri ... What made you mention him? Just so that you can excuse yourself by accusing me.'

'I don't accuse you. What makes you so angry? That you're having your fun spoiled?' Artemis waved cheerily to Katerina's mother, who was promenading on painful feet along the beach under her violet parasol.

'How can you be so cynical? So cynical and so sarcastic. Stop waving, stop it, do you hear me?' She grabbed his arm down. From the beach they seemed to be flirting. Katerina's mother shook her finger. 'You loved me yesterday. Or you said you did. Or was that just one more of your cynical little games, well?'

'No, Katerina, but then – '

'How can you be so cruel?'

'How can one be anything else?'

'Ah, you admit it. Then you admit it.'

'Does a man play a game within a game? Is a man in a game playing a game, or is he serious within the game? I meant what I said, I wanted you, I loved you, yes, but you say, "Was it a game?" You might as well ask, "Is it all a game: birth, death, and marriage in between?" '

She laughed harshly, though a moment earlier she had seemed set on tears. 'I thought I loved you too.' The harshness of her tone, a willed meanness which seemed to roughen her skin like a bitter wind, caused him to blink behind his spectacles. 'You're such a plain little man, Artemy, why should anyone want you if it weren't – because of all this? You're right: you deserve to be in the cold. I'm not the one who's the animal, the bought animal, the animal going to market – isn't that what you said? – it's you. You're the one in the pen, not me. You see if you can get out by yourself.'

She turned and went, an uncertain exit down the rough rocks, jolting the tense lobes of her cheeks.

Before the retreat the men were told to destroy all photographs and personal papers. There was a kind of brutality in the order, a deliberate punishing rudeness. It was a promise and a reminder that the seriousness of the committee's revolutionary purpose was untarnished (Brasidas). They were determined to believe, and to have the men believe, even more than before in the significance of every step they took. Everything personal must be burned. A new army was to be made of new men. And this burning was the brand that would bind them in a brotherhood without memories. Artemis himself choked on the order. It proved to him how much even such an army as this longed in its separate hearts for a return to what had been known and enjoyed before. Now that particular nostalgia was challenged and exposed. The men were raw with the surgery of it. The formal justification of the order offered some consoling element of good will for the past. When the army was operating in its guerrilla phase it had been possible to foresee the shape of an operation. There were quiet periods between specific missions. Only when the men sallied into the populated areas and found that the peasants had not seen any of the Royalist forces for days, only when it became clear that they had won the war in the countryside, had the army come together in formations of more than a hundred or so men and realized, in a dance of dust which filled the plains leading towards the capital, their strength and their triumph. There was a kind of resentment then in the guerrillas that they were so many and had thought themselves so few. Previously they had fought the war with a certain scrupulousness towards the peasants and even the small shopkeepers on whom they depended for communications and for knowledge of the enemies' arrangements. They had thought it necessary to recruit supporters. But when they saw the columns of their own force, their own veterans, it was as if they had decided to close the lists. On that victory march to the capital, always a little farther away than they remembered, a threatening vindictiveness arose among them. They no longer marched like liberators, but like conquerors. The shopkeepers in the small towns were treated as suspects. Stores were paid for, with a kind of victorious defeatism, in notes redeemable only after the complete subjugation of the country. The 'ordinary people' were no longer trusted; they were no longer needed. The first cases of deliberate, celebratory rape were reported. The Political Committee was saved from its confusion at this new turn of events by the news of the British intervention. It returned them to familiar fields. Artemis was mortified by their ill-concealed relief. They preferred the abortion of their advertised hopes to the unpredictability of a new life. They styled the retreat an advance because it avoided the crisis of their own authority. The committee elected not to see that the men stood on the brink of victory and how angry they were at its conversion to defeat. The Political Committee was proud of its refusal to be dismayed, but its pride disturbed Artemis more than open despair. He saw the nostalgia in it. They had turned on their own men. It was then that the troops began to call the officers once more by their ranks.

Artemis asked Brasidas whether he could be relieved of his command. The doctor mocked his sentimental egotism. Nothing could be more selfish than to think that there was time now for mortification. The revolution was not interested in saving souls. Artemis had never expected anything else. He looked for denial. Brasidas was impatient at giving him so obvious a present. Because of the severity of their orders, the officers were made uncomfortably conscious of themselves as a class. They would not have Artemis abandon them, just as Dmitri would always resent it, in the old days, when one of the gang preferred to go home to study or to see a girl he loved rather than come to Helen's. Yes, the Political Committee was taking a guilty step and it resented those who tried to abscond. Privacy was treason. Of course no one had expressed it in this way, except Artemis, his own sour policeman. The habit of articulacy was the beginning of his nightmare. His conscious education of himself to the movement was responsible, as soon as contradictions began to appear in it, for his failure to ignore its flaws. Before the war he had lived in that bright envelope of impressions which was the container of educated sensibilities. The flame which burned so brilliantly, as he could not help thinking sometimes, about his head, that passionate sense of his own situation which could make him so vivid and so sardonic a companion, was like the waste gas which flags an oil refinery; the burning consumed what could not be assimilated. The jaggedness of the flame denoted his inability to define himself or his life, a flag not of defiance but of dissidence. He believed during the years in the mountains that he had learned to be cold. But how could he tell the men that there were good reasons for burning out their roots? How could he uproot the olives of their past and tell them that the field would be fruitful again and with a better crop in fifty years, when they would be as gnarled as the growth he was forced to deride?

The official argument was that when the guerrillas had fought from bases in the hills, hills which the regular forces never dared to approach, everything of a personal nature could be left in the caves and effectively guarded. Bodies were recovered whenever possible, both to deny the enemy the comfort of hanging them in the villages, as had become their custom, and to avoid the photographs which might have led to the denunciation of relatives. The lack of corpses became so irritating to the Government that in some instances they re-dressed their own dead in the shabby clothes of the 'rebels' and displayed them in the villages. Now the soldiers were told that the danger of reprisals was enormously increased. An army in retreat could neither recover its dead nor be sure of when it might be attacked. The Government had aircraft now – the very planes used in the last stages of the patriotic war when the Germans were being driven from the country. Air attack could mean bodies left behind, names and origins established. The risk was too great. There might have been force in this view had there been consistency in the other orders for the retreat. If it was now intended to spare 'the innocent', why were the men encouraged to a policy of provocation? There was no possibility, so far as Brasidas was able to tell them, of their friends forcing the Government and its western Allies to pull back. Whatever tactical victories might be won on the way, whatever successes scored against the Royalists, there would be no going back on the strategy of retreat. Certainly the day would eventually come when they would again surround and this time capture the citadel, but it was a day without a date. The men were not defeated, but the Political Committee was. It had been forced to accept the logic of salvation instead of that of power. The seed had been scooped from the furrow and thrust again into the sack. The men were told to cut the trees and destroy industry in their path. The rape which had been punished (where unavoidably detected) on their advance was to be tolerated as they withdrew. They were to brand the country as they themselves had been branded. And where did this leave the committee? It left them an elite, men who had digested the future in their heads like gourmets hungrier for the menu than for the food.

Artemis paced the hills above the capital during those days of hiatus, days when the crest of the wave hung and hung in the still air before falling back. He walked as young men do to avoid spilling themselves over the memory of a breast. If he sat down he threw up his mutinous desire in a plume of words. He did not fear to be judged – or even to be killed – but he could not permit himself to weaken his companions by talk. He saw art returning to his way of life in its most debased style, artfulness. He saw the end of his season of purity. In his mind he had already begun to caress himself. As the army planned to turn back, so did he. During the hours following the order to destroy all personal papers he had a strong urge to write.

One of his walks was through a village in which there had been some fighting, a village close to the gulf where salt was winnowed from the sea. The low walls of the salt basins were of a red volcanic stone. Behind them mounds of salt bled white, drained of the glutinous sea which had carried them. The top layers glinted in the sun; the lower were as grey as used sheets. The army was encamped two miles farther up the hills, a natural amphitheatre round the capital. Occasionally a truck with supplies hammered by, the skirts of its engine-casing drawn up, the driver in a uniform taken from a Government depot captured on the way. The sight of these soldiers, humming at the death of an enemy which would soon be allowed to rise up and drive them back, filled Artemis with remorse. It would have been better to be crushed than to pull back unbruised. Artemis vaulted the roasted wall into the saltyard and walked along the path between the mounds. The scalding brilliance of the salt, stinging his nostrils with its tang, the remoteness of its lifeless cultivation from other kinds of farming, gave him pause from the confusion of events. Was he betraying the revolution by musing on the futility of the broken buildings in the town itself or on the particular misfortunes of the café-keeper whose new chairs had gone to roast a pair of sheep bullied from the fat butcher down the road? (He had doubtless earlier let his upstairs to the girls who followed the Government troops.) The salt which was both vital to men and the symbol of sterility, the spice of their being and the weapon of the conqueror who wished to abort the fields of his enemies, lay around him in frosted heaps. As far as possible from the road, a shadow within a shadow, an old man was raking a wet section in the lee of a barn. Artemis saw him as an enemy. He understood and embraced his fear and his indifference, but he was an enemy. Artemis could willingly have gone to bully him. He had an urge to go to the man and snatch away his rake and unbalance him. Oh, he felt no pity for those who were not going to suffer! How could one sterilize salt and kill its savour? He felt his powerlessness like a reproach. He hated nature. He hated this unfeeling and necessary salt. It even lacked towers that might be toppled: banal, essential tapioca! The old man might have been a deserter. Artemis was the policeman who, years after the escape of a criminal, sees a face constitute itself on his trained retina in a pattern of dots which immediately calls to mind the warped photograph of a wanted man. Yes, Artemis wanted to bring this old man with his wooden rake to justice, to demand of him how long he thought he would continue to get away with it. He would have liked to refuse him the rudimentary kindnesses that even the condemned enjoy, the right to see his family for the last time or to take a blanket. He would make him come as he was. He would be stripped to the thin bean of a creature he had become and his limp cock would be pointed out and cursed for its undeserved pleasures of the years between.

The old man grew aware of Artemis staring at him and lifted his chin, questioning but docile. Artemis came over to him, his anger dwindling, to his dismay, like desire when a prostitute pointedly chinks her key and whispers her price. 'Is this place yours?' 'No, sir.' 'You have no need to fear me.' 'No, sir.' 'Nor to call me sir. You work the place yourself?' 'Yes, sir.' 'And why are you working now? Has the owner fled?' 'He lives in the capital, sir.' 'Rich man?' A shrug: 'Perhaps.' 'And he leaves you to do all this alone?' 'I had my son.' 'And where is he?' 'I don't know. He was in the army. They took him away.' 'Who did?' Again the man shrugged. 'Was it the Government? Was he arrested?' 'I can't say.' The old man resumed his raking. The slosh of the chaff through the sluices revived Artemis's anger. 'You must know whether he was arrested. I might be able to help you.' He paraded a tender cruelty. 'They put him into a lorry and drove him away.' To the old man there was no distinction between arrest and service. 'Why do you work when there is no need to work?' 'What else am I to do, sir?' 'Do you know what's going to happen?' 'No, sir.' 'You haven't heard what is going to happen? You haven't heard that the army is to withdraw?' 'Yes, sir.' 'You have?' The old man gestured towards the capital. 'A month ago.' Artemis's anger was like dysentery. It convulsed him with contempt for himself and for the world, especially for this old man with his wooden rake. He wanted to take the bent rake with its trident joint and smash it to white splinters across the old fool's back. The man stared at him, lidded with the inert suspicion of a lizard. Artemis wanted to clap his hands and have him scamper, like the warder who receives again his old prisoner all these years later and proves to him with some prompt threat that he has not forgotten how to make him jump. He dragged the leather strap of his Sten down into his shoulder. 'Is this where you live?' 'Yes, I live here.' 'Alone?' 'With my wife.' Artemis was angry with the woman, who already in his mind looked so like this creased old lizard, this dry stalk of life which had so long ago dropped its tail. 'What do you keep in here? In the barn?' 'The cart.' 'And you live upstairs?' 'Yes, sir.' 'May I see?' Courtesy came like a cure. The old man took Artemis up a wooden staircase, straight as the side of the triangle it made with the cobwebbed wall, into the loft. There was a single large room to the roof and a smaller bedroom, visible through an open door, icons over the bulging bed. 'Do you have any paper?' 'Master?' 'Paper. Writing-paper.' 'There's no paper here.' It was as if Artemis were searching for arms. 'An old notebook? Something from – ?' He indicated the saltyard. There were ledgers on a table by the head of the stairs. Artemis took one and flipped through; pages were empty. 'May I write here for a little while?' He was ill at ease in this dusty room with its buckled floor, dusty with polish, and the round table with the wooden chairs tight against it as if the thinnest of ghosts were sitting there, nose to nose over the first communion bouquet yellowing in a silver-throated vase. Above a battlemented sideboard were photographs of dead ancestors, great moustaches, swathed busts, accusing stares, the men hairy with warlike promise to cover their domesticated presence, the women swollen in mild and draped triumph. Artemis turned his back on them and sat at a small uneven table overlooking the shaded quadrant where the old man had been working. 'A pen and some ink by any chance?' The old man nodded like a café proprietor from whom a policeman has reassuringly demanded a commonplace. He came back and stood with the required things by Artemis's side. 'Thank you. I shan't disturb anything. Please leave me now.' 'You're going to live here, sir?' 'No, only for an hour or so.' The old man took a last look at the place. 'I want a little peace, that's all,' Artemis said, disturbed by that impertinent dread he saw in the slow pan of the old man's eyes around the walls. 'Only an hour or so.' The old man nodded without believing him and went down the stairs. Artemis sat with the quill in his hand and the account book open on the ridged table. The old man had found his rake again and was continuing his work. Artemis was unable to write. He took from his pocket a letter and unfolded it and placed it over the ruled columns of the ledger.

My dear Artemis,

I expect you never thought you would hear from me again, but, as you once used to say, it's a small country. The war has divided us, that goes without saying, and I have no means of knowing whether this letter will ever reach you. I am torn between wanting to tell you everything, including that I still love (?) you and that I still hate you, and wanting to say nothing lest I betray myself here in vain and write things that will make some messenger laugh when he grows tired of carrying them. You may think that I have forgotten all about you. No, I don't suppose you think that. You may think that I am ashamed to be sitting here in (comparative) comfort while you are fighting, but then I think you chose to do what you are doing and I can't feel sorry for you. I don't even feel sorry for you when I think of you being dead, which you may easily be.

Asteris was very ill this last winter with pneumonia and

if I had not been able to get some drugs for him which are normally (!) unobtainable here he would probably have died. I think you would have let him die rather than take the drugs which no one else could get, but then I'm not like you. I can't live a moral life. Can any mother? Don't think too harshly of me because I wanted to save my child's life. You see, you still do affect me. I try to defend myself and I get angry; just like the old days. Oh, what a scowler you were! Are you scowling now, I wonder? I bet you are. Oh, I sound like a girl again and I'm not. You want me to be grown up, or you used to, and that always makes me feel like a baby again. Are you wondering what purpose I have in writing this? I wonder myself. Don't give me too much credit for plans. I never really had any plans, except to marry you and even that was just a sort of outing, at least you thought so, didn't you?

Artemis, we've been apart from each other so long and yet I still think of you so often. When I look up at the hills where your camp is, I can't imagine anyone there but you. I don't see an army, I don't see all those dreadful rebels everyone is so afraid of in the city. I see one man all by himself, a sort of gentle but rather cold monster eating all by himself in front of a fire that has gone out. Oh, will you see all kinds of meaning in that? I promise you it's an idea of my own and isn't half as complacent as it sounds. I pity you even though everyone else is so terribly afraid. They think that you want to kill us all in our beds. Well, as long as it's there, I shan't complain too much. Oh God, how can one write so fluently and still put down things that don't come from any part of oneself that one is aware of? I'm terrified of being hurt, as you know. Perhaps that's why I wanted to hurt you. You know how women will have spiders squashed as if they were dangerous.

Artemis, is it true that your army is falling apart with sickness and quarrels? We hear so many rumours and I don't know what to believe. I don't know what life to lead. You think I should have come to the partisans, I suppose, and nursed the sick. Well, I don't believe I would have been any use. It wasn't until this last illness of Asteris's that I've been able to stand looking after sickness and he is, after all, my own flesh and blood. I didn't enjoy it. Am I a monster? Why do I care what you think? After everything that's happened, you'd imagine that you were the last person whose judgment I'd care about. And yet you are so much in my thoughts. I'll tell you why I've written to you. I hear that the rebels are going to have to withdraw, that you haven't any choice and that you will have to pull back or be destroyed. You can imagine that I have good reason to believe that this is true.

Now Artemy, believe me, don't frown, believe me that I'm saying this just because it's true, quite as if I was a married woman writing to an old flame and proposing a meeting in some hotel in a provincial town: I want to see you again. Artemy, I can't explain it, but I can't get you out of my mind. I want to see you again before you leave your camp and go wherever you go. I want to see you before you're killed. I can't pretend that I care if you are, I care only that you might be killed before I see you. Will you come into the city and see me? You'd be surprised if you knew how easily people moved about in the streets these days. We are all still afraid that the rebels will break into the city before they're finally driven back, but things are much easier than they were, food and fuel I mean, and some of the cafés are again open till quite late. I know it sounds mad, but you could come to the house and see me and no one would ever know. I'm quite alone almost every evening, as you can imagine, and if you were to telephone me – you know some of the lines are still open, don't you? – I could tell you when to come or arrange to be alone. If you like I'll meet you somewhere in the city. I suppose you might suspect a trap, seeing that you're quite an important man. I can't say anything that will convince you that there isn't a trap, but there isn't. I want to see you, though I dare say that when it comes to it we shall find it hard to say anything to each other. Perhaps all of the past seems irrelevant to you. Perhaps you won't even remember who I am. You'll look at the bottom of the page – as if you didn't know already – and you'll wonder who this woman is who dares to write to you as if nothing had changed. You'll despise me for not having changed. I've done so little, you'll think, when you've done so much. You'll think me weak for the life I've led. You won't trust me. I know there are good reasons why you shouldn't. I suppose you've killed people. We're told of all the terrible things that have happened in the war. I suppose you've seen them, taken part in them. I suppose you're used to them.

Can you ever come back from the war, Artemis? Can there ever be anything for you but war? Is that a foolish question – how you used to hate it whenever I *talked*! Oh yes you did! – or is it true, is peace gone for ever? We have not suffered in the capital as the helpless have in the country, I know that, and there has been no triumph for us, no pleasure, so in that sense we are still at peace, in spite of the Germans, in spite of the war since, we still have something here I don't believe is entirely worthless, a sort of longing for things to be easier which may be selfish but also means that we fear and don't want the violence which has made us so helpless. We are people of peace in the city, Artemy, you must believe that, whereas for you war has become the only life. Can you honestly say that you long for the fighting and the killing to end? Can you honestly say that you have not enjoyed it? When I think like this about you, I feel that I hate you, that you have brought trouble on us all for no good reason, for a kind of conceit, just as you could spoil a dinner party without 'doing' anything by simply wearing a certain kind of frown or making one of your famous 'humorous' remarks. You talked about how inadequate our kind of love was, how you despised the arranged passions of the notables, but how adequate is your love? It's not the opportunities for love that you found inadequate, but the opportunities for hate. Are you still full of hate or has the 'revolution' satisfied you as far as that goes? Do you still want to kill me, I wonder? I suppose you have more reason than ever. Then what am I inviting to see me? And then again – oh, I can see your smile – why? Will you come into the city? I swear to you that I am not trying to trap you. You wouldn't believe – or would you? perhaps you walk the streets every night! – how normal things are here, no patrols in the centre, only at the outskirts, and the usual police. I'm lying, aren't I? Of course there are dangers in your coming and I'm lying about how safe it is. I want you to be the old Artemis, with that shy swagger of yours, coming across Independence Square with one of your unwieldy parcels, some nonsense you'd found in the market, or a cake with that flaky chocolate top they used to do before the war. Do you hate everything about those days? I can't imagine you different and yet I feel I must believe you to be. How awful for you if you've gone through all you've been through and must face all that's to come without being any different! I can imagine how painful that would be for you. Do you really still believe that people can change? Perhaps I want you to be right and to be different and to be sure that you are right, as usual! I'm writing like a girl again, all exclamation marks! I'm nervous at thinking of you. I want to see you, Artemis. There are things I can't write. Please come. K

Michael Shaw had taken command of the dig with a show of reluctance. He told them several times that archaeology was only a hobby with him; his actual line was textual emendation. He was quite sure that any trained archaeologist would be appalled at their lack of organization. It was as the tribute which enthusiasm paid to scholarship that he insisted that they attempt to follow, however crudely, the lines of a proper investigation, take one layer at a time and ticket the sides of the main trench and of the subsidiary excavations with tongues of wood to mark where each discovery was made. The dig began like a pick-up game which a bunch of friends initiate lightheartedly and which at each step becomes more serious and more energetic. The rules are forgotten to start with, but become gradually more obtrusive. Light-hearted fouls, once a joke, are sharply penalized; the score matters. The violent attack one of the young sailors launched on the chosen trench-line was brusquely interrupted and a demonstration of correct method given him. The independent scratching of Demosthenes and his sister was denounced as piracy. The Minister seemed to have the idea that the whole excavation could take place in a few hours, rather like rummaging through a loft for amusing relics of past days. He was told that it might be weeks or even months before a real find. The party would probably have to dig for several days before they could hope for even a fragment of pottery, unless they were exceptionally lucky or given more precise information. Two families lived locally, but neither the goatherd who crossed the beach with his chiming flock nor an old woman tottering on legs roped with swollen veins, a turban of twigs on her head, had clues to offer. The goatherd shrugged and grinned and was soon leaping up the slope at the far end of the beach, whistling his dogs, while the old woman seemed to parade across the wide beach on one held breath and had no voice for them at all. 'I'll bet she knows exactly where they get the stuff,' Michael said to Artemis, who had not joined in the dig. Shaw had come over to him with something of the same ingratiating suspicion he had shown towards the peasant woman. He resented the pull Artemis had on him. Perhaps he even wanted to silence him, just as ambitious people tend to befriend people more to abort the threat they feel from them than for the sake of any positive comradeship. Their address-books are full of names in every city which they must call, not out of common interests but to allay common fears. Sophistication assumes that there is a limited circle whose opinions are decisive. It craves a nobility without titles and its cowardice can be inferred from the urgency with which any ambitious person sharpens his perception of where the power lies in any group to which he is introduced.

Michael feared in Artemis a scale against which he could be measured. 'You don't think much of this idea, do you?' he said, as they watched the dusty scene below them. 'No.' 'Why not?' 'I truly can't say.' Artemis was suspended like a balloonist above the others. He did not have any feeling of superiority, but there he was, swinging in the vapid air, powerless and elevated. 'You think people shouldn't mess about with the past?' 'Tomb-robbing? No, I don't feel that at all. I don't much care about the dead.' 'Perhaps you just don't like being one among many.' 'But then what?' 'I don't follow you.' 'When one's said that, what has one said? One can't go through life accepting that as one's character, as something immutable, a fact like ten toes.' 'Try and get out of it,' Shaw said, 'easier said than done.'

'You're telling me something about yourself,' said Artemis irritably.

'I'm still trying to apologize – '

'There's no need. Please forget it. And go on with your dig. They need you down there.'

'I realize that I annoy you. Don't imagine it amuses me. If I didn't feel some need of you, I'd hardly humiliate myself by persisting like this.'

'You disgust me,' Artemis said.

'I realize that too. I'm sorry. Why?'

'Because you want to destroy me, because you would have nothing to do with me if it weren't for your fear and your vanity. I speak like a friend.'

'Well, I must say! Only I know what you mean. It may be true. If you were simply yourself, whatever that might mean, I suppose I shouldn't be very interested in you.'

'You're so powerful,' Artemis said, 'and yet you can't bear to be doubted, I can't think of another way of putting it. You want to disarm me. That's what disgusts me. Not your desires. Your fears.'

'I've admitted them.'

'As a means of recruiting me. As a means of weakening me.

You want to strengthen yourself by weakening others. I'm not only thinking of you but of what you represent.'

'I hope you'll treat all that as confidential. What we talked about.'

'I was thinking of the Powers, their need to believe that their wealth has some purpose. They express themselves in action over others, just as these old men do when they buy their women, not even to do anything with them or to them, simply to prove that their fortunes are not pointless. You're wrong to dig up the past, because it's younger than you are. It's you who are old. It's you who ought to be dug up.'

'Do you think one wants to be old?'

'And soon you'll be drawn into a counterfeit war. A counterfeit more noisy and more impressive than the real thing, but a counterfeit all the same. The war you'll fight will seem to you to be a fight against a great tyranny. You'll fight this war like a sacred drama in which you have been favourably cast, without realizing that the battle will reveal not the truth of your religion but its futility, even if what you think of as the right side wins. Whoever wins, the metaphysic will die. The image, the counterfeit will outlive the genuine idea it once served. But for how long? For how long? For as long as the money lasts and not a moment longer. You try to dig up the past here to prove that it's still alive, but it's as dead as you are. It will not comfort you. You'll not find your immortality here.'

'Why are you so keen to drive me to despair?' Shaw asked. 'Why don't you ask yourself that question, if you think you're so blameless?'

'I never claimed to be blameless. I'm quite willing to drive you to despair. In fact I'm quite keen to do so, now I think about it.'

'I believe you're really quite a dangerous little man, Mister Theodoros,' Shaw said. 'I believe you could be quite a stiletto merchant!'

'You should keep away from us. You shouldn't visit your sickness on us. I say this out of friendship. Cure yourself. Believe in your sickness.'

'And you,' said Shaw, 'are you perhaps now talking to yourself through me, well?'

There was a shout. Someone was waving from the beach. The diggers had struck something. 'I shall have to go. Coming?' 'No.' Michael went stumping down the slope, muttering angrily, though by the time he had reached the others his diplomatic smile had been produced like a corkscrew at a picnic. Artemis scanned the even bay. 'Not enough water to drown in.'

After a supper grilled on the beach by the crew from the yacht they asked Kosta, the young guitarist, to play for them. Stars badged the cloudless sky. Artemis was unwilling to be of the party and sat apart, watched by Katerina, at whose side Dmitri, sprawled like a head and shoulders of driftwood, gnawed lamb chops. Kosta wooed them, in private communion with his music, like a girl with her untouched beauty, tempting the world to admire it and yet content to be alone. The time for dancing seemed to have passed. The dinghy had rowed the older people to the yacht, with the exception of the widow, whom Dmitri managed to command at a distance even while he poured his attentions on Katerina. Artemis wondered whether there might be a boat from the harbour which he could reach by walking all night under the senseless stars. How exhilarating to walk oneself out across the crusts of the mountains, to pass the little farmhouses and the stone circle where they had sat and to find some foreign fishermen crouched over their coughing engine in the bay, to take ship with them and to find oneself at the end of the world, or simply in the capital the following evening, and to walk among the streets of the whores, to take the cheapest of them, to fuck, to contract some repulsive sickness and to be obliged to sever oneself, for treatment, from everything one had ever known! He would read great writers speaking of love while his own sickness leaked itself away under the unindulgent prescriptions of an expensive and illusionless doctor. He did not want to be punished, he kept thinking, he wished to be forced to act. And in the course of this romantic dream, almost as if he had merely reshuffled his legs in order to prevent them falling asleep, he was on his feet and moving to the music, which now seemed to be matching itself to him, the pretty girl at last fastening her cautious attention on a single person. Yes, he danced by himself and drew smiles from the others, though there was, in his own mind, in his grace, in the very tender exactitude with which he picked his steps, a measure of hostility. If he had not hated them, he could not have shown them such tact. He danced in the circle of the young in bitter derision. The motions of his body, obedient to the traditions of the tavern, assured them, as they began to sway to the same music, encouraging him, of their control over him, as an audience will be glad to clap to reassure itself that a performer belongs to them. A man who longs for applause is a man who longs to be captive. He is framed by those who admire him. Artemis then seemed to be captive to these young people who encircled him. They rejoiced in his new humour, they were as quick to admire as they were eager to ensnare him and the humour, the humour which played gravely about his lips, approving of the beat of the sailor, that humour appealed to them because it appealed to them, but behind it, behind it, behind it as he moved to the guitar and hummed its cadence, behind it was a restlessness which could not be sustained by applause, and the movement of his feet, the small shuffles of his feet, the jostling of the sand which was all there was to be seen, what massive kicks and leaps they signified to him! He danced his loneliness for them and they took it for companionship, they swayed to his loneliness as if they understood and he allowed them to believe they understood, which was the humour of it for him, especially the humour of seeing Shaw unclasp his smile like a boy releasing a knife gently in the darkness, recognizing the shape of the game. Oh, there was violent rejection of them in his wooing, violent derision in it and a warning, the warning that a talented young man gives when he falls silent in front of his critics and seems to accept their world when all the while he is scheming something pitiless, something not even worth discussing with them, so that when they ask him, with that adult unease about silence, what he has in mind, he answers, 'I'm working on something, but it's very difficult,' and they suppose that he is planning to please them, that they have set him high standards, and all the time, immaculate to their eyes, learning his craft, he dreams of a new world and sharpens a knife for their throats. Artemis danced as lightly as the sea which makes curtains of sand in gentle scollops along the shore. His feet fretted the sand in the circle and invented nothing. He moved as regularly as the scansion of an old metre, each line and each caesura in its place. He danced with his hands held up, like a puppeteer, and drew the eyes of the others after him. Michael Shaw met his gaze but could not sustain the duet which Artemis threatened to play with him. He beckoned to Shaw like one of those painted boys to be found in certain bars and he grinned at Shaw's fear. He drew him towards him and then with a shake of the head offered him that final insult, a whore's distaste. The girls clapped and laughed, Eleni and Eudoxia, and he trod their skirts, the hems of their spread skirts, into the sand with his bare feet. No one knew this Artemis and they thought he had concealed something from them. They might have cancelled their applause, since he seemed to elude them now, had they not been committed to it. They stirred and waited for his move. He took Dmitri by the hands and drew him to his feet. Dmitri, clumsy Dmitri, whose whole life would be perhaps a parody of elegance to hide his disquiet at this kind of direct and physical challenge, he came up like a deck-chair in the hands of a child, falling this way and that in stilted commotion, until Artemis, eyes glinting with the memory of that evening on the way to Helen's, controlled him and, offering him the end of a strangled napkin, drew him into silent conversation. They turned and rode on the swollen sand, turned inside and under each other and Artemis schooled Dmitri in elegance with a mastery the other might find more unforgivable than violence. He could match violence with power, but there was no matching this slim and humorous pedantry. Kosta began to hum and moan like a wire in the wind, the first promise of the storm, while Dmitri was exhausted by the soft precision exacted from him. He gasped as if he were dodging walls, as if a court was tight about the dancing pair, tighter than the loose circle of sand, and some penalty was due if one touched the cold face of it. Artemis defined Dmitri for Katerina that night. He defined the man's limits in front of the girl. He defined his own superiority and he abdicated his share of the world of Stratis and his thick millions. He danced Dmitri as a man and a partner might run down and bewilder a bull with alternate goads. Katerina was his partner, but a partner promised a separation. Artemis allowed Dmitri every chance to command the steps. He bowed and yielded, as a lover will sometimes hesitate in a caress to allow its rejection or will lie back and give his partner the chance to discover the frontier of her own temerity, to assault herself with his body, but Dmitri could only guffaw at such times and make a gross imitation of some grand gesture which he knew to be beyond him. And then Artemis, so gently, so politely that Dmitri never suspected his callousness, would tilt his head at Katerina and ask her if this was the lover she wanted, if this was the man whom she wanted in her bed, not that she knew, of course, of such things, if this was the man she wanted, who imitated the actions of the lover he would never be and satisfied women by a gross impersonation of a man they would never know. Dmitri brought the virility of the brothel to the dance. He invited scorn for the desire he could not repress, that he did not want to repress but which he could not enjoy without pissing on the passion which might have accompanied it. He skipped like a goat given the floor, he hopped and grimaced; he avoided criticism by crushing it with patronage. Katerina, who had been clapping and laughing, suddenly burst into tears, like a woman in a play who is at last reached by a messenger who has been making his way through the crowd in full view, loaded with doleful intent, but whom she has never supposed to be coming to her. Michael Shaw had been asking her, with a frown, the name of the dance, like a naturalist who doubts the beauty of a specimen until he can tabulate it correctly. And she was answering him, checking on Artemis's posture, when she suddenly burst into tears.

She threw herself back from the circle, without moving from her place, like someone suddenly retching over the side of a ship. Eleni leaned to comfort her, but Katerina flung her away. Artemis signalled to the faltering Kosta to continue the music and its stride resumed, its ambiguity more taunting than ever. Was it covering Katerina's embarrassment or jeering at it? Was Artemis her lover or her enemy? Now Dmitri drew Michael Shaw to his feet, glad to find someone incapable even of parody. And then Artemis was cruel; he broke the chain and left the two to confront the music alone. They stammered and Kosta laughed and raised the rhythm to double and quadruple time till there was something savage in his fingers, something indifferent and immodest. He flung down the last phrases like an insult and clapped his hand over the mouth of his guitar. And then Artemis was like a ghost. As they looked he was dancing again, but beyond them now, down by the sea, he was dancing with the sea, he was measuring himself against the sea, stepping on its skirt as it sipped the land, courting the sea as he had courted Katerina, so that finally she ran to him and the others smiled. She struck him across the face, jealous, this way and that, and he never ceased to dance. He danced to the measure of the blows and listened to them gravely, nodding, never losing his footing, never false to that unfaithful rhythm he found in the sea. She hated him with all the force of her body and then she laughed. She laughed, exhausted (the arms of her dress were tight, sewn for a girl who was not supposed to raise her hands), and just as the others were ready for Artemis to falter or to strike her back, as they smiled for some nasty conclusion, she too began to stitch the hem of the sea with her feet and Artemis took her hand without looking back at her and led the way towards the glistening white chapel on the far side of the bay. Kosta raised his guitar and then put it down. He sat there on the beach and reached for a wine jar, while Artemis led the girl down the hem of the sea.

Dmitri came and sat by the widow. 'Love!' he said. She turned her molten eyes up at him. Tears hung there like daggers. He took her hands and fondled them. 'Your hands are cold. I'll warm them for you.' The daggers fell blunt. Dmitri sipped them from her hand and she pulled back, vibrant with terror. He had smiled at her like a devil, deliberately, and she gasped in the dark air. 'There's nothing to be afraid of,' Dmitri said. 'You are a terrible man,' she said, meaning every word but in a tone of such throaty emphasis that Dmitri could only smile. 'A terrible man.' 'No, my dear, I am not a terrible man. You are in no danger from me. I desire you greatly. I desire you more than anything except the future, but I shall always desire the future more than the present and for that reason you have nothing to fear from me. I shall preserve myself and so, without meaning to do so, I shall also preserve others. I shall never spend myself. I am not like – ' he gestured up the beach where Artemis and Katerina pursued their grave dance. 'You can give a woman everything except yourself,' the widow said. 'That is precisely my condition,' said Dmitri, 'and, what is more, it is the condition of all sane men. He knows nothing of that girl. He imagines that he is educating her, that he is drawing her out. No. It all leads nowhere. Dancing is a waste of time. I'm not ashamed of being no good at it. In the end I shall have everything and he'll have nothing. I shall have the future to please myself with, he'll have only the past. He's a captive, you'll see.' 'He dances like a flame,' said the Algerian woman. 'A flame is tethered to its wick,' said Dmitri. 'The image of a flame is an image of futility. Let it burn all it likes, in the end it can be controlled.' 'I would sooner be burned', she said, 'than be in the cold with you.' 'That's nonsense,' said Dmitri, 'there's always central heating where I live. No one need be cold. The alternative is not to burn; it is to be warm. I don't believe in extremes. Things are controllable. Come for a walk.'

He stood and offered her his hand. She took it, with a deep sigh which made him smile, and pulled against him. He drew her to him. 'Don't you see how wise you would be to accept my protection? I know my limitations. I don't demand devotion. I don't ask for undying love. It doesn't even please me to think of it. I love you, if that pleases you, because of your indifference to me, at least in the first place. You prefer my mother. I know that. You can think of me what you like and I shall think of you as I like. There need be no confessions and no confusions. I believe in being grown up. Artemis is a child. He believes in totalities. I think he is doomed to a life of disappointment. I'm quite sure that I am not. Let me kiss you. Let me kiss you. I don't mean it to signify anything. I mean you to taste me. I have no particular taste. Let me kiss you. It need not promise anything.' 'No,' she said, 'I don't want you to. People will see. Please!' 'You fear to betray your husband, my love, but you've betrayed him already by surviving him.' 'I never wanted to,' she said. 'The weapon is in your hand,' Dmitri said. 'You can't kill me when you refuse to kill yourself. I refuse to be your death. I intend to be your life. You've chosen already. There's no one to blame except yourself. Allow me to kiss you, Françoise. Accept me. Accept me like a poison if you can't accept me any other way. I must kiss your mouth. Give it to me.' He knew that she would yield; that was the attraction for both of them. He fulfilled his own prediction and so magnified himself; she found a new source of the inevitable and so healed herself to her wound. He did not take her there on the sand, of course, with all the children around them, but there was a promise which contained the tenderness of menace (as when a peasant strokes the pounding necklace a small goat makes, hung round his shoulders, when he carries its death closed in his fist), the promise of a definite event. Dmitri had that feeling for anyone who came within his compound, who incurred his protection.

'It's the last time,' Katerina said, 'the last time I make a fool of myself for you.'

'You've done nothing for me. You've done something. Why are you so mad to enslave yourself?'

As the moon mounted the headland and unrolled a torrent of silver down the shadow-logged slope they stood where rock hardened under the sand and the music went out of them, as lost as when a foreign station, caught on a radio, fades and leaves a roaring void. They faced each other and were themselves again, without the music. 'I hate you.' She rehearsed a memory. 'I hate you.'

'Ah,' he said, 'what a relief! What a comfort! Now you can treasure your hatred as more fortunate women treasure their love. It would hurt you to love; it delights you to hate. That's why you're incapable of anything great, anything valuable for a man, because you look for an excuse to be cold. You don't dare to love. It isn't I who have failed you. You've failed as girls like you will always fail because you want to believe that your parents are right, that men are cheap and that only what they bring is valuable. Your beauty, the heat your body can't help having, that warms you over for a time, but underneath there's a coldness you'll always be loyal to, an appetite for seeing men fail. I used to think girls were fine and natural, better than men. I thought I saw that in you but I only saw my own fear of the cold.'

'Now I do hate you. Much more hotly than you think. Much more. I'll make sure you never ... never ... '

'Eat in your house? Join the navy? Speak to your sister? What?'

'I shall find out things about you. I shall discover what you're really like.'

'Fallacy! You'll do no such thing because there's no such thing to do. I shall discover what I'm really like. I shall decide who I am, I mean, and no one else. Spare yourself the expense of a private detective. Save him for your husband. He'll need watching if I'm any judge, your husband.'

'You pig, aren't you, a destructive pig? That's you at your worst, at your cruellest, throwing someone away and leaving a splinter in them at the same time. And what's going to be your magnificent destiny? To run off to England with your little pansy friend, is that where you're going to discover your great future? Good luck, Artemis. Good luck!'

'I've no intention at all of going to England. And he is not my friend.'

'Ah, shall we have the pleasure of your company then? And what will you do here? Assassinate the Marshal? Marry a warmer girl? Devote yourself to the academic life? Get rich and prove us all wrong after all? Come on, what is your destiny, Artemis Theodoros, when all the hating comes to an end?'

'I don't know. I'm still young,' Artemis muttered, and she laughed a coarse, divorcée's laugh, a laugh that mocked her own naivety, coarse in its claim of experience she had not yet had.

'You're frightened,' she jeered, 'you're not a man, you're not a proper man.'

'Or I would have taken you the other day? I loved you then. I was younger.'

'Yes, all those days younger. How old you've grown suddenly! You'll never come to anything in the capital. What can you do? Perhaps you'll work on one of Dmitri's papers and become a *terrific* journalist. You could be a critic.'

'The papers aren't Dmitri's yet, Katerina.'

'Oh, you could talk your way into anything. No one talks better than you do. Perhaps you should be a lawyer. You can only take what you don't love, then? Is that what you're saying?'

'I can't be what you want. You can't be what I want. Why go beyond that? Only because it's embarrassing. Because this is a political occasion and we must agree on a joint communiqué. Nothing could more clearly demonstrate the futility of pretending about feelings.'

'Nothing could more clearly demonstrate your priggishness, your conceit, *your* coldness! How can I be what you want when you don't know what you want? You want your mother, that's what you want, the warm woman. She's warm enough. She's a double blanket, that's the warmth you want. You think you want a woman, you want a *burrow*.'

He smiled sheepishly. 'I don't know what I want, perhaps you're right.'

'I'm going to bed. I'm tired of going round and round in circles with you. Don't worry. I'll tell them that we can't get married. I'll tell them you're going to "stay with your mother".'

She ran to where Kosta, bent like a servant now, was sitting in the dinghy waiting for the females who were to sleep in the yacht. The sea was ruffled. It slapped, like a master patiently training a dog, against the curve of the boat. Artemis hated the pain he felt, the tears that pricked him, he hated them like pins and needles, silly pain that humbled a man without involving anything cardinal. He hated the tears and let them fall for contempt of himself. How beautifully she ran and how little she cared for him! How fast she ran and in what a skilful imitation of carelessness! How deliberate she was! He could conquer her again. Meaning that she could conquer him? Neither would happen; they could not play the same scene for ever. Their subtlety would never extend to it. Yet was that not exactly what a relationship was, two people who could never progress beyond the first scene, like philosophers who work so exactly at their early chapters that they can never finish a book? The repetitiousness of such a life forged a chain, each fetter identical, a chain which seemed to have extension but which slipped about one's ankles and shortened one's stride. Artemis tried the door of the snowy little chapel at the top of the ridge (its whiteness almost oily in the moonlight) but it would not yield. He sat down on the low wall around the flagged courtyard at the front and let the moon droop against his face, a drunken man with a flower.

By the next morning the weather had changed. Clouds swarmed over the rim of the bay in narrow skeins which thickened and filled the air as if blown by a bellows. The beach was stamped with breakers, thrown forward across the apron of sand like carpets violently shaken by a housemaid and breaking into frothy fringe before being dragged back for the next onslaught. The yacht stood out on its anchors. The tent in which the young men had slept stretched and snapped like a tethered animal. Dead fish were flung from the sea. Others lay drowning in the air. The new trench in the floor of the bay was sweaty and discoloured. The old people shivered and would have been glad to go home, but the yacht could not dare the open water. It was too far on the mules. 'And now what do you propose, young man?' the Minister asked

Michael. 'At least it's good weather for hard work,' said Shaw. 'I've never known a day like this at this time of year. Can you explain it?' 'Nothing to do with me. It's your country. And your element, Minister!' 'Have you, my dear Sophocles, known a day like this?' 'Never. Democrats or Oligarchs on this island, Mr Shaw?' 'I beg your pardon?' 'In classical times. Mr Stratis and I were discussing it last night while you young people were listening to the music. Who controlled the island?' 'I imagine that it was under both at different times. These things varied according to external pressures and alliances. Though on the whole sea-going areas tended to favour democratic regimes. The land-based powers were inclined to oligarchy. But of course, with the smaller islands, they were at the mercy of bigger events. They had to take the medicine they were given, I'm afraid.' 'Perhaps we shall be able to tell when we find more evidence.' 'I doubt if the bones will offer much indication of their political allegiance,' Michael said, 'unless you were thinking of finding inscriptions.' 'I was thinking of finding inscriptions,' said the Minister.

Artemis left the beach and walked on his own. The women had spent the night on the yacht and would not dare the passage to the shore. Katerina's captivity aroused Artemis's desire for her. He dreamed of rescuing her, but he could not think of any place to which he might take her. The beach was drab, the world too inaccessible. Dmitri was on the *Pegasus* too. He had taken the widow on board. Had he plumbed her mouth? Had he enjoyed those lips? Artemis took a trowel which had been left by the trench. He had not gone very deep when there was a clink. He began to scoop and struck stone – sections of squared marble. In a hollow, which sand confused like blood at an operation, were more pieces of marble. One was a triangle with a neck: a head. The beach ended a few yards behind at a stone wall barbed with bundled thorn. Artemis dusted the head and held it up. There were no indentations on the face, but two little protuberances, almost at the top corners, definitely stood for ears. Artemis took it to his lips; the marble, in the listless light of this particular morning, was the colour of dough, but the face was warm against his as he took it to his mouth. He smiled at this expressionless female stone and pressed it like a seal against his cheek.

When he turned to the yacht (as if to announce a new mistress?) he saw that the storm had brought a new vessel into the bay. It was a small steamer, of the type used as a ferry to the nearer islands, but beige and without any commercial trim. The port-holes wept rust. There was something strange about it: the narrow third class of the ordinary island steamers was caged to prevent spillage into the better accommodation; in this one the third class included the whole of the rear and midships section. And it looked crowded. The rest of the ship was empty. As if he had known all along, so that there was no shock but a kind of chilly decomposition, as if he had suddenly digested every scrap of food in his stomach, Artemis realized that it was a prison ship. Beyond the shelter the storm convulsed the sea. The prison ship unshackled its anchor to the bottom of the bay. The sailors on the yacht grew busy. Artemis picked out men with rifles and batons on the prison ship: the *Aias*.

The Minister was disturbed. He paced the beach and inspected the newcomer through his German field-glasses. He was anxious about its position: would it run down the *Pegasus*? Did the captain appreciate where he was and who was watching him? The Minister consulted Kosta about rowing out. It might be possible, but they would probably be drenched. It was frustrating; it was even un-nerving, in view of the conversation which had taken place between the three triumvirs. Perhaps pure chance had brought this dun-coloured packet into the bay, but the hand of the Marshal could be seen in it. How terrible to exchange exalted impotence for bleak degradation! The Minister wondered how things were in the capital. He ought to go out to the ship, establish his own position, discover, of course, whether there was anything the captain needed, possibly even take a look at the prisoners and see for himself that they were being properly taken care of, in every sense. There were women not a hundred metres away. If the prisoners were to break loose, what was to stop them gaining control of the island?

He insisted that Kosta prepare the dinghy. The prisoners watched him as he sat on his wooden seat in the sea and was pushed out towards the *Aias*. Two officers came on to the bridge and one ducked inside for a megaphone. The Minister sat as he had in his car, staring seriously in the wrong direction, while Kosta caught the blast of the group leaning over the canvas-sided wing of the ship. Finally, when the Minister still refused to turn, a rifleman was summoned. Kosta told the Minister. The Minister would not hear. The rifleman fired: a much louder crack than expected. The Minister jumped and shouted with all his might, 'Cease fire at once. I am the Minister of Marine.' He then signalled to Kosta to continue to row and absolutely would not have any further argument. The men on the bridge had not heard a word of the Minister's announcement. They ordered the rifleman to fire again. The bullet whined over the Minister's head and pricked the sea. He indicated to Kosta to return to the shore, maintaining as well as he could the appearance of a man who has never deviated in the slightest from his original purpose. He paced up and down for a few seconds and then instructed Kosta to return to the *Pegasus* and send a signal to the *Aias*. He waited on shore while this was done. When the *Aias* had been given to understand who he was, he re-embarked in the dinghy and was rowed, with waves coming slap over him now, out to the prison ship.

Artemis folded the letter and stared at the unmarked page of the ledger. The strict columns inhibited his pen. The nib the old man had given him was scabbed with dry ink. It was impossible to write. He went into the bedroom where the icons were hanging. The larger was a blue-grounded St Sebastian, a halo of hammered gilt about his acquiescent head with its leer of pain, his body fulfilled with agreeable arrows until he had something in common with those elaborate prints prostitutes show undecided clients in which a single woman takes on a dozen or more men and accommodates them in every crease her body can afford, a cold buffet of positional ingenuity from which he may take his pick. A burnt sugar glaze covered the curved figure of the saint with his brochure of wounds. It was as certainly of recent manufacture as the one next to it was ancient. Artemis took the smaller icon from its hook and wet his finger to brush the face alive. A brown old man (Luke?) with a grey beard and drooping moustache held his gospel in his hand, his eyes averted to the right. The pages of the book were stylized in three black lines, pale between, which had the appearance of a clip of ammunition. With this in his hand the saint confronted the world, his red lips pursed in confidence of his rightness; his robes, red lines stencilled over the gold, filled the bed of the picture; above it his halo too was outlined in red. He characterized a purposefulness which went beyond martyrdom and showed no zeal for anything but mastery. Luke it must have been, the doctor, with that practised and unselfish authority. Wasn't there something of Brasidas in him too, had it not been for Brasidas's sulphurous complexion? Artemis did not want to see anyone but himself in the mirror of that particular icon and he glared at the cheap St Sebastian, like a sailor who has been landed, as he always feared he would be, with the ugliest tart at the dance. Had he to be a constituent of that lolling sensualist of death?

He turned and saw the old man, a sickle shaped like a bow in his hand, standing in the doorway. Artemis had unslung his Sten in the other room and laid it on the floor by the desk. He despised the old man for not taking it. 'Are you going to attack me?' he asked. 'Old man?' 'What are you doing here?' the old man muttered. 'Do you think I want to steal your icons?' 'Why are you in here?' 'I can go where I please,' Artemis said, 'I'm an officer of the revolutionary army. Let's have no nonsense. I want none of your things.' He offered the old man the icon. As he came to take it, Artemis took his arm in an easy lock, and snapped it behind his back. The sickle fell to the ground with a base clank. Artemis threw the old man back towards the window. He stumbled and began to babble that he had been working, that was all, and meant no harm. 'How does it happen that you have two icons, one so beautiful and one so – ? Will you tell me that, old man?' The old man said, 'That one we have had in the family for many years, very very many years, but that one,' – and his voice found a reverent register – 'that one was given to me by my son last year.' He passed his hand over St Sebastian like a mother retracing her baby in a returned soldier's face. Artemis's rage was switched from the old man to the icon he so treasured. All these ugly things, this reverence for ugly things ought to be destroyed too, in the retreat. He saw why the country had to be destroyed and yet he could not, out of shame, begin here. The frustration of his violence was like the frustration he had suffered before the war when he sat alone in his bedroom and fondled himself for Katerina, when his desire for her had humiliated and dominated him. The logic of the retreat recruited him, as a boy can be won for mathematics by 'seeing' a theorem. 'Age is a class too,' he noted. 'Sir?' 'Nothing.'

As Artemis was walking back to the army he decided not to go into the city. And no sooner had he decided than he was determined to go. He swore to himself that it was not desire which made him want to go but a will personally to have conquered the city, to have entered it, even though his triumph be unscored. It was a private conceit, he recognized, but a harmless one, to go and take the city himself. It excited him as the prospect of adultery excites a loyal husband, a man to whom 'that kind of thing' is foreign. It is not the woman he desires, but the deception. Every step he takes, every instant of infidelity proclaims his allegiance to what he betrays. After all these years of loyalty Artemis was sullen that the order to destroy the past coincided with the decision to retreat. He had not burned Katerina's letter. Why should he? It compromised only those who were compromised already. It would be a concession to the past to burn it. It would protect only what need not be protected. Katerina was not family. She was not his past. Was she his future? Not that either. Then his present? Or nothing? If nothing, how could he be going into the city to see her? There was a larger motive, that he could truly claim, the desire to take the place himself. But that was vanity, a nostalgia for private satisfaction almost as disreputable as those memories which the command hoped to expunge from the army. He would go. He would go to test the truth of the view that there was no chance of taking the city. The ease with which he could dispute the verdict of the committee would renew his loyalty to it.

It was a night shingled with stars. The hugeness of the heavens magnified what lay beneath them. The country was a world of immense horizons. It matched the planets in its diversity, the stars in its provinces. How could anything outside exert an influence on it? Artemis took a German pistol and a belt of bullets. If he met a patrol he would bluff and then shoot. There was no other way. Without alternatives, he was ready to concede the odds. They would be surprised; he would not. He wore a fisherman's sweater and carried a canvas bag he aimed to fill with melons. He would be welcome as a smuggler; anything so long as he did not appear an honest man. His fear, despite his calm preparations, was greater than before a battle. He feared the gravity of the city. He feared its senseless pull. He set off down a track through the twisted steel foliage of a derelict factory. The war might never have been. He came to a section of market gardens he had seen through the glasses, where striped melons lay unexploded amid the dead fuses of their foliage, filled his sack and went on. He heard voices and saw a group of peasants sitting in the walled yard of a cottage, a bottle beside the lamp. He kept in the shadows on the far side of the dusty track, the smell of resin in his nostrils, smiling to himself at how often the conversation of strangers, especially peasants, seemed to be conducted in a numerical language. They exchanged numbers – 'two hundred and fifty.' '*Seven hundred.*' 'Six hundred.' 'Six hundred?' 'Six hundred and fifty; four hundred.' 'Four hundred, never.' 'Four hundred, sometimes five hundred.' 'Five hundred?' 'Five hundred' – as wits exchanged epigrams.

Artemis entered the city like a needle through sacking. He never knew the moment when he passed through the line. He came to a bar and then to a street where refugees were encamped under cardboard. He walked on towards the centre, doubting the necessity of his melons and anxious now to be approached for them. He recalled his early days at the university when he had longed for those fierce and significant debates about ultimate principles of life and style which he had been promised, when he had carried his intellect cocked like a pistol only for Dmitri Stratis to ask him whether he was coming down to Helen's with some of the others. He could not dump his burden; to give it to refugees seemed a treachery both to his role and to the army from whom, however misguidedly, they were in flight.

'Katerina?'

'It can't be.'

'It's you, then. Yes, it's me.'

'Where are you?'

'In New York.'

'Stop it, Artemy. Where?'

'I don't know. Are you alone?'

'Alone. Yes.'

'I received your letter.'

'I can't believe it. It's you. Are you all right?'

'I'm very well. Can you come and see me?'

'Where are you?'

'You sound very eager. It's nice of you. I don't know where I am. Will you walk along in front of Fontano's, is Fontano's still there?'

'Fontano's is still there.'

'Walk along in front of Fontano's and go on towards the Sophia Palace. I'll pick you up somewhere along University Street, but come alone. I shall be watching and if I see anyone with you, or anything like that, a car following, and believe me, I'm pretty good at it, I shall disappear. I don't think you'll be able to surround the area without me knowing, so don't bother to do that, will you?'

'Oh Artemy, if you knew how much I wanted to see you! Of course I shan't come other than alone. What do you think I am?'

'I don't think anything about you, Katerina. Past Fontano's, then towards the Sophia Palace, all right?'

'I'm with you.'

He left the bar like a citizen. He confirmed the gun under his sweater, but he was a confident citizen again, moving casually, without his sack of melons, sold to the proprietor, as though he had no doubt of his rights in the place. Fontano's was a famous political café. It stood on University Street, at the opposite end to the Sophia Palace. Artemis had enjoyed the note of practised strategy which he had inserted in his conversation with Katerina, but he had no idea of where he would intercept her; perhaps there was calculation even in that; it was impossible for him to betray himself. He hurried to Fontano's, less eager to see her than to see it. The café had the air of an exclusive club. Its windows on to the street were several feet above the pavement and its leather chairs à l'Anglaise gave the customers a lordly view. The central window had been cracked diagonally by some bombardment, which cut across the picture of the yellow and brown interior like an awkward scissor-wound, incorrectly angled to the surface. Several old faces were visible inside, including a group with three seated figures, one of them reading a document in a hand that trembled faintly, while the others exchanged looks over his solemnity. Behind stood three younger men (to whom Artemis could extend none of the indulgence he felt at once for the old genre figures at the centre), sharp in the suits of the conventionally ambitious. A waiter, carrying a silver tray suspended from a ring by three stirrups, was about to unload coffee and narrow glasses of water. Artemis stared at this picture as one might at a group of old Dutch burghers in an exhibition. Their fortunes one knows to be founded on cold speculation, not only in the usual commodities, but in slaves (as the nigger heads displayed on the lintels of their houses testify), and in the sale of strategic materials to the very enemies against whom their patriotic bands have been formed. The modesty of their dress, the dark clothes, the clean linen appear to suggest the un-ranked solidarity of men convinced of the righteousness of their cause and the justice of their society. To the casual observer their uniformity looks like equality, but a closer look will see that the smallest distinctions of ruffle and embroidery, against all that dark material, are full of significance. The announced readiness of these men to accept the inspection of history, their commissioning of this public record, confirms their lack of doubt and their will to resist all efforts to dispossess them.

Artemis gazed at this insolent exhibition with a terrible tolerance. He recognized the man reading the paper and he could almost entitle the scene 'Decision'. The reading of letters was a commonplace in paintings of the kind he was remembering. The crisis of the bourgeoisie was to be found not in action or in emotion but in the moment when a man decided his interests. At no time did a group become so tense as when the most powerful member weighed the evidence offered him. His decision was their fortune. Yet there was not quite that richness in the present scene, not quite that self-assurance. The ships in the gulf, the power in the embassies, the degree to which the country was slashed open by the war, bound to the operating-table over which competing surgeons threatened each other at the same time as bleeding the patient, this lack of independence in the true sense had its effect on the composition. The central figure was Colonel Aristotle Democritos, Minister of the Interior. The paper he was reading might have contained news of the greatest consequence: a confession from the head of one of the party cells in the city, affording the kind of opportunity for a sensational round-up which a policeman suspects of being false because it is so spectacular and because he must mount a huge operation to avoid being accused of missing it. On the other hand, that serious narrowing of the eyes, that contemptuous consideration of the attitudes of his subordinates might be greeting the lofty appeal in an ambassador's letter for the reprieve of a party of partisans or of some luckless smugglers, capriciously sentenced to the extreme penalty in order to warn those who lived on their wits that a period of licence was coming to an end, a public announcement in the form of an execution. And that smile on the Minister's lips, what did it say but that he would hang his criminals because there was no other reply to the condescension in the ambassador's letter? It was not so much that he wanted to curtail the influence of his allies as to make its exercise more expensive.

Artemis recognized the Minister of the Interior as that same Colonel Democritos who had commanded the police as a lieutenant, when the strikers threatened to assault the offices of Theodoros and Sons after the attempt to overthrow the Marshal, and who had been captain, two years later, of the squad detailed to prevent disorders outside the Sophia Palace at the signature of the armistice and the departure of the young king. A year after that Major Democritos assisted at the transportation of the city's Hebrews, but his decision to take his entire force over to the resistance at a critical moment during the last month of the German occupation was decisive in the expulsion of the enemy from the city and in saving it from destruction. The partisans had been very ready to excuse his earlier behaviour; they were being heavily pressed by the Germans. The most political of the committee took a certain pleasure in such an unprincipled *rapprochement*. It gave them confidence that power was almost theirs. True chastity is possible only for the impotent. That a 'criminal' and a policeman should come over to them convinced them that the whole apparatus of government would soon be theirs. They misjudged their man. Democritos fought well against the Germans, but the committee had no time to infiltrate or even to divide his forces. The Government, including those who had collaborated most willingly with the Germans and against whom the colonel declared his 'undying hostility', were slow to disavow him. Democritos not only saved his own reputation at the last minute; he did something to salvage the ministers'. They claimed that they had instructed him to defect. The better he fought to disengage himself from their taint, the more credit he brought them. In the first hectic days of the liberation they were able to pose as cunning heroes who had timed 'their' insurrection at the right moment to topple the enemy without bringing him down on the heads of the 'innocent'.

The Allies were as eager to accept the excuses of the old guard as the committee had been to recruit the colonel. Experience proved that it was easier to blackmail a government with a shady past than to deal with a prickly association of self-righteous heroes. Nothing more alarmed the British than men who were indifferent to wealth and had no sins to hide. The old gang had, of course, to be purged of the worst collaborators and several were sent to the islands, but the younger element was promoted and the more able loaded with allied uniforms and decorations and advertised as having been in constant and courageous touch with Allied intelligence. The predictability of the excuses and the astonishing obviousness of the new developments were evidence less of the scientific than of the farcical trend in historical events. There were only so many doors and so many characters; no man could enter more than once unless he went out before he came back, but it did not follow that he re-entered by the door through which he had left and it was wise to bear in mind that windows were also exits, and could be entrances. Democritos had avoided treason by a brave show of patriotism. Having saved both the partisans and the Government, he was able for a short time to hold stock in both camps. His decision to revert to the central authorities was taken as proof of his insincerity in coming over to the partisans in the first instance, but it was probably, from his personal point of view, a wise one. As many of the Political Committee wanted to arrange a fatal accident for him as supported his incorporation in the inner councils of the movement. The revolution, which proclaimed a new morality, feared that he was not venal enough to be loyal; the Government, when he returned to the capital, feared that he was not loyal enough to be venal. How could they be sure that the price they had paid had completely bought him? Democritos might, in a more confident period, have found himself at best honourably discharged, but the British general, Gabriel Pick, needed someone to whom he could delegate authority. The civilians in a devastated economy were untrustworthy, since it was unclear what could be taken away from them. The colonel had rank, which in troubled times is better than cash. He was appointed governor of the city. He was lectured about his duties, but it was clear who was grateful and who was granting a favour.

Democritos now sported the dignified moustaches of a man who would prefer to be doing more philanthropic work. Artemis could have taken out his pistol, he supposed, and, despite the two guards by the marbled door of the café, shot the colonel as he came out. Democritos had in fact been sentenced to death by the revolution when it became clear that he could not possibly come into the game again except as an example, but Artemis doubted whether his execution would be welcomed. 'The revolution is not interested in justice as an abstraction.' He walked on past Fontano's, not without reluctance. He felt a kind of guiltless fascination with it, the interest a dealer gives to articles not really of his period and which he would normally swear to find distasteful but which, in the part of the country where they actually originate and displayed in a traditional setting, rather intrigue him. Artemis turned away and almost bumped into a policeman at whom he shot an irritated glance, much as Dmitri would have in the old days while eating a peach he had whipped off the stall of some flustered greengrocer an instant before. He crossed away from Fontano's (the road was in a wretched state; probably it had been repaired by his father) and entered an arcade on the far side of the street where homeless people had boxed themselves against the night.

Katerina was in the light outside Fontano's. She was wearing a long black cloak, such as smart women wore to the opera before the war, and a fur hood about her ears. The winter was almost over, but she held a hand at her throat as if to protect herself against exposure. She walked along, her head averted from the window, and entered the shadows. There were lights but no warmth in the capital. The cafés were golden with lamps, but offered nothing but barrelled wine and black adulterated coffee. She was alone. Only official cars ran in the streets. It was impossible for anyone to follow her without being either noticeable or too far away to be effective. She was alone. He could have crossed to her at once, but he allowed her to walk along the uneven pavement, smiling at her stumble, all the way from Fontano's, past the old Parliament building and the Ministry of Foreign Affairs to the railings in front of the Sophia Palace, until she came to the darkest part of the street, where a steep hill led up to the popular section. She was remote from what she knew and turned unhappily. She looked at her wrist and his heart leaped as she snapped her lighter to see the time. The light flared on her face, giving him no clear sight of it, but reminding him of the plump petulance of past years. He stepped into the dark road. She turned, scanning the shadows, and walked back across the dark front of the Sophia Palace. He stood between her and the end of the fence. She seemed slighter than he remembered. He was touched by the slimness of her body. No, he was touched by the slimness of all bodies. He had a sentimental sense of the fragility of life and of the endurance and courage of men and women in holding to it at all.

'Good evening.'

'Oh my God! I thought you weren't coming. I thought you were joking with me.'

'Well, here I am. How do you do?'

'You haven't changed,' she said.

'Oh wait, wait a minute, please. Don't condemn me so quickly!'

'I was frightened. I was as frightened, in front of Fontano's I mean, as if I were on the wanted list.'

'And I, who am, was not frightened in the least.'

'Are you armed?'

'Would I take a risk like that?'

'I was certain you'd never get the letter. Wasn't it ridiculous sending a letter like that and it getting to you? Fantastic. Where is it, the letter, did you destroy it or what? I hope it didn't endanger you. I mean, I hope that you weren't questioned about it.'

'Questioned? No. I was brought the letter.'

'But from me, after all. Wasn't there a chance that someone would think you were corresponding with the enemy? Do they know you've come here tonight?'

'What a lot of questions you're asking me, Katerina! What shall we do? Where shall we go? Let me ask some questions for a change!'

'Did you come alone?'

'I came as you did,' Artemis said.

'I've got a key, to an office in town my husband uses.'

'The Prime Minister uses an office! What does he use an office for?'

'Oh Artemy, Artemy, you haven't changed.'

'Yes, I have. Don't decide so quickly, Katerina, or I shall have to accuse you of the same thing.'

'Which of us is the bigger fool, I wonder, the bigger dupe, the bigger sentimentalist?'

'And this office, where is it?'

'In the old *Times* building. It was blown up, you know, but there was a section they shored up. A corner. It suits him to have somewhere no one knows.'

'And how do you know he isn't there tonight?'

'I know. He's … somewhere else – I can't tell you where.'

'We could have killed him if we'd wanted to … Is there still a curfew? Perhaps we ought to move off the streets. I should hate you to get into trouble.'

'Oh there're some patrols, nothing rigid. The Government are very confident these days.'

'Why did you want to see me? Do you want to come back with me?'

'Come back with you? Whatever gave you such an idea?'

'I've come to see you. I can't understand why. I hoped *you* might have a reason for this rendezvous.'

'We're old friends,' she said.

'I'd sooner you came with me than that I had a chance to kill your husband.'

'So you do have time for private emotions, then? I was afraid you might have become a soulless automaton. Shall we go to this office or not? You decide.'

'How do I know I shan't be walking into a trap?'

'You will,' she said. 'I set it myself this morning.'

'How do I know I shall ever get out of it?'

'That's not a very gallant question.'

'Are we going to make love?'

'Oh now! What a long time since you were with a lady.'

'I don't want to go back to that, Katerina. Shall we part now?'

'I want you to give me a child.'

'You said?'

'I want to have your child. I want you to give me a son.'

'You're serious. About a child. Sons, well … that's what you want of me?'

'I want to have your child before you die.'

'You think I'm going to die? I'm not convinced of it. We shan't melt like snow, you know. We have more endurance than you think.'

'I don't care about that. Come on. It's not far from here.'

She walked away across the avenue. The devastation of the capital, even in the thicker darkness which followed curfew, came home to Artemis. He was like a man returning to his house after having let it furnished. At first sight it seems little changed, so relieved is he to find it still habitable; it is only after congratulating the tenant on how he has looked after his things that he notices the damage. Artemis felt no responsibility for the ruin of the city; it was not the partisans but the liberating Allies who had bombarded it. The partisans suffered more than the Germans, who had already withdrawn their main force. The suspicion remained that it had been aimed more at weakening Papastavrou than at finishing off the invaders. The British military command had no intention of allowing an independent national Government to take office. If this state of affairs outraged the partisans, it was easily borne by the notables. They were as keen for Allied 'backing' as the Political Committee was wary of it. The 'fair' solution of a coalition was fiercely rejected. The conventional politicians accused the Left of being unwilling to take 'real responsibility'; the Left retorted that the Government was unable to offer it. The Allies sighed and proposed to mediate. The Political Committee attempted to have separate meetings with General Pick, the Allied commander. They were still prepared to believe, seeing how well known was their own fighting record and the notables' collaboration, that the British could be persuaded of the bad faith of the old politicians. The British were easily persuaded of it; it was the foundation of their policy. The Left partisans withdrew from the talks and the disorders began. The British were compelled to inflate the reputation of General Athanasiou, who had commanded the 'Royalist' partisans. His army was reinforced by recruits, supposedly to continue the war against the Germans, actually to provide, under British officers, a force to resist Papastavrou and to warrant charges against him of flouting the will of a free people. The return of the young king (who could scarcely expect to be congratulated for leaving his compatriots to German occupation while he broadcast defiance from the security of a friendly country) had to be engineered with some care, especially since the royal family was of German origin. The British had made sure that he saw some 'war' service in a destroyer, later donated to his navy, and they staged his arrival to coincide with consignments of food. The crown prince was nervous of his reception and appalled by the ruin of his country. His reign had been so short and so unlucky that he could not seem too proprietorial, but he worked hard to get further help from the Allies. It was not for entirely cynical reasons that the press welcomed him more warmly than the people did. Yet he came too late to heal the split in the country. Whatever his personal hopes, he could depend only on those to whom any compromise with the Left promised summary eviction at the best. He could hardly go entirely to the Left without losing his value as a symbol of the country's unity. He grew distant from his ministers without getting any closer to their opponents. The Political Committee preferred to blame the Palace rather than to evaluate the 'honesty' of individual bourgeois politicians. Once they had rejected a coalition, it was simpler to denounce the old gang *in toto* than to toy with the possibility that King Paul was sincere when, like his father years before, he began to speak first of a 'royal peace' and then of a 'new society'. The Left had campaigned for social reform, but once they had quit the capital they could not afford to have it come about without them. From being the promoters of economic recovery they became its adversaries. The capital might once have welcomed them as liberators; it was soon weary of their gloomy threats. Rape, if inevitable, could be enjoyed; impotent seductions could not.

'Are you coming in?'

'I used to come here quite often, when I wrote criticism for Dmitri. I used to deliver it here. There was a bar over there where I used to correct my proofs. The Yellow Bar. What about that?'

'Come on, Artemy, there's a car.'

He hesitated and then crossed to the thick door she was holding back with her foot. 'Have you got a torch?'

'Of course. Anyway, there's light. Once we shut the door I'll show you.'

'Are you betraying me, Katerina?'

'How can I betray you when I'm not married to you?'

'Still the same Katerina! You can betray me.' He stepped inside. She shut the door and twisted a knob; a pale bulb shone. Steps climbed to an office Artemis remembered as the 'small ads' department of the paper, a forbidding countered room with the atmosphere of a State pawn shop. He listened to the building (from which the whole rear section had been shorn) and climbed after Katerina. She looked at her watch under the bulb. 'Won't someone see the light?'

'It's all blacked out,' she said, 'anyway no one comes round here. Don't be so jumpy! I thought you'd be hard as nails by now.'

'I'm not used to being shut in.'

'You're trembling.'

'Never mind. Never mind. You still imagine that you're immune, that you can watch the game and never be involved. It's not so. I warn you.'

'But of what? Poor Artemy, you're the one who talks as if there was still dry land somewhere. I have no such illusions.' She threw back her hood. Her face was older. Her cheeks were still plump but there was a bruised look under her eyes. The brows were less straight, but the eyes were still bold and lustrous, capable of that pettish sullenness he used to love and dread. He had not touched a woman in two years, in two whole years he had not kissed a woman. The men took village women but a bitter resignation deprived him of such pleasures. A peasant woman had slept with him during the severest period of the war against the invaders, but he had been so feverish during most of their time together that he had come to fear her. Katerina shook her head and he stood away from her, sullen, like an adolescent who has been promised. There was no scent of sunlight in the room; it seemed to have been heated in shadow. Night brought out a smell only of staleness. Behind the counter a pair of tables faced each other like the ghosts of chess players. Beyond them, under the calendar of a pre-war year, was a buttoned leather sofa, its arm saddled with an ashtray on a strap. The scar of brown tobacco in its centre had polluted the room. Artemis watched Katerina rather as one watches an official who has said that there may be a last place on an aeroplane. Is it a favour that is being promised or a kind of callous tease? If a place is found, it will prove one's charm, one's luck, but if that head is shaken, then what hatred and what resentment will follow! To be turned down when the chances of being accepted are extremely remote is more painful than to be rejected in common circumstances.

'Did you ever really love me?'

'I wanted you. If loving you means only thinking of nothing else, I loved you.'

'Why do you say it so bitterly?'

'Because we could never be alone in those days. (Can we now? Can we ever?) My bitterness came from a sense of the limitations of the feelings permitted us. Not by edicts or authorities, but by the narrowness of our language, our world. My bitterness found a centre in you, but you weren't really the target, that's what I have come to realize. You were both more and far less important than I believed, because I had no other means of understanding society, at any passionate level, except through my feeling for you. I loaded you with reproaches I felt against our social situation; I hated the social situation because of what I wanted from you. I never understood either.'

She was within a phrase of mocking him, her lips shaped for some patronizing rejoinder, but the uncertainty with which she had come to this rendezvous, the ambiguity of her motives (which had some quite distinct elements) were lost in a sudden access of tenderness and self-pity. She began to undress. 'You haven't changed, Artemy, have you?'

'Oh please, Katerina. Not that. I've changed.' His tone was softened by the anguish of this decided action of hers, the yielding, as a demand, not a concession, of her body. The anguish was his, not hers; the anguish was not of the present but for the years that had lapsed, for the crassness of her reluctance all those years before and for the changes that had wrung her during the years they were parted. He did not see this as the great reunion of lovers who had never 'really' been apart. He recognized the separation which their meeting celebrated and it stabbed him like an assassin. His desire was almost an afterthought. It aged him, this awareness of her as an event, not as an object of desire. He took off his glasses. 'But perhaps not in relation to you. It's like an author trying to resume an old drama. He tries to become his old self again. He does it without knowing quite where he is or what he is, whether he admires that old younger self or pities it. Is he recapturing the past or consoling it for its deadness? The great mistake in psychology is the assumption that men know what they are doing. We concede that they don't always know why, but it's hard to see that they don't, quite often, know what either. That was the heart of our youth, the fact that we quite literally did not know what we were doing because the language was kept from us. I look forward to my own death as the last of a generation which was capable of thinking in an unthinkable way. The revolution, when it comes, will hurt more because of the silence which it brings than because of the hardship. It must come to grips for ever with the language question, strangely enough, just as my father and his ridiculous friends realized all those years ago.'

'Do you still talk as much as ever, Artemy? I'd forgotten how talkative you were. I thought of you always, I've always thought of you as a man with a gun and a cold smile on your lips.'

'I'm only silent in company,' Artemis said. 'I speak a lot when I'm alone.'

'Poor Hamlet,' she said. She seemed to have been undressing for a long time without having revealed herself. Her clothes were laid on the sofa, but her body was still mantled in the long coat which she had about her shoulders. Her face was the most naked thing about her, as if it was from her mouth and cheeks and eyes that all these garments had been removed. She looked paler, a woman stripped by forces beyond her, ready for a search, for pain possibly. She lowered her eyes. Her feet were naked. One of her big toe-nails had turned opaque. It almost made him cry. He went to her and put his arms round her under the tall coat. Her breasts were soft. Her body seemed so familiar to him that he could hardly believe this a virgin occasion.

'Funny Artemis; funny, funny Artemis.'

'There is no love like the love of two people who do not desire each other, but desire a new world, a different world. That's what I want, Katerina.'

'Oh Artemy, you always made such lovely speeches, such moving poems, poems I never really understood. I've re-read them again and again.'

'Yet you've stayed here in the city, Katerina. Nothing that I've thought or done – I'm not going to talk about suffering, which is a kind of accident, like colour – nothing that I was becoming moved you, at least not literally. You never budged, did you, or took part?'

'Did you want me to come and look for you in the countryside, when all we heard were stories of murder and rape? I don't want to be raped, Artemy, at least not by just anyone. I don't mind you.'

'You sent a letter like men used to send messengers. Messengers who were killed or rewarded by the messages they took and according to how they were received. You risked your letter, but never yourself.'

'I'm here now, Artemy. I'm not hiding anything. I'm uglier now but I've learned that, haven't I?'

'You accuse me of wasting your beauty, but you weren't prepared to spend it then. You thought it might become more valuable. You're beautiful now.'

'Because you like seeing things collapse, fail, weaken. You're a cruel man, Artemy, that's what your tenderness says, that it longs to be cruel but restrains itself, all your loving is a kind of restraint, isn't it, because you want to go further than you dare?'

'I like your breasts because they have given suck. I see you as a woman now. I'm not sorry for the years or the waste.'

'You do think me old and ugly! Obviously.'

'No, I no longer have eyes for those things. Bodies talk and men talk. They have different languages. The confusion is mixed metaphor.'

'You're young and old, yes, I see that now. I don't know whether it's nice or not. I don't know whether I'm with a dead man or a god.'

'Neither,' said Artemis, 'as you know very well. If you're hoping I'm a god because they always impregnate mortal women first time, don't! Of the two, incidentally, man is the higher being.'

'How it used to madden me when you said things like that, especially when you said "incidentally" in that way!'

'It's not the man–god idea that upsets you but the hyphen that joins them!'

'Must you write poetry now? Do you really want me, Artemy?'
'Aren't I here?'

'Will there be marriage when the revolution succeeds?'

'What's this? Treason? Did you say "when"?'

'Don't flirt with me, Artemis. Don't make me the strong one, the one who has to yield. I prefer to be a stranger, a slave to you, than to have you mock me. I ask you like a stranger.'

'There are no male oracles; that's the female portion, the cleft

187

that gives access to the centre of things. Will there be marriage? I don't know. I shall never know. I look forward to a world in which I can't take part. That's why I'm here.'

'What do you mean?' She was lying on the black coat, her breasts fallen flat, one knee raised, her legs parted, her open belly faintly striped by childbirth. She turned her head to him, rolling it on the hard floor, urgent for humiliation perhaps. 'What're you trying to say?'

'Say? Nothing. I'm making myself a traitor to the future. By being here with you. Surely that's obvious.'

She shut her body against him.

'It's not you,' he told her, between reassurance and brutality, 'it's me. Whatever I'm doing here, I'm admitting the past, the call of the past, the continuity, in spite of everything, that makes me one of you.'

'You do admit it, you do admit it.' She huddled herself against her knees, drawing a cloak of her own flesh about her, closing off her sexuality. She might have been across the desk from some official.

'You believe the revolution will win, then,' he said, 'do you? You speak of it so convincingly in the future tense!'

'It hates women, doesn't it? It makes no distinction, isn't that what you say, between men and women, but that's not true, is it?'

'We have women fighting with us. We –'

'Lawyer! How long can your revolution last? Tell me, Artemy, don't attack me! I want to believe.'

'That means you don't. That wanting to believe is the negation of belief, because it assimilates learning a language, a process, to accepting something, like a rich woman choosing a painting or a hair-style, inspecting what's offered and *accepting*. Wanting to believe is a false expression, or rather it expresses very clearly what it doesn't intend to express: the passive greed of a certain kind of person, waiting in a spiritual restaurant for the service to improve, for the menu to come. No, Katerina, you don't understand the situation at all. You've sat there throughout these years, as if you were suffering, as if you were helpless, but you weren't and that is why you can't escape judgment. If you could send a letter, you could send yourself.'

'I never said I wanted to. I never said I agreed with the Movement. I don't say it now. I was asking you about it, not applying for membership.'

'The sincere question applies at the same time. There's no exterior and interior to what is going on. That's your mistake. You're trying to spiritualize the conflict, to make it an argument, a metaphysical matter, whereas it's a physical thing; it's happening. You're dead when you try to rise above it. Your immortality, your withdrawal from common life, isn't a way of rising at all; it's a kind of collapse, it's a surrender. Christ would have been greater if He'd refused the luxury of resurrection. Your husband would be a greater patriot if he allowed himself to be shot like a mad dog than if he brings in a foreign power and foreign ideas and destroys for the sake of a temporary "improvement" the ability of the people to make their own world, their own language.'

'Can you seriously say that there's no foreign element in your precious revolution? Are you really able to say that?'

'The question of boundaries is extremely difficult.'

She really laughed then and he glared at her.

'I'll try to say something about it if you're capable of listening.'

She had drawn the black coat about her shoulders. He squatted beside her like someone opening a grave. She was now as remote and impassive as her laughter had been animated. Her skin had the texture of an old book. Her eyes were closed, but they bulged under the creased lids. Her hair hung, shaken free of its brushed lustre, against the collar of the black coat. He tore the coat from her shoulders as if he were wrenching the skin from her back and jerked her jaw towards him. Her eyelids fluttered, a patient waking to death at her bedside, and he kissed her lips and drew her head back by a handful of hair, uncreasing her face, which was lit by a fearful searching blankness.

'You don't need it explained.' The words bit her like light too bright for vision; they stabbed her as she twisted to blink free of their violence. 'You know.'

He tore open her mouth, hooked fish, and she gasped and jerked. Her eyes searched for what she could not see. He flung her back on the floor and her head bumped; her body yielded; cunt moist, she could not resist him. 'Love! My sweet!' And yet he suspected a cunning in her. His suspicion sapped his desire. She had gone under too quickly. She had welcomed the excuse, not because she wanted him but because she wanted a cheap victory; she wanted to be able to go home having spent less than she had budgeted.

'What is it? What's wrong?'

'There is a difference, but it needs a conscious effort to understand. It needs good will, that is, the will to be good and that means, I admit it quite frankly, the willingness to see how much stronger and truer our arguments are than yours, his. No argument can really take place about the merits of two distinct logics unless it is seen that there is something more substantial than argument which is the world itself.'

Katerina shook her head, the patient required instantly to join in a discussion about the technique of surgery. She knew the pleasure he took in this abrupt disjunction of probability. She knew the same pleasure. It was what made this meeting either an irrelevance, this part of it, or the supreme moment of her life. It would never heal to what lay either side of it, not without it proving a conquest for one and the destruction of the other. A married man, alone in a foreign city, can meet a woman. He is capable of choices which have the freshness of a new life. What really rejuvenates him is not the pleasure he finds but the right he enjoys to accept or to decline it. The guilt which may later envelop the whole affair is absent from its actual elaboration. Guilt is a part of criticism, not of life. His eyes may allude at the time to his hesitations, to his familiar responsibilities, but only to salt the humour of the occasion. He is like a man who can speak two languages but who feels uneasy at his private fluency and warns himself that he must think in one language or the other if he wants to have a real language at all. The urge to reconcile life to a single official history is a kind of emotional centralism against which the autonomy of sensations constantly rebels.

'I haven't understood a word, my love.'

'But do you want to? Don't you really prefer not to understand? Isn't there a greater pride in your refusal than in confessing your failure? You hang on to your intellectual virginity still. You daren't give yourself away, you daren't yield without that old feeling that you could have got a better price. That's what you mean when you think of life as being full of opportunities. You wait all the time for the top of the market, so that you may be said to have succeeded, to have done as well as you could, without ever seeing that it's dead stock you're dealing in. You sell yourself to the slaughterer. You can't survive to read the tributes to your own smartness. It's a false calculus, all that, it's part of what we shall see lost to the world, not refuted or argued down, just unlamentably lost like the dinosaur.'

'So everything that happens is for the best, is it?'

'Ah, there you go, quick for the kill. Why must we be talking about everything when we talk about something? You go leaping boundaries like an imperialist! Oh, but laughter, what does that laughter mean? Doesn't that have a meaning too? I'll say! It's an appeal to absent friends, to the crowd that isn't here, it proves to me how dressed you are, how much of a sacrifice you're making, how keen you are to betray me.'

'That's not true.'

'It is true. Your laughter tells me it is. You laugh because you daren't come beyond your own doorstep. You've made a property of yourself. I'm not saying it out of jealousy. In your terms, Katerina, I could take my vengeance now in every way your world understands. I curse myself with belonging to you but it's not altogether true, that's the gift you've given me this evening; I see that I truly do stand beyond you. I no longer belong to you. You laugh like someone trying to learn a new language, speechless after the teacher has finished, afraid to mouth funny sounds in case they become too natural to you. That's by the way. I was trying to tell you the difference between "foreign" in my language and in yours. You know how it is that when we say "no" and nod like our people do, inexperienced foreigners, tourists in the old days, take us to be agreeing, to be saying "yes"? Well, now there is a distinction between our foreigners and yours, the help we are given and the bribes you take, which is just as great as the division between the nod we give and what it means to foreigners. The distinction isn't difficult; you could retain it very well if it were a tip on the stock exchange. If it were not for the money which the so-called Allies are giving you, if it weren't for the concessions they are buying and the promise of wealth they are offering, if it weren't, above all, for the partiality of their help, the hidden provisions of which will be obvious only when they have achieved their first objectives and pruned the alternatives, there would be no appeal in their presence at all. Humanitarian motives may fill the Liberty ships but they aren't the same motives which unload them. So much for the notion of strings as a simple, unchanging machinery. The raw materials which are shipped from certain markets to the industrial nations change their value in mid-passage according to the commercial and taxation laws in force in the powerful countries. A crop can leave a port cheap in order to evade the duty of a weak and dependent country and arrive expensive, in the same ship, as a result of having been "sold" in mid-passage by one "independent" company to another. It can then be sold high in the home market without having to pay tax since no "profit" has been made. Yet the logic of "aid" remains as simple as the idea of barter. I'm sorry; I haven't talked to anyone like this for a long time.'

'Is it forbidden?'

'It's unnecessary. We know these things. It's only in this company that it needs to be said. What you receive are bribes; what we receive is aid.'

'And I'm forbidden to laugh. Am I a reactionary if I laugh?'

'Yes. Not because of what you are; because of what you won't be. Because you can't see that there is a real situation involved. It's not a matter of motives. Even if everything which we are given was given to us with the worst motives in the world – and because of the systems involved I'm inclined to doubt if it could be – even if our allies wanted to be as cynical as they knew how (they simply couldn't be as cynical as the capitalists know how to be, because they lack the machinery, the language if you like), even so the weapons, the food would be going towards the next stage of human evolution; they would be as much on the side of the future as the young are, not because they are better but because they are younger. At every stage of human life, of life on the earth, the future is outnumbered by the past, and yet the future is what is coming and the past is receding. Does that help you at all?'

'Thank you. But what I'm asking is, when the future arrives, when it outnumbers the present, when the revolution wins, how long can it go on? Doesn't it have to go on unless it's going to go into reverse? Or is it just going to go on correcting itself, becoming more and more punctual like a railway that runs perfectly except that it has no arrivals and no departures, only a perfect timetable?'

'This is a fine time for worrying about perfection, now! When – '

'And it's a fine time to worry about motives, about hidden provisions, when people are dying in the streets. Do you *want* them to die?'

He sat there, a refugee from his dilemma.

'You don't, but you daren't admit it. What a way to live, not daring to admit that you don't want women and children to die!'

'I'd prefer men not to die,' he shouted at her. 'So damn your women and children. Damn that pathetic absenteeism, that neutrality, that resignation.'

'Oh, all right!'

'If it weren't for men do you think you'd all be happy, all be contented and loving, with a kid at each tit? Try it and see. That's the biggest lie of feminism, so-called, the biggest piece of docility and cheating.'

'What makes everything "so-called" so-called?'

'The idea that women have no part in aggression or exploitation, no influence on the world, or have a desire for a separate world! It's a lie and you ought to know it.'

'I hope you're not fighting this war just to get your own back on me.'

'You hope I *am*. But never mind. It's of no great consequence whether I have those motives or not, whether I'm really free of them or only "imagine" that I am. I wouldn't be here, I don't think, if I thought we mattered that much. Can you really imagine a more wasteful scheme of things than one which made everything a man did in his life valuable only according to why he did it? I really believe that we may come to the end of all that, to the end of morality as a private allegory, and finally to the end of the idea of a single life altogether. A soldier, after all, isn't judged according to his whole life in one, but according to his usefulness, his effectiveness in specific actions. The whole idea of a soldier's record as a decisive, important document only arises out of the polite division between civilian and military control. The civilian control of soldiers only asserts itself finally where a man has a discharge from the forces, where he returns, as if to the more important or more substantial world, to "civilian life". The army, as an army, doesn't care a damn about a man's moral record. The army is a process too, without a purpose. In fighting armies men never retire. They go on until they drop. That is what is meant by fading away in the old proverb. There's no other life for them to go back to. The same applies to the revolutionary army. To ask why we don't resign or see the futility of our fight, when it seems to have become futile, is as empty as the idea of heaven. What makes us meet here is not the greatness of what we felt, or even feel for each other; it is its irrelevance. We're both dead already, in a way.'

'But not in much of a way. Not as anything but a luxurious metaphor, like a "fatal" perfume, something that excites rather than kills.'

'Am I betraying the revolution by being here without them knowing, and are you betraying your husband? And does it matter? The idea of a woman as the crucial moral instance can't survive much longer, can it really? As if this were the definitive sin!'

'We haven't committed it yet. Will you tell them about me, will you undress me again for the comrades?'

'I'm still a bourgeois,' he said. 'That doesn't come as any shock to me. I've known all along. So have my friends. We're less snobbish than you like to suppose. We would even have kept Democritos if he'd stayed with us. It's propaganda that we expelled him. We didn't.'

'I hate that man. I'm sorry you mentioned him.'

'Why? Because he really believes in the society you find so comfortable, because he has actually *chosen* something you prefer to think has no alternative?'

'Because he has appalling teeth and won't have anything done about them, even though he could if he chose. He has a skinned face too. Have you seen him recently? He seems to have made himself conspicuous in order that he shan't escape his fate and in order that we shan't escape him.'

'I saw him tonight.'

'Where? Artemis, where?'

'In Fontano's reading a letter like a good shopkeeper. What frightens you about Democritos is that he will commit the crimes for which you'll be judged – and insists you know about them.'

'Oh stop it, Artemy. Artemy, I'm frightened.'

'You're tired of thinking, you mean? You're going to become a woman again, all apprehensions and intuitions?'

'We must go. Quickly. Now. Before it's too late.'

'What've you done? Who knows about this place? Democritos? Katerina, answer me.'

'He was supposed to be dining on board the English cruiser. Dmitri told me, with the admiral.'

'Is he your lover?'

'Does it matter?' She laughed at him, glazed with tears.

'Are you afraid of a plot or are you in one? The answer's both, no doubt, as always. You slept with Democritos?'

'You said so. I didn't.'

'But you did. Didn't you?'

'Artemis, please. Let's get out of here. I never slept with him. You and your intuitions! Democritos!'

He pushed her down by the sofa where a black curtain was draped over stacks of back numbers. She fought him, but she was disjointed by that crick of laughter. He forced desire into her, a rescuer wrestling a drowned man alive. The more she kindled to him, the more surly and ferocious he grew. The desire to force her was not eased by the melting of her flesh or the practised lift of her legs. He was not appeased by her surrender; he was driven on by it. He squeezed her weary breasts to the tautness of youth. He beat her with his body. Their bodies smacked as they parted. Yet he longed for her pleasure, if only he could expel that bubble of contempt, of self-certainty, from her. He wanted her to complete her pleasure, but at the instant of not knowing where she could ever find it again. He wanted to devastate her. He fucked her knowing that she would not be his. She might as well have been a stranger; they might as well have been two dogs. No, because he did remember. He did remember her as a girl. He remembered her breasts when they were guarded. He remembered her face a palimpsest of family portraits. He knew her from before, but he would not know her again. He was not merely fucking, for he was determined now to do what seemed so fantastic, so selfish of her: to give her a child. He did not fuck for pleasure or out of desire; he had no future with this woman. Ah, she was moving under him and her fingers fought his back, searched angrily for some secret extra pleasure with which to crucify him! She grinned at him like a torturer; like a torturer? He wanted to see her stripped of that family likeness he hated in her (the likeness to *any* family), he drove her beyond pleasure and pain into painless agony because he wanted to rasp the mask and have the raw face revealed.

196

He wanted to give her a child, though there was a defeat for him in it, in that treacherous fury. What was he betraying? Was he lodging a traitor in her, a son that might grow up to despise her? Was he planting a conspirator in the palace, a bastard with the best cover a man could have, a consistent story from birth itself? Or was he betraying the Movement? How would the traitor know what he was supposed to betray? The perfect spy never springs his cover. He never leaves his safe house. He lives in absolute uniformity with the society he undermines. The bourgeois who goes through all the motions of propriety is a better agent of the future than the one who half-heartedly puts sand in the works. He is true to the order of things. He shows no divine propensities. His 'honesty' prepares the way. He doesn't rise up in the middle of the operation and glare at the surgeons. He yields. Was it a yielding child that Artemis forced into Katerina? Or could it be her death? An untimely child who would be born in blood and survive for revenge? It would be a child, blank as newsprint. She cried out his name, horrified, like an informer she yelled his name, screaming, and beat her head against the floor, this side and that. She came and denounced him, her body an arched bow for the arrow he drove into her. He caught her under the hips and forced himself into her. It might, of course, all come to nothing. He tore himself loose and she fell back and threw her head sideways against the black curtain, which lifted like a floodgate and allowed the piled papers to slump across her like a breached box of fish. She reared up and hauled herself together, hands between her legs, head hooded with hair. She threw the hair back and turned her blanched face up at him. 'You must go.'

'Come with me.'

'Yes, but be quick.' She frowned at her watch. 'Hurry.'

'When are they coming?'

'Who? Coming?'

'Democritos and his men.'

'Don't. No one's coming. But you must go. Or you'll never get out before it's light.'

'Then let's go.'

'If you think it's safer.'

'Safer?'

'If we're together. They'll think we're lovers. They won't worry about us. The patrols.'

'I meant come all the way.'

'I can't. I can't. You know I can't. Don't try to trap me, don't try to quarrel with me now, Artemy. I can't. If I could've, I would've much earlier. I wouldn't have waited for now. Get dressed. We must get out of here. I should never have asked you to come.'

'Isn't that why you did?'

'It pleases you to suspect me, to make me feel a traitor.'

'No. It doesn't please me. I'm not blaming you. I'm trying to understand.'

'Oh, you'd swallow the world if you could, and digest it into – '

'I'd sooner it swallowed me,' he said.

'No, Artemy, you're a bone. You're indigestible. You'd stick in the world's throat.'

'What have you arranged, you whore? Tell me.'

'I don't know what you mean.'

'Here. When you brought me here. With Democritos. What?'

'I told you, nothing. I'm afraid, that's all. Because he told me he was dining with the British admiral and now he hasn't, so what's he doing?'

'And who wrote him the letter I saw him reading?'

'Once it's light you'll never get back. The city's full of informers. How should I know what he was reading? We should've gone before.'

'Why shouldn't I stay here if it's so safe? If there's nothing to worry about?'

'I said we had to go. I never said it was safe. Do you want to stay?'

'And when will they start to look for you, Katerina, for the important lady? How long does your freedom last before you're hunted like a criminal, for the sake of the family and the Prime Minister's dignity?'

She dragged open the door as if against a great head of water. The tunnel of the stairs fell away, a throat of darkness. She seemed to have only so much time, dragging him like an anchor, before she would have to breathe in her death. 'It's not a joke, Artemy.'

A car was coming along behind the office, behind the caked wall which contained the open entrails of the old buildings. She backed against the stairhead behind the street door. 'You fool. We've left it too late.' She turned and saw Artemis smiling, and the gun in his hand. 'You haven't come with a gun?'

'Oh of course I've come with a gun. What did you expect?'

'Something more intelligent. Anyone who stops us now is bound to arrest you.'

'And you?'

'I don't come into it.'

The car came closer and then seemed to hesitate before driving across in front of the closed street door, with a clank of uncertain springs, towards the Street of Heroes. 'Friend of yours?'

'Any car's dangerous. You know that. If I'd arranged anything, do you think I'd be in such a hurry to get away?'

'One's able to change one's mind.' He caught her by the arm, captured her flinch of fear like a distinct frame of life, and kissed her again and again on the mouth, his desire as straight as if he had never enjoyed her. 'Stop it, Artemy.' But he forced her against the wall. 'This time,' he said. 'This time.'

'There isn't *time*.'

He thrust her against the wall and drove himself between her damp legs. She had to put her arms round his neck for him to get into her. She collapsed on to him like a slung sack and worked on him. As soon as he had come, he opened the street door and they left the building. She was weak. She stumbled. He caught her around the waist and set her on her feet. She looked at him dumbly and now he would have taken her with him across the lines if he could. If he could have lifted her directly to the other world, he would have taken her. He hurried her like a hostage or a prisoner, but someone he would take with him. She fought her feebleness and slowed him, like weed in a stream. She brushed against him and clung and held him back. 'They've got a road-block, a checkpoint in the Street of Heroes. They stop people going down to the harbour.'

'Where, then?' It aggravated him to have to revive her, to yield to her knowledge. He wanted to know the city better than she did. 'Where, woman?'

She swung round like a released compass, spun and steadied and started down a dark alley parallel to the Street of Heroes.

'You're being too dramatic,' he said. 'What're you so frightened about? Since you don't come into it. Perhaps we should part here. Leave me to find my own way. I've been in this city before, you know.'

She pulled him into another narrow street and they came out on the corner of the main road. There was a café on the far side, choked with smoke, soldiers and women; it was where the English troops sold cigarettes for cunt. Not yet coupled, the soldiers and the women resembled opponents in a rigged fight who have yet to be told which is the loser. Artemis and Katerina, their deal already closed, dodged through the crowd and reached the corner which would take them into what was once the furniture district. Katerina had caught something precisely of the whore, the set little face with its air of brisk but temporary mastery. She swung her hips and took short, quick steps. He enjoyed her expertise.

'You were once quite interested in whores, do you remember? Asking me about Helen's?'

'All young girls are interested in travel.' Her face was shining now, as if made up; the risen moon powdered it and caught the whites of her eyes. 'In things they think they'll never see or experience. I used to treat you like the encyclopedia. I thought you knew everything.' All this she said without slowing down.

'But you're not interested in them any more?'

'I know what they do. I know how they do it. No.'

'But you knew then. You said so.'

'I thought they did something wicked, something deep. I know they don't now. That tunnel's very short.'

'Yes. That's what I meant just now.'

'Oh, I knew what you meant.'

'But money isn't the only alternative.'

'Tell me the difference between money and power, Artemis.'

'Where are you taking me?'

'Back,' she said. 'Isn't that where you want to go?'

'How will you get back?'

'I shall walk. If anyone picks me up, any of the patrols I mean, they'll take me. Don't worry about me.'

'I want you to have the child.'

'Oh, that … ' She aborted it like turning off a light, that subject. 'You're such a prude, I knew you wouldn't do anything for *fun*!' They entered a section of streets without lights; the windows were blinded with moonlight.

'Fun?' Katerina took his arm; a car was coming from their left, up ahead, along a wide street where clutches of eggs had once hung in spherical cages. Artemis remembered them from when he went with his father to the Theodoros office in the harbour. Eggs were now quoted at twenty-two times their pre-war price, though that was a technical matter, since there were no eggs on sale. A man had recently been sentenced to three years' imprisonment for raiding a rooftop chicken run private to the Minister of War. The market had been bulldozed by the Germans. Since they had needed the harbour and the labour quartered there too badly to be able to raze it, they had decided on a *cordon sanitaire* to prevent partisans from passing freely between the city, where 'outrages' had become more frequent every day, and the harbour, which offered them an almost unsearchable haven. The Germans made the city and the harbour two distinct towns once again, as they had been in ancient times, and prevented all uncontrolled passage between them. It was this empty quarter which was one of the great theoretical hazards to a successful attack on the city. The defenders would have a clear field of fire in the one direction from which the guerrillas might hope to infiltrate. Artemis was astonished to find it almost without defences. It was possible that the Government had concealed their tanks and heavy guns in secret lairs, but such method hardly chimed with the slipshod security in the rest of the city. Artemis's 'defence' of his present escapade as a reconnaissance grew more plausible. Could he reopen the matter with Brasidas and the others?

'There must be a regular patrol?' he whispered.

They entered the shell of a merchant's house. It had been only partially flattened. Even destruction grows tedious. The place was burned, but the pattern of its rooms was clear. They crouched by a wide chimney in the Venetian style. The uneven beat of idling engines throbbed in their ears. Katerina was huddled under the fireplace, where shadow was thickest. She put out her hand to look at her watch.

'Late for something?'

She turned to him, her face brimmed with moonlight.

'You should get back,' he said. 'I can get through this. You're not doing any good. Can you get back from here?'

'I might.'

'What the hell are you playing at?' He touched her face. 'Katerina?'

'I want you to get back.'

'Thank you. But shan't I manage better on my own?'

She had the blanched, staring face of a remote goddess, the kind of figure to be found in uncatalogued numbers in the National Museum. 'I know the way. Please. Trust me, please.'

She steered him through the islands of houses. The slur of caterpillar tracks was clear now. Artemis was relieved; there was armour in the district. He would not have to carry the burden of believing that there could have been a successful invasion of the city. He was like a saint who is reassured by the discovery of the devil going about his business. They came to a street in the middle of the ruined district. The paving had been torn open by an explosion. A large tunnel was exposed; a trickle of sewage striped the bottom.

'Follow the tunnel, it'll take you under the cordon. When it branches to the left there is an inspection cover. Go out through that – there's a ladder – and you'll be near the Raffi Monastery. You know it from there, don't you?'

'I don't like tunnels. And I don't like sewers.'

'Artemy, please. It's the only safe way. They'll get you otherwise.'

'I don't believe it, Katerina, not for a moment. I got into the city without any trouble.'

'Believe me, Artemy. You heard the cars and the soldiers – '

He knew that he would go into the tunnel. He could imagine a hundred arguments, a hundred prolongations, but he would go into the tunnel. He would go alone along the darkness, like a rat. It was humorous. He laughed and she took him to be laughing at her determination.

'And you'll go back?'

'Of course.'

'Goodbye, Katerina.'

He went down into the tunnel.

'Artemy – '

He smiled as he walked into the black.

The siren split the silence. They struggled with the unremitting blare of noise as if bars of debris had fallen across them. Artemis crawled out of the tent and saluted the beach, rubbing his forehead. The prison ship was howling with light.

'What on earth is going on?' Michael Shaw produced question number one as soon as he had dashed the sleep from his eyes.

'I don't know,' said Artemis, delighted to imitate an unhelpful peasant, courteous and blank.

It took longer to lower a boat quickly, of course, and some minutes passed before the first party from the ship reached the beach. The officer in charge, a captain in the army, was hunched with anger. He had only a half-dozen men and he was aware of the futility of their mission and of the recriminations which would follow. Two men had escaped from the ship: a terrorist called Leonides and an eighteen-year-old, Spiro Papadopoulos. The storm had eased. A boat came soon from the yacht, containing the Minister himself, in his blazer, Asteris Stratis, wearing a thick brocaded dressing-gown, and Dmitri, in a sailor's sweater and white trousers.

'Report to me, Captain,' said the Minister as soon as he had been helped over the wet remainder of the sea and had collected himself on shore.

'I have my orders.'

'Report to me when I tell you, Captain. In case you're not aware, I'm the Minister of Marine.'

'I'm sorry, sir, but I'm ordered to begin the search at once.' The captain was furious at the presence of these civilians. Furthermore, as his manner was intended to convey, he was a military, not a naval man.

'Is your commanding officer coming ashore?'

'I don't know, sir. I'd very much like to know if anyone has seen or heard anything which could help our search for these men.'

'Your name, Captain. I'll call you that as long as you hold the rank.'

'Miltiades Nikolaos.'

'Thank you. Has anyone seen or heard anything?'

Artemis and Michael Shaw shook their heads. The late arrival of Dmitri and his father gave them the commanding advantage of asking the questions.

'At least there are no women sleeping here.'

'They can't be far, Captain, if you look lively.'

The eagerness of all parties to blame each other delayed the pursuit. It would be light in a few hours, however, and Captain Miltiades was content to stall, provided he had a good excuse. Since the Minister was convinced that no one could long evade capture on the island, he was keen to take charge of the search himself. On the other hand, it was possible that determined and desperate men could conceal themselves for some time and might finally escape by boat, should they be able to capture one. He therefore sent Yanni the muleteer across country at once to the harbour, in order to warn the harbourmaster. Then he insisted on being rowed out to the prison ship, this time in the boat which had brought Captain Miltiades. He paraded the officers who had welcomed him so suspiciously before and whom their present embarrassment reduced to guilty subservience. The Minister insisted on a thorough report of the means by which the two men had unlocked their irons, removed the solder from a battened porthole, oiled the screw and slipped through into the sea. This zest for details presaged only too obviously the course of a possible court-martial. If the Minister failed to recapture the men, he would certainly pillory those who had been his gaolers; on the other hand, a successful hunt might secure their immunity provided they united in conceding him the full credit for it.

'For what had this Leonides been sentenced? And to how long?'

'Fourteen years, sir. Fomenting disaffection among the dock labourers and concealing dynamite and other arms in his dwelling.'

'And the other? The boy Papadopoulos?'

'Eight years and six strokes of the whip, sir, for taking part in a military conspiracy, sir, to subvert the Government and impose a new regime.'

'Eight years and six strokes, I see. These are desperate men, then?'

'The boy belonged to a garrison in the Mavro Country, sir, where there was some trouble, if you remember. A number of men were disciplined, several officers reprimanded and the commanding officer sent to an island – '

'How many men do we have to spare?'

'There are two hundred and fifty prisoners on board, sir, and forty men to guard them. You could hardly say there were any to spare.'

'No wonder this kind of thing happens.'

'Thank you, sir.'

'What?'

'I don't see how we can leave less than half on board, sir, even if we keep everyone locked in all day and rations to a minimum. The ship has to be administered.'

'Have you reported this to the capital yet? Good! Don't. I want to try and help you avoid trouble. If we can recapture the men without letting anyone know, you can rely on me to keep silent. What kind of armaments do you carry; small arms? And have they been checked?'

'Nothing missing, sir. We've got enough rifles for all forty men and some sidearms, sir. Nothing else.'

'And if we keep the prisoners locked in, need we arm all we leave on board? You see what I'm getting at? There's our party here, we can arm the men, and there are my people in the village. I think we should send a party up there at once, most of the men've got hunting guns, quite enough to overpower a couple of ruffians. What's needed here is a swift and successful operation. The island's not large, if you're familiar with it. There's not much water on it at this time of year. Guard the wells and get the sun to search the felons out, that's my advice. I don't mean, of course, that we shouldn't conduct sweeps through the countryside. We must, to keep them moving, get them tired, hungry, thirsty, obviously. Keep it on the island and the search can't last long. At first light *Pegasus* can coast round and make sure that all boats are either properly beached and guarded or rendered unseaworthy. There aren't more than a dozen fishermen living outside the village or the harbour. Any comments?'

There were none. By daylight the *Pegasus* was standing out to sea. The wind had dropped. The even pumping of the yacht's engines lent a purposeful rhythm to the hunt. There was little disappointment at the disbanding of the archaeological expedition. The present excitement promised a more dramatic climax. The only problem was the women. The practical mission on which the *Pegasus* was bound removed all luxury from the idea of being on board, but the Minister would not hear of them staying ashore.

Could one rely on the chivalry of desperate criminals? Eleni refused to be delivered to the harbour like the mothers, and Katerina was hardly less keen, though less outspoken, in her desire to see how the pursuit worked out. The Minister turned on Artemis and said that as he was engaged to Katerina it was his duty to stay with her. His petulance proclaimed his inability to force her return to the *Pegasus*. Katerina might normally have obeyed her father, but a quarrel postponed the need to tell him of her breach with Artemis and the end of their engagement. She could also demonstrate to Artemis the mistake he had made in assuming her to be the docile daughter.

'I hope they get away,' said Eleni, when elaborate plans had been set in motion for the quartering of the island and for the steady elimination and 'securing' of one quadrant after another.

'I should think nothing is more likely,' Artemis said.

'Oh, you're such a cynic,' Katerina said. 'It's not as if you were doing anything to find them yourself.'

'It's your presence which stops me, Katerina, and no one else. If you and Eleni had only gone back on the yacht as any intelligent person would have, I could be out with the others.'

'Directing the search!'

'Personally, I hope they do get away, don't you, Artemis?'

'I hope they find you if they do and take you as a hostage, and then perhaps you won't be so silly about it another time.'

'I wouldn't mind. What would I care? Better than being cooped up with the family. I'm a hostage as it is.'

'You wouldn't think so, Eleni, once they'd got you.'

'Oh, I wouldn't mind. I'd look after them. I'm not like you, Katerina, I'm not so high and mighty. I'd like to know what they're like. They've got a lot more courage than we have anyway, you must admit that. I mean, all these men with rifles and things going out to hunt down two unarmed men – '

'They're convicted criminals. She doesn't know what she's talking about.'

'They're bound to be caught,' said Artemis.

'I don't agree. All they have to do is get a boat and they might easily get away. There are lots of uninhabited islands where they could live. I don't suppose they'd mind much what sort of place it was. They're not spoiled like you.'

'Listen to her! I suppose you're not spoiled? The things you've got, the things you get given.'

'I'm not as spoiled as you are. I don't get things specially made for me like you do. I only get things when you don't want them any longer. What kind of fun do you think that is? I hope they get away. It's not fair. All those people hunting two men on their own. I don't know why the villagers join in. I hope they refuse. I hope they absolutely refuse to help in any way. I don't know how they can stand us here, coming along – '

'If it weren't for us they wouldn't be able to stay here at all. They'd starve to death. If it weren't for Daddy this island would be uninhabited!'

'In which case they could have lived here for ever without bothering anybody!'

Artemis had ambled towards the chapel where he had sat after his dance the previous evening. The girls exchanged sour looks ('You *see*?'), each accusing the other of responsibility for the 'draught'. Artemis climbed the bluff. From the top he could see the whole valley and the threat of mountains on either side. The sea was striped with paths of clear and weed-backed water. There was little current; could the men have swum across to another island altogether? It was almost certainly too far. Then where would they head? The jagged peaks offered little shelter, but from there at least they would have notice of the search. The two girls, irked by Artemis's solitary departure, were coming up the slope after him, bending and straightening, lurching left and right, like women exercised about their weights. The beach was deserted. When they reached Artemis, full of reproachful gasps, as angry with each other as with him, since their simultaneous arrival prevented either from excluding the other, they had to assume that he had made some discovery.

'Have you had an inspiration?'

Mentally he shared with the prisoners the exhilaration of new freedom and with their pursuers the thrill of the chase. He could have been with either party. He was interested in seeing the men outwitted; he was amused by the discomfiture of the Minister and his minions. If only the two girls had gone with the mothers! They were like the female interest in a film which would have been neater without them, girls who scheme themselves into the script and then grumble at the woodenness of their scenes.

'I wish there was something we could do.'

'You should have gone back to the house, like the others.'

'I wish we could find them ourselves.'

'It would be amusing.'

'You want everything to be a joke one minute, Artemy, and serious the next. The whole world has to keep changing, just so that you feel at home in it. If I'd said it would be amusing to track them down, you'd be furious and say that I had no respect for human dignity or something like that.'

They were in the shadow of the little church. It must have seemed as if the bay was deserted. The *Aias* had stood out to sea since the wind had dropped, to deter anyone who might fancy his chances of following the two escapers overboard. Artemis emerged from the shadow, more from restlessness than with any watchful purpose, to see a man creeping on the landward side of the stone wall behind the beach. His furtiveness kindled Artemis's hunting instinct. There might be a case for one of the prisoners doubling back to the little camp if they were short of food. Artemis turned his eyes to the hills for any sign of another figure. The morning heat was growing. The shadows withered. It was hot. He could imagine Dmitri stamping up the hills, peering for shelter or water, dashing the sweat from his reddening brow and creaking in his chocolate-coloured boots. The military would be hoping to exhaust the civilians, the civilians to outwit the soldiers. Meanwhile this singular figure was crawling (to avoid the binoculars from the *Aias*) towards where the archaeologists had been digging. Artemis switched his eyes from the man to the camp, as one waits for a figure who has entered an alley to reappear in a window. Where would he make his dash across the open ground? Artemis put his hand into his pockets and made a fist with the triangular head he had found in the sand. The girls were arguing about what they had said they would do that night, whether they would walk to the harbour or wait for the *Pegasus* to return. The man had stopped short of the camp. He was scooting himself forward to where Artemis had made his private, ill-humoured excavation. Then he started to dig in the sand with the urgency of a small boy racing for water.

Artemis took the head out of his pocket and consulted its blind face. The man on the beach was not one of the criminals; he was a peasant who had been in the habit of digging on the site and who had buried his cache where it would be easy to recover and had been unfortunate enough to have Artemis, who might have preferred the humours of disappointment and to whom the head meant no more than a lucky charm, dig in the very place he had selected.

'I wish there was something we could do,' Eleni said. 'It's so boring!'

'Let's walk back to the house,' Artemis said. He wanted to distract them before they asked questions about the peasant. 'There's not much food left in the camp and we don't know whether anyone is going to come back tonight anyway. It's pointless to stay here.'

'You want to get rid of us. I wonder why.'

'Don't flatter yourself. Artemis wants to get rid of everyone.'

'Some people would be quite glad to have two girls all to themselves.'

'Two girls are the same as none.'

'That just shows how conventional you are!'

'Stop it, Eleni, when you don't know what you're saying.'

'I think Artemy's very conventional, otherwise he wouldn't put up with you. I wouldn't if I was him.'

'You're the one who's responsible, I wouldn't be surprised, for the whole thing. Nothing would surprise me about you.'

'What whole thing? What are you talking about, Katerina?'

'She's right. You *are* conventional. You want to break our engagement in secret and keep it up in public. Why do you have to be such a hypocrite? Do you think I don't know you two have been flirting ever since we set out? It doesn't take much seeing. I don't know which of you I blame more.'

'Ever since we set out!'

'Since that very first night.'

'So you were awake!'

'So there was something to be awake for, was there? Well, well!'

'Damn you both.' He ran away down the hillside towards the vineyards behind the beach. He ran and only as he ran, blindly and hopelessly, did he realize how desperate and yet what a liberation to them must be the flight of the fugitives. The hopelessness of their prospects failed to mock their temporary freedom. In the long run, everyone is dead. He shared their exhilaration and their despair. He was with them in that sense, but there was a sensuality of malice that came over him too: a desire to refine their experience, to tighten the ring on them, to make it more exquisite. He wanted to hunt them down as certain men compel women to their pleasure. Such a lover loves best the pain that his own withdrawal will cause. He enjoys her loneliness at being deprived of him more than he enjoys actually having her. That is the divine sensation, to contrive that another's world perish without one. Artemis realized how rapturous would be the terror of knowing that a great mind was bent on one's destruction. He understood the delicious duet, the *pas de deux*, between Jean Valjean and Inspector Javert. How could a man take true delight in his own skill if no one was there to mark it? Every evasive twist of Valjean was a test for his pursuer, but it was also a tribute to him. The criminal genius dies unappreciated if he hears no foot on the stairs coming just too late to arrest him. Would those two men ever have made a break for it if they had not heard that the Minister was in the bay? No wonder the old man was in a state; they had slipped between the bars of his authority and he had to prove himself by their capture. He had sealed the island to make the game as apt as possible to his vanity. Yes, Artemis's vanity was involved too, and also his dissidence: he wanted to track the two criminals, but he hardly knew whether it was to recapture or to join them. It was to recapture them. He knew.

The girls were coming down the hill after him, laughing, tripping, drawing his attention back to them as if he were on a rope. He would cheerfully have killed them, exactly that. What a mistake to think that killing is always a serious matter! He would have killed them quite happily, choked them with their own laughter. Ah, what he would do for an unsmiling world! He hated their laughter like spittle. It festooned, laced, clotted on him, he wanted to fling himself naked into fire to avoid their tinkling happiness, both of them. And yet his steps slowed. This escape was too petty, to cheat two laughing girls.

They found the mothers already at home. Both the Minister's wife and Mrs Theodoros were exhausted and irritated by the stops which the *Pegasus* had made on the way back to the harbour. Several of the crew had been detailed to join the search, so the service had been lamentable. The ladies were both afraid of an alarm, with few men to protect them, and disappointed that there had not been one. The two convicts had literally disappeared; they said it in a tone of astonished grievance, as they did of a child who ran away rather than accept a beating. The real naughtiness lay not in what was done but in dodging punishment. Society will accept a criminal, like a chimney-sweep at a wedding, provided he performs his duty in exemplifying the proper scheme of things and makes no dirty marks. Those who bare their teeth at the hangman and wrestle with his assistant unsettle all who stand around. The governor and his guests are flattered by courage; it salutes their rank. Cowardice leaves them thoughtful.

Artemis left the girls at the house. They had had a dusty walk, flushed with surprising good spirits which had led them to chatter all the way, tease Artemis and giggle together with better humour than they had shared for years. It was a country stroll in the midst of a battle. They hugged themselves under the hot sun and skipped to their own rhythm of complacent innocence. Artemis frowned. He smiled only when he had returned them, like library books both overdue and unread, to the safety of the house and saw them stamped with the measured gaze of their mother. He skipped out of the linen-room window and across the carpet of drying geraniums to the boundary wall.

The pure problem of where the men could be perplexed him like an anagram. Little could be done to solve it by intelligent steps; the ingredients had to be left in the mind to resolve themselves. One tugged at strands of possibility like a neurotic fretting at a rug. Artemis climbed the ridge where he had gone with Katerina the day the Stratis family arrived. The double beach, with its fair and foul shores, was deserted. He went and sat down between the seas. Would they shoot the men? Would they punish them for their escape? He remembered Sallust's Jugurtha, thrust into the condemned cell, surfeited with cruel attentions, and his cry, 'How cold is this bath of yours!' The hour before execution, it haunted him. Yet when he heard that voice, that black voice from the pit, he was of the guards who stood around. The cry squeezed his heart, but it was the heart of the executioner, not of the victim.

He lay flat on the spit, toying with the unresisting sand like a watchful, amused lover with the flesh of a sleepy mistress. His head, rolling on the soft surface, produced that granular grating familiar to lovers who grind their heads together in a final tender gesture of touching disillusion; bodies fuse, heads resist. He undressed and strode into the thick sea. Plunging down gladly into the chill, he swam along the coast towards the flat saucer of rock beyond the promontory whose fallen fingers stretched and failed to reach it. The sea rose and sipped at the island, jostled it, like blood about a splinter. The anagram fell into an intelligible combination. Artemis headed for the flat and glistening saucer. He understood local gods as he approached, for the sea here seemed to breathe with a distinct cunning. It raised him high and dropped him towards the green teeth of submarine rocks. He swam the long way round, to find the sheltered side, but still the lift and fall daunted him. He flung himself forward with the rise and felt the heavy hammer of rock on his leg. He hoisted himself and peered into the island, his shoulders up to his ears. He scrambled up, his good leg given a lift by the returning sea. The whole flat face of the little island was clear to him, with a still pool at its centre and the grey badges of a minutely raised plateau drying, but never dry, under the frustrated sun. He crawled forward, gasping, the deadness of his knee an iron ball to his progress. He resented the men's absence because it made a fool of him, like finding that the solution one has intuited contains one letter too few. There was no cave, no hollow, nothing but the slop of the idiot sea, the local god powerless either to ignore or to conquer this dripping plot. His leg hurt; he frowned at it like a Government official at a pessimistic estimate. A wanton lethargy possessed him. He had an urge never to return to the mainland. If he allowed his life to be timed by the machinery of the Minister's vanity, he would be consumed like plankton by an amoeba. There would be no moment to scream, no sharp teeth would rend him; he would be painlessly surrounded by colourless, hungry jelly, jacketed in blubber. He might as well stay on the rock. When would he die? And what would they say of him? Most men would die happy if they could read their final notices. The obituary reveals the partiality of all other criticism. The dead are treated generously because no advantage can be wrung from them; they cannot advance a man's vanity or be touched for an invitation. Heaven would be full of kindness, not because of the fine characters of its inhabitants but because they would have nowhere better they could hope to go. Artemis examined his body with unsensual diligence. The smallness of his naked sex bent him to pull his foreskin, without pleasure, as if he had never seen it before. His testicles had retreated into an enclave of skin. It was a trick of civilization to make the thing so big. It was not natural, the closeted obsession of the city. Suicidal fantasy was a form of divinity, the masturbation of the soul. It played with the right to life; only man knew of it. The lemmings went in a crowd, merely misguided, but the intelligent suicide was a creative act, surer of its mark than the grapeshot of conception, and therefore more artistic, more perfect. Artemis lay there, an object of bone and gristle, shrivelling under the drizzle of spray and the caustic sun.

The shot stiffened him, but he was like a man in a crowd who fancies that someone is being shouted at and wonders who it is some time before he realizes that it is he. Someone was firing at him from the top of the hill. The bristle of long-gathered wheat made spines against the sky. A man on the summit was joined by another. Pebbles of shot fell like hard rain and sprang into the sea, short of Artemis. He frowned at the man as a goalkeeper might at a ball which scarcely rolled to his feet. He was being fired at. It had never happened to him before and, like Fabrizio del Dongo, he quickly analysed his experience. He encountered no jostle of alarmed ideas. He was simply in touch with the external world: they were firing at him. They fired and looked at the figure on the rock and then they fired again. Artemis stood up and faced them. The situation lacked irony; it was just a mistake, unless he ran. He could turn himself into a hunted man by the process of running. He dived into the sea. His flight excited the men high on the hill. They seemed to believe that an innocent man would not have taken exception to being a target. It was interesting to him, as he flailed for the beach, to consider why he had been sexually stirred by the shot before he appreciated himself to be its aim. He looked up towards the hill and saw that the men were still pointing and, to judge from the puffs of smoke, still firing at him. What better than to be sentenced to death, to be aware of the unmalicious murderousness of the pursuit, and to be out of range of the firing squad? He landed, drew his clothes over his wet body (so as not to wake from the dream by too much consideration of its logic) and ran along the spit towards the land. The gang were now running along the horizon, in the hope of cutting him off. His only line was along the path towards the farmhouse where he and

Katerina had met. He dreaded not so much being run down as simply being recognized, seeing the running men tail off with disappointment. If he had been two men, himself and a ghost, he could have deceived them beautifully, but now he could hear cries and saw another party, looking not for him but for those who had fired the shots, galloping to the guns with all the brave hurry of those who outnumbered their prey. Where was he? He could never pass the beach and make the game really interesting. He scampered down the steep donkey-path to the back of the farm. And then, as he jogged into the lee of the buildings, he was puzzled to see two men running back the way he had just come, towards the beach. He gasped with laughter, taking them for two of the pursuers who had outstripped the others and overshot him. Then he realized: it was the two convicts. He had flushed them. They were running behind the farm and were still invisible to the on-coming men. He watched them go, lurching with the wounds they had yet to receive, fighting the swell of the ground. Artemis crouched for breath, sobbing with laughter (uncertain whether it was 'genuine' or not) and then ambled forward to the plateau of sunshine in front of the collapsed building. He bowed to the two groups of men which were toiling to him, a modest star taking a solo call. He shook his head in mournful apology, like a man wittily but incorrectly accused of having done it in a game of murder. He denied misleading them and asked, laughing, whether they really expected their quarry to lie out on a rock and wait to be spotted. 'You were a damned fool anyway,' said Dmitri, who turned out to have been the first to see him. 'You must've known anyone on his own'd be likely to be suspected.' He was squatting on his haunches. 'I haven't run so much for years.'

'You made very good time, considering.'

The Minister was on his way on a donkey, drumming his heels. They waved to him to relax and pointed to Artemis, but he pressed on.

'Had any luck at all – I mean apart from missing me?'

'Nothing. As you gathered. I must say, I don't think much of you sunning yourself when everyone else is breaking his back. You certainly believe in letting other people do the work.'

'Report to me, Lieutenant. Is there a sighting?'

'Captain Asphelides, sir. It was all a misunderstanding. This party fired on our friend here thinking he was one of the escapers.'

'What the devil were you doing?'

'I beg your pardon?'

'Getting yourself fired at.'

'We've been into that.'

'Have we indeed? I'm beginning to have enough of your insolence, young man. You've diverted these men from the pursuit just at the most critical stage, just as we had them boxed.'

'Whereabouts did you say they were, sir, then?'

'I said nothing. If you must know, my belief is that they're now pinned in a triangle between the village, the monastery and the valley road.'

'Ah! Well, I just saw them running up that path towards the double beach.'

'You saw them? When? What do you mean you saw them? Is this another of your jokes?'

'I think that's where you'll find them,' Artemis indicated.

'I shan't forgive this.' The Minister jerked his head at the captain whom he had accidentally demoted a moment before. Asphelides saluted with eyes which identified Artemis as the final enemy and signalled to his men to move off at the double. 'I'm not unaware of your activities.'

Dmitri scratched himself and inspected the barrel of his gun. 'I think I'll see if I can help. They might need some more men to take the flank. Were they armed, by the way, Artemis, these chaps when you saw them?'

'Only machine-guns.' Artemis was heavy with the knowledge that he had betrayed the two convicts out of spite against the Minister. They were to be taken *en passant*, victims of a more radical strategy than they would ever witness for themselves. 'Enough to give you a bit of fun.'

217

'Machine-guns, where did they get machine-guns? Nonsense!
'I didn't notice,' said Artemis. 'You tell me later.'

'You realize,' said the Minister of Marine, 'that I could have
you committed for trial on a charge of aiding and abetting escaped
criminals?'

This time with deliberate mockery Artemis looked round to
see who could deserve this charge. 'Me? I hardly think you'd risk
a *trial*, would you? I dare say you might have me shot to avoid the
embarrassment of my presence, but I can't believe in a *trial*.'

'You've treated my daughter disgracefully. I gather you've said
a number of intolerable things to her, things she wouldn't like to
repeat.'

'We're not going to marry.'

'Who are you to say that to me?'

'Theodoros Artemis, Minister. No rank.'

'Your insolence is noted. Your insolence is noted.'

'May I ask, Minister, since I am hoping to make my career in
journalism, what exactly took place in the discussions you have
been having with Mr Asteris Stratis and Mr Sophocles Theodoros? Was there any political significance or were you, as I am
told, merely arranging a little excursion on the stock market?' It
seemed as if the Minister had literally exploded. Pops and bangs
burst from about his head like crackers from a lay figure. The men
on the ridge behind where he was standing had opened fire. 'I'm
warning you, young man. I could have you arrested for seditious
libel. I could have you committed to an island. I have the power.'

Artemis walked the first section of the tunnel. After that, the roof
closed over him. For some metres farther it was still possible to
walk upright. Then he had to bend. His sense of smell had been
so raped by war that he was not disturbed by the sewage, but its
sluggish floor caused him to flounder and slap the fungoid vault of
the tunnel; his eyes strained to find shapes ahead. From time to
time a panel of moonlight fell in elongated lines from a grille in
the road. He struck a match to search for the crick in the tunnel.

Once he heard marching feet above him. He was aware of rats. Another smaller sewer ran into his; he quite resented the foreign sludge which frothed and bubbled through the grating. For a few metres he thought he could distinguish between the old serpentine trail and the new lumpy current. Then he came to the division. A cold tray of light fell from a grille. He saw iron stirrups up the corner. Why would Katerina bring him so far and then betray him? But why not go on to the harbour and get out there, where no one could be expecting him? The marching feet could have had a destination. They could have been there to mock him. He started up the iron ladder. He reached the top and had his hands against the plate. If she was as secretive, as delighting in deceit as she seemed to be, then he should press on. But was she? Why had she come all that way with him and fed him so carefully, like a ramrod, into this long barrel? He knew the harbour. It was visible from the hill where his section was encamped. He knew the back streets. There would be patrols down at the arsenal and the warehouses, but among the alleys? He descended, the smell of the sewer steaming at him now, and resumed his way, along the left fork towards the sea. It was a narrow walk; the yellow gas seized his strength. He stumbled through the crusted leak of sewage. He was disgusted, slipped and had to hand himself off the bottom, wristed in crud. He held his hand like a broken thing. He took a curve and saw dull light ahead, a coin of reflected radiance: bogus moon. The end of the tunnel was checked with iron bars. The sewage ran on under the beach. Another set of iron crampons climbed to a man-hole in the roof of the tunnel. From the end Artemis could see the placid waters of the gulf; supply ships lay at anchor.

His meeting with Katerina had the elusive melancholy of a distant episode. He could hardly believe that he had actually fucked her for the first time that night. He had once thought – had he ever matched such an idea with reality? – that there could be the beginnings of a new world in a man and a woman, a fidelity which promised the renewal of hope in human life. And wouldn't that time come with the making of a child? He resented, with a cold, ironic resentment, quite unlike the frustrated passion of his adolescence, the demanding desire which Katerina had shown towards him and which had wrenched his seed from him as she might have torn a green branch for firewood. She had burned him up for her own selfish warmth and the smoke of her smiling and predatory aggression smarted still. He recognized the web she was trying to spin for him; she was appealing to what she had found the most trustworthy of all motives, the cannibal greed which makes one feel more manly for the destruction of another. She had taunted him to wrestle again, not with her, but with her husband. She had egged him on to fight him. He was as frustrated of Katerina as he had ever been. He might as well have made one of those pilgrimages a romantic makes to visit the girl who tortured his youth. He has promised her that he is happy in another life and that has taunted her, as he hoped, to reclaim his attention. She is married; he is not. He has forgotten her pettiness as well as his own demonstrative derision towards her. He imagines that he is going to collect a deserved tribute. It is now the girl who is going to suffer, not he. Why would she bother to call him, why would she arrange that he come when her husband is at the office, why would she reopen the past if it is not because she regrets her error? He abandons intelligence at the prospect of a triumph. He omits to think that a woman will hardly bother to summon him from the grave of the past in order to make amends. The meeting with Katerina, that unchanged but now more expressive, more voracious woman, had clubbed Artemis like a comic ambush. He reeled with the delayed effects of it. He faced the long march back to a future which lacked form, while, despite all the force which the revolution had brought to bear against the capital, she remained irreducibly domesticated. Society understood her and backed her. Her argot was a language which could never express Artemis's hopes or fears, but it suited her, that unremarkable patois of the drawing-room. She was stronger than he.

He gathered himself at the top of the iron ladder and pushed his palms up against the metal trap. It held for an instant and then yielded into the darkness. The moon had gone out as abruptly as a metered light on a landing. On either side of the street were the offices of shipping lines, some still placarded with posters for pre-war journeys. Cheap passages to America were promised in colours which began to declare themselves to Artemis as he reached the narrow pavement. The sudden explosion of light seemed to him a mistake. It was as if he had been woken in an hotel to which he had gone for a rest, having given specific instructions that he was not to be disturbed. He frowned. He could see no one, until, like simultaneous waiters with an unwanted banquet, he saw the grave figures of men stepping into shadows which pointed, like accusing fingers, at himself. He turned and would have reached for his gun – for now there was no mistaking the situation – but for his shitty hand, which he could not persuade under his clothes. Already beginning his inquest on the business, he bothered to ask himself why he hesitated to soil himself now when he had gone through more squalid things with less hesitation. The little square was fenced with military vehicles of American manufacture. Yet there was a kind of deferential area in the centre, where he had emerged, where he might have enjoyed a longer provisional liberty had he been less confident. There was an area they yielded to him and for this he was able to be grateful. It gave him time to recover his sense of power. He awaited their violence with contempt.

'Will you come with us, please?' They scarcely touched him. He might even have escaped if he had shown sufficient sharpness, but his amazement connived at his arrest. They touched his arm as they might to guide an old banker to his limousine. They showed him into a closed van, one of the only vehicles around the place not of foreign origin. They had bludgeoned strikers into one like it after the assault on his father's office. Artemis had assisted in the defence of the building.

The van moved through silent streets. There was no whining of sirens, no sound of an escort. It was past midnight. The city was small in the absence of traffic; even in normal times it was rarely a long journey from one quarter to another. Two uniformed men and one in plain clothes rode with Artemis in the back. Two others were up front. One of the men with him was sore from shaving late in the day. The strap of his helmet rubbed. The van went between guarded gates and halted in a courtyard. The doors were opened from outside.

'You have him?'

'Of course.' Of course! If he had trusted a woman he could not trust … 'Out!'

The yard contained a few men in dark clothes, carrying machineguns. There was a white wall with potted plants in wired brackets on the far side. To the left were garages, once stables; on the right thick, dark hedge. Artemis glanced behind him, but was corrected by the man at his elbow, as a prince might be to avoid the embarrassment of his going to the wrong platform to take the salute. The courtyard rang with their steps. They were admitted through a door with light behind an ornamental metal screen.

Artemis had been trying to make police headquarters out of the forms of the night, but then another door was opened and he was led across the tiled hall to a big room with a figured plaster ceiling in the French style. There were few mansions of such pretensions in the capital. The room was lined on two sides with bookshelves; the free wall contained a marble mantelpiece flanked by two large frames of Coptic weavings. Tall windows overlooked the garden. A Persian carpet enriched the black and white checkered floor. Two flags, tattered and grey with age, hung from their staffs behind the desk in the far corner. As Artemis was brought in, a man rose and came out from behind the desk. It was Dmitri Stratis. They were in the house of the Prime Minister.

'My dear Artemis, how are you?'

'I am well, thank you, Dimmy. How are you?'

'Well.' Dmitri nodded to the escort. They hesitated, confirmed the order to each other, and went. 'So. You came.'

'I came.'

'I was afraid you wouldn't. I bet Katerina that you would refuse. I thought you less – '

'Sentimental. Perhaps I should have been.'

'She said you'd come.'

'Are you congratulating her or yourself?'

Dmitri laughed. 'Still the same little owl.'

'What do you want with me?'

'Want with you? My dear Artemis, you're a dangerous man. A convicted traitor. Why should you think I must have a reason for wanting you? You're wanted!'

'Have you had me brought here simply to gloat over my capture?'

'Slowly, slowly, my little owl. Not so fast. First, are you hungry? They tell me that supplies haven't been getting through so easily these last few weeks. They say you're feeling the pinch.'

'The capital hardly seems flowing with milk and honey.'

'But here I have both! The Prime Minister is only a working man, of course, but I have my little privileges. Like the Political Committee. Even you, they say, enjoy a drop of *koniak* from time to time, no?'

'I shall tell you nothing.'

'Of course you won't. Of course you won't. Even assuming that there's something you know which I don't. I shouldn't rely on that, by the way. Our sources are extraordinarily good. I've heard a deal about you, Artemy, these last months, quite a good deal!'

'And we about you, my friend.'

'Good. Then we're both well informed. What will you have? A drop of whisky?'

'How proud you are of your foreign connections!'

'My dear Artemy, I'm not so narrow-minded as you people. I lack your Draconian attitudes. Believe me. That's why I've brought you here.'

'I should like to wash my hands.'

'My dear friend, of course. How very unpleasant! Of course. I wonder – it would make things very much easier, very much less dramatic if you were prepared to give me your word not to escape. It would make the melodrama less necessary. Are you prepared to do that? There's such a lot I want to say to you.'

'You have a lot of faith in your enemies, Dimmy.'

'Enemies! It's precisely that I want to discuss. This whole question of enmity. Have no fear, Artemy, I don't intend to have you done away with, you're far too valuable for that. If that's what worries you, what holds you back from giving your word, please don't give it another thought.'

'I have no word to give you.'

'Artemy, must you always rush to the extreme position? I know what you're trying to say, that we have no language in common. That you are already committed elsewhere. I want to talk to you about all this. But first – ' Dmitri rang a small handbell (it came from a monastery) and the plain-clothes man came in – 'Inspector Angelou, will you take our guest to wash?'

The bathroom had a grille over the window, designed to keep intruders out, not prisoners in. Artemis washed himself. His gun had been removed on capture, of course, as a man's coat is taken from him, even as he greets his host, at a fashionable restaurant.

'Good! Better now? Excellent! Thank you, Inspector. You can do as we said now. Your men have done an excellent job.'

Angelou looked keenly at Artemis and at the Prime Minister before bowing and withdrawing. 'Good night, sir.'

'Angelou is a serious man. He never allows himself to be hurried. I like that in a policeman. Artemy, a few preliminary points. The men who captured you, who brought you here, do not know your name and except for the inspector they imagine that you are a member of my staff who has been working for us on the other side. They were told that you were returning from a dangerous mission and were there to give you assistance if there was any attempt to kidnap you at the last moment. In all of this, of course, you will appreciate there was some truth. You saw Katerina, of course?'

'I saw her. You must be proud of her.'

'Katerina? Of course. Artemis, we haven't much time. I need

your help. My understanding is that the Political Committee has decided on a retreat. Well?'

'You're telling me.'

'Artemy, this is our country. We both have positions of some influence over its destinies. If I were asking you about the dispositions of your men on the march or about your tactics in the later stages of your dispersal, if it is to be a dispersal, I'd expect you to be silent and I would either honour it or try to break it by less diplomatic means. You know what I'm talking about.'

'Very well.'

'Very well. I'm not asking you to make any such revelations. I said we didn't have much time. I'm not decided yet, but my calculations, such as they are, don't exclude your release. I give you my strongest weapon right away. I don't exclude your release. Indeed I intend it. That's why I want to talk seriously and at once. My problem is not the defeat of your forces. That will be taken care of. Your retreat is decreed; I have no doubt that it will be carried out. Please let's waste no time bluffing on that score. The question is what will happen to the country after the disintegration of your forces. That's why I wanted to see you. It's perfectly possible, in strictly military terms, for us to govern the country without any further changes in our political structure. There are those in my Cabinet who advocate just this. They include men whom you might find more congenial than I. Men who never drink Scotch whisky. Men like Democritos. He favours the eviction of all foreign influence and the imposition of a rule of true force, as he puts it. That is to say, he wants to eliminate all foreign aid and allow the country to discover what he calls, as you might expect, "the facts of life". He fears that the people will not appreciate just how strong we are if they see us constantly supported by foreign elements. Isn't there a similar conflict of views in your own ranks? I'm not asking for an answer; it's obvious. I'm not in favour of this Puritanism of repression. I don't believe in moral demonstrations, proper poverty and so on. I want to see the lot of the people improved and improved dramatically. I intend to do this as quickly as possible. I'm trying to imagine the future. In certain respects it isn't that difficult. The revolution will fade out. I don't say that it will never recur, your people's army, but I don't believe it will do so during our lifetime, yours and mine, Artemy. Very well, we shall be faced with a period of bourgeois rule. I'm not going to mince words; your vocabulary embarrasses me less than mine embarrasses you. We shall be progressive in speech at least. Take all the battles on the way for granted, your last stand, your defiance, your subversion, your scorched earth, all these things have their chapters in the future and we shall no doubt read about them in due course. They'll change nothing. The country will chase the revolution out because it's written in the stars, you know what I mean. Then what? Democritos, who is an extremely able officer, as I'm sure you know, is a zealot. He really believes, with all the fervour of a man who has nearly gone the other way, that unity can be imposed on the country. He believes that the Democratic – or Democritic – Party can govern indefinitely with perhaps a few splinter groups to its right to give it the appearance of a liberal posture and a very few to its left to be blamed for anything that disturbs the peace. He believes that the working classes will vote for us because there will be no one else effectively to vote for. The police, my dear Artemis, will thus become the ruling group. Now, look at it how you will, this is hardly comforting, either for me or for the people. I face the prospect – and I know you'll believe me more if I put this thing in a selfish light – of being evicted from office as the old politicians were by the Marshal. Democritos will stop at nothing, because not stopping is his principle, his only policy. He will engineer a crisis and he will impose a junta. But this is not South America. Those who support us may wish that it was, I refer to our Western Allies, but it isn't. The eyes of Europe are shortsighted, but we are inescapably in their view. So – Democritos threatens me and he threatens the good name of our country. Believe it or not, the latter consideration moves me very much. Vanity as well as self-interest if you like. What is to happen to the ordinary people when you withdraw? Politically there'll be a vacuum. They'll be feared and threatened by Democritos and they will be unrepresented in the state. Without any sort of organization, they'll fall victims to despair and to adventurers. They'll lack a voice and we shall have no means of measuring their feelings. I may not be the spokesman of History, but I'm trying to make things clear to you. Both you and I, Artemis, both the Party and the Government might have their reasons for dismissing the feelings and the lives of those who arc left behind as irrelevant. They have failed to march with you, so they are lacking in spirit and deserve what they get; that's your side. We could say equally that they helped you when you were winning and that they must take their chance now that you are to be beaten. Yet there they are. What's to be done with them?'

'That's your problem. We must hope that it breaks you.'

'It won't, Artemis, and I believe you know it. I realize that you're a convert and that you're attracted to orthodoxy as only a convert can be. It's curious how a convert, believing in free will – otherwise how could he be converted? – will always choose a system which eliminates choice. However … Breaks us how?'

'Through indigestion.'

'It won't, if only because there are always outside sources who can feed us – I refer to the Government and its supporters – through external means. A drip, so to say We shan't starve; the people will. How can that improve your hopes? And what are those hopes? Are they merely for power? Are they merely political? In that case, we are two indistinguishable gangs! Are they merely the gambler's hope that his predictions for a given runner will eventually pay off if he backs it long enough? Or is there a humane element in them? As usual, Artemy, I look to you for instruction.'

'We shall prevail because in the long run our system is more just and because you know it. You know very well that all this talk of patriotism is false. The system which you're resurrecting from its deathbed, just as they did the Marshal's all those years back, is a system devoted to the enrichment of a few at the expense of the

227

many, engaged in a perpetual battle to persuade those whom it exploits of the virtues of exploitation. It's a game of rape which replaces serious and correct relations through the insolent pretence that it is more natural – and by means of the vulgar argument that no one should stop it because everyone stands a chance of a turn.'

Dmitri clapped his hands. 'My God, I wish I was still as young as you manage to be, Artemy. I'd join the revolution tomorrow if you could guarantee my youth back. I don't suppose you can, can you?'

'You force me to explain it in cold terms.'

'Don't be angry with me, Artemy, I mean it: I wish I could be sure of becoming as young as you if I came over to your side.'

'It's true, you see, even though you make a jest of it. You will find no youth on your side, ever. Those who come to you exchange their blood for bonds.'

'Artemy, I realize the pleasures to be derived from turning this into a morality play in which you have the good fortune to play the Good Fairy or the Bright Future or any other enlightened role you like to choose while I am sentenced to be the Robber Chief, but there isn't time for that now in my view. I am concerned, believe it or not, motivate it how you will, with the future of this country. Can you honestly say to me that you are no more concerned with our people than with anyone else, that you can entertain the idea of a lifetime across the border without a feeling of remorse or of disappointment? Is language not a real thing, blood and social institutions just as much as class, as the productive order? Well?'

'A man isn't obliged to have answers to everything in order to have the right to maintain a loyalty. Men cannot be refuted, only their arguments, that's what I mean to say. You can't make alternatives out of the categories you mentioned. No one on our side denies the reality of blood or of language; all the same I'm very suspicious of what you're trying to make of them. What we say, if you really want to know, is that the economic role determines but doesn't fully describe, that's what I'd say.'

'Thank you. No, I'm serious. I'm serious. You believe in redemption, I gather. The irrefutability of man. I like that very much. I shall remember it.'

'Man is an incomplete symbol. Not through bad luck, through language. He could be a complete symbol only if language were given him *a priori*. If it were capable of being exhausted. Then the circuit would be closed. As it is, it can't be. That's my opinion. Though I don't know where it gets us.'

'You fought with Athanasiou's partisans, our people. At the early stages. Why?'

'I wet my pants. So did you. At the early stages. Why?'

'You regret your time with them?'

'I wouldn't be where I am now if I hadn't had the education of the patriotic war. Regrets are pointless.'

'Yet we have them. Don't we?'

'Over the war? No. I'm not ashamed of fighting with the Royalist forces, if you can call it fighting. It's no secret.'

'I want this meeting to be, Artemy, by the way. It *is* as far as my colleagues are concerned. It might give them a powerful weapon against me if they were to know of it.'

'Your colleagues?'

'In the Cabinet. They don't know of this meeting. It's an initiative of my own. Some of them think of you as a plague-carrier. They'd be afraid of your contaminating me. So you see, incidentally, as a sign of good faith if you like, I've handed you the opportunity to plot my overthrow.'

'I haven't given you my word about escaping. We're clear on that, aren't we?'

'Perfectly clear. I don't believe you'll escape, apart from the physical difficulties, because it would be like running away from yourself. And I think, apart from the question of courage, that you're too interested in yourself to let that happen. Too interested in assessing your real capabilities. What's going to happen to you, Artemy? Doubtless you'll display your usual owl-like cunning on the retreat, I m not talking about that, but despite your warrior's aspirations you're really a man of peace, a man who thinks. How are you going to spend the rest of your life?'

'I don't know. It's an irrelevance. This cult of premature biography. I see no point in ambitions.'

'But you have them. The desire to survive. To have made a mark. Even to have made a child. The facts are there, Artemy, in all of us, the evidence of individuality. Shall I tell you the real weakness of Karl Marx? He was an exile twice over. A Jew and an exile. A man without a country, living outside even the country he was born in. How could such a man present a whole picture of the world, of the springs of human action, how? And Freud the same, of course. The emphasis on the family because the country meant nothing to him. Introspection as landscape. The inclination they both had to look back, to argue from piety, wasn't it a kind of nostalgia for an Eden they never knew? They dismissed boundaries because they had never known them. They never had a language of their own. I'm not gloating, I'm not judging, but isn't it the truth? All I'm saying, Artemy, is that there are more ways of living than by adherence to abstract systems. Why give yourself up to a religion without salvation? Argue as you will, we only live once. We only live so long. You wouldn't deny that? Don't be so patient with me. You and I, Artemy, we grew up together; I grew up, you stayed young, you know what I mean. We went to Helen's together. We shared cunt. I haven't forgotten even if you have. Pilar? We can look down on the world together, you and I, and we know that things aren't as – what? – cosmic as the newspapers make out. We've been on the pinnacle of the temple together. Believe it or not, I don't look forward to ruling this country, not if it means ruling a sullen, depressed, hostile population. I'll do it, because I can do nothing else. I'm committed like a tragic actor. I can't play farce; no one would recognize my versatility. How can I bring the peasantry, the workers to life? Money, of course. But that doesn't always have the required effect. I'm asking you how I am to avoid a confrontation which you will be powerless to exploit but which will lead to the repression of the people you champion. You're going to leave them powerless. What are you prepared to do to help them?'

Artemis looked at his clean hand. 'I don't necessarily believe in private enterprise.'

'Classic! Classic Artemis. You always were a prig.'

'Why do you want to give me the power to bring you down?'

'No, no, you won't escape like that!'

'Because you know your own weakness. Because you want to expose yourself.'

'Your counter-attack comes too soon, too predictably. Please sit down. Artemy, listen to me, please. It's premature, this. And never rely on repetition as a dramatic device. It works only in farce. I tell you, my old friend, we're faced with a country which either retains its cohesion, its power of being itself, or which is sold off like bankrupt stock, given away like the island Katerina's father was given because the peasants couldn't be bothered to work it any longer. A repository is what this country can become if we all leave it. All. Yes. I shall remain only as a caretaker, like the owner of a shop sold off to its creditors where the proprietor stays on as a lackey. I see all this very clearly. So what's to be done? Artemis, let's have no illusions. I can lock you up for the rest of your life. I can have you shot now. Here in the cellars. I'm not necessarily going to be a sportsman. Just keep that at the back of your mind.'

'I pity you, Dmitri. You wish that we'd won. I wish it too.'

'Then we're on the same side, at least in your mind. I'm delighted.'

'You've got some proposal you want to make, Dmitri, haven't you?'

'What a bad girl you would have made, Artemy. You put one off by making one feel self-conscious. You display yourself too much.'

'I'm not a girl.'

'At times I see why you're a totalitarian. You lack patience. That's probably why you lost Katerina.'

'Did I lose her?'

'You lost her because you didn't want her. I don't argue that. I'm not making a triumph out of what happened. But I do know what happened, that's all I wanted to make clear to you.'

'I've never desired possessions. Those who possess things spend all their time worrying about having them stolen. Rightly.'

'You're a pedant, Artemy. You can understand only those categories which have existed for some time. You pretend to understand the future because it's so far away, that golden future you dream about anyway, that no one can ever say that you're wrong about it. It's only the actual future, which we shall have to inhabit, that you won't look at. Because, I suspect, you are profoundly ignorant of your fellow human beings. Nevertheless, because I know you, because we've been together at funny times, I want you to make an effort for your country.'

'What can you suppose that I would do for it that you could recommend?'

'You don't know how close you are to being beaten to jelly, Artemis. By me, I mean. Out of sheer frustration. For personal reasons.'

'I trust Your Honour is in health.'

'I'm not a sportsman, I told you. I should have you held.'

'Ah!'

'Artemis, the workers and the peasants require a leader. A man whom they can trust.'

'*A* leader! *A* man! How little you understand them. Hardly surprising since you never go near them, but – '

'You take me for a fool. I think that ungenerous and unwise. Allow me to tell you what I have in mind. The revolutionary army is about to disperse. Are you really prepared to abandon your seed-corn to the rats? Are you so insanely sure of the predictions in your Nostradamus? I tell you, even if you are, you have a duty to your time, a duty not to race ahead, as you always will. Isn't there a treason even to your own ideas in sitting out a whole generation? Tell me, what should I do now? Should I abdicate? What would happen? Democritos. That doesn't appal you. I'll tell you what Democritos would do to you. He'd tear your balls off. I mean it. What am I to do? Vanish into my mother's womb? Take my wealth out of the country? I have very little, believe it or not. In cash, very little. So, I must stay. The country must be administered. Artemis, I beg of you. Help me.'

'My dear Dimmy, I understand your pain. Believe me. What else can I say?'

'I'm the prisoner here, Artemis. And you're the only person to whom I can say it. Oh, don't let's be too pitiful! I can support my role very well, whatever happens, make no mistake about that. What your side finds it hard to believe and what I ask you personally to believe, because you and I share a sort of accidental but inescapable proximity, like coming next to each other in a register, is that I am concerned with things beyond myself. I'm not concerned to rule at any price and in any circumstances; I don't intend to punish the country with my authority. I want to help it. Will you help me?'

'You'll have to be more accurate if you want to engage me,' Artemis said.

'I want to work with you, Artemy,' Dmitri laughed, 'because I like you so much. Do you find that credible? "More accurate!" I enjoy your jargon, Artemy. I enjoy your pedantry. It challenges me. I mean it. I grow very tired of the rhetoric of my colleagues. All of this is off the record, you understand, completely off the record.'

'It doesn't matter to me.'

'Of course it matters to you. You're engaging in a conversation with the deadliest enemy of your movement. It doesn't matter to you? You're betraying your friends at this very moment, aren't you?'

'I'm a prisoner.'

'You look very unhappy about saying that. Does it not convince you? No, you're admitting a morality beyond your party's. By talking to me like this.'

'And you?'

233

'I have no principles! I can do as I please. There is no gospel so far as I'm concerned. You play by the rules; I don't. Unlike you, I've never claimed a monopoly of virtue. Or even an interest in it!'

'Your cynicism is completely disgusting. Have no illusions about that, Dimmy.'

'My cynicism is completely essential. It is your dogmatism which is disgusting. It's a continuation of Nazism. No, I believe that very seriously. It's social racism.'

'My dear Dimmy, you've practised it towards the working class, you and your friends, for generations. I prefer you as the ruthless self-seeker to your discordant attempts to be a thinker. Please tell me what it is you have in mind that I should do, so that I can refuse and we can proceed to the next stage.'

'It's on my conscience, luckily for you, that I've lured you into this meeting. I'm not ashamed; I think it was rather amusing, but I do have some pangs of conscience. I should hate to hand you over to the cellars of Heracles Street after getting you here in such an unwarlike way. I appealed to your vanity, Artemy, and you came. I don't blame you. Life isn't worth living if we give up all interest in ourselves. What is false is the pretence that you have no such interest. Your whole life is consumed with – what? – not self-interest perhaps, but interest in yourself. You believe yourself important.'

'That's not so. I would willingly accept an anonymous position. More than willingly; happily.'

'Which relates again to your own state of mind. Perhaps it's true. But others are not concerned with your happiness as you imagine it but as they observe it, which is why you find yourself thrust into positions of importance. You can't escape prominence any more than I can. I say: we're brothers, Artemy, of a kind. Can you deny it? Neither of us will ever be suffered to evade the limelight.'

'I can't accept this conjunction you're trying to foist on me. This merger. Our attitudes have nothing in common except that each of us prefers to be the subject of a sentence rather than the object.'

'I promise you, Artemy, that this retreat of yours will be longer than you can believe at this moment. It will outlast us both. It may – I say only may – lead to nothing. It will contain treacheries and disappointments which you cannot imagine. You will be leaving your country not for a time, but for ever. I don't have to say a word of this to you. I'm under no obligation to try to help you, God knows. Why do you suppose I'm doing it? Well? No, no, shrugging your shoulders isn't an answer. That owl-like face won't do, Artemy. Why, damn you?'

'Because you can't bear anything to be beyond your power?'

'Let that be the reason. A reason. Empty though it is. Then what? I could have you torn to pieces before my eyes. I could have you screaming for mercy. Don't doubt that, will you, Artemy?'

'I don't doubt it.'

'After some of the things your people have done, I'd be within my rights. After some of your actions. Believe me, Artemy, there's some justice on our side. I hope you're aware of that. There's some justice on our side too. If I want to prove my power over you I hand you over to the cellars. Perhaps you'd have preferred it if I'd had you broken before I spoke to you. I thought you capable of taking the torture for granted, of allowing me the force of my position and taking it from there. You seem to be unequal to that.'

'My dear Dimmy, I think that form of self-congratulation rather diminishing for a man in your position. You imagine that I am to believe that you refrain from torturing me because you want to persuade me of something. Isn't it more plausible to believe that you want me to refuse to be persuaded in order that you should be justified in torturing me?'

'There's nothing you know that we don't know. The numbers and dispositions of your men, your plans for retreat, your friends, your formations, nothing. You're a scoured vessel as far as we're concerned. There's nothing you could tell us. No fact we don't possess.'

'That's what proves you shit.'

'Artemis, I forbid this line. I forbid it. You're wasting our time, and I won't allow it.'

'Let me explain. To know everything, as you claim, and still to persist! You could kick a hole in this Government, Dimmy, from which it could never recover. You want me to come over to you. Why won't you come over to us? You rely on us – for your seriousness, for your ... your sense of ... of position in history, in life itself. You depend on us. We determine you. You don't determine us. I tell you, Dimmy, the true battle is within our ranks, not between us and you.'

Dmitri strode out from behind his desk and limped across the room. He glanced again and again at Artemis, who watched him as a physicist might the effect of an electric current on some previously inert mass. Dmitri's excitement required attention.

'The future is with us,' Artemis added, creaming an extra current into the experiment.

'I know what you mean.' Dmitri came back to where Artemis was sitting. 'I can't come over to you. I *can't*. And you can come to us. I can't bring anything to you. You can to us.'

'Consider the possibilities,' said Artemis. 'For the sake of example – '

'For the sake of example! Artemy, this is truly a great occasion – '

'I'm proposing this only as an example. I have no power to make any formal suggestion, as you well know. I didn't know this meeting was going to take place.'

'You give me faith in the future! I mean it, truly. Faith in the future. Perhaps it will have a kind of humour after all, a sense of its own provisional status, as you might say.'

'Humour is a form of liberalism,' Artemis said. 'Goodwill instead of action.'

'I'll remember. Tell me, seriously, what do you suggest? This example of yours, I want to hear it.'

'What would happen if you made a dramatic proposal? For the sake of the country. To prevent further bloodshed between brothers. You propose a ceasefire followed by temporary talks designed to allow families to be reunited, the exchange of prisoners, if there are any alive to be exchanged, the feeding of the starved or the deprived, etcetera etcetera. I would like to imagine a period of energetic tidying-up, perhaps no more than that. And following that, discussions between the sides towards a peaceful settlement – '

'This has been offered. We've offered this.'

'And coinciding with that a statement by your Government that it will not tolerate the interference in our affairs of any foreign power. The renunciation of Western aid, the complete, irreversible, deliberately provocative expropriation of Western businesses, a national coalition. A national coalition in spirit followed by a coalition Government in which the Party holds the Interior and other, as they say, key posts.'

'Fantasy. Pure fantasy. We should never be allowed to get away with it. Even if it were a conceivable policy. I mean a sensible one.'

'Given that it's a fantasy. Given that there are no other conditions under which to discuss this thing, who is to prevent us from getting away with it?'

'What you will never understand, Artemy, is that I am the very best you can hope for in the way of a prime minister. I represent the nearest thing to a reasonable choice that you're likely to find on this side. You imagine that there are dozens of men no worse than I am. It's not so. Imagine what Colonel Democritos would say if he knew of this meeting. He would shoot me even before he shot you!'

'I don't believe for a moment that he doesn't know of it.'

'What's that?'

'Am I really supposed to believe that the Minister of the Interior is not aware of what Inspector Angelou has been doing this evening?'

'He knows you've been brought here. He has no idea of the terms of our discussion. Angelou, I mean. Yes, probably he has passed the word to Democritos. But then Democritos's record isn't that perfect. He's given hostages to fortune.'

'That's what makes him her favourite.'

'Yes, yes. I realize that. Nevertheless, he can only represent interests from now on, never conscience. Which is what makes him dangerous, probably fatal to any attempt to evict the powers, as you were proposing. They will arm him and he will intervene. Interests always prevail over moralities. That's the nature of history.'

'Then he must be removed.'

'Assassinated? That's an elderly idea. There's always another man ready to serve the interests. There's no cleaning that particular stable – '

'Except by diverting the waters of history, quite. If he cannot be removed, he must be weakened. He must not be accused; he must be betrayed. The West will flinch from supporting a man who is proved to have rounded up the Hebrews and been responsible for their dispatch. Their own bad conscience makes them intolerant of such people. We can easily make evidence available to the courts.'

'We can make *any* evidence available, agreed. Very well, suppose that we manage to have this coalition, that we stun the powers into allowing it. What then? This coalition, how long will it last?'

'A very short time. I'm not suggesting anything stable. We must detach the country from the Western circuit, so to say. I tell you, Dmitri, in the long run, the West will play the part of the invaders. They will distort our society as the Germans did and ruin our morale as they did until the partisans took to the hills.'

' "In the long run, we're all dead", ' quoted Dmitri. 'What you're suggesting means the destruction of the power of the notables. Do you really think that I can't see that? The notables could never survive, could never retain even a portion of power if what you suggest were to take place. Do you think I'm such a fool I can't see that?'

'My dear Dimmy, I *assumed* you'd see it. What you have achieved by bringing the West into your camp is precisely the situation which overwhelmed Byzantium. You have welcomed the Crusaders who will eventually destroy the city, who have no care for you, who are bound to you only by greed for what you can help them get. And eventually you will be part of the prize.

It's not as simple as that maybe, but that's how it is. By God, it *is* the same story, and the same pretence of a shared metaphysic keeps you in allegiance to your conquerors.'

'You're offering me the choice of being eaten by strangers or being eaten by friends. Does it really make any difference, except that I shall be fattened a great deal more comfortably by the strangers?'

'Now you've reverted to yourself, your own position. In which case the fantasy is at an end. You asked me how the country could be saved. You end by discussing your own accommodation.'

'How long would I survive with you in a position of power, my dear Artemy?'

'That's an irrelevance if your idea of country means anything. I don't think that I should necessarily survive in the Party if this conversation were to become known as the origin of the coalition. Because, in the middle stages, I think it might well seem that the Party was the tiresome, divisive, destructive element. It might find it necessary to throw me to the wolves, to denounce the coalition itself as a next stage towards negotiating a larger share of the power. It would probably accuse me of having conspired for a sell-out. I offer you my position for yours, if that's any comfort. If my plan were to work, I should be its first victim, just as Dr Guillotine was supposed to have been.'

'But wasn't,' Dmitri said. 'Your head is too valuable on your shoulders for me to believe that the Party would sacrifice you. They've never really regarded you as one of themselves. They know your origins. They trust you only because you're not one of them. When the time comes for purges, it will be the extreme Left which will provide the victims, you'll see. You are the style of person, my dear little Artemy, who is denounced but never executed. Your death would intimidate no one, since there is no one sufficiently like you to feel intimidated by it. You may have joined the Party, but the Party has never joined you. What you seem not to realize is that however *wrong* it may be, your side is defeated. Our will prevails. Our will.'

'In part you're right, of course. But as you've discovered, you have no will. You are uneasy to have "won" precisely because you have no will to do anything. You imagine that we are going to wait; on the contrary, you are faced with the waiting. You actually wish we were stronger. You crave an answer more than you fear defeat. You dread the silent oracle.'

'I used to like your verses in the old days. You still write them?'

'Dimmy, this is not a vital moment in my life. It is a vital moment in yours. You've had the courage, the providence, the luck to engineer it. Don't waste it.'

'How could you confess to Brasidas and to the general that you had had this conversation, assuming I were to allow the force of your ideas?'

'There'd be no need for any confession. You could broadcast your generous terms. As a stern warning, a final offer. You'd show no signs of having been prompted. It would be a speech from strength. An appeal to brothers to abandon fratricidal strife. You're capable of it. Followed by a secret deputation offering much greater concessions than your public statement proposed. Something sufficient to attract the Political Committee, enough to make them believe in the possibility of a political victory more total even than the military one for which they once hoped. Freedom for the Party press, for the unions, and offices in the Government, free elections even.'

'Free elections. Does it occur to you that the Party could be swamped in free elections, swamped, Artemy?'

'You underrate our force and our organization. You underrate the amount of weight we could bring to bear, from several directions.'

'In other words, you'd have no intention of playing fair, isn't that what you're actually saying?'

'You're asking terms from death, Dimmy.'

'Damn it, I'm the one offering terms, not you. I want you because I remember you from the old days. You've perverted this conversation, you've twisted it to suit yourself, to turn defeat into victory. Damn you, Artemis, I'm the one with the cards in my hand, not you. I'm offering to rescue you from oblivion and before you even hear my terms you start proposing yours. It's ridiculous.'

'Terms for what?'

'For delivering you from a lifetime of waste, of worse than waste perhaps. Do you trust your friends across the border? You know very well you don't. I wouldn't if I were you. I wouldn't give much to be in your shoes as you cross from our soil to theirs. Remember what happened to the peasant leaders in '07.'

'When an easily intimidated king was on the throne. Truly, Dmitri, sometimes you're like a child.'

'Sometimes things are a lot more childish than your chess-player's mind likes to accept. The board can be jolted. Do as you will. *I* wouldn't come with you.'

'Thank you. I'm willing to take my chance in that direction.'

'You damned selfish prig, Artemis. You damned selfish prig. You're willing to leave thousands of your people, the people you aim to champion, to rot here while you martyrize yourself up there. It's stupidity so ... so self-righteous it's sickening.'

'You don't want them happy – whatever word you like to use – you want them controlled.'

'I want them represented. I want them to feel themselves represented.'

'Well, I've suggested the only way in which they can be represented. I don't say you're capable of it. I doubt that very much. It would require a miracle of intelligence. You must connive at your own subversion; I don't make any secret of it. Eventually, when the Government is strong enough, when the West has been sufficiently clearly warned for them to refrain from any spontaneous acts of liberation, you'll find yourself deprived of office and, probably, put on trial for conspiring with those whom you have actually expelled.'

'My dear Artemy, when you put it so seductively how can I refuse your proposals? You are an amazing chap. Let me put it to you my way. Suppose that I ask you to connive at your own disgrace – '

'I never mentioned disgrace. I don't think there would be any need for that. On the contrary – '

'Suppose I ask you to agree to your own side regarding you as a traitor – as a renegade – '

'But you have no side, Dimmy. There'll be no one left in the end to think of you at all!'

'My proposal is this, that you conduct your retreat with all the skill you possess, that you share the pains and the battles of your men, that you shirk nothing. I allow you that. I've no wish to humiliate you. Suppose I arrange to let you go – to escape, if you like – without conditions. Suppose I allow you to battle all the way to the border. If a miraculous turn-around takes place, if you win a great battle, if capitalism collapses between now and then, you have complete freedom of action. You have it all along. But suppose, as we know is most likely, that you are driven to the limit. All I ask then is this: admit you are at the limit. Admit that when your men cross the border they enter a world wholly beyond your calculations. Surely it's the truth? Well then, at that point and only at that point, I ask you to turn again and think of those you leave behind. Think whether you deal fairly with them, those who lack a voice. I ask you then to throw yourself on the mercy of the Government and to declare yourself disgusted with the Party and with the revolution. I ask you then to announce that you would have preferred to work through constitutional means and that you would, if all things were equal, be prepared to serve a social democratic party of the Left. I don't insist on the exact terminology, of course. The text can be in your own inimitable style, but what I'm after is an opportunity for the revival of the participation of the whole country in the running of the State. Can there really be anything wrong in that, Artemy? Can there?'

'You're asking that I renounce the Party and return – to what? Am I to be welcomed with open arms or what?'

'No, of course not. You'll be put on trial and sentenced to

eighteen years' imprisonment. We're not looking to an immediate solution to the political problem.'

'Eighteen years! I'm very much obliged to you!'

'Be your age, Artemy. If you were welcomed back too soon it would blow the whole thing. That's obvious. We must bide our time. I'm asking you to lie in wait on the future. To prepare a position for a remote, or fairly remote eventuality. Allow a few years to pass and in the meantime we relax the strictest of our laws and allow the unions to be reconstituted. What will follow? Most likely – correct me if I'm wrong in my analysis – most likely unrest in proportion to the degree of relaxation. No one was ever placated by placatory measures, isn't that right? Well then, during this period your martyrdom in prison becomes a centre of agitation. The extreme Left may, it's true, mount a campaign of vilification, but the democratic parties of the Left and Left Centre will be glad to have a martyr and will take you as their standard-bearer. You will distinguish them from the Government parties who are enjoying the fruits of office and are rigging the courts, helping themselves to defence contracts and generally enjoying the fruits of civilization. You can be their good conscience. A movement will grow for your release. It will become a token of good faith on the part of the Government, a proof of their willingness to submit to the test of genuine elections. We shall refuse to release you. We shall say that you were convicted for your crimes and not for your opinions. Only after prolonged pressure shall we consider, in return for certain guarantees, the possibility of a reassessment of your case. Finally, after riots and the stormy funeral of a worker killed in a demonstration, we shall call upon you to take your place in society and to honour your responsibilities to your followers. You will be released and brought into the centre of affairs. How many years will you have served? I hardly know exactly. A number. Once released, your progress to the Prime Minister's office should not take long. It will depend on your abilities. The fight which was so long an unfair one will now be loaded in your favour. You will be a martyr who has transcended his martyrdom.

The people will believe in you. They will have no reason to doubt your qualities. You would still be a prisoner, remember, had it not been for their demands for your release. They will not doubt you because you will be the measure of their strength. You will be completely unfettered. Neither I nor my colleagues will have any hold on you. You will be operating in an arena where any manoeuvre you care to make will be available to you. The only secret will be this meeting, a meeting so long in the past and so ill-documented that you will be able to denounce it as a lie. No one will believe that it took place, so you will almost certainly succeed in making our side look even more disreputable than before, should we try to bring you down by accusing you of having attended it. We shall have conspired for the good of the country. You will, it's true, be committed to a bourgeois demo-cracy, since your break with the Party will be authentic and irrefutable. And irreversible, of course, since you will not have any bargaining counter capable of bringing you back within their ranks. You are a bourgeois, Artemy. You know it and they know it. Once lapsed, you will never be able to return to them. But equally, I promise you, there will be no need to. The West to which you refer so disparagingly is still very strong and very rich. If it were not so, the retreat on which you're about to start would never take place. There's no deal which is not based on power; there are no gentlemen in politics; water doesn't run uphill: these things we know. You may be right and eventually the balance may tip far enough for the Party to impose itself on the country, but I swear to you it'll not be for another fifty years at the soonest. You'll waste your life as a spectator if you decline my suggestion. By God, Artemis, isn't it an exciting one? Isn't it, man? Imagine laying plans for the future, just you and me, imposing our game on the whole country, making history prove or disprove our thesis, isn't that something worth doing, something worth risking one's life for?

'You needn't answer me now. There's no answer to give, really, is there? You can decide at every stage whether or not you want to go ahead. You can renege without a moment's hesitation, without betraying a trust, without danger of any kind – except that you may, if you go too far, make it impossible to reconsider. Both of us, do you see, will be engaged with each other and with each other alone for the rest of the time we are alive? Artemis, it's a brotherhood of the angels. It dares the pinnacles. Can you resist it? Can you resist it even if you *say* you resist it? Well, you may wonder what proof you have that things will take the course I say – if you do surrender yourself, why I should ever permit your release? But then why do I intend to permit it now? I tell you very frankly, there's no proof, there never could be any proof that I shall be so indulgent again. If I find it unnecessary, or if I'm deposed or killed, well, you'll be unfortunate, but the chances are that things will work out as I say, because if it were not so I'd have no reason to make this proposal to you. Should I? Do you see the beauty of it? We are already involved in this wrestling match, you and I. There's nothing more to be said. You recognize it, Artemy, don't you? You and I, man. Why? Why not? We're above events, do you see that? It's a kind of provisional immortality: you provide the phrase. We shall stand to the country like the gods of Homer, above the battle and in it at one and the same time!'

Before the sun had risen, they had already crossed the first ridge and were four hours north of their resting-place in the valley. Artemis led the company, with Kosta close beside him. He wanted to keep an eye on the young warrior; a single impetuous move might destroy them. They had left pale Stelio in the valley with the ruins of the night's shelter piled on him for a monument. It was as if a splinter had been drawn from them; they moved more easily without him, but he left a raw place in their ranks. Three of the others were in the leading section; then came a gap and then the main section under Yorgis, eighteen of them, including the captured Bren and a German light machine-gun; after that was another gap and then the rear section, under old Paniotis, limping

245

relentlessly, a medium machine-gun across his shoulders, an Italian model which Bruno, the Italian Communist, had brought with him when he deserted to them. The gun was inclined to overheat and Bruno kept a jealous eye on it. He once slapped Paniotis's hand in the middle of an engagement when he fired too long a burst. They had begun to climb the far slope of the next valley when they heard the buzz of aircraft, hardly more obstreperous than the hum of a saw. There was nothing to do but to march on. The thud of falling bombs and the nattering of unseen machine-guns drove their heads down. Artemis made light of the gradient, reached the peak and assessed the next valley. It was broader than the last, with a road running down the centre, alongside the bright litter of a dry river-bed. It broadened towards the sea, a small village at its mouth. Towards the east it forked into two shallow valleys; at the fork was another village, ramparted on the groin of the hill which parted the valleys. In the monastery above it bells hung in loop-holes of sky. A peasant with two donkeys of kindling was swatting left and right as he trotted them towards the sea.

There had been times during the war when the partisans had been in just such a position after the Germans had come in, lorry after lorry, to punish a village which had been supplying the men in the hills. They would surround the village, round up the men and eventually shoot them, expel the women and children and set fire to the houses. There was no appeal. Guilt did not come into it. The purpose of the expedition, always at dawn or soon after, was to draw the partisans in outrage from the hills. Executions were postponed in the hope that the tension would break the will of the watchers. The victims were an irrelevance. Their attempts to plead or to run were handled with irritated indifference, like the intelligent questions of understudies. The burning houses, the efforts to rescue valued possessions, the snatching of children from the places they had known all their lives, these banalities were paraded, like favourite dishes in front of an invalid, in the hope of tempting the appetite of the partisans. And they had had to sit and resist temptation. They knew very well that more powerful forces were hidden at either end of the valley; once they descended, they would never get back. The German tactics deadened their humanity. Their sense of powerlessness, their humiliation at being unable to interfere, killed any belief in common decency. They hated those who were shot in front of them. That hatred was easily turned to callousness when they moved once more amongst civilians. They despised the weakness of the unarmed. They had had to watch again and again while the same tactics were used against them. And slowly they had become inured to them. Towards the end, they had ceased to cry out and to fling themselves on the ground. Artemis had never fully shared their anguish. The villagers were not his people. For him the scenes of deliberate massacre belonged almost to art, to the world of ideas, whereas his men had taken them literally. To him they were a metaphor, a warning, a paradox; he had taken them into his head. He remained an officer, he feared.

Artemis first joined the army when the Italians invaded the country. The 'triumvirs' had returned from the island with dubious intentions. The recapture of the two men who had escaped from the *Aias* had been a silly triumph, but the lesson of the prison ship had not been lost on them. Their nerve was shaken by the sight of that joyless company. Nothing final had been decided when Asteris Stratis sailed away. To the triumvirs' (and Artemis's) relief, their return to the capital coincided with the Italian ultimatum. Grateful to be patriots, they rallied to the Marshal. Artemis and most of his fellow-students demonstrated for the return of the crown prince the night before they joined the colours. The Marshal was glad to find a specific occasion to recall young Paul and conceded to the students the warrior's privilege of forcing upon him the one man whom he was ready to accept. Artemis saw action quickly and in the most exhilarating circumstances. The Italians were held, mortified and forced back. They were pursued across the border into the land of mosques. The morale of Artemis and his men (he had been promoted to lieutenant after his first battle) was so high that had the Italians thrown themselves into the sea, they would have dived in after them. The Marshal disengaged his forces; word had come from London of the dangers of too vigorous a pursuit. The army under General Papastavrou marched through the capital in a victory parade. Papastavrou had broken the Italians between the mountains and the sea, south of Boreopolis. The Marshal greeted him as effusively as a Byzantine emperor would a successful commander whom he had resolved to blind at the first opportunity. He offered the general any post in the Cabinet which he might care to name, a large pension and a huge grant of land. The Old Man even went so far as to ask if he had any suggestions for constitutional reform. The general refused both pension and grant. He declined to make any political proposals. The Marshal was appalled; he feared the general had some bee in his bonnet. And so he did; he requested that the funds offered to dull his ambitions should be devoted to the region whose sufferings he had witnessed. He asked to be made provincial governor and requested that certain of his officers and men, who could not be demobilized owing to the state of the war, be drafted to assist him. The use of the army for the improvement of the condition of the people aroused the deepest suspicion both of the notables and of those whose campaigns had been less brilliant than the general's. For his own personal use the Cabinet would have voted any amount of money the general demanded; his selflessness was blatant extortion. They discussed having him assassinated; Captain Democritos was summoned by Tomas Nikolides, the *chef de cabinet*, and briefed on the possibility of Papastavrou being a 'traitor' whose execution might prove as necessary as it would be difficult to explain. Democritos showed no surprise and reported that there would be no problem. The popular are never hard to remove. The Left would, of course, have to be incriminated; several of their leaders could probably be put away at the same time. The chances were, however, that the war was not over. It seemed unwise to incur the odium of killing the general when the enemy could be given the first chance to do it.

The sense of national pride which had united the Cabinet, the regime and the people was thus lost during the lull between the first defeat of the Italians and their later resumption of the fighting with the aid of the Germans. It was bad enough for the notables that Papastavrou had saved the country once; it might be fatal if he were to do it again. Meanwhile he had acted with practised authority in his native province. He banned the *latifundias*, expropriated the landlords who failed to show reason why they should not suffer confiscation – they included his own brother – and handed the land to the peasants. But he went farther: he organized the peasants into communes, financed factories to break the monopoly on the manufacture of olive oil, improved the roads and set up, within a few months, machinery for advancing money at low interest, a secretariat for the merchandising of local produce and a centre for communal projects. The resentment caused by these measures led to attempts on his life by those whom he had dispossessed and by the petty bankers and shopkeepers who regarded themselves as ruined by the cancellation of interest payments.

By the time Democritos was instructed to carry out his assignment without further delay, Papastavrou was guarded night and day by his supporters. Artemis had been delegated to the construction work on an olive-oil factory. He felt at once younger and older. He worked with an energy he had been able to display before only in games. He fell asleep exhausted but he arose refreshed, whereas in the capital he had tossed on his bed, unable to fight down the doubts and ambitions which goaded his mind, unready for night, only to wake in the morning sluggish and unprepared for the day. Now he was an authority on whom others relied. He cursed his lack of knowledge in practical affairs. It was a new school, where he was at once master and pupil; he had come to a subject he could approach with his full attention, something which did not make him clever, but able. He did not distinguish military from civilian duties. His loyalty to the young crown prince remained, like the childhood allegiance to a football club; it did not directly affect his activities and it promised that the past had not been a complete waste. He was inclined to attribute his new sense of liberation more to being in the army than to the social tasks he was undertaking. The renovation of the countryside and the summary changes in its economy were hardly more, in that brilliant armistice, than diversions. The Government waited for some irresistible force to give them the chance of crushing Papastavrou. When the Germans invaded, having failed to assassinate him they put him in command of the whole army. It was almost certainly impossible to win. The men who had broken the Italians were broken in their turn. The weight of the Germans made courage irrelevant. It was displayed, but it proved no more than a flag of defiance on the roof of a burning house. With the exhaustion of the army came the first intimations of political distrust. Artemis and those like him had remained innocently patriotic until the defeat. The German advance gave the Government an excuse to ask the Marshal to take personal command of the armed forces. It was thus suggested that Papastavrou, who was with the men at the front, holding the line on Boreopolis and the northern mountains, had already failed. The Marshal refused to cast the blame on those in charge, but his refusal sounded more like an act of grace than an indignant rebuttal. The Right was reconciled to an occupation; the notables preferred the Germans to Papastavrou.

The Marshal, acting out his naive morality against a background of cynical wrangling, resigned all his offices and asked for a minor command in the field. If it had never seemed ridiculous that the Old Man should lead the nation, allowing him the command of a regiment was obviously absurd. When the Cabinet, under the leadership of the Minister of Marine, begged him not to desert the nation in its hour of agony, it was clear that he was being preserved for only one role, that of the negotiator who might, by his own authoritarian history, first persuade the Germans to tolerable terms and eventually wear the horns of the nation's scapegoat. The Government had to wait for the army of the north to be defeated before negotiations could begin. The army continued to fight with that hopeless courage men display when they are more concerned to demonstrate their valour to the 'friends' they despise than to the enemy they hate. The line held for two and a half months until the release of dive-bombers and armour, coinciding with the coming of better weather, completed its ruin. Even then the army fought doggedly, a nation holding together for the last time, Royalists side by side with Socialists. The Royalists so associated themselves with their comrades in arms that they refused to allow a Government deputation, reported to be carrying an order to Papastavrou to divide his forces, to pass through the lines. The Government was afraid that an armistice might give Papastavrou time to march on the capital, evict the ministry, whose mandate was now dubious, and proclaim a republic.

The notables were set on capitulation as soon as possible; they drummed their fingers for news of a clinching defeat. To divide the army would both placate the conquerors and confirm their own position. The deputation led by Democritos was disarmed and returned to the capital. Democritos had either to rally to the army or become the 'strong man' of the Cabinet. The army was distant and suspicious; he chose the ministry. He was the first man in the country to be faced with the consequences of defeat; he was, in a sense, the first man to be defeated. He was put in charge of 'internal security' and organized a mobile corps from the toughest elements in the city. Such was the confusion of the notables that they were glad to leave decisions to him. It absolved them from later judgment and did not call upon them for immediate finesse. He became at once the keeper of the national honour (he was responsible for the safety of the king) and the author of its surrender. He had no political reputation, so, as it turned out, the invaders neither feared his cleverness nor felt obliged to make an example of him. He had not even fought against them; they had for him the sense of kinship which gangsters have for policemen. The military men, General Klein and Major-General Heinrich Bayer, ignored him, rather as visiting royalty assume those who line the streets are there to salute them, not to protect them from the crowds. To ask him too closely about his duties would be to reveal their own lack of popular appeal.

The army of the north had been finally forced to come to terms with an Italian general specially flown to Boreopolis, from which he had been evicted by Papastavrou and his men eight months before. The Government authorized Papastavrou to leave the country, affecting to believe that he would continue the fight from beyond the seas. He refused either to sign the armistice or to leave the country. He called upon the soldiers to desert with their arms and take to the hills. His call was heeded only by small numbers. Several who attempted to make off with vehicles or weapons were fired on by Royalist military police. Panicked by the German arrival in the capital, the ministry condemned Papastavrou to death for mutiny and ordered the arrest of all officers under his command.

Artemis was among those who were unable or unwilling to commit themselves to flight. The Government attempted to alert the Germans to the dangers of leaving the general at liberty, but Klein, with the magnanimity of a man who wishes to report a country quiet in order to give a better impression of his own triumph, neglected to act quickly enough. He saw the evidence of his victory in the rows of tired men, burning equipment, docile peasantry, and he was already involved in the struggle for advancement in the High Command. He left it to the Government to pacify the dissident; partisan warfare was not yet an obvious danger. Artemis was taken back to the capital and vetted by a panel of officers who had remained loyal to the Government. His engagement to Katerina was already broken, but his father retained some influence; he was acquitted of improper ambitions. After he had been cleared he became aware of his disappointment at being found blameless. The day before the Germans entered the capital the king left the country in a British destroyer. Artemis defended his action in the last great political argument which Fontano's was to see for many months. Having been released from the army by the investigating panel, he was wearing his black suit.

It no longer fitted him; he was too broad across the shoulders and too narrow in the hips. It seemed a provisional costume, something he could not stay in for long. If he had had his pistol he might have shot the man who called the king a coward, a journalist called Alexander Fokas. He challenged him to a duel, was laughed at for a fool, upset a table with six cups of coffee steaming on it and left the café. A year later Fokas was editing the *Times* under German censorship.

Artemis was mortified by the Occupation, but he could not think how to resist it. He was again in his parents' house. He had not even the secret of a woman to sustain him. A certain sly euphoria filled the city during the 'correct' period which began the Occupation. The notables could hardly welcome it, but they were not averse to profiting from it. The period when Artemis was with Papastavrou in his province had been unruly in the capital. The army's victories gave the ordinary people a sense of power. What the general had forced on the countryside was demanded in the city. There were strikes and a call for public works. When the Germans came, they advertised their determination to regularize the life of the country. They were anxious to get industry working again and they had no intention, they said, of interfering with its efficiency; by which they meant they would not tolerate its inefficiency. The notables were relieved. They were warned, it was true, of severe penalties for profiteering or for black-market activities. They were neither surprised nor disturbed; such warnings, in one form or another, had been given them by every Government they could remember. So practised had they become in the tactics of evasion that it was almost a relief that the Germans were now making the rules; it gave their evasion an air of patriotism. Artemis saw no one; he had no need to work. He despised those who collaborated; he had no contact with those who did not. Papastavrou was a hunted man. He was forced to hide in the most remote mountains and to keep on the move. He was unable even to risk himself in his own province, until the Germans began to act against the commune. Vassili Papastavrou had been quick to draw attention to its communist nature. Peasants who might never have left their prosperity now had nothing to lose. They joined the general. The Government was blamed by the Germans for this 'breach of the peace treaty' and the capital was taxed for the follies of the country. It was not difficult in these circumstances to get permission to raise a 'patriotic force' to deal with the partisans. Certain officers and common soldiers were recalled to the colours, subject to the vigilant screening of the Germans. Almost simultaneously the first round-up of casual labour was made in the city. The division between those who could come to some arrangement with the occupying forces and their victims became sharper. The lucky could at first deceive themselves, but the degree of their dependence on the Germans grew daily. The hatred of the notables for Papastavrou increased with the success of his cause. They blamed him for their difficulties and were able to believe that, had it not been for his insolence, the Germans might have provisioned the hungry and dealt less harshly with the population.

Artemis neither spoke against Papastavrou nor consorted with the Germans. He resumed his studies in literature; he would emulate the Abbé Siéyès. He consoled himself for his impotence by making private lists of those whose vulgarity disgusted him more than their treason. He had reverted to the posture of a rich young man incognito, who finds life wearisome not because of its injustice but because of its lack of style. He had perfected a nod of non-committal courtesy for those German officers whom he was obliged to meet in the streets. He entertained no expectations of the postwar world, nor had he any great determination to see it. He assumed some absurd mistake would take him off to slave labour or blow him to pieces. Papastavrou was said to have organized terror groups; explosions were expected constantly. The Right was so eager to accuse him of murder that it endowed him with exaggerated powers of life and death. During the war Artemis had been promoted on the field of battle; he imagined therefore, without undue conceit, merely with the amused secrecy of a man who has found the loss of his virginity a less transcendental experience than the literature suggested, that he had crossed the great watershed of maturity. He had, remembering Fabrizio del Dongo, seen his first dead man, but unlike Fabrizio he had not been stared at by him. The corpse was an Italian, lying on his face like a fallen fruit in a puddle of its own juice. He was going into action at the time and hardly gave the man more than a glance. The Italian infantry were unwise and ambled into shot like extras unaware that things are already rolling. Artemis got a couple before they tumbled to what was happening. The battle continued for several hours, but never again at close quarters. It was like one of those meals where the Melba toast turns out to be the tastiest part. Artemis walked the occupied streets then as a veteran. He had had his *baptême du feu*. He failed to pine for Katerina, whose marriage had now taken place, but he believed that the great passion of his life was already over. He constructed a montage of his experiences with whores and his futile feeling for Katerina and persuaded himself that his knowledge of women was complete. He watched with pity those husbands who carried children. He took again to writing small paragraphs of exact description, epigrams on timeless subjects and caustic parables. He walked the streets, part adolescent, part old man. He became interested in icons and turned over the stock of the dealers who still had stalls in the old quarter.

One day in early February, when it was still cold in the capital, he was examining a collection when he heard several shots. Either terrorists were shooting at the Germans or someone had run away from a patrol. The uncertainty roped off such occurrences from common knowledge. It put the Germans and their victims in a separate class. An hour later, Artemis found himself in a small square in a dismal section between the harbour and the Stavros Hospital. Cracked hotels, derelict businesses, workers' tenements rose from the brown ground. Each quadrant had been used in whatever way suited its owner. Some of the streets had no names; they were simply compounds. Whole blocks had once sold scrap of all kinds, but only the most useless and corroded items remained; the Germans had carted off the rest. Yet the inhabitants returned, like ants to a kicked-over ant-hill, and tried to make a living from a trade without stock. Starving women carried wailing or inert babies from one corner to the next. Several lay slumped in rags against the fences; silent, faceless bundles in their black laps. Artemis was drinking a cup of gritty coffee at a boarded-up café when he heard lorries. Germans rolled into the square. Artemis watched through the boarded windows of the café, whose owner hurried to lock the door. The lorries stopped at the four corners of the square and grey men climbed down. Two of the lorries were empty. A Mercedes containing three officers in black leather coats with fur collars was close to the café. The owner crouched next to Artemis, a small, acorn-shaped man in an unravelling brown cardigan, hair cropped, face unshaven. The officer in command confirmed his orders and lines of men moved off. The three officers stayed in the car; they passed a silver flask to each other. Artemis dropped his eyes to look at the *patron*, who was looking up at him with lustrous calculation, a kind of dazzled and sly admiration such as a naked woman might have excited. 'What cars, what machinery, what precision! Have you ever seen our people run an operation like that? They're fools, fools, the people who try to resist them, who think we've got anything to set against them. What've we achieved? And what have they achieved? Am I annoying you? It's not you they're after, is it? Can you help admiring them? I'm not saying they haven't done things I wouldn't. I'm not saying I'm glad they're here, don't think that, but can you help admiring them, that's all I'm asking? I won't betray you, I wouldn't betray one of our own people to them, don't imagine that, master. I'm not saying I'm with them because I'm not; I'm only asking you, how can a people like that not conquer the world if they want to? Who's going to stop them? You're not armed, are you? I've got a wife and children upstairs; I've got a family. You wouldn't bring them down on me, would you, because you know what they're like? I've heard stories of what they do to people, even innocent people, people who haven't done anything wrong. Why do you come here? You don't live round here, do you? You're not from the neighbourhood. Is it you they're after? I won't betray you. I won't tell a soul. Look at this place, look at this café. I've put every penny I've ever had into this place and look what's happened to it. Do you think that's fair? Who's making a penny these days? The crooks and the Hebrews, that's who. Oh, they take away some of them but don't you believe that's the lot; I know for a fact who's making money out of the black market. Not me, not people like me. When they do something, they do it; they carry it right through. They don't bungle, they don't rely on other people, they don't say they're going to do something and then not do it. I wouldn't mind being one of them, would you, honestly?' Artemis wanted to move, to make some violent gesture, to slide away, but the appealing cowardice of the *patron* stripped all energy and all experience from him. He was naked in front of this jeering, pleading flow which clung to him like rusty moisture he was powerless to brush off. The *patron* ceased to speak; he was again peering through the slats. A section of Germans had returned, escorting a file of dejected, ragged men whom they directed into a lorry. Garlic bloomed on the *patron*'s breath as he sighed his admiration. Another file of men was brought in. The German officers capped their flask and sat importantly. The *patron* gripped Artemis's lower arm. 'They knew exactly what they wanted. You see that? They go for what they want; they find it.' The man shuffled closer to Artemis. 'Will you have a drop of *koniak*? You want a drop of *koniak*? I've got one in the back.' He gestured for Artemis to wait and went through a beaded doorway into the back room. There was a knife on the bar, a triangular knife with a short blade. Artemis went for the knife and plunged it over and over again into one of the rough wooden tables in front of the bar. At last it snapped. The *patron* returned to find Artemis with the abrupt knife in his hand, fury in his eyes. 'What've you done? What do you think you're doing? Are you mad? What's the matter with you?' The slice of broken blade stuck out of the table. 'Look what you've done to this table! What's the matter with you?' Artemis threw the handle of the knife behind the bar, like a fish head. 'I go to get you something to drink. I didn't have to, and this is what you do. Are you ill? What do you think I am? Do you think I'm nobody, do you think you've got a right to behave like this? I don't know whether to offer you a glass or not. That knife was one I'd had for several years, quite a number of years. I had that knife before the war. I think you'd better get out of here, get out of my place before you do anything else. You'd better learn how to control yourself, that's my advice. I've got a wife and children upstairs, you didn't think about them, did you? You'd better get a grip on yourself, think things out, because otherwise you're going to get into serious trouble.' Artemis went to the door and tried to tear it open against the lock. The *patron* ran to join him. 'Now you're going to break the door. The door's locked. You can't open it like that. You're stopping me from opening it. I can't open it if you pull it like that. You're preventing me from opening it. Are you trying to stop me opening my own door, is that what you're trying to do? I don't understand you. I don't understand you at all. I offer you a drink and you break my knife. I've done my best to be civil and what do you do? What're you trying to do? Are you *trying* to stop me from opening it because I can't get the key in if you keep wrenching like that and getting your hands in the way. You seem like an educated person, why are you being so unreasonable, so silly about this? I want to help you. You want to go; I want to help. Now don't get violent, for heaven's sake, isn't there enough violence in the world, enough needless brutality, haven't we seen enough of that for one day? I've got my wife and my children upstairs. If you want to go, in heaven's name, let me open the door for you, and if you don't, well don't, have a drink, sit down, calm yourself. Perhaps you need a doctor. I like you. I should like to have a discussion with you. I'm interested in what you think about things. It's obvious that you're an intelligent man, a man with ideas out of the ordinary, not someone to be taken lightly, not someone to be dismissed. Are you ill? Have you suffered from some disease? You look as if you might have been tubercular. You're not tubercular, are you? How often do you see a German spit? Rarely. Very rarely indeed. They have standards we don't. They have ideas which can conquer the world. It's not that I'm not a patriot. I am a patriot. I fought in the war. I was one of the Marshal's men and I'm proud of it. I'd fight again if there was a chance of winning, but what I'm saying is, one has to be honest with oneself. Now, shall I let you out or will you stay and have a drop? Let you out. Of course. If that's what you want I'll do it. There. No one in the square. Nothing to worry about. A clear run for home! Good luck, sir, God go with you. And take care of that chest. That's a dangerous thing, a chest. Take care of it. See your doctor, a man in your position. I would.'

Artemis imagined himself unperturbed, but he missed the turning which should have taken him back towards the banking district and found himself in a section he had never entered before. It covered a small hill; the streets rose sharply, each building stepped above its neighbour along narrow pavements. Artemis had an uneasy feeling, as if he had been isolated (the streets were almost empty) by some great event of which he had not been notified. The place had the unnatural calm of a district near a stadium where an important match is due to start. Artemis might have arrived during the preliminaries, when the crowd is too happy to be inside the ground to have started shouting. The first shots had the undemanding freshness of memory. They spoke no immediate message; they were already part of the past. Then someone ran up the hill, a man with a pair of very worn bicycle tyres over his shoulder. He was followed by two more men, civilians, with guns in their hands. Artemis, even with his experience of war, was confused. Was it some kind of crime? Had they robbed a bank? He was alarmed at his own indecision, his indecision whether to pursue the men or to stay aloof. It did not occur to him to take their part. They crouched at the corner of the street and fired several times at the clatter of pursuers behind them. Artemis cowered in a doorway, a metal grille behind him. He was in the angle of two streets which intersected like the arms of a pair of scissors. The gunmen hesitated and then ran on up the hill. The Germans fired several

times, chipping lumps from the white walls, and then charged the
hill. Artemis was frightened. He could not move. He would be
shot if he was seen. He pressed back against the grille. There was
a knob in his back. He reached and twisted it. The door fell open;
he scrambled inside. He had often dreamed of being incapable of
walking, of an affliction, which he had accepted like a cripple, that
prevented him from standing upright. He could proceed only by
holding on to something, best of all a rug or some hempen railing.
Then he could go hand over hand, like a monkey, like one of those
four-legged semi-human creatures who lived on the roofs of the
village of his dreams. His legs were powerless, paralysed. He clawed
his way into the murk behind the iron door. He could hear
Germans shouting, the hammering of rifle butts. He crawled back
to the door and tried to drive the rusted, warped bolt into its thong.
He could not do it. He stiffened behind the angle of the door at the
patrol's approach. The door was kicked, the knob twisted. Artemis
was slim as a broom in his corner. A helmet leaned in, was recalled,
sniffed and withdrew. There was a burst of firing, the clash of
boots, shouts, more firing. Artemis was afraid. A bullet clanged
on the door like the snap of an iron knocker. Artemis feared to die
like a rabbit in the wrong trap. 'What're you doing here? What's
happening?' 'I'm sorry –' 'Stay where you are. Don't move. I'm
going to call the police.' 'It's nothing to do with the police.' 'How
did you get in here?' 'The door was open. I opened it and I came
in.' 'Are you armed? Have you got a gun? What were those
shots?' The man was holding a scimitar. He filled the trough of a
stairway that came down from a terrace to the small dark area
where Artemis was standing. There was no room for him to slash
at Artemis, but neither was there room to evade him. 'Don't you
know?' 'I'm asking you.' 'You know what they were.' 'I believe
you took advantage of what was happening because you wanted
to steal something, that's what I think.' 'There's no truth in that at
all. I've no wish to steal anything. No need either.' 'No need?
Don't pretend you don't know who I am.' 'I've no need to
pretend. I haven't any idea who you are. As soon as the Germans

have gone, I'll be on my way.' 'Are they after you, the Germans?' 'I don't know who they were after exactly, if anyone. I don't imagine they knew themselves, anyone who ran, that was all, anyone who happened to be in the way.' 'What made you try that door? Well?' 'I was standing in the doorway when the firing began. It was that or to be caught in the open. I tried the door.' 'What're you frightened of? You're frightened. I can see; you're shaking.' 'It's true.' 'What're you frightened of?' 'Not you. I'm not frightened of you, it's all right.' 'Have you done something wrong?' 'I'll be going now. I'm sorry if I alarmed you. As I say, there was no cause.' 'Don't move.' 'Now really, Mr – ' 'You don't live in this quarter, do you?' 'Correct. I'm passing through. I'd be glad if you'd tell me how to get back to the Street of Heroes.' 'Is that where you live, the Street of Heroes?' 'No. But I can find my way from there.' 'It's dangerous, leaving your own quarter in the present state of things. It's not wise.' 'I'm beginning to realize that.' 'A man should stay where he belongs these days, if he doesn't want to get into trouble. I'm interested though in what you said: there was nothing you needed.' 'What should I need?' 'Fuel, food, clothes. There's nothing you need?' 'Nothing.' 'You're a lucky man. You have your own sources, I take it? That's very interesting.' 'What would you attack me for now? Why are you still threatening me with that? What could I say that would bring you to use it? I mean, why not put it down? I'm not going to do anything.' The man was bent to look under the floor of the terrace at Artemis; it was as though he had a more important appointment going on simultaneously above. The man would have been handsome if he had been shorter, but his good looks were implausible on so tall, so stretched a frame. He had the good looks of an idiot. 'What would I want to steal, if I'd come to steal something? What business are you in?' 'Who sent you here?' 'I told you – ' 'But I don't have to believe you, do I? You're after something, what is it? You're not in the police yourself, are you? *Are* you? I haven't seen you before.' A note of neutrality softened his voice, though he tightened his grip on the scimitar. 'I have friends in the police,' said Artemis; 'why?' 'Friends? Who?' 'Captain Democritos is a friend of mine, for instance.' 'What kind of a friend?' 'A friend and associate.' 'I've taken care of Democritos. He and I understand each other. What's your name? I'll ask him about you. I'll find out about you and then – then we shall know each other again. He didn't send you?' The scimitar wavered as the man came down a couple of steps. Artemis reached and caught his wrist and jerked him down the stairs, hurling himself wide, like a passenger avoiding the vomit of a man who has been looking seedy for some time and now suddenly flings up. The man was astonished and confused: he did not know whether he was trying to stay above the level of the dark or whether he should hurl himself at Artemis. He was too affronted at the sudden treachery to be capable of decision. His mouth was open to protest as Artemis broke him across his leg and clubbed him with his fist as he fell. The man was unbalanced; there was too much of him for the space. He crashed his head against the door, dropped the scimitar, banged his knees and began at once to grumble for mercy. Artemis had tricked him and knew he could never trust him. As he spoke, the man was reaching for the scimitar. Artemis grabbed it and shortened it. The man realized that it was no longer win or draw, but win or lose. He scampered on his heels and Artemis stabbed his chest. Outrage preceded pain, horror death. The scimitar snapped at the second stroke, so that Artemis reared back, the tongue of steel standing out of the man's striped shirt. The heels trotted and subsided. The huge body sprawled in the well, arms up, folded like a crayfish. Artemis squeezed out of the iron door, which the body closed behind him, and walked down the steep hill. The form of the city now appeared clear to him; he had no problem in finding his way to the Street of Heroes.

There was little sense in hesitation. They had no real choice. They hesitated only as long as the illusion of power remained to them; it was a minute of nostalgia, as they considered the two villages, the two donkeys with their bundles of brush, and pretended to the terrible patience they had once shown. Artemis shuffled off the peak and followed the yellow path between slanting rocks. 'We shall cross the valley as near the sea as possible, a third of the way between that village and that one. It looks to me as though they're more likely to be in position there' – he pointed towards the village that straddled the groin where the two valleys sloped together – 'than there. And if they've bluffed us, well, I still think we've a better chance on level ground.' Kosta checked his Sten and was ready to follow. Yorgis was frowning at the little harbour through his German field-glasses. Paniotis glared at the higher village, as if it had been reprieved from a fate he would have liked to see it suffer. 'We shall proceed in the same order, but at wider intervals. Each section will cross the valley alone, from those bushes there up to the wall there, above the ruined hut. No section moves before the other two sections are in position. Understood?' Paniotis agreed; Yorgis lowered his glasses and passed them to Artemis. A small coasting vessel, of the size that would take fish from an island to the capital, was warped to the mole. 'Why?' Yorgis wondered. 'I don't know, but there's nothing to be done. We must go. The planes may be here soon.' The distant bombardment had stopped. A fresh mission was probably being prepared. 'The only question is – ' Artemis paused. The men were not going to help him. 'It seems to me that we must be here.' He indicated a place on the scuffed map where two villages were shown in positions similar to those below them. 'In which case, we head for here. If we go on through the night, we should be there by dawn.' Yorgis and Paniotis dropped back to their sections. Artemis began the descent. The two donkeys had cleared the road. It was possible from the slope to see almost directly behind the wall which bordered it for most of the way. No one was hiding. Artemis's steps became less heavy. The valley flattened. When he saw the rest of the men down and aiming he nodded at Kosta and the section crossed to the road. The sun was sharper now. They vaulted the wall and hurried across knobbly fields to the far slope. They mounted the Bren on a terrace about twenty metres above the valley floor. Artemis stood and waved. The main section rose, checked its weapons and followed the same route. Artemis went down behind the Bren. It was a relic of the help which the British had once dropped.

While Papastavrou's 'army' remained small, nothing was done to supply it. The British were unwilling to have anyone succeed where they had failed. They took part in the operations in the islands because it helped them to believe that they had never really been driven from them, but their miscalculations on the mainland upset their vanity and they preferred to forget it. They changed their policy only when it became clear that Papastavrou had recruited a substantial force and could not be discounted in the political struggle which was sure to follow liberation. The officers who had been operating in the islands were more deeply involved in the passions of the islanders than their superiors liked. The fighting was very savage; the Germans were unrestrained even by the small scruples which made them behave better in the capital than where no famous eye could fall on them. They remained susceptible to the illusion that all high-ranking persons belong to a freemasonry which will see to it that no one worthy of a long obituary finds it in print before it can be helped. On the other hand, the deaths of those who live in outlandish places always come cheap. The British officers like Michael Shaw, whose first fighting took place among the mountain-people of the larger islands, became fiercer partisans of their particular culture than anyone from the central Government could ever have been. Michael found the warrior a gladdening fellow. The comradeship of the hills had a fuller range of responses than that of the Senior Combination Room and more binding secrets than those of bought pleasure; there was a belief among the officers who lived for a long time with the partisans that they had found a permanent and cleaner way of life. They did not look forward to a return to 'civilization'. They were happy to ascribe virtues to their companions in arms which they would not so willingly have conceded to those who spoke their own language. At the same time they knew very well that what was theoretical to them was reality to the native. They watched the burning villages; the locals watched their villages burn. Nevertheless these British officers identified ardently with 'their' islanders. Nothing pleased Michael more than to be taken for one of the locals, to use so exactly the inflections which normally distinguished an islander from one who lived in the capital that a sentry would ask him when 'this Englishman' was coming. His bravery, which delighted him without convincing him of any personal merit, came of his awareness that he was not running quite the same risks as his fellow-combatants. No doubt he would be tortured if captured, but he would be treated more apprehensively than a partisan. He might not expect mercy, but he was sure of recognition. He was not intimidated by the execution of hostages. It tore him, but not in his flesh. It hardened him.

When in due course Papastavrou sent a mission to make contact with the island partisans, it was not warmly welcomed. The islanders distrusted the mainland. In the past it was always they who had to make concessions; the weak majority had prevailed too often over their isolated strength. The Occupation had restored their separate pride. The Germans had severed them from affectations of unity. There were those among the British who would actually have rejected Papastavrou's 'sly overtures'. Michael shared their feelings but saw through their sentimentality. To encourage separatism among the islanders was tempting but it was self-indulgent. However Homeric the British officers might seem temporarily, they would become foreigners again as soon as liberty was won. Shaw could not believe in any reliable sympathy from Whitehall for the interests of so notoriously 'difficult' and unproductive a section of the population. His love for them forbade, and his intelligence deplored, the vain short-sightedness of his colleagues who were happy to recover their chivalry in the mountains of a land whose history blanketed them in a glorious patchwork of ancient myth and modern misconception. A special providence seemed just in time to have fleshed their classical learning with this romantic incarnation. The relationship they maintained with H.Q.

was like that they had had long (or not so long) ago with senior staff at school; they ran their own show and won the cups to prove their zeal and keenness. But Papastavrou wanted to be more than a new house in the existing scheme of things; he wanted to modernize the whole establishment. His radical politics reminded the romantics that their days were numbered. Most of the British officers resented his ideas; Michael regretted them, but he saw that regret was a luxury. The partisans on the mainland were all of the Left. If the British were to have a chance of re-establishing their influence, a Royalist force with credible battle honours had to be created. Meanwhile Papastavrou had to be endorsed. How else could he be contained until a way was found of displacing him? Shaw reported favourably to H.Q. on the mission from the mainland and proposed that Papastavrou be supplied with small arms in sufficient numbers for him to have no call to ask for aid from elsewhere. His arguments were not directly challenged, but his fellow-officers took exception to them. It was arranged that he be recalled and dropped into a part of the country where Royalist partisans were operating.

After Artemis had killed the man in the doorway he returned home, collected some clothes and left. He went to the house of Dmitri Stratis. 'I've decided to join the partisans.' 'Excellent! Now we shall certainly be victorious. Artemy has made his decision.' 'Foolish as it seems, I have no idea how to set about it.' 'All Artemy's decisions have to be intellectual. No one is less affected by opportunity.' 'Dimmy, I've come for your help. Where are Nikos and the others?' 'I can't tell you exactly. I have my responsibilities too, believe it or not. But I'll tell you where to go. Someone will meet you there. You have my word.' 'You're in touch?' 'Everything will be taken care of.' Artemis nodded and stood up. The two men embraced, strongly. 'Leave the capital the day after tomorrow by train for Boreopolis. You are going to report a Trade Mission which is coming from Berlin at the end of the week. Come tomorrow morning first thing to the office, you know, where you used to take your articles, and collect your pass and papers. When the train stops at Hagios Stephanos, get off and report to the local Kommandantur that you would like to write a piece on the successful pacification of the vicinity. Put up at the Hotel Drakos in the square. Someone will contact you there.' Dmitri took Artemis by the hand. 'Believe me, my little Artemy. I love you well. Are you afraid that I shall betray you? You have me as close as I have you. You know that.' 'You have my love,' said Artemis and turned to go. 'Will you be there in the morning?' 'In the office? No. But Yanni will know what to do. Fear not. Are we not brothers?' Artemis went out on to the landing. An oil lamp was burning over the thick door in the hall. 'Artemy? It is you, isn't it? How are you? What a long time it's been, hasn't it, since the island?' He felt the girl's breath against his face. Did he imagine the wanton warmth in it? 'What're you *doing* here?' 'And you, my dear, are you living here these days?' 'Living here? Of course not. I never thought we'd ever see you again.' 'You may well not,' said Artemis. 'You're leaving the city. You're going to join the partisans, I know you are.' 'You've been listening at keyholes.' 'It's true, then.' 'Eleni, if you say a word to anyone – ' 'Take me with you.' 'Don't be a fool.' 'Take me with you. I'm not a child. It's only being here, being in the city, being in my parents' house that makes me a child, don't you see that?' 'Very clearly. But there's no question of it. Even if it were true – ' 'Why must you lie to me, pretend to me, why?' 'Two people travelling together are always suspicious.' 'A man and a woman are less suspicious than a man on his own.' 'Yes, that may well be so,' said Artemis, 'but I'm not going to be responsible for you.' 'Or for anyone else. Then why are you going to fight?' 'Eleni, if you say a word to anyone – ' 'I've told you. You can trust me. Why should I want to betray you?' 'To Katerina – ' 'I shan't say anything to Katerina. Katerina's in the country. For the baby.' 'Then what're you doing here?' 'Visiting. Aren't you inquisitive! I'm visiting. You can't go out any more. Dimmy's brother and sister are here. We're going to play cards. Don't you believe me?' 'Yes, of course.' 'Take me with you, Artemy. Please. I shall die here.' 'You've no idea what it's like out there. I've very little idea myself. But then I'm a man and – ' 'I want to go with you. I want to be with you. I want you to take me.' 'You're playing, Eleni. You're hoping to enjoy yourself.' 'Oh and why not? Must it be unenjoyable, life? Why are you going, Artemy?' 'That doesn't matter. I don't know. Motives aren't interesting.' 'Oh, I do love you! You're so pompous! Do you know that, how pompous you are? You want me to be worthless, don't you? You want women to be worthless because it justifies your neglect of them. It puts down your need of them and it excuses you belittling them. You welcome the war. You'd prefer to die rather than to give yourself to anyone else.' 'I don't know, Eleni. A man and a woman, that needs a world. A battle, that only needs a gun, an enemy. You may be right. Domestic life is the more demanding. Or is it merely the more crippling? I can't say. I don't know. But of course to discover the answer is already to be beyond escape.' 'Oh Artemy, it's so good to talk to you again, to hear you talk; it's so – serious. You're so funny! Don't be angry, I like it so much. You make everything so important. Dear owl! Do you mind if I call you that?' 'Not at all.' 'Help me to grow up. Take me with you. Tell me how to get to you and I'll come. Don't say there aren't any women in the partisans, because I know there are. They do have women to cook and be nurses, even to fight sometimes. Don't sentence me to stay here.' 'If you want to grow up, you must do it on your own. At least you *can* do it on your own. If you're serious about it, you can make your own way to the partisans.' 'I can't. You want me to stay here, that's really it. Oh you live in the abstract!' 'You've been talking to Katerina about me.' 'No, I've been listening to you. Take me with you, Artemy. I won't bother you. I won't complain, ever. I swear.' 'I know. I know.' 'I'm not like Katerina, whatever you may think.' 'You're a remarkable girl. I recognize that.' 'Which means that you're refusing.' 'Eleni, I'm afraid myself. I'm afraid of myself, of what I shall find myself to be. I have to go alone. I only have enough strength to take myself. It'll be bad enough to be my own judge, without having to live up to what you expect of me. It's not because I despise you that I can't take you, but because I can't go at all with you in judgment over me as well. I haven't the strength. Please understand that. I'm not treating you as a child. This has nothing to do with your qualities. I must get away from what knows me. I need time to be – invisible.' 'How can I be anything to you? You're rejecting me completely, aren't you?' 'Not because I mean to.' 'No, I see that, but in fact. There can never be a time when you could have any use for me, not unless you fail and then you'll be too bitter to. So there really isn't ever going to be a time, is there? Do you know how much that hurts me?' He kissed her face strongly, but without sensation. She tried to find pleasure, but then twisted from his arms. 'You see I'm right, don't you? You're denying me a life.' 'That's an absurd exaggeration!' 'So stiff, so formal, such a judge!' 'I'm not the only man, heaven knows. We hardly know each other.' 'I know you very well, very well.' 'You think you do.' 'I've thought about you more than you can imagine. I can do things for you. I'm not a child. You think I am, but I'm not. What would I have to do for you to take me seriously?' 'I don't know. I don't know. I don't know what it means to take someone seriously. To include them in one's life? What I'm going to do now I have just enough strength to do; I told you. I can't include anyone else.' 'You're going to submit. That's what you want to do, isn't it, to be punished, to be tested, something along those lines?' 'Possibly.' 'And will it ever end, do you think, your punishment?' 'I can't say.' 'You hope to be killed, I suppose?' 'Not consciously. Certainly not.' 'Then you'll come back and resume your life?' 'Resume? There's nothing to resume.' 'You know what I mean. Will you live the same old life? Accept all this again, will you be able to?' 'I can't make predictions. Predictions are vanity. I don't know.' 'You hope you'll be killed and don't have to find out. Take me with you. If you won't take me with you, tell me where you're going and I'll come on my own.' 'How can I do that?' 'What's to prevent you?' 'It's not fair on you, nor on those who are going to help me.' 'I could betray you tonight if I wanted to.' 'Of course.'

'So why should I betray you later?' 'There are ways of making you talk, everyone knows that. We needn't go on about them. I can't give you knowledge that might endanger you.' 'You refuse to liberate me, that's what it comes to.' 'Then, my dear Eleni, that is what it comes to.'

He turned to go downstairs and she leaped on to his back. He tottered, danced on the vanishing steps and reeled against the wall where a series of prints of national heroes, from the War of Independence, went down towards the hall. He reared and plunged before collapsing on the tiled steps, throwing her sideways against the banister. She lay panting, her skirts over her waist, hair shaken loose. 'Coward!' 'Perhaps.' 'Coward, aren't you?'

He took the train to Boreopolis, left it at Hagios Stephanos and presented himself at the local Kommandantur. He was greeted by the major in charge and drank coffee in his office. He listened and took notes while the major, whose name was Haller, told him his problems and the measures which had had to be taken to curb those who 'wanted to take advantage of the situation'. The major did not conceal the willingness of certain elements to frustrate the German war effort nor did he deny that foodstuffs were being removed in quantities which left the local people short. He had a clear conscience – he felt able to talk frankly – because he was under orders himself and because the food was necessary to an effort from which he personally derived no benefit. Artemis sat without shame or alarm with the major; he was able, without difficulty, to be the man the German took him to be, sympathetic to the problems of Occupation, a student rather than a critic. He asked pertinent questions and wondered what impression the major had of the local character. He prompted the other to jokes and admitted his own sense of strangeness in the company of peasants. One never knew what they were thinking; one never knew the best line to take with them. He wondered whether it might not serve the partisans' cause if he were to remain on terms with this Major Haller; he could imagine a situation where he became a kind of referee on whom the civilities of combat depended. He was in no hurry to go to the hotel where he had been told this suspended state of his would come to an end and he would meet his contact. He remembered the efficiency of the Germans in the square and the tailored charm of their officers in the big car, the glint of the schnapps flask; it seemed as though it was in the light of that secret glimpse that he was able to compose himself with such affectations of intimacy with Major Haller. He felt as if they had seen common service. What greater misconception could there be than to suppose that a double agent had some true allegiance? Artemis's sympathy with the major, with the whole beauty of the German style, was no more false than his enmity was true. He had never given the Germans much thought; he could hardly claim that he had always known of their wickedness, always condemned them, always expected to have to fight them. No, until their invasion he had liked their music and some of their scholarship; he could find a wilful, even narcotic element in the *determination* to find their destruction the only purpose in life. It was likely to be a protracted business; it served in the office of a lifetime's ambition, but it was hardly enough. Between him and Major Haller, sitting by the iron stove in the Kommandantur, there was a kind of openness which could come only from a certain wistful duplicity on both their parts. Haller too had his music and his philosophy; no single German officer could be encountered who did not have his music and his philosophy: he was equipped to lose as well as to win. Only the complete barbarians, always on another front, lacked this capacity for alternatives. It was pleasant in a bleak landscape to theorize on possible forms, to inhabit possible worlds. An intimacy, born of casualness, joined the two men. Artemis lingered; he prolonged his questions; he was grateful: he did not so much play the part of the effusive collaborator as, provisionally, become him.

When he left the Kommandantur he walked across the square and looked back to see whether the major was watching from his window. The Hotel Drakos was cold. Was he to take a room or not? He went to the desk across the marble vestibule. A bank of keys rose behind the reddish woman bespectacled over her accounts. 'You have a room?' 'Your papers?' 'Of course.' 'How many nights?' 'One. Two. One, probably.' 'Mr Theodoros?' 'That's right.' It seemed a flimsy disguise, to travel under one's own name. 'Journalist?' 'Correct. Are there any messages for me?' 'Messages? Are you expecting a message?' 'It's possible. My paper may have told someone to find me here.' 'Your paper.' 'I've just been with Major Haller at the Kommandantur. I'm writing an article on the district.' 'Major Haller?' 'Yes. I was sent to see him.' 'Will you be eating at the hotel? Have you got coupons?' The room was so icy that Artemis wrapped himself in the blankets with his overcoat on and lay there as cold as a roll of linoleum. He dozed and dreamed; woke and dreamed again. He dreamed that he was sitting laughing with Major Haller, declaring quite openly to him that he had come to join the partisans and that he now had doubts, that he was willing to work with the major subject to certain safeguards: obviously he wasn't going to be party to the death of any of his compatriots, but he would like to be given the arguments for not opposing the German presence; he was willing to be persuaded that there was more merit in the German case than he had been prepared to admit. This discussion had a more settled logic to it than most dreams; a strain of realism, of thoughtful definition ran through it. Artemis could recall the arguments when he woke. He dozed off again with the distinct intention of clarifying a point or two, like a lawyer pencilling a query on a crooked knee before going back into chambers. It seemed only as a certificate of unreality that he noticed that he was sitting naked from the waist down with Haller, who was identical with his genuine self except that he wore a military overcoat with fur facings and toyed with a silver flask which he held out several times to Artemis. Artemis was embarrassed at first by the display of his genitals, but the major absolved him from shame. He raised his hand to forestall apology and continued the discussion on a lofty philosophical basis. Music came from the street. Artemis was impatient for an agreement, and kept looking out of the window, but the major was maddeningly pensive, either through a sly knowledge of Artemis's timetable or from a misguided desire not to shorten his pleasure. Artemis knew that he was dreaming, in the common sense, yet he believed in the reality of the major. Artemis could swear this imagined Haller had independent feelings, said things he himself could never have imagined. He dreaded an interruption which might deprive him of further intimacy. He believed that he was about to sign not a separate peace but a general treaty whereby the problems of the world could be resolved. He claimed to sympathize with the German position, to be ready to allow her grievances and asked only that the major 'understand why we are bound to resist if things go on in the present way'. Artemis's dream was without ornate symbolism or the sudden shifts of location which dreams traditionally display. He and Haller endured long dialogues and gave each other the polite attention typical of last meetings. When Artemis felt himself shaken, when he was bound to acknowledge a third force in the situation, he shuddered and stayed rigid and did his best to keep the major's eye, hoping that he would not terminate the discussion. He leaned forward with his hands across his genitals, minimizing the area of bare flesh. The major was shaking his head – 'My dear fellow!' – and wiping the mouth of the flask when Artemis was finally prised into consciousness. It was dark and colder than ever. The reddish woman was at his shoulder. There was someone downstairs. She took him to the yard at the back of the hotel. The man was wearing a suit and had a look of cupidinous short-sightedness. 'Let's go, let's go.' Artemis went back for his bag. He was almost surprised to be allowed to return upstairs. It seemed an indiscretion, as if an arresting officer had permitted him the chance to escape. His teeth chattered. He could not stop shaking. The man had not altered his expression when he returned with his bag. 'I'd better pay the bill – ' Artemis looked apologetically at the woman; he might have been afraid that she would think that he had given her hotel a bad name. There was a cart in the yard with two barrels on it. A big mule stamped in the shafts. They climbed up. 'What am I to say if we're stopped?' 'Show your papers and say we're going up to the monastery. It's all cleared with Major Haller.' Artemis had taken this man for an emissary from the partisans. Now he was less sure and, simultaneously, less hostile. He had yet to cross the frontier. They clopped forward along the cobbled street and bumped down on to a track. The landscape was frosted, as if a dull bulb was glowing under layers of old laundry. 'What about patrols? Are there any?' 'Not in this weather. No one goes out in this much.' The man handled the cart efficiently, but Artemis had the impression that he was a townsman. He was doing somebody a favour. The monastery was on a steep hill a few miles from the town. They were about to start the ascent, Artemis blowing on his hands and huddling under the sack on the box, when the man gave him a nudge. 'All right. This is where you get down.' The place was among stones, black and dead as a frozen plant. 'Here? Are you sure?' 'Of course. Down you get.' What possible reward could the man gain through deceiving him? Artemis got down. 'Well, thank you.' 'You're welcome.' The mule stirred; the cart creaked; the barrels lurched out of Artemis's view. The last creak of the harness died on the wind. He was alone. Artemis crouched at the edge of the road by a wayside shrine he was now able to pick out. He blew on his hands and tried to find amusement from the fear which shrivelled him, like a schoolboy who hopes to fill a blank in his verses by some wilful hyperbole. A mournful hooting kept him company. Then there was the poop of a toad. In this weather? A snort of laughter affronted nature. 'Who's that? Who's there?' 'I thought owls liked the dark!' 'It can't be! It can't be!'

Konni was stronger and broader than he had been as a student. His face was less fine; he might have been a featherweight late in his career, the lines thickened over cheeks and brow, the body harder but no less agile. If he had lost the slightness which had been so attractive, the loss had its charm. It amused them to see each other; Konni enjoyed the authority he now carried and to which Artemis was willing, temporarily, to defer. In the days which followed their passion was replaced by friendship, but Artemis's ambition was fired by Konni's new seniority.

General Stavros Athanasiou was an officer of the old school. His only contribution to the tactics of resistance was to insist on correct military forms. Regular discipline was his panacea; he attributed the national 'disgrace' to a failure in morale and his solution to the hardships of his men was artificially to increase them. A stiff grey-haired man with the square head and cold eyes usually ascribed to the Junker, he had the rigidity of mind which combines un-questioning patriotism with scornful suspicion of one's compa-triots. Artemis was to find him obstinate and short-sighted (like most men whose eyes are fixed on immutable ideas), but his idiotic probity was not unlikeable. He had the charm of the antique; if he was cracked, he was not cheap. Did he have visions of being the post-war Marshal? Perhaps no military man could censor entirely such noble manifestations of a warrior's final belief in himself, but he was perplexed and wounded by the condemnations of the Government radio and found it hard to accept that those in the capital had little choice but to strip him of his rank and decora-tions. He was seriously troubled by his degradation and spent several hours debating whether or not he should remove his medals. Artemis took advantage of the general's piety towards the old army to reclaim his old rank, but once possessed of it he clamoured, with a vigour bordering on insubordination, for more imaginative action. Athanasiou and his officers seemed to think that they were doing their duty simply by establishing an indepen-dent force; they were reluctant to endanger their positions by excessive provocation. They argued that they were incapable of resisting a full German assault and that they would therefore be unwise to engage the enemy too vigorously. If they fought too aggressive a campaign, the civilians would suffer most from it. The speed and zeal which the Germans showed in carrying out reprisals were proof enough of that. Athanasiou was caught in a fork. He felt himself abandoned by the Government to whom he looked for encouragement (and promotion) and he lacked that enthusiasm for an untypical future which strengthened Papastavrou. If he broke up the traditional structure of his army, he might lose for ever the power to return it to its traditional allegiance and to claim the traditional rewards. Young men like Artemis, whose loyalty to King Paul was still avowedly sincere, filled him with misgivings. Paul had agreed to leave the country under pressure from the British, who wished to preserve him for post-war purposes. If Artemis's allegiance had not been broken by the king's flight, it was hardly confirmed by it. The passive attitude of Athanasiou's army, with its tortuous tact towards the enemy, gave Artemis time to distinguish the strands which bound him to the old order. There was no cause to snap them and no sharp edge against which to fret them. For many months they remained slack but unbroken, while the partisans endlessly rehearsed operations and drew conclusions from the rehearsals as if they were real parts of the war. That they bore arms convinced them that they were honourably embattled, but cold and hunger were more consequential enemies than the Germans and took greater toll of them. They persuaded themselves that the Germans dared not attack, whereas it was truer to say that they were glad not to have to do so; their force could be concentrated elsewhere. Artemis's first discontent grew not from social but from military considerations. He pleaded for small groups to break away and form fighting patrols which might dislocate German communications and attack targets which could be destroyed without the risk of a pitched battle. It did not occur to him for some time that the malaise which had caused his breach with Katerina, his dissent from the rationale which united the notables, could relate to his present disquiet. He was not openly critical of the command until he was accused of challenging it. He had suggested his ideas to Konni, relying on the sentiment which gave them both a secret pleasure in each other's presence without renewing their desire. What could be more humiliating than siege tactics when one was not even besieged? Konni agreed. The morale of the men, granted neither action nor responsibility, was failing. Discipline was the traditional method of 'understanding' the common soldier. The only vigorous action the command undertook was against their own men. Artemis and Konni were both ordered to take part in the court martial of three men who had attempted to desert. The charge against them was that they had hoped to make contact with the enemy. Artemis was able to convert that into a bitter jest, much to the disapproval of the other members of the court, and the charge was reduced to simple desertion. Konni was appointed defence counsel, since he knew the men. He was thus enabled both to express the disillusionment of the rank and file and to remain within the proprieties; it was his duty, after all, to speak up for the defendants. However, Artemis was on the panel of officers and his contemptuous analysis of the reasons for the breakdown of enthusiasm and good order provoked the embarrassed dislike of his colleagues. He and Konni expressed the same point of view, but the one felt that he had done all he could, while the other was left ashamed at his futility. Artemis could not refrain from telling Konni how disgraceful he considered the verdict of the court and how strongly he opposed it. Konni was disturbed by the impropriety of a member of the court apologizing to counsel. Artemis was impatient. 'The court? What's that but a way of escaping from the realities?' 'The men were punished. Detention. Bread and water – hardly different from our normal diet. It wasn't very severe. They might have been shot.' 'If they'd been shot, you wouldn't have seen me again in this army.' 'I won't listen to this, Artemy.' 'The blame rests with the command, you know it yourself. You told the court: the men couldn't see any point in staying with the army. I ask you, a sergeant and a corporal, both long-service men, and they can't see any point. They're right; the army's become simply a way of living outside a society that happens to be suffering. It's a self-indulgence, this apparatus of command, the maintenance of formal discipline, military justice, it's a charade, Konni. Can't you see that? What're we fighting for? To survive, which means simply that we've deserted the ordinary people who don't have the chance to absent themselves from domestic responsibility. Do

277

you remember Eleni, Katerina's sister? She wanted to join me coming here. I told her it was going to be dangerous! I thought the Germans were hushing up the seriousness of the situation. I thought Major Haller was a mouthpiece, full of fake figures, but no. What's Athanasiou doing? He's waiting for the Allies to bale him out, he's preserving his force intact so that he can call the tune in the capital when the war's been won by other people. How can we recover our self-respect like that?' 'Artemy, you mustn't talk to me in this fashion.' 'What're you fighting for, Konni?' 'I know you're clever, Artemy. I refuse to be cross-examined; I've no doubt you can show that there are inconsistencies in my attitude, but you won't change me by pointing them out. A camel may be absurd but you won't talk him out of his hump.' 'Listen, my friend, one assumes one knows somebody because of – certain things, and one finds one doesn't. I want to understand.' 'Oh, you think there're words behind everything. You treat everyone like an old billboard. You want to strip off the layers and come to something basic, but all you do is rub and rub like an eraser on thin paper until there are holes everywhere, and then you want to write on them. You're wrong about people. You make them so important. You want them to be full of motives like a pillow with feathers.' 'All right, I accept that.' 'Oh, damn you.' 'Konni, I mean it. I appreciate what you're saying. You're probably right. Only I don't see why that makes it wrong to want to understand you, especially you.' 'Oh you're so romantic, it's really funny. It's funny, Artemy.' 'I loved you. I shall always have something of that night in my heart.' 'That's something private. You make a mistake to try to make it convertible. It's irrelevant to the present.' 'You still think about your father's estates.' 'That's quite untrue.' 'No, I don't believe it is. You won't hear any criticism of Athanasiou and the *vecchi* because you share my disillusion.' 'Artemy, I warned you – ' 'But they remain your only hope of reconquering what you think of as yours. You prefer to remain with them, wrong as they are, because you needn't have any scruple in peeling off from them in order to settle your old scores when you're strong enough. Become a general, you think, and you might gain enough influence to insist on a change of the borders; you might be able to "rectify pre-war injustices". Can you deny it?' 'I never thought of any such thing.' 'Think of it now. Doesn't it fit your behaviour like a mould?' Konni might have struck Artemis if he could have decided with which hand or which weapon to hit him where. Indecision left a strand of malice in him. His face was yellowed and sour. His defeat endeared him to Artemis. He felt fond of him, wanted to fondle him now for the first time since they had met again. He was so touched by Konni's confusion that he took it for endearment; his vanity ignored its unexploded resentment. 'I shall always love you, Konni.' He let his hand fall on the other's shoulder. Konni did not break free. He was bowed by a kind of docility which seemed to concede victory to the other. He waited until Artemis removed his hand. Artemis had smiled, uncertainty clouding his eyes, and moved off with an awkward salute.

Some days later British planes bombed the railway line at Hagios Stephanos. A few days after the first raid came another. During it a single plane detached itself from the main force and flew over the partisans' territory. Three British officers, of whom Michael Shaw was the senior, dropped into the area, together with a modest load of supplies. Shaw's arrival was not widely announced to the partisans. His mission was to liaise between the British command in Cairo (the other two men were W/T specialists) and between the forces of Athanasiou and Papastavrou. Athanasiou was formally welcoming and presented a list of requirements. Michael was anxious to get the general to commit himself to positive action, but that very anxiety encouraged Athanasiou to delay, with the knowledge that more could be gained from an urgent than from an indifferent ally. Major Shaw was not encouraged to circulate among the army; he was entertained at headquarters. The senior officers feared that he might call the men to arms prematurely; when he protested his loyalty to their cause, he only encouraged their suspicions. The more arms the Royalist forces received, the less willing they proved to employ them. At first,

Michael's tact was equal to the situation. He argued that the army could scarcely pose as the liberators of the nation if they had no scars to show for their struggle. How could Athanasiou match Papastavrou's claims if the one could parade an army of veterans, the other a collection of wallflowers? The only force which could command the peace was one which had made a contribution to the war. Athanasiou's calculations were different. The British would never understand the politics of his country because they were incapable of an accurate translation of its terms into theirs. They would continue to think of the Church as a spiritual force and of the army as 'military', whereas the former was also a political system and the latter a mystique. The British had the common habit of sentimentalizing the morality of a country whose destiny they intended to shape without reference to it. They were expert at overriding rules which they believed others would keep. The general promised action and amused himself by playing Penelope to his British suitors, organizing a plan one day and finding a reason to postpone it the next. To deceive his friends became a more rewarding game than to damage his enemies. The messages from Papastavrou which had at first been understanding and even solicitous became more peremptory. Finally he warned Athanasiou that indignation was growing against him, especially with the worsening conditions in the countryside and the starvation in the capital. The British imagined that their efforts to supply arms to the insurgents and food to the hungry would earn them the gratitude of both; Papastavrou, whose munitions increasingly came from the north, remained, in fact, their most loyal supporter, constantly making allowances for the sloth of his compatriots and pleading their case to Cairo. Athanasiou was more afraid of Papastavrou than of the Germans. Everyone would combine to drive out the latter, but he would probably be on his own against the former. Papastavrou was apparently persuaded, even when he became openly impatient, that Athanasiou needed an excuse to move and that he would do so if action was made unavoidable or hesitation dishonourable. Accordingly Papastavrou led an army across the central mountains at the beginning of spring and attacked against the German garrison below Hagios Stephanos, right under Athanasiou's nose. He was confused in his tactics and paid the price for it. He wanted at once to demonstrate his strength by smashing the Germans himself and at the same time to make the strongest call one general could to another theoretically on the same side, to let him hear the sound of the guns and challenge him not to march towards them. The army of the Left passed under Athanasiou's outposts early in the morning and was immediately ordered into battle. A request had been made for facilities for treatment of the wounded, if they could be evacuated, and for supplies. Some food was waiting for Papastavrou's men, but the ammunition was 'mislaid'. They had to go in with what they had brought. Athanasiou had given the word for his army to stand to; it was in full battle order when Papastavrou passed through the lines. The sounds of heavy-artillery fire breached the morning. The Germans were ready for the partisans and engaged them in good order. By mid-morning the battle showed no signs of resolution. Artemis requested permission to take out a patrol in strength with a view to establishing the situation. He was told that the battle was being satisfactorily surveyed; there was no point in such a patrol. After an hour, when the battle below showed no signs of easing, he went again to headquarters and saw Michael Shaw. Unwisely, he appealed directly to the Englishman. 'You must get them to intervene in force at once. Given reasonable luck, we should be able to smash the Germans, gain credit for ourselves and redeem our honour.' 'I should like nothing better. I've been arguing for them to do it for the last hour and a half. I don't know what they're waiting for.' 'I know and so do you. They're waiting for the Germans to smash Papastavrou. I don't know how you can stay with them.' 'How do you?' 'I'm one of them. Why can't you threaten to withdraw all aid from them if they don't march?' 'Because my orders are to afford them all possible assistance. I have no discretion, Artemy.' The staff officers listened to this exchange with furious resentment. If they could not understand English, the tone, like the sound of a poem according to some authorities, conveyed enough for them to feel both criticized and uneducated. A colonel told Artemis that unless he returned to his unit at once he would be placed under arrest for desertion in face of the enemy. Artemis laughed and asked loudly for the order to advance. The colonel drew his pistol. Artemis shrugged at Michael Shaw and walked away. He ordered his men to prepare to move off. He was on the extreme left, almost overlooking Hagios Stephanos, perhaps an hour below. The colonel did not trust him and sent another officer, Zanti, to check on his behaviour. Zanti, a heavy man with short legs and the apologetic surliness of a policeman not yet equipped with a warrant, attempted to intervene between Artemis and his men. Artemis drew his pistol and demanded that of the other officer. Zanti called on the soldiers to disarm Artemis, but he was unknown to them and lacked authority, since he already had his arms up. Artemis told his men that he was going to the help of those in the valley. He called for volunteers to accompany him. The men were bewildered and reluctant at first, but once the bravest had stepped forward the rest followed. When Artemis led them down the hill, Papastavrou had already been defeated. His men were unused to complicated manoeuvres; they had lost touch with each other in the unfamiliar landscape and they were shaken by the cohesion and fire-power of the Germans. Courage was insufficient against troops who were better armed and who seemed to expect them. The partisans had forced their way up to the railway, but they had merely insisted on entering a trap which, on a less demonstrative occasion, they would have been wise enough to evade. The first soldiers Artemis and his company met were Papastavrou's and they were in retreat. Stunned by their reverse, they mistook their compatriots for Germans and opened fire. Artemis lost three men killed and several wounded. He could not prevent the others from returning the fire. He ran out into the middle of the confusion and shouted to both sides to hold their fire. He was wounded in the thigh before he could manage to control them. By then it was a victory to have imposed a sullen armistice.

Both sides had been hurt by the exchange. All but a handful of Artemis's men demanded that he lead them back to the redoubt. Artemis knew that he would certainly face a court martial and probably execution. Men who had followed him so reluctantly would give evidence against him with alacrity. 'I am staying with the army of Andreas Papastavrou,' Artemis shouted. The battle continued behind them. 'Then you're a traitor to your king and your country!' cried a corporal and levelled his rifle. Artemis shot him and then ran to join the others who had vanished in the smoke. He was almost irritated when three of his original company trotted after him. The rest hesitated and were lost in the confusion. For a half-hour or more the four renegades were free to act on their own initiative. They managed to engage a German patrol from the flank and matched their tactics to suit those whom they had come to support. The Germans were less eager to follow up their advantage than they would have been in a regular battle. They feared that Papastavrou planned to draw them under the guns of Athanasiou's redoubt and they knew that they had only to have their strength dissipated and their artillery balked by the risk of its falling on their own men for the balance to swing towards the enemy. At one moment they seemed about to annihilate the partisans, the next the field was empty; the battle was over. Artemis and his men, now in the best of humour since they had seen action and avoided loss, joined the retreating army. Artemis was fortunate enough to fall in with a captain whom he had known in the war against the Italians. He assumed that Artemis had been with Papastavrou for some time (the Left partisans' style of fighting meant that there were long periods when a man could be away from the main body) and by the time that Artemis had explained his recent arrival explanations were superfluous. Papastavrou himself discounted Artemis's account of Athanasiou's treachery. He had a higher proportion of killed and wounded than usual: he was relying on the shelter of Athanasiou's positions. Surprisingly, he lacked rancour. Artemis actually feared at one stage that he would be surrendered to his erstwhile friends without Papastavrou considering what might happen to him. It was not easy to argue for by-passing Athanasiou when some of the wounded were unlikely to last much further. Artemis was fresh, the general weary. He hinted that the partisans might encounter a cooler welcome than they hoped, but even he hardly expected that they would actually be fired on. Papastavrou's men headed for the hills in three loose columns; they were in each instance met by rifle and machine-gun fire. Yet so shaken were they by their misfortunes and so relying on the good will of those in the redoubt that they continued their dejected retreat into the guns. The fire was not sharp; some of those on the slopes refused to open up, but the story in the redoubt was that the Germans had disguised themselves as partisans and that unless they were resisted they would overwhelm the garrison. Only when Papastavrou's men were within earshot did their unmistakable accents cause most of the defenders to falter. Their officers ordered them to honour their oaths as soldiers and continue to fire against their compatriots who, it was claimed, had 'sold themselves to the Germans'. The new losses were as heartbreaking as they were disgraceful, but Papastavrou gained command first of himself and then of his men. They were not recruits; they were capable of facing treachery with the same determination that they faced the Germans. He told them not to condemn Athanasiou's soldiers. They should pity those who were being misled by guilty and frightened men. At the very moment when Papastavrou saw that his battle must now be openly political as well as military, at the instant when the great break came between the army of the Left and the Royalists, a breach which was to lead to years of civil war, he was mild and understanding. He would detach from the Royalists all those who had been deceived before dealing with their deceivers. For the time being he imposed on his men the whole burden of their own salvation. The retreat was painful, but they would never again expect help either from the British, whom they suspected of engineering their betrayal, or from Athanasiou, who had so stonily ignored them. It was a sign perhaps of their respect for the British that they could not imagine them impotent, only deceitful. Michael Shaw himself crossed the central massif in order to remonstrate with Papastavrou when the Central Committee formerly denounced the Royalists, but no reconciliation began to be possible. Shaw had time to speak to Artemis, who was distinguishing himself in the new army, and was able to convince him that if he were free he would have preferred to stay with the Papastavrou contingent. He was not free; after leaving all his chocolate and a W/T set with Artemis (theoretically a form of negligence which might have landed him in serious trouble), he returned to the Royalist camp. By the time that the army had reached its mountain strongholds Artemis already assumed that the future of the country lay with the Left. There was no blinding conversion. His loyalty towards the young king which he had once imagined so passionate fell away like dead skin. He neither knew the young man nor cared about him; his character and his principles were like cardboard left in the rain. The march simply revealed to Artemis how little he knew of the country he had imagined he understood all his life. It was not only the future which was open but the past too. He was as misguided about the one as about the other. The march placed him, without the comforts of deception, exactly in his social context. If his situation was inescapable, his exact knowledge of it released him from its bounds, at least intellectually. It made his history a little joke, an encapsulated wart, hopefully non-malignant, which marked him indelibly but which might, suitably cauterized, not affect the rest of his life. He could see himself released from a logic of position into a logic of action. His 'courage', which later became an endearing (because almost inadvertent) characteristic, ceased to be the result of discipline, the expected behaviour of an officer, and became the sport of freedom. This period of skittish courage was limited, but it certainly existed. He was like a traveller who realizes that it is not his personality, not his character as defined in school reports or paternal chats, but the luggage with which he has been burdened, the tedious wardrobe of precautions (in case it turns cold, in case it gets hot) with which his background has furnished him that prevents him passing into the world of possibilities, from living in the present.

The second section crossed the road and climbed to where Artemis and the advance party were waiting. The two villages showed no new signs of life. With the balance of his strength now swung to the northern side of the valley, the Royalists had either missed their chance or were not in the area. He spread the men wide along the ridge, one section facing each village, and gave the signal for Paniotis to bring his men across. He gestured fiercely to the new arrivals. They had a duty to cover those who had just seen them across. Paniotis and his squad ambled towards the road. Artemis stood up and shouted, 'Run. *Run.*' He was without clear motive, but his anger was unfeigned. He saw something personal in their indolence, something deliberately crass, the glazed smile of a child who refuses a lesson. He saw Paniotis's face enlarged with derision (as a woman's with accusing tears) and the old sailor rolled, in a parody of a run, towards the wall behind the road. The section vaulted it and Artemis watched for them to come up the slope. Paniotis was not with them. The section approached and then wavered. Paniotis was lying below the wall. Artemis yelled at the men to take up position with the others along the ridge and went leaping down towards the wall. Paniotis was huddled against the bottom of the wall like a bundle of sticks fallen from a donkey. He smiled at Artemis. 'What's the matter, what's happened?' 'I fell.' 'Can you get up? Get up, man.' 'I fell. I'm sorry. I was clumsy.' 'Try and get on your feet.' Artemis put his hand under Paniotis's shoulder. He was inert. Even helping him was a struggle. 'I think my hip's out.' 'Your hip?' 'I've put it out again. I didn't know how far it was to the ground. I misjudged it.' 'Are you sure?' 'It feels like it.' 'Try and get up, will you?' Artemis stood up and frowned at the ridge. He was like a referee in a game where stern measures have been necessary and where the likeliest offender, the man he was told to keep his eye on, has now been injured. 'Will it go back?' He was waving for men to come and help. 'Can we get

it back?' 'I don't know, Captain.' 'Well, what did they do before?'
'I had two operations on it.' 'Why the hell didn't you look where
you were going? Well?' 'I was hurrying, Captain.' 'I didn't tell
you to – oh, well, what's happened has happened, I suppose.'
Kosta and young Adonis arrived. 'Get him away from the wall so
I can look at him.' 'What happened, old man?' 'Never mind. Get
him away from the wall so that I can have a look. Does it hurt?'
'Yes, Captain.' Paniotis's courage was unendurable. 'Adonis, go
up and tell Yorgis to take command. He's to send three men up to
the top of the hill to keep a lookout. Tell Paniotis the shepherd and
Michali to get down here, they'd better bring Yanni with the
tommy-gun – and Bruno too. Hurry. And then come back here
yourself.' 'You'll have to leave me behind.' 'Shut up. Shut up,
Paniotis, will you please while I think? I want to have a look at
this injury. Does it feel like it did before?' 'It's out, Captain. You'll
have to leave me behind.' Artemis tore at the old sailor's clothes
as if he were going to rape him. Only a gasp, the first indication
of actual pain Paniotis had given, restrained him. 'If only Brasidas
was here.' The dislocation was obvious. His injury brought a smirk
to Paniotis's face. He was like a useless animal that knows it has
ruined its master. 'You'll have to leave me behind.' 'Is this your
village you seem so pleased about it?' 'This? My village?' The
sailor raised his chin: never. 'Then I'll decide what we do with
you.' Paniotis the shepherd, smiling as usual, 'a moon without
a hidden side' Artemis had described him in a poem, had crabbed
swiftly down the slope and was standing there. 'I want you to go
into the village and see if you can find a handcart – ' 'It's no use,
Captain, taking anything with wheels. You'll never get across the
hills with anything on wheels. You'll have to leave me here. Don't
worry.' 'Worry? You've already held us up. If we leave you here
and they capture you they'll know exactly how many we are and
where we're heading.' 'They know that now.' 'Probably. Go into
the village and see if you can find a stretcher.' 'Pointless. You'll be
slowed up. You'll never carry me across the mountains. I'll do no
damage if you leave me behind. I'll not tell them anything.' 'That's

287

not the point.' 'Then what is?' 'I won't leave you here. It's not far to the frontier. We can get you there, can't we, Paniotis?' The shepherd would agree to anything; his encouraging smile was no encouragement. 'If you run into any trouble, get back here as fast as you can,' Artemis said to Michali as they moved off towards the village. 'What did they do to your leg? Can we force it back into its socket? If it's only a case of dislocation –' 'I was in plaster ten weeks. Captain, it would be simpler if you'd leave me here. Get me into the village if you like and I'll take my chance.' 'Chance? You'd have no chance. It only needs one man to know who you are and tell the Government. Can you really believe that there's a single village today that could keep such a secret? They'll shoot you.' 'What's the matter, Captain?' Artemis had forced his hands into his pockets, consulting the time by the sun, his plans burning away, and felt the crumple of paper. He had kept a few of the pamphlets dropped by the aeroplane. He yelled to Michali and the others to come back. They failed to hear. He sent Adonis after them. He was alone with Paniotis and Kosta. 'I'll stay with him,' said Kosta. 'No need.' Artemis smoothed a leaflet and handed it to Paniotis, who frowned to focus. 'When they get to you, show them this.' 'What is it, Captain?' 'Never mind. Paniotis understands. You get on up the hill and tell them I'll be there in a moment. Get them ready to move off tell Yorgis.' 'You're going to leave him here?' 'He's going to stay here. He'll be all right.' 'They'll kill him.' 'Not with this. Do as I say now, Kosta.' Artemis appealed to Paniotis, for the last time perhaps, to obey him. The old sailor nodded at Kosta, who threw a look of heavy contempt at Artemis. 'From now on,' he began, 'I watch you –' 'Get up the hill.' 'I'll stay with him.' 'You're needed. He'll be all right.' 'What is this?' Kosta made to take the paper from Paniotis. 'Up!' said Paniotis, withholding it. 'Up!' Kosta looked again at Artemis as though it were he who was keeping the paper from him and then he bent and kissed the old sailor on each cheek, his own face scored with accusing tears. He stormed the hill so meaningly that Artemis and Paniotis smiled together, like parents. 'You'll use it, won't you?'

'Goodbye. Good luck. May you live long years.' 'Panioti, God protect you.' He lapsed into the ageless phrase. 'Be well. May you live long years.' He too bent and kissed the old sailor who did not put his arms around him, long though he held the embrace. Artemis stepped back and raised his clenched fist. Paniotis, eyes on the distance, smiled at the situation, not at Artemis. He rejoiced in this prone victory of his and left Artemis the loser. The men were ready. On legs almost too stiff to force themselves against the slope, Artemis stumbled towards his command. The old sailor sat there frowning at the paper in his hand. The line moved up the ridge towards the heat. Artemis counted them past him over the hill. He turned and looked again for some sign from Paniotis. He saluted and waited for a moment. Paniotis raised the white paper. Artemis smiled, relieved. The old sailor tore it into strips in the air, took the fragments with his teeth like an animal and spat them away. Then he lay back against the wall.

> 'He goes out of life ill-tempered
> And slams the door on my fingers.'

Artemis muttered to himself as they started into the next valley. The urge to write glosses in the margin of his present experience reminded him of the days when any stimulus could be the excuse for an erection, when even to be aware of the absence of a stimulus was a stimulus. The body was in open insurrection against conscience and conscience itself became its accomplice, just as at the later stages of a revolution the police, while seeming still to be loyal to the old order, become so accustomed to conferring with the leaders on the other side that they are more familiar with them than with the remnants of the Government. The police are insensibly recruited to the new scheme not because it is more just or more enlightened but simply because it is more coherent. The tangled history of Democritos lost its ravelled uniqueness as soon as it ceased to be a moral and was read as a social text. The policeman does not change sides; sides change him. It was the prosaic element of that scholarly character which Artemis had never wholly lost that led him to compose the apologies of those against him. He could not prevent his mind from springing to their defence. Before the retreat, this capacity to impersonate the thinking of the other side was a positive advantage to the understanding (and confusion) of their strategy. It won him his place on the Central Committee. There might come a time when the door was closed on the past and mastery of their dialects would cease to be creditable, but only when the past was no longer a threat to the future. If the revolution had swept the board, Artemis might have found himself on trial; he would have embodied a memory whose only function would have been subversive. The committee would have turned on him without rancour, but with the ruthlessness of a manager junking old machinery: nothing personal. The retreat was a reprieve for him. Dmitri imagined that he would waste away with boredom, but he would at least retain a use across the border; he understood a language which was still current and would remain a common tongue in the state Dmitri and his friends had resurrected. No interpreter, whatever his 'real' sympathies, dies before an army has done with the territory to which his tongue has the key.

The firing came from the east, artillery and small arms. No planes had flown directly overhead, but the drone of bombers could be heard, parcels of bombs. Artemis felt a strong urge to march to the guns. The contempt of the men for their own situation was directed against him. It was convenient for them to make his decision free and so to remain in the comfort of bondage and accusation. He crossed the valley without a glance towards the east and began the next ascent. This valley had no houses, only a single stone shelter high on the slope where a goatherd could rest. The men were so aware of his cowardice (how else could they look at it?) that they were convinced that they would reach the frontier without incident; it was the greater humiliation and so they took it for granted. They passed the shelter and continued to climb. They had not noticed that this peak was higher than the earlier ones and they were unprepared for the view it gave them. They were on the roof of the province. The sea was away to the left, four scalloped bays visible to them, while to the right a wrinkled plateau stretched fifteen to twenty kilometres, maybe more, valleys and villages open to their eyes, a living map. Behind the plateau were snowy mountains; ahead of them, on the farthest horizon, a town with icy minarets hanging from the sky. The bombers twinkled like needles through blue silk. They were attacking a village a full fifteen kilometres to the east. Away to the north, where they were finishing their run, puffs of anti-aircraft fire smudged the air. Who could be firing at them except the 'traditional enemy'? The frontier could not be more than fifteen kilometres north of Artemis and his men. They started down the slope which would take them on to the roof of the plateau. The wrinkles which seemed so mild from above were higher than they expected. There was hard marching ahead. Artemis led them north-west, away from the fighting. He guessed that Brasidas and the others were holding off a thrust from the east while the main body (and stragglers like Artemis's group) made for the frontier. Artemis felt no gratitude but a wry affection for the jaundiced doctor, who would take the most dangerous mission for himself as if he were impelled by a kind of greed and deserved no thanks. Or would Brasidas see that such courage was not admirable today and prefer to play the coward and lead the main body to safety, leaving the glory for Alexander Pavlides? It was likely that he had done just that. And now Artemis did feel grateful to his unattractive colleague, whose skill was always disposed to make others seem more praiseworthy than he. He was a sublime Thersites, ennobled with courage, but careful to retain the appearance of a charmless opportunist. Artemis was happy for the first time in weeks, keeping step in his imagination with Brasidas, sharing a joke only the two of them would have the wit to see. They crossed the first shallow step of the plateau and took the low ridge into the next. The firing was more sporadic, but louder. The Government troops had either lost touch with the partisans or had

been outdistanced by them. Artemis had forgotten a third possibility: the Government had disengaged to allow the bombers a
clear run. The new planes came low and in two waves. This time
their axis was east–west and they finished their run by machine-
gunning Artemis and his group as they crossed open ground. No
one was touched. The planes overshot their marks and were out to
sea before they could recover. As they banked to come back, the
men reached the boulders of a river-bed and were in the caves
behind them. The planes came low over the wrong valley, firing
aimlessly, and were on their way. It was now midday. The small-
arms fire resumed. The Government was in command of a minor
road which had major importance. It enabled their motorized
infantry to outflank the main force of the partisans by looping east
and then coming north-west towards the fortress at Hagios Loukas
which commanded the main road into the territory of the traditional enemy. This was not immediately disastrous. Papastavrou
had always intended to excite the Government troops on the right
and get his main force across in the centre. But the pressure was
greater than he had expected and the partisans were more bunched
than he would have liked. The high plateau gave them little
shelter; they were a ready target for the planes. Papastavrou was
caught again in a dilemma which exposed his main weakness. He
would have preferred to turn and fight, but the decisions of the
Political Committee had held him so long to a distasteful course
that it would mean treason (and disillusion) to break from it now.
The committee members were dispersed; it was hardly the time
for a debate. Now and again their paths did cross, but each had
held so firmly to the obedience which had cost them so much that
the more questionable it became, the less they dared question it.
The retreat must go through. But if the disciplined cohesion of the
army was too firmly maintained (a curious anxiety for a military
force), the absurdity of the retreat might become too plain for the
men to accept it. There was a danger that, at the last gasp, they
would turn and shatter the Government. Papastavrou was obliged
to make the Royalist forces irresistible. Even now when he could

see that a thrust to the road between Hagios Loukas and the Boreopolis junction – an area not unfamiliar to him – would cut off the optimistic motorized infantry from their support and allow him to crush them, he had to hesitate. Pavlides was ready to move, but the fear of victory was as powerful in Papastavrou as that of defeat in lesser men. To break the enemy now would make it next to impossible not to follow up with the capture of his air bases. In a situation of that kind, how could he order the retreat to be resumed? Papastavrou had to keep the enemy threat credible without allowing it to become overwhelming; it was military tact in place of military tactics. If he allowed the enemy to believe that he himself was not broken, they would ease off and so weaken the pressure which could carry the army over the frontier. If he allowed them to believe him shattered, they might come on so strongly that he would be forced to counter-attack. It was an exercise of the most delicate kind, confused by the terrain and by lack of communications. Personally Papastavrou had committed himself irreversibly to the decision of the Political Committee. His march had taken him, by his own deliberate decision, through the lands of his fathers. During the whole civil war he had protected the co-operatives from the Government with a paternalism not strictly in accord with accepted theories. For as long as the Revolutionary Army was going forward, Papastavrou fostered the co-operatives as models of the development he intended to encourage in the country at large. When the retreat was ordered, he took his own army through the Mavro Country (as the district was called) and personally supervised their destruction. The Revolutionary Army generally gave no explanation of its violent policy. It demonstrated simply that it did not accept its defeat and that it could not agree to a 'decent' withdrawal. Papastavrou persuaded himself that the peasants of the Mavro were different. He had educated them to a higher degree of revolutionary awareness and therefore he tried to explain to them that he could not allow the improvements which he had brought to their district to go to the credit of the capitalists who would certainly appropriate

them. He hoped for their participation in dismantling the co-operatives. He was disappointed. A victorious army would have found
willing help, but how could the peasants offer their support to men
who advertised their own reverses? The very effectiveness of
Papastavrou's innovations, the fact that they had rooted themselves so firmly, made the peasants determined not to forego them.
The 'storehouse of the revolution' (such was the Mavro's rhetorical
title) refused to be torn down. The peasants armed themselves for
resistance. The co-operatives were blown up, the villages burned,
the trees cut down, the leaders of the resistance and their persistent
followers executed. For Papastavrou it was like mutilating himself.
He could not cry out, for that was the first of his mutilations, to
silence his own pain. He gave the orders as if these people were
strangers to him, the men whose lives he had seen in decay, whom
he had rescued and resuscitated and now condemned. Would the
army obey? The army obeyed. This very obedience was poisonous
to him, for it meant that there was envy and a love of disorder, an
unexpected charge of malice in the soldiers, that they could turn
with so good a conscience against those who had worked for them
and on whom they had depended. Papastavrou did not question
his own motives. He was stone in those days. It stripped him once
again, this ruin he unleashed on the land. His own family were in
the capital. He refrained from destroying their castle. He drew
down the odium of the peasants and even the suspicions of his own
men. The castle was left. It was important to make it as tempting
as possible for the old regime to reimpose itself. If one ruined the
whole place, the Papastavrous might renounce their lordship, but
they could scarcely resist its comfortable resumption. As a result,
they would soon engrave their own vanity on the district once
again and re-create the social conditions which would make their
next eviction final. Brasidas came to Papastavrou's headquarters
in the midst of the repression and offered to take command.
Papastavrou rebuffed him. For once his greed for dirty work
insulted the man he had come to help. Papastavrou ordered him
to press his retreat with all speed and to be the first across the

border. Brasidas bowed to the rebuff and stayed several days ahead of the next group in the order of march.

The drift of the land forced Artemis farther to the east than he wanted. He was now able to set his map. His intention was to keep towards the coast and reach the frontier at Foutsani, but the valleys slanted towards the north-east. Unless they were to climb constantly against the grain, they had to cross in the next valley, at Monasteraki. Towards three in the afternoon, with the sounds of a growing engagement to the east, where the minor road climbed to Hagios Loukas, they met the first comrades they had seen since leaving the central plain. They said that they had been ordered to retreat along the valley westwards. They were all strangers to Artemis. He told the officer in charge that his present course was taking him away from the frontier. 'From what I hear that's no bad thing.' 'Meaning?' 'Brasidas and his people crossed five days ago. I hear he's just broken out again.' 'Broken out? Broken out of what?' 'They say they're disarming our chaps and putting them in pens.' 'They say? Who say?' 'Some of the people we met back at Kolnaki. A major and a bunch of chaps, they say they saw our people being disarmed as they went across. They've got heavy machine-guns mounted. One lot refused, they say, and they opened up. That's what they say.' 'You're to turn north at once. Has anyone actually seen Brasidas?' 'I'm not taking orders from you. How do I know your orders mean anything?' 'What future is there in moving towards the sea, I should like to know? Also your name.' 'We might find a boat.' 'I tell you there's no future at all unless we obey our orders and cross the frontier.' 'They're bombing the hell out of everyone. We'll never get across.' 'You said yourself Brasidas is across already. There's a contradiction there, isn't there? And who's been firing at the planes if it isn't the people across the border? They're our friends. Well? Well?' The newcomer was fair, with dark eyes and beard; he could have been a German. 'There is another possibility.' 'In what sense?' 'That no one is firing at the planes.' 'Then what are those?' 'I said "at". I don't deny there's firing going on, of a kind, but – ' 'Look, forget the enigmas. What do you mean?' 'I've heard – ' 'What a lot of conversations you've had!' 'I've heard that the people across the border are pathfinding for the planes. They're not firing at them, they're firing for them. Indicating exactly where our people are heading.' Artemis looked again at the dangling puffs in the sky, as if by inspecting them more closely he might deduce their real meaning, as if their motive might be implicit in their appearance. The landscape explained itself in a different light, as a text in indirect speech will to a boy who is asked to take the object for the subject and see how it works that way: the very syllables seem to recompose themselves. This stranger, with his brazen scepticism, was abruptly the master of the afternoon. 'May I ask your name?' 'My name is Spiro Calabresus. Lieutenant.' Artemis said, 'You're not really going to take a boat. Where can you possibly go?' 'Up the coast. We may find friends there.' 'These stories you've heard, you believe them?' 'I believe there's a danger they may be true, yes. I don't say that they are. I accept they could be rumours. But one must concede a certain plausibility to them.' 'You were at the university?' 'In Vasiliopolis, why?' 'The vocabulary. I hope you're wrong, but I shan't try to stop you. I hope you succeed.' 'You won't join us?' 'There'd be too many of us. It's better that we should try as many routes as possible.' 'Good luck then.' 'Have you had any contact with the enemy, Calabresus, recently?' 'They say there are some groups operating between here and the border, but the main army's to the east. Our people seem to be holding them.' From a panorama of the border country, they had descended now to the base of the plateau where small hillocks and the deeply scored beds of winter torrents prevented a large view. The firing seemed to have veered north, though the echoes among the hills made precision difficult. Calabresus and his party continued their westward march. Perhaps they had done the right thing. Artemis resented their independence even as his common sense endorsed it. If it was permitted to use one's own judgment, the whole retreat was dubious again. If the people across the frontier were guiding in the bombers, perhaps they were also capable of shooting the exhausted fugitives. What response was possible to such treachery? Having failed to best the Royalists in one's own country, could one properly overthrow the Central Committee in another? As evening deepened the valleys, Artemis and his men, now surely no more than five or six kilometres from the frontier, sighted another group of thirty men. The two parties crossed each other without saying anything. They might have lacked a common language. Speech was pointless; all was known except the unknown. Clouds had gathered. The smoke from the anti-aircraft fire still hung in the air. Now it seemed to swell into thick banks, like racks of seaweed, hanging and fattening in a currentless lagoon. The sunset was coral behind it. The men walked on. The shots came from a small church on the hillside in front of them. Artemis was down and returning the fire, bringing up the main group to his right as if he were waiting for the cue, as if he had rehearsed the move. His morbid sullenness vanished on the instant. Perhaps he had dreaded a safe passage. He walked over to where Yorgis was behind the heavy machine-gun. 'I'm taking Kosta and Michali and a couple more round to the left. There's a valley that should shelter us. Paniotis, Yanni, Adony, take your section right, keep well down and go slowly and obviously – take care but make sure you're spotted. Don't get there before we do or you'll spoil the whole thing – ' 'Let me take the section, Captain.' 'We'll continue to obey my orders, Yorgis, for the moment. When I'm killed, that'll be your chance. You'll attack in exactly – half an hour. Yes, half an hour.' They started to move off. Yorgis and the remaining men would give covering fire, as if Paniotis's section was the only one on the attack. The enemy machine-gun by the church continued to fire at the centre. Artemis had recovered his energy. He was happy. Kosta was watching him, but he was equal to the warrior's challenge. They backed away over the ridge, worked left and found their way behind the church. By now the sun was very low; the shadows fitted their advance. Heavy firing from the east suggested that reinforcements for the Royalists by the church would have a hard time getting through. It also suggested that they were not part of a large group. Some impulsive officer had raced ahead of his colleagues. Artemis and his section heard continued firing: exactly as he had hoped. Kosta was for rushing straight into the church, but Artemis was determined to coincide with Paniotis's section. Intelligence mastered boldness. The enemy could be seen now, more than a platoon, half of them with automatic weapons. The church had two small houses and a barn behind it, cypresses rising from a dusty clearing between them. The enemy main section was forward, facing Yorgis; another had worked left to meet the flank attack from Paniotis; a smaller group was out to the right. Artemis's section was twenty metres behind the barn when Paniotis broke cover and charged in from the left. Yorgis and his section opened up as if this was the big moment. The section on the Royalists' left rose and sprinted across the open ground towards the threat. Artemis and his men killed them all and were in behind the church, firing into the heavy machine-gun emplacement before anyone realized what had happened. For a few seconds they were actually taken for reinforcements. Nothing is so uncertain as the morale of those who expect an easy victory. When the Royalists realized their predicament, the joys of the hunt yielded to fears of a silly death. They were now in the in-glorious position of being about to die on what could be the day of victory. Convinced that they were outnumbered, they turned and ran, faltered when Artemis and his men picked off the front runners, and stood, perplexed and pathetic, while their officer, waving his pistol, shouted to them to regroup. Artemis was obliged to ease his fire because Paniotis and his section were now charging the slope. The action was confused. Kosta fired merely to disobey and Artemis knocked his rifle aside. The Royalists rotated like models trying to locate the camera and raised their hands while the officer shouted and threatened them with his pistol. He never noticed Kosta hurtling at him. Four or five men had taken to their heels. The section had captured a dozen. Kosta was rolling with the officer on the ground, cudgelling him with his own body as though to beat him to death. Artemis prised him away. 'Enough,

enough. I need him.' The officer sat up, his bloody face in his hands. His pistol lay on the ground under a cypress. Kosta picked it up.

The prisoners were terrified. Since they would certainly have shot the partisans had they captured them, they were sure that their own execution was imminent. They had been led to believe that the Reds would shoot them 'on principle'. In fact, if they were shot, it would be for no ideological reason, but because they were an embarrassment to their captors. They could hardly be taken over the border. Nothing would be less welcome, even if the stories of the Revolutionary Army's reception proved false, than prisoners whose existence would give the capitalists an excuse for violating the frontier on a crusade of liberation. To meet more of the enemy while escorting them would only hamper movement and give them an opportunity for tripping their captors. The Royalists would be even more likely to shoot Artemis and his men if only to conceal the humiliation they had suffered. Even if a threat to shoot the prisoners, unless free passage was granted, were to reach the Royalist command, it would not necessarily hobble the pursuit. Athanasiou had been replaced by a career officer who might have ambiguous attitudes towards the common soldier. A man who allows himself to be captured could be said to have 'gone over to the enemy'. An ambitious leader like Levko, with no shortage of recruits, might be tempted not to miss an opportunity for displaying 'iron will' in circumstances which would add to his fearsome reputation. He would very possibly call the 'rebels' ' bluff. If the hostages were killed, it would prove the wickedness of the Reds. If they were rescued, it would demonstrate his strength of character. He did not care about these conscripts as individuals nor did he expect to have to use them again in battle. He might want to parade the force they gave him, but not in open combat. He was concerned with the future in a sense not unlike Artemis; he foresaw a political struggle in which the army itself would fight for its interests, in which it would impersonate the country rather as the Reds impersonated, on his analysis, the working class, without being identical with it.

Stelio Levko had been a young officer during the victory over the Italians. He had not fought on Papastavrou's front and he had not shared in his triumph. He had distinguished himself, but he had not found glory. His admiration for Papastavrou was as great as his envy. He observed him with the patient discipline of a passionate rival. He had never quarrelled with Papastavrou; he was opposed to him. When the country was overrun by the Germans he fled to Cairo and joined the forces which served with the British. He fought ably and with unmistakable courage. As distinct from those British officers who found their freedom through working in the mountains, he liberated himself from local considerations by belonging, temporarily, to a larger world. The British were disillusioned by their own country because they knew it too well. Levko never knew Britain, but he campaigned with an elite which fought as if the qualities of resolution, courage and honour were actually to be found in the Britain of which, secretly, they had despaired. They convinced Stelio Levko of the vitality of a tradition they were almost parodying in defiance of its decay. Levko took the dying blaze of glory for the natural colour of the world he had never known and became the last disciple of a doomed school. He was more than a careerist; he was a romantic of the Right, believing all over again in crusading ideals whose source he assumed Britain to be. The British always admire those who ape them; they can both recruit and despise them at the same time. Levko was rewarded with British decorations and British praise. He was groomed for the staff position he deserved and inculcated with those grand neutral affectations which bound him to support the Government and the king in the conviction that he was following the British model of unselfish and apolitical soldiering. He returned to the country too late to see the Revolutionary Army as anything but a band of disruptive insurgents. He had missed their exploits; he was in time for their effrontery. How could he regard as having any legal status an army which offered him no place? The capital was in the hands of an army the British recognized and were ready to help. Papastavrou, whom he had once so anxiously admired, was now condemned as a criminal. Soldiering, as the British in the mess used to say, is a trade one must practise if one hopes to rise in it. Civil war is ferocious not least because the military men on each side know that they can hope for no further employment in the case of defeat, whereas in wars between nations it is often the defeated generals who suggest themselves as trustworthy caretakers for their conquerors. (One need hardly fear the leadership of those whom one has just outwitted.) That Colonel Levko proved an able commander was enough to convince Dmitri Stratis that he was also a loyal one. It was not so simple as that; Levko was ambitious in the service of a Government which wished to establish only its independence from those who were assisting it. The next menace to Dmitri's regime would come from the Allies and from those who could convincingly accuse him of being their puppet. Stratis knew that he must find a commander who could credibly be given the honour of having defeated Papastavrou. Athanasiou had already been relegated to the Inspectorate of Infantry. He was too committed to the Right to be its popular champion. What was needed was a man who could be hailed as a hero, not one who had already announced himself to be one. In Levko, Dmitri had a man who had fought bravely against the Germans without either supporting or betraying Papastavrou. Dmitri realized that as the years passed there might be a reaction in Papastavrou's favour. It was necessary to prepare for that situation by condemning only his recent 'treason'. Levko enjoyed the battle with the general without apparently having any political animus. If he guessed that Papastavrou was not devoting his mind simply to defeating the Royalists, that did not prevent him from feeling that he was engaged in a duel of wits at the highest level. The opposition flattered him and he would not have been human had he not returned the compliment. He too had his contradictory impulses. He disliked the police activities in his sector of the country. The arrests and rumoured executions of partisans who tried to merge with the peasantry disgusted him, yet there was little that one could do with prisoners of a war which was about to end and who had no convenient foreign origin. He transported a number to one of the islands, but he could not prevent their ill-treatment unless he claimed a decisive role for the army. He was not averse to allowing Papastavrou to escape (certainly he was appalled by the prospect of capturing the great man, though not by that of his accidental death in battle) and so he was reduced, like the revolution, to aiming for some kind of 'moral' ascendancy. Since he was debarred from political sentiment, he found his best tribunal in his principal opponent. He wanted to earn from Papastavrou the kind of honourable concession which a Grand Master, running into time trouble, makes to a young player by resigning while at the same time pointing out a more subtle variation than the other has actually contrived. To find no place in his final dispositions for scrappy forces like those Artemis had captured would be in keeping with this abstract aspect of the end-game. He would not like Papastavrou to be able to point out such a juvenile error as allowing his minor commanders to outrun their support. He looked for more advanced criticism than mere spelling mistakes.

As soon as the action was over, Artemis ordered the common soldiers to be locked in the barn and told Yorgis to put the officer into the church. It was a small building, a single barrel vault with only the smallest aperture for light above the door: a crossed triangle, alpha. There was a screen for the icons at the east end and a narrow passageway behind it. The place was no more than eight metres deep and two wide. Two icons, one in a silver facing, were nailed to the screen. A candlestand, marbled with fallen tallow, was leaning against the wall. Artemis, undecided in his own mind, gave an appearance of decision. He told the men that they would keep their prisoners till midnight and he would then judge what to do in the light of the situation. He wanted to interrogate the officer separately. 'I shall see him alone.' 'Is that wise, Captain?' 'Do you think I can't deal with him? I shall be armed.' 'I'll leave two men within earshot.' 'I want the men to guard the prisoners in two shifts. We've stopped to get some rest.' 'Yes, Captain.' 'Yorgi?' 'Captain?' 'Have you seen one of these, to read I mean?' 'What

you gave Paniotis?' 'Yes. Well?' 'No, Captain.' 'Take it. Read it.
Discuss it with the men. If you were to hand me over to the
Royalists, you'd probably save your lives. No, don't demonstrate
your – simplicity, not so quickly. I want you to consider this
document, all of you, and come to your own decision. I've hesitated to give it to you, as you can gather, but I feel I must. I can't
conceal the facts from you without creating in our ranks just the
kind of ignorance against which we are fighting in society. The
military situation is very unclear, but not as unclear as the political.
I hope to find something out from this officer, but we shall see. If
I have anything to tell you, I shall do so. You must decide between
yourselves what you are to do. But don't imagine that I shan't act
too. I may not agree to be captured by you – no, think, Yorgi. I
insist on it. Personally, I believe that we should continue the retreat
as we all agreed, but that agreement was made in the assumption
of certain constants. I'm not convinced that they have remained
as we were led to think. Treason is always more plausible than
constancy. So – think.' Artemis turned and went towards the
church. He had the door unlocked and ordered the sentry to lock
it behind him. He smiled as the bolt ground home.

'One can't be too careful.'

The enemy officer was looking at the icons.

'Are you a believer?'

'You know me better than that. Are you accusing me of having
changed? Surely not so unsubtly, not you.'

'Are you all right? Have you eaten? Are you thirsty?'

'Our army's well supplied. I'm short of nothing.'

'This is the most damnable thing.'

'Oh spare me that, Artemy. You're delighted.'

'To see you, of course, but you're the last person I want to have
on my conscience at this moment.'

'Am I on your conscience? Why? Because of what you intend
to do to me?'

'Because of that, yes, but not because I know what I am going
to do, precisely the opposite: because I don't.'

'You're going to shoot me.'

'You don't believe that.'

'In one sense no. But I believe that you'll come to that conclusion. In time.'

'We haven't much of that. I'll tell you exactly why this is damnable. You've come on the scene precisely when I'm at my weakest, my least certain. I need you and here you are. That's profoundly demoralizing. You're the only man in the world to whom I could speak honestly tonight.'

'You could speak honestly to any man who was entirely in your power. Anyone whom you'd bought. In that sense we're all willing buyers of flesh when we can be, not for the power only, for the freedom.'

'You once accused me of wanting power. That seems a modification. Do you want to smoke? I don't, but – '

'Such a little Puritan! If there had been Protestants in our world, your ancestors would have been among them. I can imagine you in black. When you shoot me you'll want to confess me as well. Or rather to hear me admit your moral superiority, which is the Protestant equivalent. I was simple when I was a student. I thought in terms of our class, of the continuation of our rationale. I see now that I was wrong; the game has new dimensions.'

'And you're still among those who play it on the old squares. Do I detect a note of regret in that?'

'Because it's never too late to repent? I know that smile, but I know you too and I'm right: you long to hear me submit.'

'The damnable thing is that I still love you. I'm a fool to confess that if you like, or at least so soon, but it's true.'

'No, Artemy, it's not true at all. You desire me now – '

'Love you, I said. You're not as beautiful as you once were.'

'That's irrelevant (though I resent your mentioning it). No, the truth is that for many years you were indifferent to me, as for instance when we were in the hills together, but now, now that I'm once more your prisoner, your desire returns, your love for yourself, your desire to command and to be commanded, which is still the essence of power. I didn't understand metaphor clearly in those days, but I got my facts right.'

'You were never my prisoner before.'

'You only realized it vaguely. And the situation was less coarse, I grant you that. Yet I wanted you. I sensed something in you, if you like to use that schoolmasterly image, something you haven't failed to demonstrate in spite of everything, leadership if you like, ruthlessness more probably. If we must make confessions.'

'As you say, they precede conclusions.'

'How genteel, conclusions. You still intend to shoot me.'

'If you believed that, would you still be so cool? If I were really going to kill you? I doubt it. Why do you put it in my mind?'

'I don't; it was there already. Why pretend?'

'You have no business with them.'

'What do you know of me?'

'You know it's true. The fact that I can talk to you, care about you, that proves how different you are from the rest of them.'

'What you're resisting is the realization, at this stage, that it is you who have no place with the people you're with. What hurts you now is the fact that you are so much easier with me, with anyone from your own class than with any of them. The love you think you feel for me may be real inasmuch as I'm your prisoner, but it's only a particularization of something else, the pleasure of talking to someone who can understand you.'

'That doesn't throw me as much as you think, pointing out our affinities. I've never supposed that I could find myself wholly over here. Probably if the war hadn't come, if circumstances hadn't polarized things so brutally, I'd still be playing politics in the centre and imagining that I was exerting myself to the full. It may be that I would be, but that would only be because the crisis had been postponed, that the future was getting here more slowly – '

'The future! You're like an old man waiting for a young bride, you people.'

'Don't you feel impoverished, awaiting your inheritance only from the past? Try and understand. I concede something to you,

305

this ease of speech, and it means that I can never be a complete person, I see that, however much I try to persuade myself that I can be remade each moment. I know it's not possible. I'm not proud exactly for that reason. It makes me uneasy, but it gives me a good conscience, being split. Because I reject a part of myself doesn't mean that I'm wrong. I'm sure you can see that.'

'I distrust those who distrust themselves.'

'I don't distrust my intellect. I don't distrust what I know. I won't yield to you there. How can you be on the same side as Democritos? How? Or even Dmitri? I even include him.'

'But more slowly, I notice. You include Dmitri more slowly. On the same side? How used you've become to monoliths, Artemy! I don't discount the possibility, even the likelihood of future political battles in the capital. I'm sure that there'll be plenty as a matter of fact –'

'You know you should be with us,' Artemis cut in. 'You know it. Tell me the truth, if you'd been near us that day in the mountains when Papastavrou attacked Hagios Stephanos and Athanasiou let him down, wouldn't you have come with me?'

'Yes, I would.'

'Well, then.'

'I fight out of a total distrust of everyone, Artemy. I fight for my family, for a lost cause. I know very well that we shall never recover our lands –'

'The lands that your grandparents, your great-grandparents, I don't know who, filched from someone who had filched them from someone else. What a waste of your intelligence, of your energy, to fight for something you know to be lost! It's a tragic confession.'

'Yet you wish that you were the prisoner.'

'I wish that you weren't. I want to find out certain things. Will you help me?'

'It hurts you even to allude to a morality beyond your famous polarizations, the absurdity of these enmities –'

'No, I conceded their absurdity. I can see a future without them –'

306

'Oh, damn your future! It's like marriage in the old novels, that great and golden future where everything will be all right. I tell you, you sentence the inhabitants of these economic paradises of yours to all the same inevitable disillusionments the old novels offered their married couples. How can the future be as good as you make out?'

'We have no quarrel and yet we're mortal enemies. Isn't there an even worse absurdity there?'

'On the contrary. We have a quarrel and we are not mortal enemies. We have a quarrel. I don't agree with you. I haven't the smallest urge to kill you. You, on the other hand, have, to kill me. Because you're always looking for a philosophy of finalities, something which will make life important enough to be worth living. You believe in your great cause out of a disenchantment with the particular. I have some zest for the particular and so mistrust your even moralities, the great shadowless murals on which you project your heroic future. It's because you have so little aptitude for detail that your ideas grow bigger and bigger. You want a science in which each atom is as big as a melon, and a morality to match. Only then, my poor Artemy, will you be able to remove your spectacles. But alas, such a science would be a grotesque misrepresentation of realities, specially confected to suit those who can't see straight.'

'So you knock me to the ground and break my spectacles,' said Artemis; 'is that really the best argument you can offer? I believe myself to be beyond redemption, that's what I've been trying to say. I don't for a moment ask that the world conform to my addled vision. I deny that charge entirely. Will you tell me the truth, Konni, if I spare your life?'

'In other words you're asking me for information.'

'Don't cheapen this, I beg of you, for the sake of – '

'A night of adolescent passion? Are you still so naively sentimental under all your dialectic?'

'I'm flattering you – '

'That's dangerous – '

'I'm flattering you, you – impossible fellow, by assuming that this matters, this issue between us. I want us both to take the right decision. Has it not occurred to you ever that we on our side must be in the right, that you're making the most disastrous, wasteful mistake? Can't you dare, in this bizarre – this freakish purity – '

'Purity!'

'Must I kill you for not *listening*, out of sheer ill humour? Assume that I love you – '

'But that's a social assumption, Artemy, isn't it, love? Doesn't it say something about material circumstances, unless it's just a synonym – '

'You know it isn't that – '

'Why do you trust me so?'

'Do I? Do I trust you, for what?'

'To play this particular game, this end-game of yours, to make this some kind of crucial encounter. Isn't that your final vanity, the vanity of the painter who gives his model values to tone with the background he's decided on? You try to make the flesh conform to an aesthetic, but it's irreducible in that sense. It won't conform to euphony; it doesn't scan. The spheres have no music. Can you never accept that? All this selflessness of yours, it's to give you an extra chance, an extra way of being right, of imposing yourself, of exerting power – '

'Are there no objective situations, is there no sense in prediction? Is all planning, all strategy without any sort of justification? Language itself promises the opposite.'

'Something you've said troubles you. The voice perhaps. The voice is not language. Which is why arguments are not persuasive and men are. Is it the voice?'

'You mustn't think that I'm threatening you,' said Artemis, after several seconds' silence. 'Of course the fact is that there's a material, a physical problem between us – '

'What to do with me.'

'Yes, and I was tactless to refer to it so quickly, if it was me.'

'I disagree. We would both have been waiting for it. It's like before. It's nothing to be ashamed of. It's a fact, as you say, and may as well be declared, though it hardly needed to be stated, since it's so obvious. Again like before.'

'I need to know what lies ahead. No, it isn't that funny, and I don't mean it threateningly. I need to know the facts, the immediate facts; I don't mean the historical future. I have a group of men here. Can I get them over the frontier or not, and what's happening up there? I'm being quite practical, you see. Are your people between us and the frontier?'

'I don't know, Artemy, and if I did – '

'You wouldn't tell me. Why not? Can't you see how frivolous your opposition to us is? I can understand it up till the moment when you're disarmed, but can't you now see how empty your bravado is? What're you protecting, Konni? You say yourself that you're fighting for the sake of purging your own disillusion – well, something like that – but now that you're not fighting, can't you see how immediately unimportant the whole question of sides becomes? For you. The Government will never support your interests in your own absence. You can't blame it; it's a company of brigands you joined and only those who are on the spot share the spoils. There's no continuity of purpose, no community of intention. You're alone now as I could never be alone in your position – '

'You'd be waiting for the comrades to gallop up and rescue you, I suppose?'

'I'd still be able to take an intelligent interest in what was happening, whereas you, as soon as you're unhorsed, you've no further part in the battle. There's literally nothing for you to think about. Not a single word can be written or thought on your side which makes a contribution to life. All speech in your world is excuse and deception – '

'And private life – '

'Even that's a deception, full of false promises, not because the people are false necessarily but because they can't live up to the rhetoric they're bound to use. Love, marriage, the rest.'

309

'My God, rhetoric!'

'Yes, I agree. We over-use it too. But I truly believe ours is less dangerous than yours because its falseness, I mean its gaudy qualities, its blatancy if you will, is so accessible that it can be easily separated from the rest; it announces its own exaggeration; it's like floats in a parade. Whereas your rhetoric, the rhetoric in which we grew up, is pervasive; it concerns true feelings but it associates them with false institutions. The truth is that the love which our – our old society most admires is a tragic love which flies from organized life as if from a plague. Doesn't that nostalgia for flight suggest something to you of the contempt which we really had for the family and for all the polite, sensible feelings we tried to associate with a "worth-while" life? Our most envied, most committed lovers are those who have no use for that world at all –'

'Are they running to yours?'

'They're running, they're running, that's all, because they realize that the world which is supposed to give them what they want, the freedom to "live their own lives" is so completely hostile to true feeling, so aggressive and so demanding that only blind flight can preserve them from its taint.'

'You're fighting to make a world free from taint, a world safe for lovers, is that it? Really, Artemy, isn't it a little late for that kind of froth? Lovers always want to get away; there's nothing very surprising in it, and I'm sure very little critical content. Or are you going to tell me they take off their clothes as a protest against sweat-shops? What will happen in your famous future, will lovers no longer run to the woods and the beaches? Will they fall together where they stand, gloriously at one with their society?'

'You're too quick to mock. I'm not saying that. I'm saying that capitalism pretends to have a specially tender place for the highest feelings, the deepest passions, pitch them where you will, and that it justifies itself by proclaiming its special relationship with freedom, freedom above all to express oneself. And I'm saying that there's something supremely vulgar in those pretensions, something which is exposed as soon as really strong feelings occur, since those who feel them always want to run from this gentle, considerate, happy society. It affects to favour the best and it doesn't. You don't agree, you don't agree. There's no sense in pursuing it. I credited you with imagination enough to see the point. I distrust, I regret a world in which parody is the natural form. Mockery, the habitual criticism, seems a waste, a perversion, that's all. Ordinary life as it is lived in our old society *is* a parody; it conforms in no way to man's essential needs, his essential nature. And criticism is equally flippant, derisive, *personal.*'

'Then why doesn't man give up our form of society more willingly? Why must you fight to separate him from it?'

'You know very well. Because the object is not in the singular. Because there are interests who profit from others' bondage. These are things that don't need explaining. You're trying to hobble me with arguments to which you yourself know the answer. That, if I may say so, is typical of the world you come from. You should be ashamed. No man should – '

'Oh, stuff it, Artemis. You're beginning to weary me with your high-mindedness. Let's get on to the torture.'

Konni was leaning against the white wall near the candlestand. His face was blanched except for a scabbed swelling under his right eye, his head bowed under the curve of the vault. Artemis was against the icons. He glared at Konni, whose tiredness reminded him of his own.

'There's not going to be any torture. Torture – Why should I want to torture you?'

'Now it's your turn to use your imagination and not to cheat. Why did you never come near me again after that night?'

'That's not true. We did meet, several times.'

'Not alone. Not in the sense I mean.'

'Why didn't we make love again?'

'Why did you not want to?'

'I'm not sure. It's not as easy to be honest in this as you may think.'

'Let me answer for you. Because you could not imagine a relationship which did not become a fight, which didn't continue until one or the other was broken. You run from every singular experience for the same reason. Because you lack the ability to stop. Because under all your selflessness, your intellectual candour, there's a huge, unexpressed greed, a temptation to brutality which appals and excites you.'

'No, you shan't answer for me. I accepted that night exactly as it was. I refused to draw conclusions from it. I refused to try to repeat its pleasures, because I didn't want to think of them as pleasures. I didn't categorize them at all. Perhaps that was the height of my romanticism, to think of them absolutely wordlessly. I believe that's a real part of what I did. I wanted not to squeeze the thing dry, not to flatten it to a conclusion. Must you find something evasive, something disreputable in that? I don't see why, except for the sake of the present.'

'I on the other hand was wounded by your silence. You treated me like a woman. Like someone you'd bought. As if we'd gone on to Helen's –'

'No –'

'I understand your saying no, but it seemed so to me. You desired me like a woman, but I wasn't one. I'd wanted you for some time because I craved your company, your attention; I believed that I could learn from you. But your instinct was to despise what you desired, to think that close acquaintance must disappoint you. You talk about embracing the future, but you run from it whenever it applies to you. You crave the mass because you hope you can lose yourself in it – You should give me the pistol.'

'And what would you do with it?'

'Relieve you of it, my dear Artemy, to begin with, simply relieve you of it. You could have been over the border by now. Why aren't you?'

'Because we had the misfortune to bump into you.'

'Nonsense. You're delighted to have done so.'

'You flatter yourself.'

'Be your age. You could have killed us. It was a good move, that of yours, not that I shouldn't have been up to it. To tell you the truth, I expected you to back off and try and slide round us. I never thought you'd come straight at us. But capturing us, what was the sense in that? You've loaded yourself with an anchor just when you ought to cut and run. Why?'

'Come, you're making too much of the psychology of the thing now. We captured you because it's difficult to shoot men down at close range with their hands up, especially when they've inflicted no casualties on you. Isn't it?'

'You said you needed the officer. Did you know it was me?'

Artemis raised his chin. 'No.'

'The frontier's five kilometres away, anywhere in a northerly direction. So what is it that you need?'

'I want to know what's been happening.'

'As, for instance, Brasidas has been shot.'

'What do you mean, shot? Killed?'

'Shot, by Papastavrou.'

'You beastly little liar. You cheap little liar.'

'No, Artemis, as a matter of fact. It's common knowledge. Brasidas was the first over the frontier. His men were forcibly disarmed and put into camps in the highlands. Not very warm up there. When he protested at the conditions he was told, roughly speaking, in the old phrase, that beggars can't be choosers. You know Brasidas, he's got guts and he felt responsible. He'd brought the word, hadn't he, that the retreat was on and that your people would be taken care of across the border? I don't know if this is the kind of information you wanted from me – '

'This had better be true.'

'Yes, well, he broke out of the camp. It was rather ineptly guarded, I gather. Perhaps even they have some shame at putting their glorious comrades in the stockade. He broke out, collected a group of other escapees and stragglers and people like that and headed back for the border. They had to shoot their way out and that seems to have really set things alight. Your mates across the frontier weren't too charming at the outset but this gave them a chance to be self-righteous as well. Their people were never eager to have a foreign army on their soil, for reasons that anyone but a sentimentalist could have seen. (Funny how hard-headed people are always sentimental to a degree when it comes to expecting generosity from others! Just like you imagining that our having been to bed together makes us friends beyond time and place, isn't that right, Artemy?) Brasidas lost his sense of the inevitable a bit late in the day, but, like most of those who give up the Church after wasting their youth in it, he was eager to make up for lost time. He doubled back after the dust-up at the frontier and released a whole camp full of rather angry men, armed them as best he could and crossed back into Boria only to meet Papastavrou on the road. Well, you can imagine.'

'Imagination doesn't come into this, you bastard, and well you know it. What happened?'

'Oh, sorry, I thought it would be obvious to the unclouded intellect. Brasidas had all the patriotic assumptions you might expect of someone who's spent a large part of his life abroad. He also assumed that Papastavrou would see that a change of plan was essential even at this late date. If a political mind was willing to change, how could a general agree to the humiliation of his army and put political dogma before practical sense? Brasidas imagined himself, if you like, the last metaphysician and supposed that it only needed him to give up his illusions for the whole world to become realistic. Well, Papastavrou was committed to the retreat so deeply that he couldn't pull out. Brasidas seemed to believe that the tide could be stemmed, the hinge turned, whatever you will, whenever the general wanted it. He never believed, in other words, in the inevitability of the withdrawal. He always saw it as a political decision. Now that he'd seen the consequences, he wanted to go into reverse. He believed that as he'd been the most fervent supporter of the retreat there'd be no difficulty once he himself had changed sides. He didn't know Papastavrou, did he, after all? As soon as Brasidas ceased to be the mouthpiece of the Most High, Papastavrou had no interest in his opinion. He arrested him, disarmed his followers and drove them back towards the border. Brasidas was shot as a traitor to the Movement, since he was the only man capable of saving it. Meanwhile your friends over the way had panicked and decided that they didn't want any of your people coming into their territory after all. Armed or disarmed. That was when they got into touch with us and proposed to assist us in following Papastavrou's line of retreat. Even if he found out, he had no choice but to continue. No doubt he's still funnelling his men across, as best he can. And maybe those who make it will get a warm welcome from the Central Committee. Maybe. And that, more or less, is the sum total of my knowledge.'

'You're lying.'

'You believe me then?'

'What you say is certainly believable. In that sense, yes, I do believe you.'

'I'm the messenger in the play. You confuse me with my message. Well, it's true, Artemy. Not that I take any pleasure in it.'

'Naturally, since it makes no difference to what I've been saying.'

'Oh how you do go on believing that winning an argument is all that matters! Typical of a man who could have been an academic but failed to persist. Your speciality is being right.'

'I'm not unaware of this tendency. It's pretty severely controlled in the Central Committee, I promise you that. I don't get away with much. Nevertheless, motives aside, there is such a thing as being right. I hold to that.'

'A mathematics of life! I doubt it, I doubt it, Artemy. What would make a difference to anything as far as you're concerned?'

'To be proved wrong.'

'By what means? To the pure everything is impure! Nothing could ever touch you. It might destroy you, but it would never touch you, not in that hard little head of yours.'

'Pure! It's you who suppose that I expected perfection, unalloyed devotion from our friends over the border. I never expected anything of the sort. Your news doesn't surprise me at all. I feel as if I'd already heard it. That's why I'm not sure whether to believe it.'

'It makes your internationalism absurd. A complete illusion, a figment of faith. Sooner or later they know that we shall want to rectify the border and undo the King's Peace. The people they have in their power speak our language. It may be that the borders won't be challenged until your people finally take over – '

'Ah!'

'It doesn't damage my – my ideas to make such an admission. All things are possible; it's you who deny it. Well then, why should they nurture the viper that will sting them when it's recovered? Of course they'll disarm you, disorganize you, do their best to demoralize you. And what're you going to do about it once you're over there? I tell you, Artemy, you'd do better to stay here and you know it. You're not powerless here; over there you'll be worse than that – you'll be meaningless.'

'I've given my men the chance to stay. They're discussing it now. This isn't, however, the crisis it amuses you to think it is. Boundaries, languages, these too are kinds of money and will need to be – '

'Analysed?'

'Yes. The thing can't stop at borders. We shall eventually see that class can't possibly be only an internal matter, boundaries sacred, concepts invariable; how can they be? And how can they be changed without upheaval? Impossible. Quite impossible. Is it madness or *folie de grandeur* to foresee such things? Or simple intelligence? The pain of the upheaval, that's another thing entirely.'

'You're going to tell me in a minute that surgery isn't necessarily painless. Did you have a medical when you entered the army?'

'Of course.'

'Then can you deny that there's something particularly unpleasant about being handled by a doctor, by a stranger, when there is nothing wrong with you, when you're not suffering? When,

316

moreover, you know that the man has no wish to help you, but is merely concerned to justify your use by authority? Why do you have such a grudge against the world? Why do you give yourself over so gladly to those who care nothing for you? I wish I could understand that. I can't. This endless desire to operate on yourself, what self-love it really is, what a flight from other people!'

'It can't really matter, I take it, to your people, to Levko, whether he catches us or not. If our friends are also our enemies, it hardly matters whether we reach the border or not.' Artemis went on with such a brief break that Konni was startled; his mind blinked at the abrupt new light Artemis flashed on the situation. 'In terms of what happens to us: why should we suppose that we should be favoured across the border? That we wouldn't suffer. None of us expected that. Are you accusing me of a death-wish? If so, I could as justly accuse you of one. Am I the only one who wants to be in the power of the other side? If so, why are you here at this moment? All your daring, what is it but excess, a sort of over-enthusiastic assent which becomes dissent by sheer... well, exaggeration? You think that you're justifying your claims on life, but that kind of self-justification is self-destructive. In a way it's as immoral as cowardice, as socially treacherous. Personal acts have no morality, by definition.'

'Which is the reason for the flight you make so much of, Artemy, the lovers' rout.'

'No contradiction.'

'What a relief! What a relief! I've never pretended to be other than a man on his own. But you have. Are you? At this moment? Where's your society? The world's let you down rather, hasn't it? Whom are you going to blame? Me?'

'Blame? No one.'

'How you wish I'd told you nothing! How you wish there was something you could rack out of me! If only there was a barrier instead of a cul-de-sac! You claim that I should capitulate, that I should act the midwife to the future and confess that your side is the only one with a future-perfect tense. I disagree. I think it's you who must concede me the right to a future, since I at least have some plans for one.'

'You know very well that we should have swept the country if it hadn't been for the Allies.'

'*All* the Allies, that's what you must realize. There's no one who supports you. No one can be bothered. What might have been is surely irrelevant, as irrelevant as God, Who is also a decent hypothesis. Your friends sold you out, Artemy. There's no inheritance coming to you. With me it's different; the world may be imperfect, but I'm willing to take my place in it. I know what to do with it. I have prospects. If there were one bullet in that pistol, there'd be more justice in putting it through your head than through mine. Which is the reason, perhaps, why in the end it is I who'll be killed with it.'

'Why should either of us be?'

'Shall we run?'

'Run? Where?'

'Was that in your mind? That we should escape together?'

'No, well – perhaps. Perhaps I had thought of it. But then you might say that that would be only a more *recherché* way of – I don't know. Together? I don't know.'

'It makes no sense. You know it very well. Where should we escape? And for what purpose? *Per far l'amore?* To found a magazine of opinion? To agitate for Freedom, a children's crusade of bearded children? You see the curious thing, it's only as alternatives that we're coupled; one of us must replace the other, swallow the other. If we were cannibals there would be no problem. You'd eat me, since I'm your prisoner, and so achieve your synthesis. In this moral world you're associated with there's no such happy solution. Truly, I see you longing to sink your teeth into me. You're exhausted with frustration, Artemy. You haven't nearly come to the final analysis you're so keen to achieve. The animal evades your refining zeal. You can't assimilate me, isn't it so? You dread the cannibal in you, which is why you urge the other – me or Katerina, I've heard a bit about that – to be strong, to be strong

318

enough to fight you off, to deter you from what you so much desire and so much dread. Well? You don't accept pleasure because it's never complete enough to satisfy you. Death might just be your *métier*.'

'Tell me, Konni, are you only trying to save your own life? Or are you wasting time for some bigger purpose, the loyal lieutenant?'

'Bigger purpose?'

'To keep us here until we're cut off entirely.'

'But you are cut off, Artemy. Where can you go? I thought you'd realized that already. What's happening now is a parenthesis. It can't affect the main narrative. It's an improvisation this, isn't it? Necessity has run out. We're skidding, can't you feel that? No rails.'

'Is there something I don't know, Konni? I mean to find out.'

'So, you want to improvise a reason to torture me. I thought you would.'

'Will you shut up to hell about torture? I'm here alone. One man can't torture another – '

'Which proves my earlier point – '

'Oh damn your points. No more than he can rape him – at least I can't you – '

'To be specific, which is so diminishing. No wonder you insist on being the servant of necessity! What a pity it's broken down! What a pity for you that you are no longer of the smallest importance! Since you've rejected the world of feeling – '

'Spare me, Konni – '

'You're left with nothing at all.'

'You think me incapable of feeling?'

'You have feelings only to reject them. Your ideals are so beautiful that they excuse your contempt for what you actually encounter. Your search for reality is a flight from it, all the time, it always has been.'

'Did you expect us to last for ever?'

'It was you who had the expectations. You were so overwhelmed with your own desire, so astonished by its actually coming to something, that you had to make it a great passion that would be contaminated by any long contact with its object.'

'With you.'

'With me. You made me a whore. I didn't mind. But you did. Because you're a prude, Artemy, and a prude always prefers death to ... to the possibility of accident, to pleasure – because pleasure has no shape, no defining frontier. Your appetite for politics is an appetite for anathemas, for trials, for verdicts, heresy and orthodoxy, dramatic categories, tragic costumes. Life without costume, without impersonation, you can't face, life as an animal that lives and dies.'

'Why do you want to die? Or at least want me to kill you?'

'I don't –'

'Except?'

'For moral reasons, as you might say.'

'Oh no! As you *have* said! Don't try to get out of it that way.'

'Because it would finally prove to you that you've nothing left. That you're completely isolated. However, as I say, I don't. I don't care enough for you to sacrifice myself on your behalf, for something so negative as your education.'

'If I let you live, then –'

'I don't think you can ever see the futility of your – I don't know – your course, your ways, your ideas –'

'I stand to you like the narrator to the critic. I shall prove I care for my work more than for its reputation only by destroying those who are able to understand it. I shall show my indifference to fame only by killing the only person who might be capable of celebrating it. And someone I love.'

'Coldly and without regret.'

'God Almighty!'

'Oh yes! If you killed me, it would have to be because logic demanded it, and in logic there are no tears. Logic demands nothing of life, Artemy; it is life which demands that logic exist in order to conceal its arbitrary nature. *Évidemment!* You've reached the point where every practical instance destroys your faith. Resurrection is your only way out; the sublimation of all mundane things, a world in the sky!'

The exile, his preparations made, has a few hours to walk in the city. His mind is calm. He is like a husband, long deceived, who has decided on practical steps. He will no longer sit at home under a burden of anguish, pretending to know nothing of what eats his heart. He has a scheme; he has accomplices who are not exactly certain of his motives but who will certainly arrange that things go smoothly. Vengeance was his dream; action displaces it. It is not the only motive which now stimulates him; there are also the pleasures of secrecy and of surprise. It is he who is the deceiver now. A plot makes every movement of the plotter significant. He might be detected at every moment; every moment when he is not is a minute triumph. Freedom is deception. The future has a shape now; the new diary is not a succession of empty leaves but is marked with crucial, if innocent-looking, appointments. The exile feels fully grown at last; he is leaving the scenes of his child-hood; he will be distant from those who would write off his present opinions as the obvious fruit of a past they can trace only too easily; he turns his back on those who mutter that the apple never falls far from the tree. He breaks out like a figure in a tapestry from the stitching which makes him a mere shadow in a landscape. He will no longer be goaded to indignant pain by the sound of prattling passers-by in the main square who parade unaware of the oppression under which they live. He will no longer have to walk under the walls of the military hospital where his comrades are tortured by those who lack not only humanity but even serious purpose. He walks there now for the last time, imagining that his resolution will be strengthened, his energy for the fight recharged by his disgust. But he is not disgusted; he dreads to lose the stimulus of these familiarly abhorrent walls. He is like that husband, his murderous plans perfected, who hears of the death of his rival. His hatred is more precious to him than his love. Deprived of it, he fears the loss of all sensation. He hopes that it is a rumour, an example of adulterous cunning, something which can call for even more meticulous punishment. The exile plans to deliver the city from its tyrant. How can those who remain in it bear their slavery? At the point when he most needs to believe in their misery, during that last walk in the streets, he sees in the smiles of friends, the kisses of lovers, the prolonged handshakes of businessmen, the very betrayal of his purpose. He loathes his fellow-countrymen for finding so tolerable the conditions from which he is pledged to liberate them. The city itself – the palaces and the prisons – remains true to him; the stones do not shrug at his passing, the towers do not nod to each other nor the Government offices giggle like shopgirls. Even the sentries at the torturers' gate are more loyal to his vision than the frivolous crowds. What would Samson have done if he had found that the temple had no pillars? The exile finds himself hoping that things will get worse before he returns to make them better. He hopes that the regime will nail the smiles on the faces of the indifferent masses. Earlier he believed that he was going to join the real battle, that the fight was elsewhere, but as he wishes his fellow-citizens ill his conscience is stirred. He resolves that his exile will be hard; he will allow no cushions between his spine and the cold surface of outer darkness. He must make things worse for himself than they are for those who remain behind. How he despises anyone who thinks of settling in a foreign country! He swears that he is recoiling only to jump more effectively on those who have purloined his homeland. He imagines a new society in these streets he is walking for the last time. He looks to the women, who seem, with their solemn dark eyes, to understand the tyranny that overshadows them, he binds them with his meaning, passionate gaze to wait for the new dawn, to show the same contempt for their temporary masters as they once had for the foreign invaders. He sees the addresses, the visiting-cards which the men exchange, their limited and rectilinear identities, and he promises them punishment, but the women are different: they are waiting, in their dark naturalness, for the bright liberation he will bring them. As they pass him on their spruce brown legs, dark passion unkindled in their lustrous eyes, they lend him strength; he will show them; he will come back to them. The truth of the nation, its buried promise, lives in their undeclared allegiance to a deeper premise than advantage. How much he has talked about the intellectual responsibility of women, what a virtue his party makes of it! And yet, at the last minute, he relies on their mysterious, uncontrollable nature. He rehearses the details of his journey. Why does it pain him so much to part from the eyes of these women and yet lighten him to think of freedom from the pull of his own involvements? He has rejected the girl who wanted to come with him. He has been cruel to her for the doubts she has roused in him. She came to him and asked him to take her with him. He told her that it would be hard, this exile. 'And have I asked for a soft life?' 'The arrangements are made. I'm expected alone. I don't know whom I might endanger by changing the plan at the last moment.' 'And do you expect me to wait for you?' 'Did I ever?' 'Any woman to wait for you – even as an idea – when you're so indifferent to what happens to us? You're interested in a world for men alone. You're glad to go.' 'I've arranged to go.' 'Ah, then you might as well have arranged to stay; you're morally no better than the men who serve the regime.' 'I make no claims; but I do have a purpose.' 'You're afraid of the future. You hope it will never happen.' 'You talk as though there was something ... something permanent between us – ' 'But that's how you talk about the whole country, as if there was something permanent between you! You're afraid to love me.' 'Ah, my dear!' 'No, it's true. I don't say it out of vanity. I don't need to believe in your love. I mean I'm not short of admiration, as a general thing. I've seen what you're like with women. I don't take it personally that you don't love me. You're afraid of anything that would make you personally accountable. You're used to getting out of things.' 'And that's one of the things I want to get out of, accusations of habitual failings. How can one ever defend oneself against them?' 'Oh you want to make a new world just because certain things aren't fair to you, or perhaps just aren't *agreeable* to you.'

'How noble you are, women of your class! How willing to help us see our faults! Is it to strengthen us, do you believe, or to weaken us, to put us more in your power?' 'Do you really believe that you'll ever come back?' 'Yes, I do. If I didn't – ' 'What?' 'This would be the evasion you think it is. It isn't a slight on you; it isn't a slight on you that you have no penis, or that women don't fight like men. There are things women can't know.' 'It's men who prevent it, women knowing, to hide their motives, to hide their pleasure even, I do believe that's part of it. You never want to come back.' 'There's no arguing here. Imagine, though, how much I should achieve with an argumentative woman at my side wherever I'm going! Imagine how clear a head I should have!' 'Oh, you should have been a monk! Why don't you have yourself hauled up to heaven in a basket like Socrates in the play and hang there, eternally good and eternally useless?' 'I have particular objectives. I have plans. I'm not going to hang anywhere, at least not in a basket.' 'You want us all to keep our eyes on you, you want to be the white horse in the hills. No one's going to watch you. No one cares.' 'I realize – ' 'And resent it. You resent it like death. Worse. If only – you're a lover of men, aren't you, really? No woman could produce a child general enough, perfect enough, to please you. No womb could contain anything worthy of your potential.' 'Imagine prolonging this argument for the next fifty years!' 'I don't want to come with you only to be with you.' 'That I've heard before. I'm not convinced.' 'You make me into a shrew. A vixen.' 'You're not going to get everything you want. Get that into your head.' 'Your whole life is denial, can't you see that? Denial. You want to attract the attention of the world only to shake your head at it. Because it isn't good enough for you. Well, maybe it's a damned sight better than you are. Maybe it's you who's missed your chance and not the world.' 'It's possible.' 'You're condemning me to a life you can despise. Just like you did my sister. That's what amuses you. And exposes you for what you are.' 'Why can I not be allowed to drown in my own way? Why must you keep thrusting my head under the waves? And then

324

trying to haul me out. Leave the night and the sea to take care of me, my dear, and spare me your assistance.' 'When you go on the street you want them all, you say so yourself, but what are they all but fantasies? Here's one of them and what do you do? Take me, please. Take me now if you won't take me with you. Prude! Snob! Prig! You can't get it up, I suppose, for something that wants you, that really wants you. Whom shall I blame? Your mother? Why do you make it so important? For my sake? Or are you thinking of my family, the family you so despise, are you thinking of them? And snubbing them in me? Traditionalist! Son of your father!' He passes the house of her father. His walk seems to create its own scenario. He waits there, remembering how many times he has hesitated, cursed, dreamed, stared at those lighted upstairs windows, how even on his way back from the brothel, with the hairs clotting in his pants, he has divined shapes against the blinds and hoped for a glimpse of the sister. While he waits, a limousine carrying her father, now once more a minister in the Government of his son-in-law, drives up. The Government, arrogant in its modesty, no longer parades its potentates through the streets with an escort of white-booted motor-cyclists. It has 'settled to the tasks with which the nation has entrusted it'. It affects the attitudes of serious businessmen, the decorum of those neat officials who distribute aid from their elegantly designed new embassy in the international style. The Minister's house is watched by a single figure in a pale blue rain cape, rather crumpled, and a waterproof beret. He salutes the Minister, who allows his driver to pull up at the kerb because the limousine is too wide for the chained gateway. How easy it would be to kill him! One could be abroad before suspects were even listed. Is there any sense in such an assassination? And is not its possible senselessness part of its attraction? One would have the amusement of seeing the newspapers attempt to fit it into a pattern, a new terrorist policy. The Minister has a kind of innocence. Is it that which one wants to rape? He walks so unostentatiously from his car (finding time to bend and salute the chauffeur, whose wife has had a little girl that very afternoon) and keeps his ears down in his astrakhan collar; these spring evenings can be deceptive. He wears gloves and grey spats. How little of him shows, especially with those thicker spectacles! So much paper-work! He is scarcely a man at all. He is like one of those insects which bleed a blanched liquor when they are split and to which one would like to apologize for having doubted their animal status. Rape with those little feet in the air, those blind eyes groping for a description of what will soon be blotted out for ever? The exile turns away, disgusted, from the natty symbol of the regime with whom he can no longer bear to share his native soil. The Minister's puny appearance, his dutiful precision, these minuscule attributes are more depressing than the screams of the tortured. Torture, one's humanity cries out, cannot continue; it demands revenge and challenges men to wrest the iron from the executioner's hand. The exile can believe in a struggle against barbarism. It is more difficult to go fiercely into action against the petty, the prim, the pale. There may be glory in assassinating a tyrant, but his painstaking minion? The Minister stands by his front door waiting for the maid like a shopkeeper posing beside his new shingle for a local newspaper. Can he really be worth plotting to overthrow? Come, is there any real difference between a cunning lackey and the interests he serves? Already the exile is forced to paint reality in gaudier colours than it wears. No, there are, there must be abuses, persecutions, brutalities crude enough to sustain, if need be, an eternity of indignation. He walks now to the square in front of the School of Philosophy. Here a demonstration of students was attacked by mounted police. A martyr, one of the most brilliant logicians of his year, was beaten to death against the railings of the Freedom Statue. 'On this spot my friend was done to death. On this very spot! I must never forget it.' But another voice, more convincing because less noble, is saying, 'To think that I shall never be seen here again! Am I not also a martyr?' How much more tragic, because so freely chosen, his own survival may prove than his friend's murder! As soon as the exile decides to leave he substitutes his own history (his life and letters) for that of

326

his country. He will judge the progress of the nation by his own fortunes. It will have turned from its wicked ways if it readmits him to the centre of the stage. It will have failed its destiny if he is permitted to waste away in a foreign land. The exile, no matter how cruel the circumstances which expel him, no matter how unquestionably right he is to quit, no matter how blazing his defiance, is a moralist; he carries everything in his head. How else can he remember Jerusalem?

Passing through the capitals of Europe, he confines himself to the most relevant visits. He refrains from admiring cathedrals and art galleries. He recruits his strength by permitting himself to go only to certain shrines of liberty. He makes contact with others who have fled before him. He is as thorough as possible in briefing them with the information he has brought with him. He is brisk when it comes to personal messages or news of those who are still in the capital. He refers almost with embarrassment to having seen the Minister and is distressed at the affectionate contempt with which the old bastard's persistence is remembered by former opponents. He expects the other exiles to sharpen his political will; their questions about the tea at their favourite cafés, their dismay at the reconstruction of the harbour which has razed the brothels of their youth, their eagerness to see the latest issues of the literary magazines which, in a degenerate form, are still published monthly, their greed to squeeze from him the taste and smell of the city fill him with alarm. He exaggerates the unpopularity of the Government and the need of the people for a lead from abroad. To hear him, it might be thought that disconsolate crowds huddled about clandestine loudspeakers waiting for the word to rise. Already, when his walk was meant to fix in his mind with photographic accuracy the true state of the city, he is abandoning precision for rhetoric. Hungry, he refuses food; thirsty, he will have nothing to drink. At last, in a fury to get things organized for action, he lands in his country of refuge. Nothing will persuade him to call it his new home. He is determined to seek out only those who hold social and political views like his own. He resists the idea of a common front. How can it make sense to work for the bogus freedom which men of the Right and the Centre can pervert as soon as it has been restored? He will not dilute the strength of his own convictions for the sake of a polite coalition. As for the country he has come to, he gives it the curt nod one offers a fellow-lodger with whom one does not propose to have breakfast. He lives in a rundown district, near the restaurant where his associates have formed a debating club and above a tobacconist where he can buy émigré newspapers, at least until they go broke. The newspapers from the capital are also on sale there; at first he resists, but then he buys them: one must, after all, not close one's eyes to the worst. And football, at least, is not political. The better the news from home, the more severe his frown: the censorship is obviously becoming more stringent all the time. Those of the extreme Left analyse every facet of policy. At last they have the opportunity to clarify their programme. It is only after some months that repetition begins, but once it has begun it continues. What else is there to discuss when everything has been discussed, except everything all over again? How small now seems the cabinet of friends! How unsurprising are their opinions! One longs for a new face. If only some one of them had stayed at home so that they might have the excitement of welcoming him! The exile is torn between reproaching those who have not made the break and dreaming that he had stayed to share the darkness with them. He wishes he could see the girl who wanted to accompany him. What would she say to a dingy room above a heel bar? How would she like to sleep with a man too cold to wash himself at the tap on the half-landing and who can afford a municipal bath only once a week? Is this the exciting, free life that he denied her? Would she like to have his baby here among these grey-faced foreigners with their fat infants loaded like parcels in unoiled wheelchairs? The politics of men who have no prospect of power are as tedious as playing bridge with those who have no money. He is galled by the hours he spends in conversations whose thread he loses, leaning against the cold doors of washeterias or the opaque

328

glass of a solicitor's consulting-room while another exile rehearses his grievances against a third or exposes a plot to bring out another 'free' news-sheet whose first issue will be its last. The wealth of certain other émigré circles is highly suspicious. Anyone who can raise a few pounds is thought to be in league with the regime or in the pay of the Americans, or both. The exile resents the exigencies of his world, but how can he live except by keeping his straw in the narrow glass into which well-wishers pour their sporadic funds? He finds a club where he can play bridge. He makes his bread at low stakes, partly because he cannot afford higher, partly because it avoids entering a classier world. He has made some contact in broadcasting circles, where amiable sympathizers find him work monitoring programmes sent out by the regime. He rejects hospitality, however, and returns to his charmless digs. If he begins to take a quiet interest in the life of his temporary resting-place, he tells himself it is only because he is tired of keeping everything in his head. What a relief to have a frame of reference outside the word! He notices the habits and linguistic peculiarities of his neighbours with the attentive skill those who speak a narrow language show in mastering the minutiae of another. In this academic way he begins, *ex improviso*, to find himself at home, just as the tourist becomes familiar with the district round his hotel when he is forced to go out in search of a restaurant. Appetite obliges him to make order out of what surrounds him. The exile reads the books of local authors and, with the distant dream perhaps of an embassy or of the Foreign Ministry, realizes how foolish it would be not to take advantage of his enforced stay to acquire a critical knowledge of this remote place. Why leave it to sailors to be the only travellers to see more than national monuments and the best hotels? He finds it ironic to be better informed about local politics than most locals are. Because he prefers to hide his partialities under a mask of scholarly inquisitiveness, he gains the reputation of a pedant. He wants such precise answers! He is quite a comparative historian! He is embarrassed by his own professorial quietism and returns to the arena of exile politics. He has forsworn the company of women (there are few among the exiles, only one or two wives who live hard lives, type, keep records and cook communal meals, determined not to complicate their husbands' political existence with passionate adventures) and he finds it difficult to resist the comfortable homes of hostesses where he can relax in an atmosphere of physical and emotional warmth. These women seem more sympathetic to the exile than to their own husbands. Their parties are enhanced by a tragic guest, while an interest in his cause excuses their incidental interest in him from seeming unwise. The resentment they feel against their busy and powerful husbands and the apprehension of irrelevance which deadens the hostess the morning after justify a blameless rendezvous with the morose stranger whose quizzical look and uncanny lift of the chin so gently dissented from the successful company around the dinner-table. The exile has considered buying a woman; in his country such things are not unmanly. He is put off by a world where a man may buy sex only if he confesses himself a dupe. He recalls the pretty tarts of his adolescence, who undressed with trite but professional coquetry and looked from their cunts to him with a tilt of the head, yes? Is it the climate or the men themselves who cannot enjoy what they have purchased but must, like diners in an inferior restaurant, await hungrily what they know will disgust them? What a strange country indeed is this where the menu is the best part of the meal! While dining at fashionable houses, he loses no chance, of course, to denounce the regime in his own country. He is touched by the quick indignation he arouses. He is obliged, however, out of common courtesy to listen to stories of visits to the temples and oracles which other guests have made during their holidays. He is even asked to recommend restaurants and, ducking that, finds himself suggesting out-of-the-way expeditions to the scenes of battles or to the birthplaces of those who died for their country in the War of Independence, things they must see one day. This last hurried postponement deprecates going while the regime is in power. He listens with embarrassment to the apologias of those who believe that their local friends will be hurt by their 'unexplained' absence or who maintain that a flow of foreign tourists through the capital reminds the regime that the eyes of the world are watching. He does not quarrel with these views because it would be folly to alienate the powerful over a matter on which, it has to be admitted, there can be several opinions. He leaves the house both excited by the new contacts he has made (a member of parliament has promised to attend a meeting as soon as he has a spare evening) and shrivelled by the awareness of how peripheral to the powerful are the misfortunes of the weak. He is aware also that he has made his appeal to men for whom, were they politicians of his own country, he would have no time. Simultaneously he sees how fruitlessly puritanical his associates have become in limiting their own plans to men of the Left.

He resolves now to call a meeting of all exile groups. He is rebuffed from the Right. Having determined not to conceal the will of the Left to announce its own programme, he now must face either failure or compromise. He decides, without altering the essential programme, precisely in order to preserve it in fact, to call a meeting without prejudice; a meeting of protest not of dogma. The Right is less obdurate; the Centre, as always, proclaims its open-mindedness, which means that it will wait to see which wing is the stronger before weakening it with its support. When he is attacked by his own comrades he is stung into ridiculing pedantic snobbishness as a form of political purity. He feels that he is the one who has taken the risks. He persuades himself that the all-party action committee he is so busy organizing will prove the platform he has so long sought, from which the rotten regime may be levered into perdition. Only these months, perhaps years, of gloomy sectarianism could have led him to think that all that was necessary for a successful revolution was a united émigré front. When they meet in the hall which they have hired, there are more people on the platform than in the seats. The discussion does not begin in the present but insists on excavating the past. It is a bourgeois drama in which the final curtain falls on a situation which, after protracted hostilities and senile memories, is precisely the same as it was when the characters first took the stage, save that one has had a heart attack and a boy has run away to become an artist. The regime has been accused of all the usual crimes and the most gifted orator present brings everyone to his feet, waving and shouting, by describing the public celebrations which will greet the Government's fall and the miserable tricks which ministers will try in order to disclaim responsibility and retain office. 'We shall say to them all: be gone and good riddance. It's a better fate than you offered us. Be glad of it and get you gone!' Without a single decision taken (better to arrange these things, it is said hurriedly, in private), without a single durable gesture of fresh good will, with the same stiff courtesies and muttered malice, the meeting dissolves. The exile, like a man in the habit of suffering agonies from the desertion of a woman whose good points he finds it increasingly hard to recall, goes home and curses his comrades more heartily than the tyranny which expelled them. He considers again whether he should not take the offer made him by a gentle banker, regretful over a cigar, to assist in a project, necessarily a small one, to bring commercial know-how to underdeveloped countries. The bank cannot, of course, disburse its money to charities, except in the most limited way, but it is willing to put its knowledge at the disposal of the less fortunate. Would such a position interest him? His languages would be helpful and the very fact that he has had no long connection with finance might allay unfounded suspicions. The bank would have no objection to the establishment of non-profit-making agencies in certain ex-colonial capitals (provided they were also non-loss-making!) with a view to long-term collaboration in works of national importance. All of this was said so diffidently, with the same caution that might be shown in inviting a man who might or might not be married to accompany a certain visiting lady to the opera, that the exile could hardly refuse at least to consider it.

Lying on his cold bed, the exile remembers the girl who might have come with him. What good did it do to deny her? His hand goes for warmth between his legs and his shelved sex peels from his thigh. He lies on his back and blinks at the plaster ceiling, with its cracked cornices, the shadows sweeping across from the night traffic. He thinks now of his hostess of the previous night, her powdered arms and, yes, her powdered voice, dry and carefully modulated as if it had been separately washed and anointed. Her whispered intimacies promised how much she longed for the liberation of his country from its *wicked* rulers. He recognized how her eyes kept darting to the door in case some important latecomer had appeared, he heard her use the same tone to congratulate the director of a film which had richly scandalized America with its outrageous and undemanding brilliance; her congratulations to the director had a more devoted tone, since they embraced money as well as fame, but the exile cannot afford too complete a cynicism: he likes to think that this woman, with her black silk arms and her firm white flesh, lacks only the opportunity to be the Liberty on the barricades. Come, does he not also welcome the taint of corruption, the sweet odour of compromise which floats up to him from her filmily covered breasts and powdered armpits? He needs her to need punishment, for then he will be right in using her. Her willingness to meet him (she has agreed to come with him to an exhibition to raise funds for Freedom) might put him off if he were tempted only for sexual purposes, but he has, after all, a higher purpose.

Her costume is more modest, almost severe, when she meets him in the street. He is touched and a little disappointed. It is a long time since he accompanied an elegant woman. The exhibition is poorly attended. She promises to speak to some friends she has in the press, one of them with a column of his own, brilliant. Someone should do something. The exile talks for a long time, or what seems a long time, with the girl who is running the exhibition. He asks about numbers and whether she has enough assistants. He longs to root out some outrage, something that needs doing, but he fails. He is excluded from concern. He shrugs and leaves, after several hesitations in the doorway, while his rich lady waits on the street, her little fur collar up about her ears, her face promising noble immunity to the weather. 'You're frozen,' he says, 'you must allow me to get you some coffee.' He utters the cliché sincerely, but then feels that flutter of excitement a young man experiences when he asks casually what he realizes to be a testing question. 'You must let me make you some tea,' she replies. 'On the contrary. I live near by. Well, not too far. If you don't mind my hovel.' How can she not come now? She is shocked by his room. She cannot take off her coat, it is so cold. He goes and borrows a fire from a neighbour, offering excessive gratitude to make up for his habitual gruffness. 'Here we are, here we are!' 'You speak our language so marvellously. How I wish I had your gifts!' 'You can see where my gifts have got me!' 'It's a crime, a man like you not being able to extend yourself. Do you think there's any chance of an armed intervention by the great Powers?' 'An armed intervention? My dear lady – no, I do not.' He stands by the gas ring (which is hidden in a cupboard) and waits for the turgid coffee to boil. 'You know, I don't mean to criticize, but – you should have somewhere less depressing to live. I don't mean that as a criticism, but you should. In case people have to come and see you, influential people. I know it's wrong, but how can they know how important you are if you're in a room like this?' 'Important?' 'A future Prime Minister, maybe. How can they? I may know how brilliant you are, but not everyone will. People are such snobs. It's not right, but they are. I'm surprised your friends haven't realized. Have you thought of taking this job that I overheard that man – I don't like him very much but he's very powerful – that he was offering you? Perhaps you should and use some of the money for a bigger place, warmer, where you could have your books. I expected you to have a lot more books.' 'Books cost money. I borrow mine or go to the library. You have excellent libraries.' 'Yes, it's such a good thing. Well, that does look appetizing, I must say. Look, we've steamed the windows up! It's nice.' 'A small room soon warms.' 'It soon warms up, yes, doesn't it? I think I'll take my coat off. You live all alone here then,

334

do you?' 'Oh yes, all alone.' 'You must have made a lot of friends here by now though, I expect?' 'Friends? No. I don't meet many people.' 'A lot of people thought you were very charming the other night. Very intense, challenging, I think they liked it.' 'It's always a comfort to the fat to see that the hungry can walk.' 'Oh, that's naughty! Are you starving? You're not starving, are you? You can always come to my house. Any time, there's always something to eat. I'm going to take my coat off. If you're hungry, you can come any time. And your friends. There's always masses.' 'I believe it. You're very kind.' 'What are the chances, truly, of forcing the Government to restore democracy?' 'Very small, I fear.' 'And you're not planning armed intervention?' 'Not from the great Powers.' 'How cryptic you are, aren't you? I can never tell exactly what you're planning.' She hesitates and then sits on the narrow bed. She leans back and shakes her hair loose. 'Have you learnt how to be secretive or is it the way you always were? I can't imagine you ever being exactly – I don't want to sound unkind – forthcoming. You seem very suspicious, somehow. Perhaps you don't give yourself the best chance, like staying in this place, by being so determined not to give yourself away.' 'I don't want to become a symbol.' 'Then what are you, if you're not visible, if you're not noticed? I'm sorry to say so, but aren't you simply useless?' He sees how he could be like the famous homosexual whose honesty has reformed the law and restored the idiom of a love that was once unspeakable. His gallant advocacy has legitimized a passion he is now too grand to be allowed. He longs again for the nocturnal dangers, the bold whispers in certain notable lavatories, the silent taxi-rides while one considers the pale profile of the man who will soon be in one's bath, he longs even for the blackmailer's camp sibilants, the few friends who are planning to meet in a suburban house, the quiet 'Are you doing anything?' and he frets at the unashamed reputation which debars him from secret pleasures. 'I should be useless', says the exile, 'if I became so well known that the underground didn't dare let me into its plans. If I become the ambassador-in-exile I shall have the ground cut away from under me. Passion can't be put on show. It wilts.' 'It wilts! Are you a very passionate person then really? I suppose you must be. Were you tortured when you were captured?' 'Would you like to see the marks?' 'Were they very brutal?' 'You do want to.' 'I think anyone who tortures anyone –' 'What should happen to them?' 'I don't know how anyone can do it, that's really what I can't fathom, how anyone can bring themselves –' 'Sometimes it's a necessity; sometimes it's a job. How can people clean sewers or cut throats? Virgins wonder, no doubt, how they will ever open their legs and … *mais ça s'arrange.*' 'That I find less difficult to understand. Seriously –' She tosses her hair, in case he takes the reversion to the previous subject to be too earnest. 'Everything which hasn't been done seems impossible; everything which has seems banal.' 'Are we talking about sex now or about torture?' 'It's all the same.' 'That sounds rather frightening.' He puts his cup on the floor and goes and stands over her. 'It's a long time since I had a woman. You mustn't tease me.' 'Am I?' He kisses her throat and feels her hair against his cheeks. 'You're a very attractive man but you frighten me. You won't hurt me, will you?' He finds her mouth, impatient to stop these throaty whispers, impatient to have done with words. She pushes him away as his hand finds her breast. When she stands up, he realizes that she is blonde and wonders what colour her cunt will be. The inconsequentiality of this afternoon is its attraction and its futility. What is this woman whose body is now displayed to him? He feels no betrayal of her husband because, as she sighs and touches his body with her practised flutter of daring, searching his face for a promise she insists on finding, he knows that he feels nothing for her but unmilked desire. Her body draws his. He crowns her breasts with kisses. It's a pleasure. She allows him to kiss her belly and her thighs and her breath shortens as he butts her cunt. *Ça marche.* Persuaded that they are past all restraint she takes his penis to her lips like a typist getting the hang of a new machine. And when finally he consents to finish in the usual way she opens an eye and sees him, this glaring swoop from one side to the other

336

is meant to tell him, in a new light. 'You Mediterranean men!' Already there is a briskness about her, as if she were already clothed and making sure that he knew her engagements for the next few days. She is content to have appropriated him. Although her glance assures him that he has given her all she has hoped for, he is as depressed as if he had come on the counterpane. How nimbly she makes use of his amenities! She bends to his mirror and prompts her hair into shape. She examines his comb – with a bright smile – and thinks better of it. 'May I have my bag?' She is more polite after being fucked than before. 'Well, I suppose I ought to go. This has been nice.' 'Good!' 'And I do think you ought to think about that job. And moving. Not only for my sake. You can't stay here for the rest of your life. You're very naughty not to use your talents! You are, you know.' She is not in the least aware that he wants to kill her. 'Now don't you go looking so fierce or I shall think I've done something wrong!'

'Now you will sit down by the iconostasis and put your hands on your head.'

'Really, I – '

'Do as I say and keep your voice down.'

'This is absurd. What do you hope to gain by it?'

'Gain? Nothing. A change of key.'

'The key is in the pocket of the young man outside. He's not likely to let you out. Give me back the gun.'

'Out of the question. Why did you bring it in? You intended to shoot me.'

'One carries arms because there's nowhere to put them down. This makes no difference to anything.'

'Because you're doomed already.'

'Because this place is surrounded. Because you'll never succeed in getting away. I thought you were capable of something more imaginative.'

'Just as you were once before when you hoped I'd be scandalized.'

'What a lot you make out of that! Give me the gun and we'll say no more about it.'

'Doesn't it occur to you that a desperate man is unlikely to play fair?'

'I could never have killed you. I never intended to. Not that I object if you don't believe me. I was hoping that our story might end on a note of more than wrestling and absurdity. Not that I care if you kill me. It's because I don't care that I find all this pointing of guns so irrelevant. Presumably that's why I allowed you to jump me. Silly. But not very interesting. Hitting a man over the head with a candelabrum. My dear Konni!'

'Never mind the aesthetics.'

'Would you desert your men? They'll certainly be executed if you get away, whether you kill me or not.'

'It doesn't appeal to you, the idea of our both getting away?'

'Both of us? In tandem?'

'I fire a shot. You call the guard. When he opens the door he assumes me dead. We grab him and run. The rest of them are in the barn, you said. We must have a good chance.'

'*Und zen?*'

'There are other places in the world. Why shouldn't we get away? A boat? I don't know ... '

The shot was fired. Artemis knocked on the door and shouted for the guard. It was the simple Paniotis. He slid open the bolt, unlocked the door and was hauled inside and crowned with the pistol. Konni smiled at Artemis. Artemis recognized Konni in that instant and with a lame courtesy, the ritual of a court whose king has been irretrievably overthrown, he bowed the other through the door. As Konni stepped out, Artemis saw what was coming and cried out, in an urgent, present voice, his hand already behind the thick door to close it. The shot came too soon. The shot came at once. Artemis fell back through the doorway and palmed the door shut. He lay inside the church, a bolster against the door. Konni knocked from the outside, head on wood. He had been shot through the lungs. The bullet had pierced him and taken Artemis in the chest. Effort was needed to force the door of the church. Artemis's mouth was a hoop of blood. Kosta stood over him. 'I told you I'd be watching, Captain.'

At his trial, for which he has been prepared by several months in the military hospital, a political prisoner is condemned to death for crimes committed during the civil war. He is kept in solitary confinement. He refuses to see his mother. He claims that he has no family. He hears the shots which execute others, but he is reprieved. The authorities are convinced by their foreign sponsors that it would create a scandal to kill him. The prisoner is a poet. His works have been published in larger countries. There is credit in not executing him, but the authorities begrudge him his life. Their clemency makes a foreigner of him. They despise him, not least because he failed, during his trial, to give any notable display of defiance. The drama lacked fire. There was no chance for them to demonstrate either their power or their compassion. He was unmoved by the tears of his mother. He neglected to challenge the competence of the court or the qualifications of the judges. He did not even accuse them of torture. He endured in silence. They wanted a self-aggrandizing martyr or an evident beast. He declined to be either. He seems now to be unimportant and it displeases the authorities to reprieve a nonentity. Yet they distrust him. He has not confessed enough. His intelligence makes them fear that he is tricking them. His lack of gratitude offends the Governor of the prison when he brings the news of the reprieve. The prisoner receives it more like an extension of his sentence than an easing of it. The Government does not announce the commutation publicly. The prisoner is driven out of the capital by night. It is as if he had been killed at home but kept alive abroad. From the window of the van he is able, when dawn comes, to see neat villages and cultivated slopes. They are driving through a part of the country the war has not touched. The prisoner weeps at the unspoiled countryside, the neat grapevines, the busy peasants. His guards doze under their heavy helmets. He is shackled day and night. The guards are not interested in him. A condemned man is sacred; a man sentenced to life imprisonment embodies a story without a climax. They come at last to a small fishing village at the head of a gulf. A huge fortress of black stone commands the harbour. Opposite it the foundations of a modern hotel have been excavated. The prisoner is taken to the fort, where an old dungeon has to be prepared for him. The weather is too bad for the crossing to the island where he is to be kept.

The new governor of the penal colony is due to be taken to the island at the same time as the prisoner. He is a man of correct views, whose record has been blemished by his refusal to execute a party of guerrillas amongst whom the poet was later identified. A storm in the gulf keeps them in the little town for several days. The men who have brought the prisoner from the capital are not to be part of the garrison on the island. They are impatient to dispose of their charge and return to the city. Only the major and the prisoner watch the sea with the same eyes. At last the weather clears. The sea drops. The boat comes from the island. The major and the prisoner are escorted aboard, where the regular crew is waiting. The poet is designated 'particularly dangerous', although he is physically frail. He is locked into a special cage on the boat (the crossing takes three hours) and special quarters have been made ready for him on the island. The officious precision of his treatment seems calculated to prove to him the capacity the Government has for punctilious behaviour. They insist that the major live an austere life, as if to show that their officers expect no favours. The Government itches for the admiration of its enemies. The major himself waits, as months fatten into years, for news of a fresh appointment. His resentment towards his superiors makes him moody. He cannot complain to his assistants. He complains to the prisoner. But he also complains of him. The prisoner gives him no chance to reveal his qualities. He would like – he would like the prisoner to announce his recantation. He would like him to write some patriotic poems. And then again, quite honestly, he would like him to try to escape and to be shot in the attempt.

Meanwhile the country recovers its economic strength. Rich countries contribute richly to its development. The Government decides to permit free elections. Large new amounts of aid are provided from abroad in order to dramatize its achievements and secure its 're-election'. In a sense the Government is right to claim responsibility for the country's revival. Were it not so arbitrary and so uncertain of its popularity, its rich would have less need to help it. Before the elections an amnesty is announced; most of the poet's fellow-prisoners are taken to the mainland and released. The poet is officially permitted pen and paper (though the major has 'forgotten' his own pen and notebook several times after his visits) and he is given an extended exercise period. He finds no impulse to write. Regret disgusts him; hope is sentimental. The present lacks resonance. He prefers to brandish his sterility at the major rather than to conquer it. The outside world has become a supposition. On the mainland the death penalty is abolished for political crimes. The civil war is officially over. The prisoner learns of this from the major. It is hard to say which of them is more dejected by the news. The prisoner feels more abandoned than ever; the very category to which he belongs has been erased. The major is degraded by the relegation of his prisoner. The past no longer has any historical lacing; it is reduced to a series of incidents and acts.

Before the postponed elections the Government is liberalized. The hard men are retired by harder ones who realize that a softer style is advisable. This ingratiating liberalism disgusts many who were prepared to accept tyranny. The army fears demoralization. The officers who remember the civil war are suspicious of those who do not. Some of the ministers, even those who are not dismissed in the reshuffle, give covert support to the 'officers with memories'. What do they have to lose? The Government is lulled into believing that it can win a fair election. Its generosity in tolerating other parties will surely be rewarded by their defeat. The major brings his prisoner the results. The Government has been beaten by a coalition of the Centre and the moderate Left.

The major is confused. He asks the prisoner to analyse the situation for him. Now that his old superiors have lost office, he fears that his chances of promotion have gone with them. He is bitter at being out of favour, no matter who is in power. The new Government is anxious not to alienate those whose wealth has transformed the country. 'Continuity will be maintained.' As a proof of new standards, however, all political dossiers are to be burned. 'The Inquisition is over.'

The fate of the prisoner is ignored. The major shows a new and sarcastic side to the prisoner. He speaks all the time of 'your friends'. The prisoner asks how they are friends of his. The major writes to the capital for a clarification of the amnesty. The new ministers want nothing less than the return of a hero of the Left. They snub the major, who can, as a member of the old officer class, scarcely expect their favour. He is ordered to take good care of his prisoner, for whom he will be held completely responsible. In addition, for the sake of economy, the garrison is reduced again. While the extreme Left was willing to find nothing surprising in the tyranny of the tyrannical, it is infuriated by the hypocrisy of the moderates. Popular expectations of a new Government can never be fulfilled. The ministers enjoy only the briefest popularity. The mass of the people demand a continuation of the boom; the politically committed demand a legitimization of the old Left which would certainly lead to the cancelling of aid. It is hardly to be wondered that the new ministers conclude that moral rectitude is a luxury to end all luxuries. If it is to retain control of the army, the regime can hardly make concessions to the Left. It must prove itself more patriotic than the patriots. It is easier to tolerate treason from the Right than sedition from the Left. The continued detention of the prisoner is part of the Government's reserves against a run on its credit. His cause is taken up by the Left, although few of them have ever known him and they would be unlikely to find him a place in their counsels if he were released. One day, while exercising on the battlements of the prison, he is amazed to see a yacht sailing close in to the island with a banner carrying his name. The people on the yacht wave and clap. There is the blare of a loudhailer. The major arrives with his pistol and hurries the prisoner into his cell. The yacht must belong to rich people. The major is unnerved and suspicious. If the prisoner escapes (what is there to prevent a landing?) he will be ruined; but if these rich anarchists gain the day he will also be ruined unless he can get the prisoner to plead his cause. The prisoner is not exhilarated. He knows that he is not the man these young sparks imagine. It makes no difference to either man who is in power on the mainland. Neither will ever be welcome there.

The major is now the only active gaoler. Another change of Government occurs in the capital, without fresh elections; then fresh elections without a change of Government. The prisoner is a slogan to the crowds, who have set an untypical poem of his to music, but events fluctuate too quickly (ministers are replaced before they can open their files) for any positive action to be taken. The major suggests that the prisoner, if he doesn't object to the term for the sake of the record, comes to his quarters as a servant during certain parts of the day. It will relieve the monotony for both of them. The poet is now the sole prisoner, the major the sole gaoler. Rigid hours are no longer kept. They are more anxious not to be caught out by a surprise visit, no matter by whom, than apprehensive of each other. The major retains a certain command over matters. If it were not for him, they would not eat. When the supply boat comes from the mainland (the prison boat has rotted from disuse) it is the major, as governor, who signs for the stuff. Everything must seem as before, in case a check is made. The two of them cannot enjoy the island, for that would make them want to leave it. They share its oppression. They fear the future. They discover the past. They compare their school and student days, experiences in the mountains. They begin to inhabit each other's histories. They could almost have been lovers. They have a nostalgia for the past which sweetens their despair. The prisoner continues to try to believe that he wants to escape. The major tries to believe that there is a danger that he will. He locks the prisoner

343

in his cell every night with a little smile of triumph, as if he has tricked him into it. He walks away tossing the key freely from hand to hand. One morning the major is late. The prisoner thinks that he is allowing him an extra sleep, but as soon as the door is open he realizes that the governor is ill. They return to the house. The major goes to bed. The gun is under his pillow. The prisoner tends the sick man, who regards him with suspicion. The major insists on the prisoner giving his parole. He does, protesting that it is meaningless. The major grows worse. The prisoner demands to be allowed to take the boat and go for help. The major reminds him of his parole and begs him, in any case, to stay. The prisoner is alarmed by the major's illness and yet it provokes him to derision. He accuses the other of being an alarmist and a hypochondriac. The major orders the prisoner to go back to his cell at nightfall. The prisoner refuses; his parole does not promise obedience, only that he will not actually escape. He tends the sick man through the night. At dawn he dies. The prisoner is furious. He kicks the body out of bed. It sprawls on the ground with a flag of orange blanket over it. He despises the major for dying. He tells himself that his parole can no longer apply to a dead man, but the body excites his anger; it is alive for him. He takes the gun from under the pillow and laughs at it, a contraceptive without a cunt.

When the boat next comes from the mainland with the provisions, there is no one to meet it on the quay. The officer in charge climbs to the major's house and finds the body. He runs to the cells. The prisoner is lying on his bunk, covered in an orange blanket. His door is locked. After a search, the officer finds the key below the barred window.